THE STEEL GAVEL

THE STEEL GAVEL

ADAORA OGUNNIYI

Troubador Publishing Ltd
Unit E2 Airfield Business Park,
Harrison Road, Market Harborough,
Leicestershire LE16 7UL
Tel: 0116 279 2299
Email: books@troubador.co.uk
Web: www.troubador.co.uk/matador

ISBN 978 1805141 341

British Library Cataloguing in Publication Data.
A catalogue record for this book is available from the British Library.

Printed and bound in Great Britain by 4edge Limited
Typeset in 11pt Adobe Garamond Pro by Troubador Publishing Ltd, Leicester, UK

Matador is an imprint of Troubador Publishing Ltd

Dear reader,

May rays of love light your every path...

PROLOGUE

Ijemmili and Urenmma, at the command of a group of five men, lay sprawled on the ground. The hot dust of the quiet noonday filled their mouths and noses as they took desperate gasps.

With the men of Afoku out warring against a distant town, today presented the perfect opportunity. Fiery-eyed Ajoafo warriors looked set for vengeance. Two of the invaders stomped in and out of huts, collecting cowries and ornaments. At last, her defeat at the native court, three years ago, in the long-standing Ocho-River dispute, would be avenged. The other three men darted their eyes around as they kicked and stepped on the women on the ground. Silent tears flowed down the women's faces. This invasion did not come to them by surprise. They suspected and mentioned their fears, but Afoku chiefs waved away their wives' concerns as mere worries.

The pressure from the warrior's leg would not let Urenmma see their faces, but she sensed their rage. Like a hungry lion in wait for its prey, Ajoafo town licked her wounds as she watched her women and children walk miles to Obeleanu river, two towns west of theirs, enduring endless hours of wait, with the sun biting their skin, to fetch water for their homes. Not more than a fortnight ago, Ijemmili told her husband what she overhead at the market square; how the people of Ajoafo smarted. 'Nobody is buying their seafood. They decay after such long treks from the river to the market,' she had said. Indeed, the scorching heat of the tropics of Eastern Nigeria did not afford their goods any fighting chance at freshness. No longer able to sell her fish and crab for sustenance, let alone maintain her integrity as the famous commercial hub for seafood, poverty caused Ajoafo to grit her teeth for three years. And like a sodden cloak, she wore her identity as the least among the string of clans on the other side of the River Niger.

One of the men kicked Ijemmili on her bottom. 'On your back!' he said, the veins in his neck pulsing with the strength of his vocal chords, his Adam's apple bobbing up and down.

In rasped whispers, Ijemmili begged for mercy. 'I beg of you; the baby may come to harm.' After Six harmattan seasons of agony-filled supplication to the gods, she was going to be a mother in only eight market days. By now, the two looters had joined and were casting leering glances at the women. One started towards Urenmma.

Urenmma's legs pulled her back as she ran. Tree branches and thick forest shrub stumps made it their sole mission to thwart her flight. The men in hot pursuit were closing in on her, and all hope was lost. Although not an overly adventurous woman, Urenmma made up her mind to dare the five-man band when they slit the throat of Ijemmili, her friend and next-door neighbour, because she chose to fight. At first, she thought her friend stopped pleading because her throat was now coarse from the dry-season dust. Only the sticky red fluid gliding from Ijemmili's throat told Urenmma that her friend and neighbour was dead and that the time had come to flee or follow.

Strange squeaks and sudden bursts of forest bats joined in, making a swine meal of Urenmma's escape to safety as she cast her eyes back, again and again, at her assailants' menacing charge. She did not see it in time and slammed headlong into a white one-legged she-goat. It looked graceful as it cast what looked like a pitiful glance at Urenmma and walked off, every inch unperturbed by the ominous grunts from the men in the distance. Picking herself up like a wounded squirrel would, Urenmma kept running, unseeing, as new streams of tears began to course down her face. Today may be the day she would die. Too far into the wilds, she could not say which way went east or west. She feared her husband would never find her in the belly of the forest.

A strange-looking hut in the distance stalled Urenmma's now numb legs and feet. With one swipe of the back of her hand, she cleaned her tear-stained face. Her forehead furrowed. *Who would build a hut in this forest?* Certain the men after her would come upon her soon, she dragged herself towards the hut, thinking it may be safer to hide there than continue running.

Urenmma crouched in a corner of the hut and shut her eyes tight, quivering like a leaf in the eye of a storm. Her fingers stuck in her earholes did not stop the sound of the footsteps as they came nearer and nearer. Her end hovered within earshot.

The footsteps stopped and after what seemed like fifty-two market days, Urenmma prised open one eye to, at least, behold the face of the one who would cut short her life. She froze. For before her stood the white one-legged she-goat with an unmistakable smile and an almost blinding orange halo over its head. Then came total darkness.

ONE

WHEN THE DEVIL IS YOUR SEAMSTRESS

A short walk from Brent Cross station, past Brent Beach shopping mall, brought Greyburtons Academy into full view. It sat on an endless stretch of snow-filmed greenery.

Before now, the academy's boarding facility appealed to the Taylors. Clean air, filled with constant wafts of deliciousness, would strike nostalgic strings for anyone. But most importantly, for Bree and Donald, the thought of their child within a managed space, offered infinite comfort and reassurance. Imagine their disappointment when, one week before Fiyin's departure from Nigeria, a call from the academy informed them that all their in-boarding facilities were booked.

Fiyin hurled herself through the heavy oak door of Greyburtons. A petite lady with green eyes and a genial smile introduced herself as the administrative manager and gave her a tour of the facility. The lady, Annabelle, showed her three conference rooms and two offices attached to the five-a-side pitch-sized reception. Annabelle held the door open for Fiyin, and they exited the administrative block.

About seventy-five metres away, the kitchen stood in majestic splendour. Its twenty-five workstations, life-size cold storages and a bevy of cooks milling around did nothing to diminish the sheer size of the cookery enclave. The boarding facility comprised three blocks and lay farther away from the administrative and kitchen blocks. Annabelle gave Fiyin a sneak-peek of the flats, and genuine regret swept over her face as she said, 'I know… we wish we had an extra flat for you.' The unmistakable class got an already impressed Fiyin astounded, but she decided to learn to prefer Paddington's light-hearted bustle to Brent Cross's crispy clean air. After the tour, Annabelle gave Fiyin a folder with a few sheets of paperwork which she could fill out and return in two days, in readiness for her orientation.

It still seemed like only yesterday when Fiyin Taylor tossed her reading glasses into her box. The smile on her face had made her look more content than the patient dog which eventually got the fattest bone. She could not believe her examinations were over. Every inch the picture of glee, she had separated the items that would not be making her homeward journey with her. *Rechargeable lamp? No. Night socks? No. Handouts and textbooks? Hell, no!* A giggle had escaped her closed lips as she imagined her parents' disappointment when they learnt she had no plans to further engage in any form of typical academic work. She reckoned her home did not need any more academic points to score as Donald and Bree possessed doctorates in agricultural economics and botany, respectively. *They should be grateful I made a second class upper. Medical rehabilitation is not an easy course!* But Bree and Donald were not surprised by Fiyin's decision to ditch her initial plans for a master's degree. Their only child's interest in food reared its head before she had lost all her milk teeth. And when it became certain that her love for food went beyond flavours alone to its presentation on the plate and texture on the palate, the Taylors realised they had a passion in their laps.

So, as they sat for dinner on that night of their child's final return from undergraduate school, Bree and Donald had presented Fiyin with her graduation present: a six-month enrolment at Greyburtons Chef Academy, London.

And after two months of basking in the euphoria of her new reality – that hard class chairs, reading glasses and the trepidation which often preceded and trailed examinations were now in the past – Fiyin Taylor was ready to leave Lagos, Nigeria for the United Kingdom.

At the airport, as Fiyin walked through the departure doors, turning to wave for the last time, a furrow had formed between her father's brows.

'Are you sure we are doing the right thing?'

'Of course, we are, dear!' The smile on Bree's face held, without the faintest hint of a waver.

'Bree, sometimes I feel we're overindulging... maybe we should have insisted on a master's first...' Donald often spoke with a slight shake of his head whenever he was worried about a decision he had made.

'This is about your talk with your brother and his supporters, abi?' Bree suspected why her husband hopped from one foot to the other. But regardless of how many furrowed brows or disapproving glares crossed Bree's line of sight, she remained resolute in her decision to support her daughter's dreams, however wild. So, 'Nonsense! Tell them to try banging on God's door for nine years, begging for one thing! Look, Don, nobody should tell us how to raise our child, period!' had ended Donald's second-guessing, as always.

'Here in Greyburtons, we are famed for combining tradition with innovation. Our chefs' passion to transfer knowledge, while ensuring all techniques taught are handed down for many generations, is unequivocal.' Enthralled by the Chief Executive

Officer's warm yet confident hybrid of English and French accent, Fiyin hung on to every word of her welcome speech. She sent out a prayer in gratitude for her parents' auspicious graduation gift, for not too far away tolled the bells heralding her career: of owning a catering outfit which may someday float a cookery school.

One week into her course, Fiyin raised a white flag in submission to the weather's capricious temperament. But Winter's incisors appeared to have suffered a trim since it did not bite quite as hard today. After ten minutes of gasping at the price tags on the shoes in Russell & Bromley at the Brent Beach mall, Fiyin strolled off to the train station, with only the shoes she wore to the academy. On the Northern line to Kennington, she joined the many commuters standing knee to knee; some eating wraps, a few drinking coffees, tea, or something liquid in paper cups, and others reading the dailies or novels. The desperation to get to wherever they were headed seemed to be the unifying factor between both sitting and standing commuters.

Still smarting from the unappealing prospect of standing through her journey of almost eighteen minutes, after her twelve-minute walk from the mall to the station, Fiyin observed a chestnut-haired gentleman give up his seat for a man bent in age. *Hah! And they still say the British are a snobbish bunch?*

'Chalk Farm.' the transport address system announced. The train crunched its brakes at the next stop. The elderly man, the recipient of Chestnut Hair's kindness, had reached his stop. Once Fiyin established Chestnut Hair's disinterest in reclaiming his seat, she dived for it. Oh no! Not fast enough! Another lady had her eyes on the same spot and sensing the odds were not stacked in her favour, flung her duffel bag to lay claim to the seat before Fiyin got to it. The bustle and battle for survival back in Nigeria had not prepared Fiyin for this primordial variant of strife.

Seething, Fiyin took one more stride, sat in the prized seat and, with a curt smile, gave the duffel to the lady. 'Sorry, you dropped your bag.' Although dark-skinned, Fiyin strained from trying to associate the too-sharp-for-her-own-good lady with any African country. She could be black British for all she cared. But when Sharp Lady, every inch displeased, retrieved her bag and gave Fiyin 'the eye', Fiyin knew without a doubt where, on the world map, her roots lay.

At Warren Street, Fiyin changed lines, sighing with relief at the empty seats in the Hammersmith and City line to Paddington. She settled in the last carriage, rested her back and closed her eyes for the zap before Paddington station. She had just started tossing around dinner options in her head when her eyes fluttered open.

Two cold eyes tunnelled into her forehead. *Sharp Lady from before!*

Fiyin's heart began a sprint. She had not seen her get off at Warren Street. *When did she get on!* With feigned indifference and something she hoped looked like a scoff, Fiyin busied herself with studying the advertisements screaming on the body of the train; *Specsavers, Les Misérables, Levi's...*

When Sharp Lady bowed her head over her mobile phone, Fiyin snatched the chance to observe her. They appeared to be of the same height. And although a tad fairer-skinned, Sharp Lady still leaned towards the dark continent. She possessed a flawless skin and a pretty face too. The way she glared at anything that caught her fancy announced, 'I-am-a-troublemaker.' And if their first encounter offered any indication, Fiyin believed every word of that announcement.

Paddington! All the commuters shuffled out. Fiyin began her walk home. The grocery store in the station did not close until midnight.

She courted the idea of grabbing a pack of Caesar salad and a toastie but walked past the store when she remembered Peri-Peri Masters' along Praed Street. A burst of wetness filled her mouth in anticipation of some spicy goodness. At first, Fiyin had fretted over the cosy but always near-empty chicken joint. But the frenzy with which the chefs grilled, served, and sent 'to go packed' grilled chicken backstage put to rest any fear of it being a bad place for a good treat.

While waiting for her peri-peri, Fiyin started a head count of people waiting to place their orders; *one, two, three, uh... four.* Heart freeze! Sharp Lady had just walked in, a lazy smile playing around her mouth as she floated to the counter. Not a glance. Now certain she was being followed, Fiyin left with her order and started towards her flat, looking behind every now and again at Sharp Lady on her tail. Mile after mile, stretched the two-minute walk to Chilfort Yards. Was Praed Street distending? The faster Fiyin walked, the faster Sharp Lady walked, until they arrived at the same building. Accompanied only by dense and awkward silence, they travelled the elevator with Fiyin all the while clutching tight to the key in her jeans pocket. *If this girl comes near me, I'll use this key to defend myself.*

The elevator doors slid open on the fifth floor. They exited. When Fiyin stopped in front of her flat to let herself in and Sharp Lady did the same two doors away, the most incredible thing happened. They both burst into tear-drawing, ribs-hurting laughter.

'I bet you thought, "This looney is set to get me for outsmarting her over the train seat," huh?' said Sharp Lady in between balls of laughter.

'I was already thinking I should have just left the damn seat alone.'

'You should have.' But Sharp Lady's tone offered a flighty element. Playful even.

'I'm Fiyin. My friends call me Fifi... you can too.'

'My name is Omoni, but you can go with Omo. I'm here for a one-year fashion course.'

'Naija girl!'

'With every bone and muscle!'

They became good friends ever since, and hardly a day went by without the two ladies comparing notes on their day's activities over a glass or plate of something: with one point of view from Brent Cross, and the other from Shepherd's Bush. Nevertheless, it did not take too long for their differences to stick out. While Omo, who plunged herself into the world of dating as early as age fourteen, understood the meandering course of relationships, Fiyin relished, without remorse, her blank page of boys and men. She remained strait-jacketed in her certainty that, at the right time, the right man — who by the way happened to be a younger and unrelated version of Donald Taylor, her father — would come to sweep her off her feet.

⌐———⌐

The soft upward curve of Chef Jose's mouth made mild the blow of his announcement. 'Your first cook-off project is in three days!' All twenty-two course attendees from varied nationalities gasped. They were to create their traditional version of an international or continental dish and dessert. Chef Jose handed them a list of meals to pick from. A French specialty nudged Fiyin's adventurous double. Tête de veaux. But Fiyin thought it typical of the French to invent a fancy name for boiled cow head. For dessert, she picked honey and tea jammers and planned to bedazzle them with chunks of walnut or peanut for her Naija twist.

Three days sped past in a whiff. Bewildered mutterings filled the kitchen as attendees unboxed their individual brown paper boxes to find mini parcels of condiments, unique to their nationalities. Packs of pumpkin leaves, water leaves and African egg plant leaves greeted Fiyin when she opened her paper box. Shelled, dried and milled prawns sat in a small square plastic container. Her main ingredient, pressure-boiled, de-boned, bite-size cuts of cow head, lay wrapped in a transparent food wrapping film.

A fifty-centilitre bottle labelled 'palm fruit oil' drew a loud whistle from Fiyin as she began to fiddle with the packs of various coloured peppers and an unlabelled inmate in her box. Her sixth sense stilled her curious fingers, and her head shot up to find pairs of eyes bursting with humour and boring into her skull. Realising what an unbecoming representation of a lady she must now appear before her new colleagues, Fiyin coughed in embarrassment. With puckered lips, she resolved to leave the surprised-whistling part of herself back at Chilfort Yards on her future visits to the academy. One item after the other, she set the contents of her box on her dark-grey granite workstation, her mind still on the unnamed inmate.

'Oven-baked and flaked mackerel,' said Chef Jose in answer to Fiyin's unasked question. Her lips began to form an 'o' for another whistle, but she stopped herself, twisting them to the right, improvising a smile of gratitude to the chef.

At four o'clock in the evening, the sun had long snuggled under the quilt of the dark clouds, but all the meals sat proud on Greyburtons' grey granite workstations. Chef Jose and the other twenty-one participants nodded in appreciation of the creative blend of spices in Fiyin's dish but also in utter bewilderment at how anybody could subject their tongues to such a spicy assault yet manage to maintain any semblance of sanity.

Accompanying each mouthful of 'tête de veaux' with loud gulps of sparkling water, they did not heed Fiyin's theory about how waiting out the spice before taking little sips of water achieved better calming results than the current method they employed. Her attempts to change their opinion on how best to quell the fire on their tongues or stop their runny eyes and noses were like pouring water into a colander. Although sincere in her sympathy for the suffering tongues of her new friends, Fiyin did not forget to scoop the remains of her dish to the last bit. She intended to indulge her longing for home-cooked meals over the weekend. Casting a rueful glance at her honey jammers as she walked out of the near-empty kitchen, Fiyin hauled her backpack on. Too bad. Not only did her cookies not grace the tongues of Chef Jose and her friends, but they would not be hiking home with her either. They came out of the oven as super-tanned versions of themselves.

Unrepentant in its savagery, winter's fangs clawed as Fiyin manoeuvred her five-foot six-inch frame into the embrace of Chilfort Yards' reception. Soft tunes floating through the unobtrusive elevator speakers washed over her frayed nerves as she travelled the four floors leading to her flat.

When Donald Taylor insisted on a studio flat, his wife and daughter thought his minimalist alter ego had started stomping about. Today, Fiyin thought otherwise, since the warmth in her small flat, which now juxtaposed with the brain-numbing chill a more spacious home would have offered, gave her the lucid definition of bliss. Although the long string of terraced buildings flanking Praed Street, where Chilfort Yards sat, took some bite out of the chill's sting, Paddington's Chilfort Yards stretched miles away from Brent Cross's Greyburtons and travelling such a distance in the cold, almost every day, filled Fiyin with dread. However, only two months of being enthralled by Paddington's lively charm and cosiness, and Fiyin's previous longing for a flat in Brent Cross now tasted like a spoonful of nothing.

Once she settled her dish on the counter, Fiyin dialled Omo's mobile number. Omo would forgo her inheritance for any meal with a remote leaning towards 'home'. She did not fancy the long train rides to Burnt Oak, where brisk walks in and out of its many stores, in the cold, offered an assortment of Nigerian food stuff, condiments, and ready-made meals. She picked up her phone at the first ring. Just out on a dinner date, Omo promised to rattle Fiyin's door knocker in the next three hours or less.

Whoever chose to call her on her mobile phone while she snuggled under the lather of her warm bath would have to adjust their timing. Fiyin entertained no thoughts about leaving her warm cocoon anytime soon. She shut her eyes and hummed a rhythmless tune as her phone rang out the fourth time. Giving up her now-tepid pleasure pod, Fiyin splashed on some moisturiser and donned her favourite butter-coloured wool robe. She started to dish some 'tête de veaux' when her mobile phone began to ring again.

The text, 'Mummy' danced on Fiyin's phone screen. It did not matter how many times in a day she heard it, her mother's voice always delighted Fiyin. Mrs Taylor wanted to know how her daughter's first project went.

'Did my advice pay off?'

'Hmm. I used as many pepper flavours as possible, Mummy, and it paid off all right.' Fiyin chuckled as Chef Jose's red nose and wet brows flashed in her mind's eye.

'Bless my angels for giving me such inspiration!' Bree shouted in excitement. Mr Taylor waited till his wife and daughter finished with their animated chatter about the infinite vastness of the African menu before he could say hello. Amused, Donald Taylor counted himself lucky. What would he have done without the genetics responsible for keeping obesity far away from his two ladies?

'I am glad you nailed your dish, darling. Now to the original reason we called. We're going away to the United States for a two-week vacation, but on our way back, we will stop by London. It won't be Christmas without you, will it?'

'Seriously, Daddy? No kidding?' Fiyin could not believe it, and midway into her elation, she slid into instant overdrive. 'Where will you lodge? Can we fit into my studio flat? How long will you stay? Maybe I'll check if Omo can move in with me… that way, you have a more spacious living space. Would you like to see the zoo? Maybe a train trip to Scotland? How much shopping do you plan to do in London?' The questions tumbled out in torrents. Amidst balls of laughter, Donald asked her to let them worry about all her worries.

The bell chimed. *Omo? So early?* Still on the phone, she peered through the door lens and let her friend in, not missing the sullenness. As soon as the call ended, Fiyin wanted to know why Omo returned so early from her date. 'What?' she asked, widening her eyes, tilting her head to the left, squinting her eye; it often got Fiyin's friends spilling their secrets, irrespective of their resolve. It was what made Omo tell Fiyin about the two hidden segments of her childhood.

'What?' Fiyin asked her sullen-faced friend again, popping a plate of tête de veaux in the oven to heat. She could not wait to show off to Omo who, quite frankly, had proven to be culinarily challenged. Although an architect by training, Omo intended to build on her real passion for all things fashion. As she often said, 'Of course I will practise architecture, but I also plan to help satisfy the ever-evolving and insatiable feminine desire for exquisite apparels.' And to give life to her plan, Omo possessed the resilience of a rock, adorned with precious ornaments of infectious optimism. Today, however, Omo's mien glowered at optimism.

But because no southbound mood could ever subdue her affinity for any food with the promise of nostalgic sumptuousness, Omo pounced on her meal with the gusto of a starved warrior. And, like always, her verdict was, 'Excellent! With a bold uppercase E!'

No matter how Omo tried, Fiyin refused to be fooled by her ephemeral lift. 'Omo, what went wrong? Why did you return so early from your date?' she asked again, her brows furrowed in concern.

A downward curve of the lips – an expression often indicative of Omo's intense frustration or displeasure – accompanied her loud sigh when she blurted, 'Is it not Ben? I do not get the guy at all! He is all cotton candies and warm milk when he calls to fix a dinner date which, by the way, does not quite fit into my schedule. But you know me and pleasant surprises, so I move mountains and fill valleys to honour it. I show up and Ben bends ridiculously out of shape because, wait for it... he disapproves of my outfit!' With her hands outstretched, Omo stood and asked, 'Fifi, please tell me, what is freaking wrong with this dress?'

Eyes sweeping over her friend, Fiyin asked, her lips curving upwards in a naughty smile, 'Ehm... with or without the jacket?' Omo gave her the eye and sat back in her chair. Fiyin continued, suppressing a chuckle, 'Besides the alarmingly low neckline, curious dip in the back, and apparent shortage of fabric which the designer must have encountered, I see absolutely nothing wrong with your promise of a dress.'

'It is in vogue, and it is classy!' Omo said, clicking her tongue. Deciding not to pour salt on the injury of her friend's ruined evening, Fiyin took her foot off the pedal on her journey down Reprimand Lane and asked to be told, in fine print, what happened on their date.

'I damned reason and left school halfway into my design class. Someone volunteered to cover for me because I had to pick up this dress from the dry cleaners before my date. Only for Mr My-opinion-counts-all-the-time to take one look at me and serve me the look reserved only for juvenile delinquents.' Fiyin listened with rapt attention as Omo told her how she endured twenty minutes of Ben's thin-lipped monosyllabic responses to her chit-chat initiatives and how, just as their main course arrived, she decided she could no longer handle her boyfriend's cold stares and shoulders for one second more. Omo said she picked up her purse and, without a word, walked out of Morgan Steak House, leaving behind an at-once-confused boyfriend.

Fiyin decided that giving voice to her uncut opinion would do neither her nor Omo any good. So, in the way she knew how, she cajoled her friend away from the looming depression, if only for a moment, with the hope of revisiting the issue of Omo's more-than-occasional squabbles with Ben, whom she thought, by the way, to be a fine gentleman. By Fiyin's count, Ben was her friend's sixth boyfriend, and that number, in her opinion, sat at five too many. But she did well to keep such opinions to herself.

Being a proponent of 'try your utmost to hit your target the first time', it came as no surprise that, at age twenty-three, Fiyinfoluwa Taylor remained innocent, partly in mind, but wholly in anatomy; she spotted not one relationship on her war bonnet. Many people explained this oddity as a total lack of interest in the normally stronger of the two genders of the human species and a probable inclination to the less strong. But for the more spiritually attuned lot, possession by a negative mystical creature lent more aptness to Fiyin's sorry state.

For Omo, her friend's decision to remain single till she met 'the one' only outlined the shape of outright cowardice. But at all three theories, Fiyin scoffed. For buried under countless layers of childlike naïveté and aloofness, stern in its discouragement of men merely seeking ephemeral relationships with her, lay, in all its latent splendour, a hopeless romantic, waiting to find expression. But so high was Fiyin's wall of expectations that even she could not afford a peek over it for an informed decision on who to let through or keep out of her castle gates.

Omo's comforter, a now-empty cup of chocolate mousse, sat in proud testament of her appreciation for good dessert. As she washed her cup, Omo decided to go straight to bed as soon as she entered her flat. That way, she would resist the overwhelming impulse to call

Ben. In truth, Omo liked Ben a little more than any of the other guys on her trail of past relationships. Something about the way he looked at her when they talked, almost like he was X-raying her soul, convinced her of his depth. But it annoyed her no end how she seemed to always be the one who donned the 'sage hat' and initiated 'the talk' each time a fight happened. *This time, I am not going to make any move, no matter what Fifi says*, she said to herself, her lips pursed in determination.

Her thoughts suffered a jolt when Fiyin said, with stars dancing in her eyes, 'Guess what? My folks are coming!' Fiyin's face radiated the joy of spring on this cold winter night, and although Omo's knowledge of Mr and Mrs Taylor came only from descriptive accounts by their child, she caught Fiyin's 'spring-bug'. They spent the few minutes before Omo returned to her flat, bouncing off ideas on how to keep the visitors occupied when they arrived.

TWO

YOU MUST LOOK BEFORE YOU LEAP

Fiyin did not want the novel to end. *Only two more chapters. Mscheew!* At the end of the third paragraph of the penultimate chapter, she slid off her bed, stretched her back, and ambled to the sitting area to peer through the blinds. After she took an apricot from the fridge, Fiyin adjusted the knife holder on her way back to her bed, to continue her reading. Of all the romance genre novels Fiyin read, only the author she christened 'the letter devil' made her bawl over words and her own imagination.

Minutes after she settled back in bed to resume her mind torture, her door knocker rattled. She let Omo in and started back to her bed.

'Babe, catch!' The paper bag Omo threw to Fiyin landed inches away from Fiyin's outstretched hands. 'Bad catcher!' said Omo with a giggle.

'No, bad thrower! What's this? Ahh!' Fiyin took out her new toffee-coloured lingerie, slipped it over her bum-jumper. 'This is lovely! Omo, but you shouldn't buy me stuff every time you go shopping!' Omo shrugged, walked off to the fridge to take a bottle of water. Fiyin ran her hands over herself, enjoying the clinging silky softness on her body. She thought Omo shopped too often.

Today, Fiyin was not going to ruffle Omo's happy place. One time, when Fiyin went didactic on her about her compulsive shopping, Omo brandished her status as an only child who never got any 'hand-me-downs'. 'I'm an only child too!' Fiyin had said, but Omo maintained her defence: they were different. And in truth, they were. Their childhood realities were daylight and darkness. Omo, the third and only surviving child of her mother – the fifth of her father's six wives – possessed no memory of her parents in any conversation unembellished with raised voices, neither did she recall her father ever holding her close. But Fiyin? Fiyin's home hugged her each time she set foot in it. The mere thought of it sent a warmness over and through her.

Fiyin asked, 'Has he called?'

'No.'

One week after Omo's failed dinner date and still no call from Ben.

'I miss him.' Omo's legs pulled her reluctant body towards Fiyin's bed. She picked up the novel on the bed stand, squinted at the title.

'*Fine Things*? Hmm. You and Danielle Steele. Why should I read other people's love story when I can act mine!'

'What? I like how she plays hide and seek with my emotions.' Fiyin climbed into her bed, tucked her ankles under her legs.

Days ago, Fiyin's words had jolted Omo. 'Hold out on Ben. Let's be sure we aren't mistaking pride for level-headedness.' Omo's eyes had grown into two tiny saucers. 'Et tu, Brutus! I kind of hoped you would nudge me into calling him!' But for the first time, Fiyin shared her friend's often-battle-ready mien. Why hadn't Ben ever initiated a reconciliation? Fiyin did not understand it.

Nevertheless, three days on and the lady warrior's resolve took a nosedive since Ben had neither called nor visited. An assortment of emotions began to wash over Omo. First, fear – perhaps she pushed too hard this time? Next, seething rage at Ben's predictable stance. In the end, she settled for steady withdrawal, to fortify herself against looming heartache.

Five more days idled by, still no call. Fiyin buckled. 'You know what? I don't think you should stretch this thing any longer. Call him. Be the adult, Omo.'

'Again! I won't, abeg!'

Before now, Fiyin had relied on her impressive IQ to deal with the emotional realities of adult life, but Omo's defiance at the ache she suffered from not talking to Ben shone a beam on her ineptitude at, and unpreparedness for, heart matters. This realisation compelled Fiyin to stick her tongue to the roof of her mouth, push all her opinions back into her gut, and join Omo in her countless shopping trips to Oxford Street. Lit in all its Christmassy splendour, carols floating through the cold winter, the crowded street and its endless string of shops allowed little room for an unmanageable degree of emotional brooding. Since Fiyin's presence made Omo's trips twice as fun, she played the excited shopping buddy. Moreover, it did not hurt the lady's purse; her father arguably owned a fifth of Benin; Omo wanted for nothing material.

⌐⌐⌐

A spike in temperature to a welcome six degrees Celsius caused Fiyin to send silent thanksgiving to the elements for their benevolence. Without question, her parents would have been shocked out of their shoes had they come only a few days earlier, for nothing would have prepared them for the sharp contrast in weather between Florida and the city of London.

Round and round the carousel, bags and boxes circled in search of their owners while Fiyin and Omo waited for their Christmas guests to emerge. And once they did, the ladies ran towards Bree and Donald with chin-splitting grins. Omo required no introductions. They locked in huge hugs, chatting as they walked out of Heathrow airport to the waiting taxi. All attempts to evade the savage arms of winter turned futile as the chill, surreptitious in its intent, snaked through their thick winter coats. Bree was certain that the thermometer in the United Kingdom's climatology department malfunctioned today. 'How can they say this is six degrees? This cannot be higher than minus six!' she said, rubbing her glove-clad palms together, her voice gruff from clenching her teeth at the cold.

Much to the taxi driver's eventual relief, silence ruled at last. He had almost grown deaf from the short-lived but loud chatter in his car as he endured the forty-minute journey to London, Paddington. He stifled a yawn, enjoying the soothing symphony of his passengers' breathing. Omo and the Taylors slept through almost the entire drive.

Now they understood why Bree and Donald had declined Omo's accommodation offer. Novotel Paddington could lure anyone into an overnight stay. Once the two young ladies set foot in number three, Kingdom Street, Sheldon Square, they understood why nobody would choose their dear old Chilfort Yards flat over this piece of elegant luxury. With the way the reception and lobby dazzled with bright lights, Fiyin and Omo could only imagine the splendour of the hotel's external features at night. But the Taylors' executive double room glowed with more subtle lighting. It kissed the heavy, rich cream drapes as they flowed from the ceiling to the warm wooden floor. Bree toned it down further by the twist of a knob.

Fiyin plopped into the queen-sized bed. A wrinkle formed on her forehead as she wondered why hoteliers associated the luxury of a room with the intensity of the backache their guests suffered from sleeping in their gravity-friendly mattresses. In silence, Omo sat in a single leather chair with a mild smile on her face, allowing the ambience to travel through her pores, to her soul and senses.

Omo and Fiyin exchanged winks at Donald's furtive glances at his wristwatch and Bree yawning into her own mouth, erupting in laughter at Fiyin's banal joke.

'We'd better be leaving,' Fiyin said, about an hour later. They said their goodbyes with a promise to return in the evening or the following morning for breakfast. Bree's eyes were drooping before they left the room to begin their trot to Praed Street.

A waterbus, the size of a little house, sat on the scenic Grand Union Canal of Little Venice. It caught the ladies' eyes and their steps faltered at the ramp which linked Sheldon Square to Paddington train station. Wafts from the restaurant nearby tickled Fiyin's senses with the promise of scrumptious meals, and she made a mental note to dine at Amole's restaurant sometime before the end of her course. After some grocery shopping at the store inside the station, Fiyin endured the last stretch of their walk to the apartment through Omo's bemoaning of her fashion course. 'I never thought the sketch module would prove to be such a tangle. It is way more tasking than I imagined!' Omo reminded Fiyin of herself as a child; those times she tried to pull her still-buttoned shirt over her head.

Unable to keep the bubble of laughter from escaping her pursed lips, she asked, 'Have you, at least, tried to sketch anything?' Omo's silence stretched for many moments. 'Well, have you?'

'Not quite. The first time I tried to sketch something, I assumed what my coach really wanted was… an idea of my sketch. He took one look at it and applauded my effort with a glare. Today is Friday and I must come up with something more dignifying by Monday.'

Fiyin was choking on her laughter. 'Idea of your sketch! What, in heaven's name, does that mean?'

Omo stopped in mid-stride, gave Fiyin a glare intense enough to clog her flippancy.

'On a serious note, Omo, type "how to design sketches for kids" on Google or YouTube. Babe, I trust you to transfer your passion into print. Ignore your coach… methinks he likes you.' Fiyin further masked her reprimand by giving Omo a light nudge on the shoulder. Omo shook her head in resignation. How typical of her dear friend to flesh out romance from rocks and irons. And to even further ameliorate the sting of her initial chiding, Fiyin agreed to Omo's suggestion; to go and play at Westfield mall, in celebration of the weekend. They were there until night-time.

Puffing with relief at the promise of warmth beyond the glass entrance doors of Chilfort Yards, Omo buzzed them in and froze the instant she entered. In one of the waiting chairs, in an obscured corner of the reception area, sat Ben, his arms resting on his thighs, his head bent forward. Omo had chosen to forget to mention a small detail to Fiyin: her phone had received a text-message battering from Ben. She had also ignored the non-stop vibration in her bag to and from the airport. Omo's eyes darted back to the door. But, guessing her next move, Fiyin placed a firm arm around Omo's waist, pulling her further into the building. No way would she let her thick-headed friend catch the flu or something worse because she would not breathe the same air with her boyfriend.

On his feet the instant he saw them, Ben said, 'Hi ladies.' He sounded like the flu already got to him.

'Hey, you!' said Fiyin, flashing a one hundred-wattage smile. Omo stole a reluctant glance Ben's way. On seeing his pink face and puffy lids, she wondered if it came from his flu. *Look how awful he looks. Hasn't he been sleeping well?* She managed a clipped, 'Hi.' After Fiyin swiped her access tab at the elevator panel, they huddled themselves in, away from the prying eyes of the front desk staff.

The ride to the fifth floor happened in deafening silence but the glint in Fiyin's eyes barked at Omo; she hoped whatever mischief Fiyin nursed as a payback plan would make Ben sweat in his shoes. *He must suffer for what he put me through. It's about time this cocky oyinbo learnt a thing or two about Naija!*

Once the elevator beeped and its doors glided open, Fiyin invited the pair for coffee as an antidote for the night's chill. Not yet ready to suffer Ben's intense gaze without company, Omo pounced on the offer. Ben hesitated, scratching the back of his neck. He much preferred some alone time with Omo, not coffee. But he raked his fingers through his wavy chestnut hair and pushed himself in, after his flighty girlfriend.

After Fiyin set the kettle to boil, she fished for cookies and cakes from her refrigerator. Ben and Omo sat on the sofa, playing tag with their eyes. The kettle whistled away the silence in Fiyin's room and soon, coffee, cookies and cakes were ready. As Ben and Omo ate, Fiyin scurried around in search of her phone. 'Maybe it's in your bag,' she said, digging through Omo's handbag. 'Oh, found it!' She let out air through her half-parted lips and started towards her exit door. 'Where're you going, babe?' Omo asked, but only the opening and slamming of the door answered her.

Another metal clanger – Omo's home keys – accompanied Fiyin's as she, who by the way had her mobile phone the entire time, slammed her door shut. *Ben and Bestie are stuck whether Bestie likes it or not.* Fiyin let herself into Omo's flat, wondering if the rumbling in her belly was happening in response to hunger pangs or spasms of excitement at her mischief. After establishing Omo did not have any cookies in her house, a disappointed Fiyin settled to enjoy *The Chase*, her favourite TV game show, with a mug of coffee and pistachio nuts. *Wow! Double episode! Those two lovebirds have a long night of talking.*

Almost halfway into the first episode, Fiyin's phone started to ring. She peered at the screen. *If it's Omo or Ben, I won't answer.* It was Ifeatu, her friend, calling from Nigeria. Since her engagement to Chike, Ifeatu called almost every other day, stressing over one wedding idea or the other. Ifeatu either called with a long list of colour theme ideas, or to fret about the near-empty receptacle of wedding concepts.

A week earlier, an argument about whether to incorporate souvenirs for her soon-to-be-husband's colleagues into her fast-expanding wedding budget occupied a significant portion of their airtime. Fiyin believed the entire concept of giving out souvenirs at parties mirrored not only a barefaced sham but monumental waste. 'Why in the world would you sell fabrics to be worn for your party to friends at more than twice the market value, all in a bid to accommodate the cost of the so-called "souvenirs" you intend to hand out?' As hard as Fiyin tried, she failed to understand the sense in it. Imagine her further bewilderment when Ifeatu's defence went along the lines of, 'It's how it has always been done... besides, it adds colour to the day!'

Fiyin picked up her call on the third ring and spent the better part of the second episode of *The Chase* convincing her childhood friend to agree with Chike's suggestion to set their wedding in Abu Dhabi.

As far as Ifeatu was concerned, Chike's suggestion did not stem from class or romance but smacked of a ploy to cut down the guest list to the barest minimum. 'He loathes large gatherings. He thinks I no longer remember how he used to lament about his cousins inviting hundreds of people to their weddings,' she said, pausing to draw air. 'I have a... a large family, and some of them are quite up there in society. How will everyone fly to Abu Dhabi for the wedding?' With mounting impatience, Fiyin reminded her friend that not everyone, as a matter of need, should attend her wedding.

'Distance will help check your crowd,' she said.

'But I don't want my crowd checked! I always wanted a big

wedding. You of all people know this, Fifi!' Ifeatu was becoming emotional, and time had taught Fiyin the futility in presenting any form of logic to an emotional Ifeatu. So, she focused her attention on the last segment of her game show, where her chest often threatened to burst with excitement as the quizzer, also called 'the chaser', answered as many questions as possible with the aim of catching the group of brilliant contestants and the cumulative cash prize in their possession. And with uncommon ingenuity, but mounting trepidation as her eyes stayed pinned on the TV, Fiyin offered the right punctuations to her friend's yammer: 'Yes', 'Okay', 'Mmhh' and 'I see!', hoping her art never loses its allure. Hunger pangs shook Fiyin out of slumber at 10:35pm. She picked up her mobile phone. No missed calls from Omo? She wondered why.

A chill snaked up Fiyin's spine as she let herself back in her flat. She clutched her mobile phone, her finger on the emergency button. Taking short, reticent steps further in, she let out a sigh through her trembling lips. On the fluffy rug, hidden from direct view by her single leather sofa, lay Omo and Ben, nestled and fast asleep. Fiyin noticed the leftover stir-fry in the saucepan and two used bowls sitting on the dining table; they bore proof of her guests' satiety. Plate of pasta and stir-fry in hand, Fiyin started to walk on her toes, towards the microwave oven when she obeyed her sixth sense's nudge to look back at her sleeping guests. Four eyes stared back at her.

'When did you get in?' A smile tugged at Omo's lips.

Ben said, 'Hi.' He rose to his feet, stretched a hand to Omo to pull her up, and sat down afterwards. Fiyin did not miss the almost shy glint in her friend's eyes as she took the sofa space beside her boyfriend.

A quick twist of his wrist to check the time and Ben got on his feet again, said he was starting back home, but Fiyin and Omo did not think it sensible and convinced him to stay till the following morning. After a few moments in thought, Ben sat back down and allowed himself to be sucked into a game of golf on ESPN.

Now sated after her rather late dinner, Fiyin went in for a shower. A while after, she joined her guests in her pink ankle-length night robe. Ben's only concern seeming to be the game showing on TV, he offered not the tiniest hint of perception when his girlfriend yawned, nudged him, and began to walk towards the door. Omo was part exhausted, part lonesome. And as she waited for Ben at the door, he said, his eyes still on the game, 'You go ahead, Omo. I'll, uh, join you in a minute!' Fiyin's eyes narrowed at the man in her flat. *This guy is avoiding Omo. Can't he watch the game at her place?* Fiyin followed Omo back to her flat.

Fresh out of the bathroom, Omo donned some lacy lingerie and slid into her bed, beside Fiyin. 'I am fagged out. My Gawd, Ben is a talker! That guy will talk for ten straight hours if you let him,' she said. Fiyin wanted the details of their exhausting talk.

'On the night of our fight, Ben's granddad died.'

'Jesus!'

'He was ninety-six.'

'Oh.'

The extra information about Ben's Poppy's age laved a balm of sorts over the heart-wrenching news. While chatting, they flirted with sleep. Omo lamented her misinterpretation of Ben's silence. As the only child, it fell on him to give his dad a hand to hold through the funeral. After suffering a chiding from Fiyin for not investing enough time in her relationship to perceive when something did not quite add up, Omo acquiesced. 'All right, all right... don't roast me. I promise to do better.' She turned over to her side of the bed when Fiyin would not let the matter rest. But by fifteen minutes past one in the morning, Fiyin joined Omo in her snoring party.

At the door, Ben beckoned. Omo walked towards him, her eyes twinkling with delicious anticipation. She snaked her arms around his neck and began to kiss him. Oh, how she loved the feel of his lips against hers. But Ben's lips, cold and unyielding, grazed over Omo's supple and yearning mouth. She became desperate, pressing into him, running her searching hands up and down his back. Ben stepped back, and with his hands clasped over her shoulders, began to move his lips in inaudible frantic speech. In the end, she trusted her eyes and mind to perceive the words she strained in futility to hear. 'Wake up, Omo, look at me, I am not me.' Omo's eyes fluttered open to Fiyin shaking her awake.

'What happened?' Omo asked, sitting up. *A dream?* Omo's recent encounter with her boyfriend only took place in her subconscious. It took a few moments for her to recollect, to string together the fragments of her dream. She sighed. A tear slid from her right eye while the left threatened to set free a drop of another just-formed tear. Fiyin's searching eyes bored into Omo's when she asked, 'Omo, what happened? Why are you crying?' This part of Omo lay buried beneath layers of self-awareness, optimism, and humour. Nothing Fiyin said made Omo reveal her source of distress, and at 3:00am, deciding that her crying friend possessed the ability to walk a terrain not at all new to her, Fiyin gave up and gave sleep one more shot.

A rattle at the door jolted Fiyin and Omo out of sleep. At 7:45 in the morning, they were running in deficit of time for breakfast with Mr and Mrs Taylor, but they remained in bed, weighed down by fatigue. Ben sent out another set of rattles. Fiyin started to get out of bed, to reach for the door, but Omo's words stilled her. 'He won't touch me. At best, he gives me a light kiss but nothing more. I am confused.' Fiyin thought she heard tremors in her friend's voice. *Is she crying?* She could not tell for certain since Omo had her face to the wall, to hide her fast-pouring tears. For the first time since knowing Omo, Fiyin scrambled for words but found none. She walked to the door, for fear it would soon fall apart from Ben's pounding.

Two minutes after Ben walked in, Omo bounced out of the bathroom where she had gone to take a mouthwash gurgle. Pasting a smile on her face, she reached for Ben, gave him a peck on the cheek.

'My apologies, sweetheart, my tired lids deceived me,' Ben said, turning towards Fiyin and continued, 'and I did not mean to deprive you of your bed, Fiyin. I am sorry. It was most insensitive of me.'

Fiyin waved away Ben's apology.

'Nonsense! We chatted until super late and woke up only this morning,' she said.

'Hope you haven't emptied her cookie jar, you rascal,' Omo said, moon-eyed and ruffling Ben's hair. She settled on the armrest of the chair beside him, so that their legs touched. Almost dizzy from Omo's switch between miens, Fiyin blinked back her surprise. She excused herself and, at the door, called over her shoulder, 'Hurry up, Omo. Remember, breakfast with my parents!'

It's so much softer than first grade human hair... so soft! Omo wanted to spend the entire morning running her fingers through Ben's hair, but she slid from the sofa's armrest, pulling Ben, by his wrists, onto the sofa with her. 'Ben, will I ever be able to earn your forgiveness?' Ben started to say it did not matter anymore, but Omo would not let him. 'I didn't call, refused to pick up your calls... gosh! I sound savage now listening to myself. I am sorr—'

Ben pulled Omo onto his lap and smothered her face with little kisses. 'My God! Omo, you drive me mad in so many ways!' The visible pulsation at the base of his neck gave away the disquiet his face and voice fought to mask. It caused Omo to wonder why Ben often retracted into his shell whenever they were alone. Most times, she wondered if her race should be called into question. But for now, she intended to glean every warmth his current passion offered.

When Ben expressed enthusiasm at the prospect of joining her for breakfast with Fiyin's folks, Omo pondered on the most probable of the three reasons behind her boyfriend's interest in breakfast. The opportunity to satisfy his curiosity about what Africans or Nigerians, besides Omo and her friend, represented made blunt the notion that Ben wanted to meet Fiyin's parents for the sole purpose of fostering a relationship. Or did he, indeed, crave for a hearty breakfast?

By 9:15am, Ben walked into the breakfast lounge of Novotel with Fiyin and Omo. Mr and Mrs Taylor were already seated and waiting. A cheery clash of food aromas, warmth and chatter filled the air, the sight of various shapes, sizes, colours and textures of food a wondrous sight to behold. Ben caught the gentle rise in the brows of the Taylors on their arrival.

'Oh, how sloppy of me! I should have called on our way,' said Fiyin, who began to make the introductions. 'Dad, Mum, this is Ben…' Mrs Taylor's elastic smile faltered an almost invisible fraction at the end of her daughter's phrase, '… Omo's close friend.' But Mrs Taylor soon recovered, and with a smile so radiant, told Ben what a pleasure it was to meet him. And to Donald's 'Good to meet you,' Ben said, 'I am most thrilled to have finally made your acquaintance. Fiyin and Omo have both told me so much about you. And please, accept my most sincere apologies for barging in on you this way, I simply could not let this opportunity slide past me.'

'Nonsense! Five is a party! Please, sit and have breakfast with us,' said Bree, pointing him to a seat by hers.

Sautéed sausages and tomatoes, scrambled eggs, steamed runner beans, French toast and cereal never tasted better. Of the many tables in the lounge, theirs ranked the loudest. Tales of Fiyin's cooking escapades and Omo's cardboard paper design adventures left tears in the corners of everyone's eyes – the chroniclers included. With breakfast over and the day only beginning, Omo suggested a walk around Sheldon Square and the canal. Paying no attention to Ben's glare, she convinced the Taylors of what an incredible idea it was to walk around in the cold to shake away the cold. Bree and Donald went up to their room to fetch their coats. While they waited for the elevator doors to slide shut, Bree took short steps further into the elevator, beckoning on her daughter to join them. Ben and Omo wondered why Fiyin rolled her eyes at her mum's invitation. Little did they know.

Once they began to travel up, Bree turned to her daughter, 'So, where is your own?' Donald coughed and moved as far away from the two women as the elevator allowed.

'My own what?'

Half irritated at her child's feigned ignorance, Bree asked, in clear language, why Omo had a close friend to introduce to them while she did not.

'Well, Mummy, isn't it obvious? I do not have a close friend to introduce to you, because I do not have a close friend to introduce to you!' Bree started a retort, huffed, and clammed down all in one short thread.

The rest of the elevator trip happened in tense silence with Bree's eyes tearing into her husband's forehead. She blamed him for not hopping to her side of the fence. Fiyin said she would remain in the room while her folks went on with the initial plan for a stroll; a thin film of tears shone in her eyes. At once, Bree walked to her daughter's side, held her face in her palms and said, 'Oya, come let's go, baby girl! All right, Mummy is sorry, I won't ask again.'

Nearly yelping at his wife's discreet kick, Donald added, 'Don't pay your mum any attention. Take your sweet time, my dear. It always pays to do so, trust me.'

Fiyin's lips lifted a fraction as, still sulking, she said to her mum, 'Keep up with this man quest, and I'll present you with the next male who glances my way.'

The week preceding Christmas burst with a consortium of activities. Since Donald and Bree were in London, Fiyin and Omo shuttled between schoolwork, sightseeing and shopping. Winter bit harder as the days sped by, so their prior plan to visit ZSL London Zoo scampered to the backseat to allow for a nice lunch with Ben's parents.

'So, tell me all about Africa. Is it as big as London? I find it incredible that you have lived all your life in Africa,' Milly Wright said, attempting to spark a conversation with the Taylors.

'Oh! Why so?' Bree asked, her eyes crinkling at the sides as she flashed a knowing smile. Ben forgot to tell his folks what an absolute witty soul Fiyin's mum was.

'Your accent sounds... uh sort of...uh different from what... I mean... uh...' By now, Milly punctuated her words with short dry coughs, making more obvious her nascent embarrassment. Bill shifted in his chair. Something told him his wife had boxed herself into a corner.

'It is Lagos, Nigeria.'

Darting her eyes to Ben, to her husband, and back to Omo, Milly blinked multiple times.

'Look at it this way,' Omo went on, hoping to draw a learning curve, but also wondering if no country, besides Nigeria, taught any geography in schools. *Or are we such a bunch of inconsequentials?* 'Africa is a Europe, the United Kingdom is a Nigeria, and Lagos is a London.' It became clear; although Milly and Bill exuded infectious positive energy, they could lay no claim to being bathed by sun rays in any parts beyond the United Kingdom and perhaps France. Ben's attempt to salvage their lunch date with a game of charades received good-natured support from Bree, Donald and

Fiyin. But Omo was not letting their hosts off easily. She bruised the rest of the evening with toasted tales of life in Nigeria; a targeted mission to stamp 'class' all over her home country. The non-Africans listened in utter awe, save for Ben's occasional, 'Oh, wow. I did not know that!'

When the two friends were able to steal a moment to be alone, Fiyin screeched into Omo's ear, 'What is wrong with you. Do you not have long-term plans for Ben? I mean… you going on and on with his parents.' At first, Omo did not understand but gawked as soon as she did.

'For real, Fifi, who are you?' It was Omo's turn to screech. In her opinion, Fiyin did not live up to the image she projected – one of a self-assured, happy and content female who thought nothing of remaining obstinate in upholding her standards. One who would never stoop for the reward of creation's so-called best work of art.

THREE

FALLING, FALLING, FALLING!

With Christmas in the recent past and Donald and Bree back in Nigeria, life resumed its monotonous symphony for Fiyin. But on this fine January afternoon, her mobile phone started to ring, rousing her from her siesta. Saturdays were almost sacred to Fiyin. They were her wrap-up-and-snuggle days.

Omo's smiling face flashed on the screen of her phone. Fiyin tapped the 'answer' icon. Her forehead remained wrinkled as she said, 'Hello.' After Omo's attempt to pair Fiyin with Ben's colleague, his supervisor to be exact, the supervening cold war between them had stretched longer than the typical life span of their fights. In Fiyin's opinion, this last 'hook-up' attempt by Omo happened to be six times too many within their four-month-old friendship. And although Omo's actions were borne from a heart of concern, Fiyin's perception of Omo's display of care for her tended towards unconventionalality and micromanagement.

Her brows went slack at the words from the other end of the line. 'Fifi, I'm at the hospital. I fell. They suspect I slipped a disc. My X-ray is not yet out… it hurts so much. The doctor is saying I may need to stay immobile for days.'

Fiyin scribbled the name of the hospital and in forty-five minutes, stood at the reception area of Edgware's St Agnes Hospital. A nurse asked for her name and address, before sighting her passport. She punched some keys on her computer and said, 'G wing, room 09.' Her voice reminded Fiyin of Penfold in the *Danger Mouse* series. She almost asked the nurse to point her in the right direction but changed her mind. The nurse's head bent over her phone and her eyes boring into only-heaven-knew-what convinced Fiyin to use her eyes instead of her mouth to find G wing.

A long hallway. Olive-green alphabet-inscribed boards on the walls indicated the ward wings. O wing, the first hallway off the long hallway, was a dark corridor covered with thick carpet and so were N, M, L and K wings. The corridor with J inscribed on its wall glowed in soft yellow lights and Fiyin spotted a male nurse wheeling backwards out of a room. Darkness ruled yet again as I and H wings sped past Fiyin.

At the entrance of G wing, Fiyin hesitated, her eyes forming slits at the unlit corridors. *How come a hospital like this cannot replace things as fundamental as light bulbs? Or is there something else going on here? And this eerie quietness. Ha!* Her mental commentary suffered an interruption when a door swung open. The instant a doctor emerged from one of the many doors, the corridor came alive under warm light. Only then did it strike Fiyin's befuddled head, *It's not the bulbs!* They were sensor-sensitive and would only come on when their laser beams encountered an obstruction. Resuming her commentary, she justified her ignorance by convincing herself of Boots store's complicity. But for their pedantically equipped stores, she would have had need to visit at least one hospital in her many holidays to London.

The doctor, blond and brown-eyed, gave Fiyin a polite nod as he went past her. Fiyin's eyes lit with surprise when she realised he had just exited room 09. As soon as Fiyin came through the door, following her tentative knock, Omo lifted her head from the pillow.

'Chick! What happened!' said Fiyin rushing to Omo's bedside, her eyes squinting with concern. When Omo tried to prop herself on her right elbow, a wince escaped her pursed lips, so she gave her narration on her back, of how she slipped on an ultra-thin film of ice on her way out of Broad walk mall. She had landed right on her butt, got up without as much as a blink. But once at the tube station, Omo soon grew aware of the slow spread of intense warmth from her waist down to her ankles. 'That was when I realised the pain and I were not mates. My legs developed a mind of their own. They stuck to the ground. The pain increased in geometric progression. Fiyin, you cannot believe it, I started wailing like a deprived baby. Babes, I swear, I've never experienced anything like this!' Omo shut her eyes in pain when she tried to chuckle.

Once Fiyin established that her friend's inability to walk stemmed chiefly from the psychology of pain, the drumbeats thudding in her chest quietened. Pain relief medication, seeping into her veins through the timed dispensing tube affixed to her wrist, guaranteed Omo could live out the rest of her day with manageable discomfort.

'Can I check?' Omo's brows furrowed in immediate alarm at Fiyin's request. But remembering Fiyin's course of study at the university and further specialisation in physiotherapy, she let her. A few winces, entreaties, and grunts later, Omo lay on her belly to endure the probing hands and fingers of her physiotherapist-turned-cook friend. Fiyin planted her left leg on the ground and her right across Omo's frame, on the narrow hospital bed. 'This may hurt,' Fiyin said, as she palmed down and worked Omo's waist, two inches away from both sides of her spine.

'*Iye meé!*' Omo yelled, squeezing the sheets to manage the excruciating pain lancing through her entire body.

'Why do you do that, though?' Fiyin never quite understood her friend's proclivity for yelling for her mum at the slightest provocation.

'Do what?' Omo's squeezing stilled for a moment, a line forming between her brows.

'Call for your Iye meé. It's not like you're a mummy's baby,' said Fiyin, easing her fingers into quick, light taps.

'It's your Iye, not your Iye meé. Iye means mother. Meé means me. Like Iya mi is to your Yoruba while Iye mee is to my Bini. I swear, Fifi, you are a real language olodo.'

'Your mouth is still sharp, abi?' Omo's distraction encouraged Fiyin to slide back to pressure-palming.

'Ahhhhhh! Fi-yin, easy! I take God beg you!'

Cooing sounds from Fiyin to quell Omo's cries yielded little. In one maestro move, she slid her left forearm underneath Omo's belly, half propping her on her knees.

'Babe, what... are you doing? Mscheew, nothing is wrong with my stomach! Abeg, if you are not sure of what to do, remove your hand and let me manage myse—' Before Omo could end her protest, Fiyin formed a hinge with her other arm. Bracing for Omo's reaction, she ran her hinged elbow down Omo's spine with a slow but deliberate technique. The shout of 'Jeeee... s... uuuu!' filled the room and, on cue, the door flung open. The same English doctor Fiyin had seen leaving Omo's room minutes ago walked in. On his tail was the most handsome man Fiyin could swear she had ever laid eyes on.

'What is going on here?' the brown-eyed doctor asked.

His companion was a dark-skinned middle-aged man, perhaps in his earliest thirties. He narrowed his eyes in unmasked disapproval as Omo tried to explain their awkward position and gratuitous noise.

'I leave for a minute to fetch my colleague and this? Surely,

Miss Omo, after my detailed explanation only moments ago, you must have understood. Complications could arise from moving without proper supervision.' Brown-eyed doctor's tongue-lash muffled Omo's additional excuses. Her lips parted, but no words came out as she ran her tongue over her dry lips in utter embarrassment.

'This is Dr Jide Williams. He will be handling your case from here on. I presume you would find it easier to obey his instructions,' brown-eyed and most-displeased Dr David Summers said, handing his companion a folder. Before either of the ladies was able to respond, Dr Summers walked out of the room, shutting the door with a noiseless slam.

The drawn silver-ash wooden shutters opposite the door, beside which Dr Williams still stood, provided an interesting object for Fiyin's observation. Her less-than-subtle evasion of the doctor's amused gaze fast turned ridiculous once he addressed her. 'So, ma'am, do you care to share what you were doing on my patient's back?' Fiyin tore her eyes from the window, but her tongue stuck hard to the roof of her mouth. 'And she does not speak!' the doctor said, walking the few steps to Omo.

'Tell me again, what happened?' It drew Fiyin's interest, how three horizontal lines formed across Dr Williams' forehead as he listened to his patient's account. A torrent of thoughts bounced around in her head. *He is so handsome. His name looks Nigerian. J-I-D-E... but that British accent, though. And why did Dr Summers pronounce it as Jyde? Maybe I should listen when he says it himself. But the way he looked at me! So... so condescending! Did I come off as stupid?*

Omo's question jolted Fiyin out of her self-dialogue. Fiyin's jaw dropped.

'Eeh? Fiyin, what did you do to my back? I can move... and... and sit!' Omo asked again, her face ready to split from grinning.

Modesty melted into oblivion as Fiyin sought to recreate her initial presentation of herself. She reminded Omo about how hard she studied for her university degree. Omo caught on, and the two ladies chuckled. But the humour did not hit any notes for Dr Jide Williams.

'Oh! You are a physiatrist?'

'No, not quite, uh, I am a… uh… I studied medical rehabilitation… with… with a major in physiotherapy.'

At the doctor's next words, Fiyin's self-esteem sank to the bottom of her stomach. 'I see, you are one of those who believe a short postgraduate degree, studying lab sciences or medical rehab grants them an instant licence to meddle with a business as sensitive as medicine.'

From a response to attraction to a feeling of rising indignation, the fast tempo of Fiyin's heartbeat switched without warning. *What conceit! Who appointed this guy judge over which course ranks superior to the other? Simply because he studied medicine doesn't give him any right to stomp all over other courses.*

'No course is inferior to medicine. They all have unique roles to play in life's journey. Although medical rehabilitation is not my first passion, I am darn proud I acquired such a training. I mean…' Fiyin stopped to let out air from her half-closed lips, a gesture she hoped portrayed self-assuredness, 'forty-five minutes after my friend lay writhing in pain in your hospital bed, unable to sit, I arrive, and Hallelujah! She is sitting and smiling, all thanks to my meddling with sen-si-tive business!'

The only reactions which Fiyin's outburst inspired were Omo's widening eyes and a mumbled, 'And she speaks… in angry bursts,' from Omo's doctor who tore his eyes from her face to resume examining Omo and taking notes. Fiyin resisted the intense urge to plant him a facer.

Dr Williams' eyes narrowed at Omo as she leapt into the air and bent to touch her toes, without as much as a wince. He did not look convinced enough to cancel her scheduled X-rays and three-hour observation. He insisted she stayed the night. Fiyin stood by the window, seething, stealing stealthy glances and scoffing every now and again. The next fifteen-odd minutes Dr Williams spent in the room with his patient did not include her.

Omo resembled a person walking on broken glass as they made the few blocks to Chilfort Yards. She worried about the possibility of another fall, fearing to make any sudden turns. After he signed her discharge papers, Dr Williams had warned Omo to keep the pressure off her legs and spine for a few days. At the reception area, he attempted a conciliatory smile at Fiyin, but she clicked her tongue at him. *Nonsense! This guy has a caustic tongue. I'm not going to give him the pleasure of subjecting myself to another acid bath from him*, she thought, her legs barely able to keep up with her intended speed as she stalked off, ahead of her friend.

⌇

Not knowing the reason for the unmistakable glint in Omo's eyes was goading Fiyin into petulance. Ben was not coming until tomorrow, and she did not impress her coach with her last design sketch assignment either; Coach Michael asked Omo to dig deeper for inspiration. So, what was it? It was obvious something was exciting her. Or at least had her attention. Fiyin stewed in her own curiosity while Omo sipped, with infuriating contentment, on her cup of hot chocolate, smearing with unbelievable ease Fiyin's white wall of fame; one which, before now, attested to her adeptness at squeezing information from almost anyone. Whatever the case, no quest for information possessed the strength to keep Fiyin up too late on a Saturday night. Sundays were one degree more sacred than her Saturdays, and she loathed arriving for church service any time later than 8.25am. So, after she gave Omo a back and waist massage, she bade her goodnight and began to see herself to the door.

'Babes!' Omo called. Pausing and giving her body a full swing, Fiyin's mouth curved in a smug smile.

'You like the fine doctor, abi? Don't you dare lie to me.'

Whaat! How did she… Christ! Am I that obvious? Fiyin opened her mouth to say something but slammed it shut again.

In one final blow below the proverbial belt, Omo said, 'Should I feign pain… so you can take me back to the hospital… so you can, maybe, see him?' She burst into rib-hurting laughter when Fiyin stomped off, rattling her entire house with the slam of the door.

Sunday morning did not find Fiyin early and cheery. Only able to rest her eyes at five o'clock in the morning after fighting her bedcovers the entire night, her eyes fluttered open at 9am. And for a service with a habit of commencing at 8.30am and spanning only an hour, the futility in trying to make it in time mocked an already incensed Fiyin. She blamed Omo. If only the girl ever went to church, she would have woken her up. Fiyin could wager her best shoes that Omo still snoozed in her bed and would continue to do so till noon if she let her.

Still in bed and crouching on her knees, Fiyin said her prayers…

'Merciful Lord, thank you for keeping me through the night, for allowing me some sleep and for waking me up in perfect health and in sound mind. Thank you because I have faith in your ever-protective arm over my parents and all those I hold dear. I am so sorry for not attending service today. I promise, I'll be more deliberate going forward. Please let your angels guide and guard me and all my loved ones… and… and please Lord, help me take my mind off that doctor. In Jesus's name I have prayed.

Amen.'

'What? I can't hear you. You need to speak up!' Fiyin screamed into her phone.

'You would if you turned down the music,' Omo fired back from the other end of the line. Ron Kenoly's 'Lift Him Up' settled to a mere whirr. Omo wanted to know why she had not gone to church and if she cared to join her on a trip to Burnt Oak for some food condiments.

'No, I missed church... too much sleep... you have infected me with your Sunday sleeping sickness.' Fiyin could not resist the jab. 'And no, I'm not in the mood to go anywhere today, but you can buy me four plates of jollof rice from Epe Cuisine, if you don't mind.' Cheery tunes, blaring at its highs, filled Fiyin's room once again as soon as Omo got off the line with a promise to buy Epe Cuisine's famous rice.

A bang on her door, so loud it defied the eardrum-bursting music, jolted Fiyin, interrupting her mid-morning dance to Stanley Kaosi's 'Jesus, I Love You Oh'. With hurried steps, she got to the door to find no one. Puzzled, Fiyin scanned the length of the carpeted hallway. No one. She made to shut her door, but her eye caught a white envelope with her flat number on it. *Hmm! Who is sending me a letter?*

Prompted by heightened curiosity, Fiyin shut her door and tore the envelope. The contents stilled her head from bobbing in rhythm to the tunes filtering through her Bluetooth speaker. After a quick scan, Fiyin strode to her speaker, long-pressed the power button and tiptoed to her bed where she sat in a corner until Omo rattled her knocker. She scurried in with three bulging Burnt Oak signature blue nylon bags; countless identical blue bags, scrunched together, occupied a substantial space in the kitchen cupboards of the two ladies, evincing their preferred grocery shopping destination. Lost in her musings, Omo neither took note of the way Fiyin's eyes darted up and down the hallway when she unlocked the door to let her in nor her laboured inhaling and exhaling of air. Nothing of how Fiyin closed the door in a hurry alerted Omo of her friend's unease. Silence pervaded the flat as Omo, close-lipped, deposited six bowls of jollof rice on the kitchenette counter. With eyes raised in expectation, Omo regarded Fiyin as she sat, chin on knee, on her lone sofa, cracking her knuckles. She wondered why Fiyin failed to notice or ask why six, and not four, bowls of rice sat on her counter. Whatever the case, Fiyin and Omo were both troubled by something.

'Fifi, I… there is something I need to tell you. Please, don't take this the wrong way. I saw…' Fiyin flayed her arms, placed her index finger firmly over her lips. Omo stopped talking. And in answer to her rumpled forehead, Fiyin pointed at the white envelope on the dining table. It read…

> *'Good afternoon,*
>
> *In case you have not realised it yet, people live on floors lower than yours. You stomping around with no consideration for other people smacks of a profound degree of thoughtlessness.*
>
> *Some of us have more to deal with than you can imagine and are not able to take any additional challenges. As you live your perfect and happy life, do employ some consideration for us mere mortals…*
>
> *Thank you.'*

Whatever bothered Omo before now sublimed and escaped through her flared nose. Her eyes glared with indignation. Right hand on her waist and flicking the note, she said, 'Who sent you this nonsense?' As soon as Fiyin narrated the drop-off and pick-up of the envelope, Omo's disposition changed again but to one of incredulous humour. She started to laugh. 'Oh, boy! I never jam this kind cowardice before! Babe, abeg, don't mind this person! Make im come touch the person wey im dey follow talk. Okobo!' Omo often spoke Nigerian pidgin when utterly miffed or mind-rattled with amusement. In her opinion, the angry neighbour downstairs was a racist who had resorted to threatening people to drive home his point. When Fiyin asked what buoyed her impetuous conclusions, Omo held up the letter. She pointed at the excerpts 'stomping around' and 'consideration for us mere mortals…'. With embellished surprise, Fiyin's eyes fluttered multiple times at Omo's elucidation. The former phrase underpinned the note writer's belief in the shared kindred spirit between Fiyin and the gorilla or other animals, famous for stomping around. Racist. The latter ended in dots, which was indicative of a threat. And who else but the normally physically stronger of the genders would threaten anyone?

'You have a rather vibrant sense of imagination. Let's hope it doesn't land you in boiling okra soup. Ehe! Let me pounce on my yummy rice!' Fiyin shrugged off her friend's theory and walking on her toes to the dining table, she opened one of her just-arrived bowls, took a sniff, and lowered her eyelids in unabashed appreciation of the harmonious smell of spices and steam.

As Fiyin savoured her third spoonful of jollof rice, a bemused Omo started towards her flat. Only then did Fiyin ask why she had bought more bowls of rice than she ordered. 'And by the way,' Fiyin said before Omo's response, 'you still haven't told me how much I owe you.' Omo's eyes narrowed. *Is she still afraid of looney note-writing neighbour?* But she did not have the luxury of dwelling on why Fiyin whispered in her own flat; something else worried her. She walked back to Fiyin, her pulse throbbing. And pinning her with a now-all-too-familiar piercing stare, she drew a lungful of air as she told Fiyin about her chance meeting with Dr Williams at Burnt Oak.

'He wanted your number… just to apologise for the way he spoke to you the other day.' Fiyin needed no further confirmation. Acrid-mouthed Dr Williams now possessed her phone number. A prickling started in her underarms. Her breathing became laboured from the tightening in her chest, Fiyin asked Omo to leave her flat at once. Omo, certain she had crossed the line this time, began to explain.

'Fifi, I swear, I did not have a hook-up in mind. For once, I didn't!' Fiyin refused to meet her friend's searching gaze.

As soon as Omo left, Fiyin exhaled. She leaped, but remembering her neighbour, landed on her toes to do a hybrid of the moon walk and the robot dance. Omo's insinuation about the neighbour's gender flashed in her mind's eye, and she shuddered. *God forbid it is a woman!* Fiyin did not claim ignorance of the extra spunk associated with her fellow female folk. Half running to the dining table, she reached for her phone. *So, why hasn't he called?* Fiyin spent the rest of the day scrolling through her phone. If Dr Jide Williams called, or sent a text message, she did not want to miss it.

That night, another battle ensued between Fiyin and her sheets. But this time, lip-smacking excitement replaced frustration as the reason for her fight. She would see, or at least hear from, the handsome doctor with the scalding wit again. When he apologises, she would have her tranquillity back. *What was it called? Transfer of negative energy?*

FOUR

NO PRESSURE

An ear-to-ear grin greeted Omo when she opened her door to Fiyin. A game of 'spot the difference' played in Omo's head as she tried to gauge Fiyin's disposition. In response to Fiyin's flash of a smile, Omo offered a placid one of her own. Perhaps she came to rattle a little more about her recklessness, her smothering?

Without question, Omo liked Fiyin a lot, often coveting her moral strength. She wondered how a babe like Fiyin maintained such a pristine dating history. Fiyin set a bowl of chin-chin on the kitchen top. *Bribe as usual*, Omo almost scoffed aloud. Most times, she extolled her friend's virtuous quality. But on certain days, like today, she questioned how much of a choice Fiyin had in the matter.

'Chick, how did your sketch go today?' Fiyin asked, walking to the refrigerator to take a pear.

'Fine.' Omo made an excellent impression of a lioness licking her battle scars. Her smooth forehead and monotone sent a clear message: she still smarted from last time. Rabbit-eyed, Fiyin set herself on the sofa, beside Omo. Her insolence the day before was utter in its needlessness, and Fiyin said as much to Omo, who did not appear to have heard her. She confessed how she had not been able to stop obsessing about the doctor's insult-splash party, how she longed for a chance to pay him back, mend and refill her punctured ego.

'Let me be honest with you... I think I got attracted to him before I was ready to admit it to myself. It's not a good enough excuse but when you wrote it in black across a whiteboard, I felt like a thief. A thief caught with her hand in the pot of meat... you caught me, and I wasn't ready to be caught... Chick, I'm sorry.' Omo's forehead twitched.

'Oh?' Omo picked up her phone to begin scrolling.

'Don't be angry now!' Fiyin made a playful effort to snatch Omo's phone. It earned her a glare.

Desperate for a bit more engaging response from her angry friend, Fiyin said, 'So he called me today.' And pretending to swallow Omo's feigned ignorance, expressed by her now crumpled brows and slight tilt towards her, Fiyin talked about the call from Dr Jide Williams. Like a spool of wool undone and left to roll down a gentle slope, Omo unravelled, forgetting her prior anger.

'Did he ask you out?' Tiny stars started to dance in Omo's eyes.

'Yes... he wanted to apologise in person... at my place, but I told him his phone apology did an excellent job.' Worry lines formed on Omo's face, her lips curving downwards. 'What? Omo, abeg, I'm so not prepared for him and his mammoth-sized ego. Didn't you notice the way he was looking down on us at the hospital... I mean literally?'

Omo began to defend the doctor. 'But it's not his fault I was sitting most of the time.'

'Not me! I stood the entire time!'

'Well, it's not his fault he is a full head taller than you, nau! How else do you want the guy to loo—'

'Omo, you've started again!' Fiyin said, wagging her index finger at Omo who raised both hands in surrender.

Not much about Dr Williams featured in their chat for the rest of the evening. For a peace offering, besides the bowl of chin-chin, Fiyin told Omo she had prepared fish soup.

'Something for the cold?' she wheedled.

The soup made the difference. Omo's spirits reached cruise altitude and refused to touch down. An episode of *The Cube* occupied the rest of the evening until 9:30pm when Omo began to yawn. At the door, before Omo said goodnight, a message alerted on Fiyin's mobile phone. It pulled her mouth into a smile as she read it.

'Who?' Omo suspected who.

'Guilty conscience pricks hard. You've guessed who,' said Fiyin, giving her phone to Omo.

'*Hi Fifi, Thanks again for letting me apologise. Please send my warm regards to Omo… Tell her to keep the pressure off her legs if she can help it. Enjoy the rest of your week.*

PS… Still keeping my fingers crossed on tasting one of those brownies you were chewing over the phone. Have a pleasant night rest, ma'am.'

'Ma'am! This doctor is hilarious,' Omo said, making to give back the phone to a smug-faced Fiyin. Provided his communication delivered a clear apology, Fiyin did not care how Dr Jide addressed her, and she told Omo so.

Nevertheless, there proved to be a clear contrast between Fiyin's recent declaration and her following reaction. When Omo hesitated on returning the phone and did only after she deleted Dr Williams' phone number and text message, Fiyin's discomfiture shone in all its elegance. 'Omo, why naa!' Her voice rang an octave higher; her eyes supressed her annoyance, and a nerve on her right temple pulsated. Indifference cloaked Omo's smile. She sashayed off to her flat saying into the hallway as she pulled the door after her, 'You need me, babes. For this one, you need me.'

⌒

Wednesday through Friday, Fiyin's eyes sparkled. In uncoordinated bursts of unwarranted excitement, her voice rose octaves higher than necessary. What about the spills and burns? Yes, Fiyinfunoluwa spilled condiments! Today, she managed to burn her time-consuming and effort-straining seafood casserole. Every now and again, Chef Jose pulled his brows together and scratched the back of his neck.

At first, Chef linked Fiyin's freneticism to her excitement over securing a coveted spot in a diploma class in Culinary Management and Administration. But the distant gaze Fiyin fixed at nothing through the rest of the day told the chef to undo his link. He shook his head in amused admiration as Fiyin skipped off at the end of yet another chaotic day. Chef Jose only hoped the weekend would afford his prized student enough time to source the necessitous reins for her exuberance. 'See you on Monday!' he called after her fast-disappearing frame.

Nobody understood the reason for Fiyin's recent disposition. While she never bragged about being the most aloof, Fiyin also did not possess a plaque for the world's shiniest sanguine. She maintained a delightful spot somewhere close to the middle.

All knots, edges, and nerves, Fiyin sat through her train ride. After a quick stop at Paddington station's Sainsbury's, she half jogged to her flat, her pulse racing faster with each tick of her wristwatch's tiniest arm. Somewhat comforted by Omo's last-minute change in plans for a date night with Ben, she hoped 'Miss Know-a-lot-about-men' would be willing to come to her rescue today.

Walking past her flat, Fiyin took the few steps to Omo's door. With time almost overtaking her, she wanted to contain the disconcerting warmth she felt spreading from her chest; to keep it from showing when the object of her disquiet arrived. Yes, Dr Acrid Tongue had managed to extricate an invitation from Fiyin. Or so Fiyin hoped Omo believed.

Try as Omo did, knowing the degree of torment a jab would inflict, she lost the duel to mischief. 'Let's agree he coerced an invitation out of you... why didn't you push for a later date? At least for some time to... ehm... comport yourself?' Omo's question earned her 'the eye' as Fiyin asked if she would give her any tips or not. Of course, Omo dropped the jabbing, and soon, donning her fedora hat of all wisdom, started an endless recital of do's and don'ts.

'Give him only a drink. Ignore his joke about your cookies.'

'Try not to initiate any conversation.'

'Don't be too chatty.'

'Listen, but don't clutch at his every word.'

'Scroll through your phone between your chats...' The list stretched on and on. Swimming in the drone of Omo's voice, Fiyin thought about what she would do with the baking flour and butter she had purchased from the grocery. She had planned on making Dr Williams a new improved version of her honey and tea jammers.

Once inside her flat, her mobile phone began to ring. A glance at the caller identification, and Fiyin kissed her teeth.

'Ifeatu, sorry I can't talk now... No, not at all... Yes. I'll call you back... maybe later in the evening... Yeah, bye.' Ifeatu sounded desperate. She and Chike were at it again. With their wedding only months away, Fiyin hoped their now-frequent fights were only borne from wedding jitters.

Although thankful for the calming which Ifeatu's call gifted the chaos in her head, Fiyin reckoned her best friend may be drifting away on the trimmings of wedding pomp and vanity rather than concentrating on the actual fabrics; if the yardage, texture, and stitches were in concordance. Fiyin's musings helped her attain a degree of calm. But not for too long. *Ah, should I turn on the TV for background noise? What if he's a bore… or I'm a bore!*

Sofa puffs in place, kitchen counter cleared and flat smelling of lemons and cotton candy, Fiyin toyed with taking a shower before her guest arrived. But she only toyed with the idea for fifteen minutes. On the mark of the scheduled time, Dr Jide Williams called flat 512. He lit her entire house as he waltzed in with an almost face-splitting grin.

Far from Fiyin's fears, not one moment of awkwardness passed between the two. They had something to say about every topic broached. Non-stop chatter reigned as they discussed life in Nigeria, parents, siblings, or the lack of them. They talked about life in London, and favourite childhood films.

A heated argument ensued when Jide mentioned his best film of all time. *Seven Brides for Seven Brothers!* Fiyin interpreted the piece as a reflection of institutionalised barbarism which thought nothing of the dignity of the female gender. But Jide dissented. He insisted the film spewed mad humour and did not deserve the extra emotion she appeared to be investing in it. The spotlight soon slid off their different views on the 1966 film.

Next on the podium, *The Sound Of Music.* Much to Jide's amusement, Fiyin exhibited a spine-breaking leaning towards the musical, which had also captured his heart as a child. She highlighted the 'girl power', against which Captain Von Trapp's macho character stood defenceless, as her high point in the film. He wondered if the lady before him would ever unravel enough for him to see what lay beneath. All the fundamental trappings of a female activist seemed to be burgeoning.

Jide's incipient perceptions of Fiyin soon suffered a nip by her next words.

'What can I offer you? Tea, coffee, juice… water?'

'Um… water is fine,' Jide said, both amused and surprised at the seamless speed with which she slid between subjects. As she handed him a bottle of still water, Fiyin gobbled the features of the fine man on her sofa, and the fast throbbing in her chest, the one she thought had bowed to her self-control and dignity, resumed with renewed purpose.

Everything about Jide delineated intentionality. His almost lazy slouch as he sat on one end of her lone sofa. She adored the delicate eloquence with which he disagreed with some of her views. Like when he maintained his stance about it being therapeutic to let out loud farts, public gatherings or not. 'How can you advocate such unbecoming behaviour?' Fiyin's voice had risen almost three octaves. The fizz in his eyes when something excited him excited her; she had seen it twice. The first time, when he saw her on Omo's back at the hospital. The second time, only moments ago, when she copied his handstand pose. Of all his mannerisms, Fiyin feared she may never forget the way he uncorked the bottle, filled and downed his glass of water in four silent gulps.

'Aha! Now, where were we?' he said, setting his empty glass on the centre table and resting his forearms on his knees. 'So, besides the films you like, your first degree in medical rehabilitation, your passion for food, your physical flexibility, and your advocacy for girl power, what else am I missing about Miss Fifi… um… I still do not know your surname,' Jide said, his eyes crinkling at the sides.

Deciding on the improbability of such a parcel of appeal being unsnapped by some smart and equally appealing lady, Fiyin willed herself to stash her hopeless-romantic soul and remain content with enjoying the company of her fine and witty guest. *I always meet them after the fact*, she thought, recalling the first time she experienced this same sense of loss.

It had been in church, during one of those forced breaks, when aggrieved university staff, in an often-futile attempt to protest the non-implementation of agreements by the federal government, went on another one of their never-ending ASSU strike actions.

Moments after the processional hymn, he walked into the church and sat two pews away from her. Save for their exchange of handshakes, when the Reverend asked everyone to welcome their neighbours to church, no interaction passed between them. But for most of the week, Fiyin thought about the man without a name. She hoped to see him again the following Sunday and beamed with delight when she did.

In an interesting web of chance, they sat on the same pew this time, next to each other, and exchanged greetings long before the Reverend's prompt. For a nation still grappling with wanting governance, the sermon, captioned, 'Your Pharaoh Must Bow', resonated with everyone. Occasional sighs, bursts of laughter and spirited concurrence punctuated the preacher's forty-minute-long sermon.

At the close of service, while everyone filed out, the man introduced himself as Dapo Olabode. 'I am Fiyin Taylor.' A warm smile was etched on his face as he bade her goodbye and wished her a lovely week before he walked off in a hurry. On the third Sunday, Fiyin spent an appreciable part of the service scanning the church for her new acquaintance. Just when she thought he may have skipped service, she spotted him in an obscure corner.

Though she found her relief rather ruffling, Fiyin hoped that would be the day they exchanged phone numbers. He spotted her at the close of service and waved with childlike enthusiasm. Fiyin meandered her way through the milling congregation for a chat. Then she saw her.

This has got to be the most flawless skin on the most graceful human being I have ever seen, thought Fiyin.

'Hello Fiyin! We missed each other today.' Remembering himself, Dapo continued, turning to Flawless Skin. 'Aha, Sweetie, this is Fiyin, my neighbour for two services in a row, the one who told the right-eye-to-left-eye riddle. Fiyin meet my fiancée, Tinu.'

A genial smile spread across Tinu's face as she held out her hand to Fiyin.

'Oh my gracious! Your riddle... I tried everything. From "the more you look the less you see" to "I see you" and "we look together". When Dapo told me the answer, I almost laughed out my lungs,' Tinu said, almost starting another bout of laughter. Someone nudged Dapo, which brought their attention to how much human traffic they were causing with their chit-chat. A chance for Fiyin's escape came at the most auspicious time. With a smile terminating somewhere between her nose and eyes, Fiyin bade them both a lovely day. She scurried off to find her parents who she suspected still revelled in the exchange of pleasantries with people they saw a day or two before. She all too soon felt cranky, but the cause eluded her. *Perhaps the long sermon is to blame*, she had reasoned.

'Fiyinfunoluwa Taylor. My name is Fiyinfunoluwa or Fiyin. But you can stick to Fifi, like most of my friends have chosen to.' They both let out chuckles when Jide said he could not agree more, since her full name would pose an insurmountable task to his tongue, lips and teeth.

'Besides, when I asked, Omo told me Fifi,' he said in his own defence. For the first time since Jide's arrival, a moment of awkward silence hovered between them, but not for too long.

'You up for a riddle?'

'Ask away!' Jide rubbed his palms in delightful expectation.

'What did the right eye say to the left eye?'

'Um... um...' Jide closed his eyes in thought.

'The right eye said, "Um... um"?' Fiyin was gloating.

'You are terrible!' Jide's tone was light, but his forehead remained crumpled in concentration.

'So tell me!'

'I will. I will... if only you would let me focus!' Jide fought it, but his lips were experiencing smile spasms. Fiyin let out a dramatically loud yawn, emphasising the fast-depleting time.

'Got it! Yes, I got it! The right eye said to the left eye, "Between us, something smells"!'

'Ah. This doctor! You are too sharp for your own good, joor.'

A while later, Fiyin tuned to Challenge for an episode of *Catchphrase*, a game show where contestants played to win luxury gifts by decrypting familiar phrases portrayed by pictures.

'I never get their phrases. This particular game show is tilted in favour of the British,' Fiyin said with a sigh. But Jide told her to write a petition to her school, demanding a refund from her English Language teacher since, as far as he knew, the phrases in play were all English language constructs.

'Says the one whose only education outside the UK is secondary school! You have unfair advantage, you brute!' Fiyin said, rewarding Jide for his jab with a throw pillow in the head.

Before Jide turned his attention to the game show, an edginess had settled over his easy exterior, but Fiyin missed it. She had let herself float away on the wings of her excitement, believing her appreciation of his company was reciprocal.

Omo made herself, her calls, and her text messages scarce and Fiyin, without meaning to, prayed it remained so. At fifteen minutes past seven, still not ready to rid herself of his company, it no longer made sense for Fiyin to not offer Jide something besides Still water. Since not many of Omo's tips remained to be broken, one more would not hurt, she rationalised.

'Can I whip up a batch of my favourite cookies for you?' Fiyin almost knocked herself on the head for asking. Jide's eyes lit up like the trees on Oxford Street at Christmas. A gentle tug in the middle of Fiyin's belly provided all the confirmation she needed; she would whip up ten batches of cookies, bread, cupcakes, and pies if he as much as asked. *What is it about this guy? I should still be wary of his sharp tongue,* she thought, checking herself. But Jide did not allow her self-check to linger because not only did he take her up on her offer, but he also offered to help. 'I have always wanted to learn how to constitute this major weakness of mine.' Fiyin smiled at Jide's twist of words, a leaning she now recognised as his road map to humour.

Once Fiyin's head bobbed up and down in assent, he cast a nervous glance at his wristwatch, walked to the counter where his host stood, and rolled up his sleeves higher. He could not remember the last time he felt this relaxed. Late in the evening or not, he would glean every nanosecond from his time with this lovely being… while he had the chance.

As they waited for the cookies to bake, Jide apologised again 'for being such a brute the last time'. Satisfaction washed over Fiyin as she told him, again, 'No worries… I mean it!' As a gentle diversion, she talked about her plans after Greyburtons and soon after, a twenty-four-piece batch of Fiyin's home-made cookies came sliding out of the oven.

Time for the cookies to cool on the oven rack idled away with a game of 'rock, paper, scissors'. Afterwards, Fiyin challenged Jide to a game of 'Ayo'.

'What is Ayo?'

Fiyin laughed and asked him if 'Mancala' sounded more familiar. Jide's brows rose in realisation.

'You this Naija Oyinbo!' Fiyin said, stifling a giggle.

'Oh, you mean "Ncho"? I know it as "Ncho",' Jide said.

'Odd. Never heard it called "Ncho",' said Fiyin, her brows pulling to the middle. They played three rounds, with Jide cementing his visit by gifting Fiyin a thrashing to remember.

To go with the cookies, Fiyin made some custard. No sooner had they descended on their meal and Jide had begun to ask how else Fiyin spent her free time than the knocker rattled. Fiyin cast a quick glance at the door. It must be Omo. She dragged herself to the door, ready to tell her to disappear. Not so easy! Omo came with Ben.

'Impeccable timing,' Fiyin said with a mock scowl.

'Don't blame me, love. I no sabi the dude. What if he's one of those organ-harvesting doctors?'

'Clearly, he's not!'

'No vex. We'll leave before you can say J-i-d-e.' Omo gave Fiyin a double wink. Ben's polite smile through their hushed doorway dialogue prompted Fiyin to exhibit more enthusiasm at her guests' arrival. She moved away to let them in. Jide's eyes lit up as soon as Omo entered. One would think they were good old friends. He shook hands with Ben and started the introductions. *This Naija boy's 'Britiko' accent though!* Omo mused.

True to Omo's promise, they were out in no time but not without three cookies each. 'If you still have any left by tomorrow, abeg, remember your girl!' Omo said, scurrying after Ben as he left Fiyin's flat.

They ate their cookies and custard in silent appreciation of the warmth of a good meal, each lost in their own thoughts. Fiyin wondered if Jide would ask her what she wanted him to ask, while Jide rumpled his brows at the warmth he now experienced. This warmth, did it come from the custard or from the cloaking of a certainty – the certainty of the evanescence of this budding friendship?

Determined ticks nudged the unwilling hour arm on Fiyin's wall clock towards 'IX'. Jide got on his feet, his hands in his denim trouser pockets. 'I have had an incredible time, Fifi. Thanks again for letting me apologise for my poor behaviour. One day, I hope I will be able to give you a plausible excuse for it.'

An inflection in his voice called Fiyin's attention to his probing eyes and the horizontal worry lines on his forehead. A nervous chuckle escaped Fiyin's pursed lips. Her underarms were clammy. 'Well, you chose my good week to exhibit your abhorrence, but don't count on your luck next time.' They both laughed.

Once downstairs and outside, the knot in Fiyin's belly loosened.

Jide had driven, else it may have been a tad tricky for him to travel to Edgware so late in the night. A drawn face and squared shoulders replaced his easy mien as Jide got in his car. Now obvious he bled with the need to say something, Fiyin watched him, slit-eyed, willing him to speak. *Ask me if I'm seeing someone, darn it!*

At the tap of his index finger, Jide's car growled into wakefulness. And mere seconds before it hit rock bottom, Fiyin's heart received a boost; Jide wound down his window.

'Um… what part of Western Nigeria do you come from?' Jide's voice sounded low, somewhat tired.

'Ondo state. You?' For a moment, the ground under Fiyin's wool-slip-on-gloved feet felt gibbous. The evening chill, formerly tamed by her warm meal and engaging companion, returned with barbaric vengeance. It made absolute nonsense of common sense. How could someone called 'Jide' be from South-Eastern Nigeria?

Words started to travel from her head but lost their will to be spoken once they reached Fiyin's dry tongue. Jide had a lopsided smile, made more obvious by his now almost-drooping eyes. The silent sliding up of his window as he said, 'See you around… Miss Fiyin Taylor,' seemed definitive of an all-too-familiar loss. Jide engaged his car in 'drive' mode and sped off into London's chilly arms.

⁓

'Anambra state!' Omo's voice rang through her flat. After a three-second interlude, she resumed with her monologue. 'How? Call him and ask him again! Uh, maybe his father is from the East and his mum from the West! Or vice versa… that would make sense, abi?' Fiyin looked on with sunken eyes, her tongue as heavy as her heart.

A few more moments of pacing around her living room and

casting quick glances at Fiyin and Omo said, 'But, uh, babes... does it matter so much where he comes from? Na still one Nigeria nau?' Sitting with her knees drawn to her chest, her arms wrapped around her legs, Fiyin struck an unblemished picture of confusion. *Where is the exact location of Anambra on the map of Nigeria? What else, besides their affinity for money and aggression, do they represent?* she thought.

One Nigeria indeed! Fiyin recalled, with growing dread, the account her father once relived of his close friend who lost his wife. The family of his late wife had insisted on 'their daughter' being brought back to her 'father's house' for the burial rites. Still in grief over the loss of his wife, Mr Kunle did not protest about where the interment of his wife occurred. He made the necessary arrangements.

Revulsion washed over Fiyin's father and other thirty friends and loved ones when the late woman's kinsmen disclosed the last requisite burial rite. Custom required Mr Kunle to revisit a certain marriage ritual before the body of his late wife could be put in the ground. Twelve years before, during their traditional wedding ceremony, the couple had skipped the part where they would go, hand in hand, to the bride's father for blessings. Mr Kunle also did not spend the night on a white-sheeted bed with his new wife.

Before Fiyin left for her house, she told Omo about the man who completed his wedding rites with his dead wife. A horrified Omo fast began a different chant, 'My God! Those people are mad! What sort of barbaric culture will make a man spend the night with a corpse! In which of the Igbo-speaking states did this happen?'

Fiyin said, 'I'm not sure. I think... it is either this same Anambra or Annua Oboo or something like that.'

Omo left Fiyin more perplexed than vexed when she, in a gruff tone, asked her to get her facts together. 'Madam! Which one come be "I think"? Annua Oboo is in Uyo-Akwa-Ibom state while

Anambra is a state on her own. Which one was it? Abeg, call your papa and verify.'

~

It lingered; Jide's mild scent. Fiyin took an involuntary whiff. One minute, she floated into dreamland, the next minute a heaviness dragged her back to harsh reality. Who was she kidding? Hot jollof rice did not just happen on one's plate, it had to be prepared or at least bought. *He appeared perfect to a fault anyway,* she mused, shutting her eyes, willing herself to sleep.

Fiyin woke up with a start. A message blinked on her mobile phone. Furrowed brows rose. Jide? At 2:44am? She checked the time stamp. Same time. *Does he not sleep?* she wondered, her heart thumping in her chest as she tapped the flashing envelope.

'Hey Fifi, *I found your company most exhilarating. Thank you again for the delicious cookies and custard. Need I say I had no further need for a meal when I got home? Before the evening ended, I had nursed the hope of seeing you again. For a moment, I swear I saw the bright spark of a beautiful friendship. But we both see the futility in pursuing one, do we not?... So, it is better killed than allowed to grow into a full explosion. Have a nice life, Fifi.*

PS It is Jideofor Williams. My friends call me Jide.'

Without waiting to think, Fiyin hit reply.

'Yup... *without question... kill the spark. Nice to have met you, Doctor Jideofor.*'

Jide swallowed hard, tossed his phone into his bedside drawer, and turned over on his belly. Life indeed sucked. He swallowed again, squeezing his eyes shut.

FIVE

POP! GOES THE BALLOON

This Saturday morning did not arrive with the usual sacral appeal. Fiyin shoved the real reason for her southbound mood, blaming it on Ifeatu's call. *She should try handling her emotional issues herself sometimes. I never bug her with mine... maybe she believes all I do in my spare time is wait around to solve other people's issues*, she screamed in her head.

With February almost over, skipping off to the neighbourhood grocery store did not pose such a daunting ordeal to Fiyin. The thought of throwing on two thick vests, a blouse and a winter jacket over two pairs of stockings, a pantyhose and a pair of trousers, all for a quick dash to Nisa Local, two blocks away, often brought out the logical thinker in Fiyin: *Can this wait until tomorrow?* So, chocolates to the rescue. *Today is one of those days*, she mused as she left for the store in a pair of jeans, a pullover, and wool slip-ons.

Her assortment of chocolates: milk, dark, white and butter, gave Fiyin the high as she let herself back into her flat. Omo and Ben were out on one of their 'am to pm' dates. So, she dived into her comfort food. Mere moments after she turned on her TV, her mobile phone started to ring. A frown crumpled Fiyin's contented face, her mouth, with butter chocolate still in it, hung open, forming an 'O'. *What! Why is he calling me? Is it an error?* Fiyin blinked multiple times to clear the fog in her head as the text, 'Dr Jide', continued to dance on her mobile phone screen.

'Hello Miss Taylor! Good morning! Sleep well?' Fiyin peeled her tongue off the roof of her mouth to respond to Jide's rather cheery greeting, considering the awkwardness of their parting only the night before.

'Good morning. Yes, I did… you?'

'Um… yes. Well enough. Are you home or out?' Jide's breathing sounded laboured.

'Out before, but I am back now,' said Fiyin. Her jaw dropped at Jide's next words.

'Tell me about it. Do you mind hanging with me today? I think I might be able to interest you with a few places… if you say yes.' It both amused and surprised Fiyin to learn that her caller, Jide, was parked outside her flat block. *Who is this guy? One minute he blows tepid, the next, steaming hot. I can't keep up.* With mounting excitement, the lady who barely caught any meaningful sleep the night before and who had planned on taking a well-deserved rest after drowning herself in chocolates, dressed up with the frenzy of a little child in a candy bar and willed the elevator to have a sense of purpose in its glide to the ground floor.

Twelve degrees Celsius did not feel nearly as cold, but Fiyin thanked her cardigan for the warmth it promised, should the need arise. The looming clouds of West London stood no chance against Jide's smile as he jumped out, nearly running to Fiyin's side, to hold the door open for her. For a fleeting moment, his brows furrowed. Her unspoken insistence on opening the car door for herself puzzled him.

Other than the curt 'hi' they threw at each other, no other words

passed between them for nearly four uncomfortable minutes. From
the corner of his eyes, as Jide meandered the streets of Paddington,
he regarded Fiyin. She sat, her back pinned into her seat, clutching
her handbag to herself; like someone protecting herself from
something. Or someone?

'Have you been to ZSL... London Zoo?' Jide's voice did not
sound quite as easy as the last time Fiyin remembered.

'No.'

'Would you like to visit?' He did not mean for his sigh to be
audible when Fiyin said, 'Yes.'

After the delightful penguins succeeded in taking their minds
off the gruesome backs of the hippos and the slithering folks at
the reptiles' arena, Fiyin and Jide were now ripe for a warm meal;
green peas with traditional fish and chips never tasted better.
Contemplative, sipping on cappuccino, Jide stared into space while
Fiyin's eyes searched his. She wondered how long he would sit there,
pretending he neither sent a parting text message some hours ago
nor sensed their tense parting note yesterday.

Although Fiyin's teeth now chattered on their way to see the
giraffes and zebras, she refused when Jide suggested a postponement
of their tour; anything but crawling back home to bemoan the
messiness of life. In a little while, she willed the chill away and
drowned herself in taking shots of the striped horses and their
incredibly long-necked neighbours, shoving aside her thoughts
about the brooding young man who trod beside her.

Jide neither cared much for the animals nor the scenery. He
had been to the zoo far too many times. Moreover, to sit with Fiyin
in conversation, or silence, presented a more appealing option. But
recalling the way her eyes dilated when she learnt his roots lay in the
'wrong part' of Nigeria, Jide was content to endure her enthusiasm
on the altar of his own disinterest. *The light in her eyes outranks any
comfort I will get from beginning such an uncomfortable discussion*, he

reasoned. An image of her fleeing with hands and feet flaying in his mind's eye drew a jaded smile from his lips.

Now admitting the folly in their reckless defiance to the mounting chill, quick steps led them through the exit parlour, where an assortment of souvenirs – stuffed toys, branded bags, keyrings, and picture frames, to mention but a few – tugged at the purses of departing visitors. Once inside the merciful embrace of Jide's car, Fiyin's teeth let loose. Oh, how they rattled. Jide turned up the temperature, blaming himself for not exhibiting more sense. Save for Yanni's *The Rain Must Fall* filtering through the speakers, the drive home was endured in painful silence.

Omo could not take it any longer. She would pound the details out of Fiyin, if all else failed. Details Fiyin preferred to keep to herself. Two weeks after ZSL and three more dates in between, neither Jide nor Fiyin now concluded their day without, at least, talking to the other. Through it all, Omo skipped about in her corner like a dog with two tails, waiting for her opportunity to ask exactly what was going on with her friend and the good doctor. With no more patience to spare, she threw courtesy out the door, invited herself over to Fiyin's house and yes, pounded the truth out of her.

'All right! I admit! I think I may like him a little more than I would like to admit.' Fiyin's nose flared as her eyes darted around the space near her friend's head. Omo beamed and, for the first time since becoming friends with Fiyin, she acknowledged the delicate state her friend waddled in; she had fallen in 'super-like'. Worse still, this was her first time.

'I don't suppose asking about Jide's position makes much sense… not with the way he shuttles between Edgware and Paddington,' Omo said, her face still aglow.

With every passing date, call, or text message Fiyin shared with her new 'super-like interest', in Omo's lexicon, their ethnic difference lost yet another layer of relevance, while an intense sense of foreboding hung above her head. It impeded her flight into the enchanted world of romance. Rejection by his parents, or the fear of it, did not appear to be the culprit since Jide, perhaps by design, alluded to his parents' ethnic blindness. In her case, a little haze hung around how tribally 'evolved' her parents truly were. Could that be it?

'Hey Fifi! Still up? A curious thing... Why do I go to bed smiling only to wake up smiling these days? Sleep sweet.'

Fiyin read Jide's text, and her mouth tugged at the corners. She started to surrender to sleep's allure when it struck her. Greyburtons would be over in under a month. At last the reason for her mood swings! *But wait... the management course! I have another two months or so*, she thought, breaking into a smile. *Afterwards, what next?* came the cruel voice of reason. Fiyin snuggled under her duvet, hoping to evade despair's snaking arms.

⸺

The familiar shops and streets had fast begun to disappear when Fiyin, shifting in her seat, asked, 'So, where are we going?'

Letting an almost four-inch-wide smile slide across his face, Jide said, 'Would you not rather I surprised you?'

Ten minutes and still no clue.

Fiyin took out her phone and sent a message to Omo. *'I'm out with Jide... He came over and whisked me away. A surprise he says.'* The way she worked hard at fusing into her own side of the car as she typed on her phone caused Jide's eyes to crinkle at the sides. He understood her caution. It would be unlike a Nigerian girl to not watch her own back.

'You can exhale… I am taking you to a concert,' he said, deciding to end her misery. Fiyin lit up at once.

'Are you serious! Which one? Where? Come on, tell me, tell me. Please!' Her heart raced with excitement. Now thoroughly amused, Jide savoured her enthusiasm.

'All in time, my sweet lady, all in time,' he said as they drifted on, leaving West London behind.

Jide reached for Fiyin's right hand and held on to it through the rest of the drive. Something about the way he said nothing but squeezed her hand in the soft way she had now become used to assured Fiyin of her safety.

They turned into an underground parking lot. Jide pulled up. 'It is Daylight Music at Union Chapel. We better hurry. We do not want to be late,' he said. Bemused, Fiyin mouthed to herself, scampering out to follow in brisk steps. *He's taking me to a church!*

Roomy, yet intimate. Gothic but spiced with the audacious eloquence of modern class. Light-emitting diodes warmed the room with varying colours of soft brightness, causing tranquillity to float from the stone walls, through the pews, all the way up to the mile-high ceilings. Fiyin's breath caught in her throat.

'This place looks nothing like a church,' she said, her voice husky with excitement.

'Do you like it?' he asked, dipping his head to talk close to her right ear. Close enough to touch it, but not touching it. Between his rasping tone, when he asked her if she liked a thing and the crinkling of his eyes or deepening of the creases around his lips when he established that she, indeed, liked a thing, Fiyin wondered which made her want to twist her feet at the ankles and push her heels into the ground.

'I love it! I more than love it!' she said. Jide meant to only smile, but a low chuckle followed. Her excitement amused him; he loved how it affected him.

After a Saturday afternoon spent in the company of great music that warmed the senses and soul, tea, decadently delicious cakes, and savoury pastries that crumbled in the mouth once they touched your tongue, Fiyin's eyes shone. They held Jide's for a moment before it hit her in the gut – she had let the caustic-tongued doctor from the Eastern part of Nigeria take down her castle walls, one brick at a time. This thought plagued Fiyin through their late lunch, did not let her be during their boat ride at the London Eye, and lingered long after their Mexican cuisine dinner adventure. But willing the uncertainties away, she clutched, with teeth-gnashing desperation, at the magical moment between them. Yet it worried Fiyin that her feelings showed. Perhaps a few dates before now would have prepared her for this strange terrain. Maybe she would have been able to tell the difference between a jerk and a true gentleman. Hmm. What if he was nothing more than some bored guy in need of company in faraway England?

On the converse, Jide would have been content to sit out the entire evening, soaking up the sight of Fiyin who, but for the two occasions when she picked up Omo's call to assure her of her well-being, remained contemplative.

In front of Chilfort Yards, still sitting in the car, Fiyin told Jide she'd had an amazing day. Although her eyes still sparkled, her voice lacked its characteristic pacing and flighty tone. He started to say how much he enjoyed himself too but stopped to unclip his seatbelt. It happened without warning; Jide leaning over, holding the sides of Fiyin's head, ever so gently, and covering her face with countless little kisses. Still wide-eyed, Fiyin sat transfixed as Jide pulled back. His furrowed brows made his gaze more intense. He ran his hands over his face, stopping to massage the sides of his nose. He squeezed his mouth with one hand, let out a sigh as if fighting some internal battle. With a start, he pushed a button to wind down the car windows, let himself out and all but jogged to

Fiyin's door where he placed both forearms on her window frame. 'Fiyinfunoluwa Taylor, I have fallen madly and impenitently in love with you... Please, tell me there is a chance... any chance,' he said between hoarse intakes of breaths. A shy smile slid across her face and in desperate want of a distraction, Fiyin tore her eyes from Jide's probing ones to undo her seatbelt. Jide pulled the door open, and holding his outstretched hand, Fiyin stepped out of the car. An awkward moment of silence passed with Jide still holding her hand. She felt him staring. *Is he waiting for an answer? Now?* Fiyin's eyes darted around, everywhere but Jide's face, looking every bit a squirrel set to scurry away in fright. But she did not run. With all the courage she managed to dredge, Fiyin took his other hand and stepped closer. Squeezing both his hands, she angled her head towards his face and held his gaze.

~~~

Where is Omo? Where is Omo? Fiyin rode to the fifth floor. Her legs felt like inflated balloons. Her heart? A clump of butter experiencing the invasion of a blistering-hot knife. She had rattled the knocker twice before she thought to dial Omo's mobile phone. She was out with Ben. *Again.* Fiyin went home to treat herself to a warm bath; a warm bath which did little to check the flutters in her tummy or her need to talk to someone besides herself.

~~~

'What!' Fiyin's intended whisper into her mobile phone's mouthpiece rang through the entire kitchen. Chef Jose called in sick today. The flu he said. Chef Blake, his stand-in, cared for not one ounce of unruliness; his rigid shoulders, clipped tone and icy glare made it spring-clear. Already having been served a good measure of the new chef's scowl, Fiyin excused herself. 'Wait a minute, Jide. Slow down! You are travelling to Nigeria tomorrow? Wait, as in, sleep-this-night-wake-up-in-the-morning tomorrow? Why? W… what happened?' It took the patience of a nun for Fiyin to listen to her boyfriend. She preferred the term 'boyfriend'. 'It sounds cool. Never used it before,' she had said to Omo who advised her not to use such a flippant term.

'Only chronic daters like me are entitled to such a term, not puritans like you, who are likely to marry the first man they date. My special someone, my man or, better still, my fiancé sounds more apt,' Omo had said.

'I am coming to you,' Jide said, and Fiyin's breathing returned to normal. She stepped back into class to endure Chef Blake's chocolate pudding class, all the while wondering at Jide's predilection for driving through half the city of London in a day.

⤜⤛

By 4:55pm, Fiyin had tidied up and suffered the agony of maintaining her calm until the end of classes. Jide had sent her a text message over fifteen minutes ago: *At the car park, waiting to see your beautiful face.*

'You look tired,' Fiyin said as soon as she slid into the car. The lines around Jide's eyes were more distinct, compared to the last time she noticed them.

'And you look as beautiful as ever, Miss Taylor,' Jide said, inhaling her now familiar fragrance. They drove on in taut silence and even when the green board with the inscription 'Edgware' came in view, Fiyin did not object. Since he never offered, she never asked. However, today presented the perfect day to know where her boyfriend lived.

High-on-the-hog best described Jide's living standards. His three-bedroom home looked neither like Fiyin's studio nor any flat an average Nigerian doctor living in London could afford. *How does he maintain his rent and this level of tidiness?* Fiyin wondered, doing her best to infuse a degree of decorum in her voracious scan of Jide's living space. She didn't have to comport herself. Once Jide nodded with satisfaction at the natural light coming through the white window blinds in the sitting room, he walked to Fiyin, who now stood peering at an artwork; the image of a lady crafted with an assortment of coloured buttons. It sat in a ten-by-ten-inch frame. 'Do you like it?' Jide asked, holding her shoulders, dipping his head to observe the craft from behind her. His chest brushed against her back and his right cheek touched hers on the left. Fiyin tensed; her heart rate tripled its beat frequency. Jide sensed her tension. He eased away from her back but kept his light touch on her shoulders as he, steering her around, gave her a tour of his house.

In the bedrooms, the shiny wooden floors were covered with lush grey rugs. All the kitchen and bathroom fittings oozed sublime affluence. A spicy orange scent floated around, almost luring Fiyin to distraction. But all the alluring scents in Europe could not subdue Fiyin's need to discuss Jide's impromptu journey back to Nigeria.

They walked back to the sitting room. Fiyin stalled in front of the button art and, turning towards Jide, the questions came barrelling.

Did something happen back home?

Why the urgency?

What about work?

'Can you just up and leave? No notice… or did you… plan to travel all along?' Fiyin's eyes were searching, her chest tightening. Almost body to body, Jide's breath fanned her forehead, but this time, Fiyin stood unflinching. It fell on Jide to concede. He went to the dining area, pulled a chair and sat. Fiyin followed, drawing a chair to sit in front of him.

Jide leaned his elbows on his thighs, slouching and cracking his fingers. Watching him purse, twist and blow air out of his mouth, Fiyin suspected she required stark attention and immense patience for whatever explanation he was preparing to give.

At last, when his words came pouring, Jide sounded like one would after a sprint.

'Remember I told you my folks are both medical doctors? Well, they own a hospital in Abuja… um… a big one… some big ones.' The frown across Fiyin's face told Jide to elucidate, but nothing prepared her for what she heard.

Not only did Dr and Dr (Mrs) Williams own a first-rate hospital in the finest parts of Abuja, reserved for only the rich and influential, but they also owned hospitals in Lagos and Port Harcourt and moved in government circles, making an awful lot of money from their 'affiliations'. Affiliations which ensured they were the sole distributors of specific high-end medical equipment across the country. Of course, their hobnobbing with the big shots often fastened a zip on their lips as certain activities eroded their own values. And why not? Did those same activities not guarantee their societal and financial status?

The rubber met the road when first, Dr Afulenu Williams and afterwards her husband, Dr Somadina Williams, had a spiritual encounter which caused them to question everything they ever believed about life and success. The dial-back they embarked on, as they expected, rocked the foundation of all they had built over the years. From licence withdrawals to contract cancellations to incessant court cases regarding past business dealings; they travelled an endless tunnel of retribution.

Nose flared, heart thumping, Fiyin held fast to the edge of her chair with almost as much strength as she did Jide's gaze, as though she feared he would change his mind about sharing so much with her. But he did not.

'Fiyin, something awful happened... an emergency. A bleeding lady... post-delivery complications. Keen on observing their first recto-vaginal fistula repair, almost half the doctors on duty decided to hover around my mother who was in theatre at the time... My father and I were away in Israel for a conference and the remaining doctors were either on break or simply absent...' At Fiyin's silent gasp Jide said, 'Trust me, these things happen.' Jide's breathing was heavy as he continued. 'A physiotherapist, rather than interrupt the doctors on break or the surgery to call the attention of a qualified obstetrician, took the liberty of "stabilising the patient"... conclusion, the woman died.'

Curiosity fast turned to boiling rage when Fiyin learnt the real reason a pregnant lady became an emergency case. The late lady's husband refused surgical intervention to deliver his wife of their baby. His poor financial health, lacquered over by his religious beliefs, did not permit such invasive intervention. So, he insisted on vaginal birth. Oh yes, she pusned all right. And after forty-three hours of labour pains, a 5.1kg baby girl graced the universe with her arrival; only she would never experience the comfort of her mother's bosom.

Not only did registering a death in the hospital rank high on the chaos dashboard, but the days following the woman's death also revealed the waiting trap the Williams had fallen into. The dead lady was a distant relative of the Senate president. And in one flash, the Williams made the headlines. Oh, what an absolute mess it was.

'Talk about harassment,' Jide said, his voice lead-heavy. 'My father spent three weeks in police custody and walked free only after we posted a bail of NGN5,000,000. Their hospitals, all three of them, were shut down. My family suffered indescribable persecution from the media and the government. Their accounts, the ones within the federal government's reach, were frozen. And for added spice, countless bizarre allegations began to hit at my father's integrity. My folks insisted I should not be caught in the web they built so I came to hide in England... as an intern.'

'What?' Fiyin's eyes widened in slow realisation. 'Soma-Williams Hospital! That's you? Oh, my God.'

'Yes. And in the dearth of options, one must take whatever is handed... I hope that explains why an obstetrician was assigned to reset your friend's spine,' Jide said, baring his teeth in a mirthless grin.

A thin film of tears formed in Fiyin's eyes. 'How? Do they have the right to... to do things... anyhow... by any means? I mean, what happened to investigations and—'

Jide let out a wry chuckle. 'Yes, sweet pea. Where you and I call home, a massive load of mess can happen. But those who do not dine with the devil seldom get smeared... My folks flirted with trouble, but even I now question the fairness in being passed through a never-ending chamber of nemesis.' Unable to withstand the sadness on Jide's face any longer, Fiyin reached for his hands and told him to stop talking if it hurt him too much. But the looming separation by endless miles of space and an ocean would not afford Jide the luxury of stopping. It was imperative for this girl, who had managed to invade both his conscious and subconscious, all in one short thread, to have a clear picture of him and his accompanying baggage before he left her alone to think him through.

After the sudden and celebration-erupting resignation of the Nigerian Senate President, Chief Clifford Orjileke, countless petitions which never would have seen daylight began to hit the desks of the House and the Judiciary. The rumour floating around was that Chief Orjileke ruled with two iron fists. Hated by the masses, despised by his colleagues, and infamous for his use of public office only as machinery servicing his already spilling receptacle of influence, power, and wealth, Chief Orjileke's reign typified a tight fist around the neck of a people. Some believed the Senate president controlled all three arms of the government – executive, judicial and legislative – from a little wooden kettle which he kept under his bed.

'The man was the engine filling the pool of heartache my family has swum these past years,' Jide said, his voice sombre and dripping with bitterness. Even after his alleged paralysis, which happened over a year ago, he would not relinquish his position. He barked instructions from his sick bed, did not make public appearances as he imported, with taxpayers' money, all manner of doctors and spiritualists from Saudi Arabia, India and China to still the Hand Of God.'

'And there I was feeling sorry for the man. I always thought he was a philanthropist… with the way he catered to the destitute. All those programmes and foundations he ran.'

Jide gave Fiyin a warm smile. 'You cannot blame yourself, sweet pea. These people run the most fool-proof PR systems. They say he gave up only after hair began to grow in his mouth. His replacement, Daniel Ikhuebor, I learnt, is a man with a heart for our country and is on a mission of reformation. Fresh court cases have been filed, old ones reopened, and I am required to give my testimony in a pivotal case… It is all one big rush, but I cannot complain. This is something I have pined for… prayed about… for the last three and a half years. You do understand why I must go,' Jide said, squeezing her hands. Fiyin bobbed her head up and down with a sense of urgency. It suggested her need to convince Jide as much as she wanted to convince herself.

⌐⁀⌐

For some would-be brides, the wedding preparation is a time for introspection, about the life behind and the life ahead. For many, it is a time to show the world, especially their detractors, how much of a diva and victor they are. But for others like Ifeatu, it is a time for both. While she looked forward, with absolute exhilaration, to life with the love of her life, Ifeatu believed a wedding ceremony deserved all the fuss and a lot more. And, in all honesty, so did Chike – except for certain aspects which, in his opinion, were utter in their unnecessity. Aspects like inviting a crowd which constituted eighty-five per cent strange faces. All other niceties, like trousseau shopping or other activities geared towards preparing his bride to glow on her all-important day, both amused and excited Chike.

But as much as the promise of Ifeatu's visit to London for her pre-wedding shopping appealed to Fiyin, it held not enough power to pull her out of the pit of despair which Jide's departure plunged her into. 'Babes, it's been a week! Try small, nau!' Omo had said, attempting to shake her friend out of her gloom. What made it worse? The fees for her two-month long course in culinary management and administration had already been paid by her rather zealous parents. To Omo's utter surprise, Fiyin admitted that, but for the heavy penalty charges involved, she would have deferred her course to a time to be determined by her emotional state.

Two bowls of jollof rice and a few bottles of water sat on Fiyin's counter, under Omo's scrutiny. 'You spent an awful lot of time for only these. Underground delays?' she asked, her brows nearly dipping to touch her nose.

Fiyin confessed she still had some rice and soup from their last trip to Burnt Oak. 'I... I went to Edgware.' Omo's eyes began to sparkle like a child watching the ice-cream man pile scoops on her cone. 'Why? Jide is back?' she half asked, half squealed. Shock dragged her onto the next available chair when her friend, in a small voice, said, 'No, I only went past his house to see if… to… to loosen the tightness in my chest.' Fiyin struggled to understand why, only four days after Jide returned to Nigeria, he had ceased any form of contact with her. She also wondered why his mobile line kept saying 'Switched off' whenever she tried to call his number.

By the time Omo found her voice, she served Fiyin a substantial helping of tough love, telling her to guard her heart and forget about people like Jide who preyed on the innocence of young impressionable ladies like herself. 'We are here moaning and mourning over him while the guy may be in Abuja, having the time of his life, impressing another Fiyin, Fatimah or Feluchi, for all I care!' Omo's teeth-kiss lasted an impressive six seconds. Only the intervention of the ringtone from Fiyin's mobile phone saved both ladies from the mortification of Fiyin's imminent bawling. Omo cared little for emotional wreckage.

It was an unknown local number.

'Hello.'

'Hi, Fifi. It's Ifeatu. I've landed.'

If Fiyin thought she had a hurricane to contend with in Omo, a tornado just hit town.

SIX

WADING THE ATLANTIC

One week with Ifeatu, and Omo's 'bestie' list grew by one. Although led by two incongruent paths, they both raced to the battle front to save Fiyin from herself. 'Bend low to conquer. Be lovable... don't display any air of pride for now. Don't mind all these female power nonsenses... Unless you want to wake up one day at seventy to find yourself in an empty house: powerful and alone. Show Jide you are a ten-yard wife material and don't stop calling him until he answers,' Ifeatu had said. Omo's blueprint underlined the rewards of flaunting a woman's sense of self-worth. 'If a man wants you, he must leave you in no doubt. The tune you play in the early stage of a relationship will determine your dance steps throughout the life span,' she had huffed. In the end, Omo won the bid for the preferred process towards Fiyin's recovery. On the night before Ifeatu's return to Nigeria, over dinner at Flehming's Steak House, Fiyin made a solemn declaration in a voice most uncharacteristic of her – 'I would rather scratch my back on a cactus plant than dial Jide's number, ever again!'

The mundanity of life after Ifeatu's departure back to Nigeria flooded Fiyin and Omo with relief; much like bringing one's head up for air after minutes of swimming under water. Gone were the shuttles between and through Brent Cross, Paddington and the labyrinth of streets in the heart of West London for the perfect dresses, shoes, gloves, tiaras, wedding favours and lingerie. But unlike Fiyin, Omo exhibited more intentionality in her plunge into the activities Ifeatu's visit imposed. In her quest to protect herself from the fraud of emotional dependence on another human being, Omo launched a calculated strategy to distance herself from Ben. 'I refuse to spend my time with someone who thinks he stands on a higher moral pedestal than I do. I will not be Ben's foil,' fast became her chant. Omo's interpretation of Ben's pursuit for her awareness of, and accountability to, the controlling force of everything in existence did not settle with Fiyin. Nonetheless, she purposed to leave the subject of Omo's faith well alone, if only for now.

Ben held to his strings of restraint, giving Omo every inch of the space she demanded, albeit without a word. Their last argument took a train ride with them from Paddington to Ben's Kensington apartment. 'Why are you so angry?' he had asked, utter bafflement pulling his brows together.

'Because it's my damn prerogative to exhibit emotions. And where I come from, Ben, anger is a healthy emotion, not a disease!' she barked.

She wants her space. I should let her breathe, Ben thought and told her so. A wail began to bubble in Omo's chest, but she managed to contain it, hoping Ben did not see the signs. And swimming against the tidal wave resolute on pushing her towards Ben, Omo left her boyfriend's apartment. With her head high, shoulders taut and heart in shreds, the words of Dolly Parton's *I Will Always Love You*, hovered in her subconscious.

With three odd weeks to spare before being sucked back into work at Greyburtons, Fiyin busied herself with touring the parts of

England, yet to grace her memoir; Brighton, St Albans and Bedford. Propelled by the fear of being drowned by boredom, Fiyin cajoled Omo into going along with her discovery of Wales and Scotland. Cardiff's Motorpoint Arena and Aberdeen's easy luxury – seen in their granite roads, walkways and buildings – gave the two ladies a different perspective of Great Britain. Omo spared nothing in thanking Fiyin for dragging her out. How else could they deal with the sudden abundance of time, seeing they had no 'distraction' in their lives? But not for long.

Nothing but sheer chance could have orchestrated the meeting, on Oxford Street, between Fiyin and Dapo. Yes, Dapo with the flawless-skinned fiancée from the church in Lagos. Overcome with the excitement of meeting an old friend, Fiyin walked up to her acquaintance from before. Face ablaze with a grin, she said, 'Are you serious! Dapo! What are you doing in London!' Only the gentleman was not Dapo at all but someone who looked like him.

'I am so sorry to disappoint you, but I am Olu. It saddens me to say, your friend and I do not share as little as the first letter of our first names,' the stranger said, his five-inch grin calling Fiyin's attention to his lips; they looked like they had suffered multiple stings from vengeful bees. Olu's clumsy attempt at humour fast concealed Fiyin's stark mortification.

Only two weeks after, fist-sized holes started to appear in Olu's web of humour and amiability. Married to a British citizen only for the apparent gains of such an association, he longed for a more 'wholesome' relationship. 'My life is like a spacious prison. I'm looking to settle down with someone who understands me… not some overtly aware and self-absorbed individual,' he said one evening as they sipped on mocktails. When Fiyin asked why he believed she fit the frame of the 'perfect-someone-who-understands-him', he answered, 'You are humble, not entitled. You're safe. The first time I met you, I sensed an instant connection, and I am never wrong.' And as fast as he secured the position of car wash – a male companion who only served as a harmless stopgap for the void caused by the plague of singlehood – dear Olu suffered an unanticipated redundancy.

～

Startled and rubbing her eyes, Fiyin answered her mobile phone. 'Good morning, Mummy.'

Bree frowned. How come her always-up-and-about daughter still snuggled in bed at 10:30 on a Saturday morning? 'Fiyinfunoluwa! You still sleeping? Are you all right, baby?' Sometimes Fiyin wondered at the ease with which her mother slid between emotions; one moment jocular, the next anxious, and yet another, roof-popping angry. One never could tell with Bree. Once her daughter said she was fine, Mrs Taylor resumed breathing with ease.

Chef's assignment suffered Mrs Bree Taylor's expression of displeasure for robbing her child of a decent portion of her sleep time.

With the end of Fiyin's course only weeks away, Mr and Mrs Taylor planned their yearly vacation to coincide with when their child would be free.

'We will be with you in a fortnight, and together, we'll go to Russia… for vacation.'

Bree heard her child's sharp intake of air. 'Russia? Mummy! Who goes to Russia for vacation?' To which Bree answered, 'We do, and you are coming along! Don't worry. I promise, you'll thank me in the end.' Incredulity soon mutated into enthusiasm, as Fiyin began to ask for specific dates and exact destinations.

'Patience, they say, is a virtue. Be patient my baby,' Bree said, enjoying her child's torture.

Omo reckoned providence tilted in her favour when she learnt her fashion course would end right about when Fiyin would conclude her management programme. While waiting to land the big job set to bankroll her fashion house, Omo intended to do some business in Nigeria. Selling the footwear and clothes she snatched off the sales counters of the stores on Oxford Street sounded like a solid plan. She threw herself into buying up the entirety of London, with the hope of dumping her extra luggage on Fiyin's baggage allowance. *We'll be flying back to Nigeria together, and Fifi doesn't care much for mindless shopping.* Imagine her disappointment when a beaming Fiyin informed her about her planned holidays with her parents. 'Oh, wow. I guess I cannot begrudge you for having a balanced family,' Omo said, her mouth forming a sloppy 'n'.

A sudden wave of pity for her friend washed over Fiyin as she held Omo in a hug. For the first time, Fiyin acknowledged Omo's vulnerability. Layered miles beneath her brash but often vivacious exterior lived a little girl. A little girl who feared the course of her life may be leading slowly but surely to the curse of an unhappy life and marriage. One not any different from her mother's. 'Don't worry,' Fiyin said, squeezing her, 'you will have a balanced family. You'll see. In the end, you'll say I told you so.' And as fast as a baby who had been given her bottle after an intense bout of hunger, Omo's face lit up. She shrugged and said, 'Yeah, I guess so.'

⁓

Plants which, not too long ago, hung forlorn, now bloomed with even more beauty after summer's gentle rousing.

'These Oyinbo people are funny, o! See how dem dey collect sun like say dem be lizard,' said Omo, in reference to the droves of Caucasians who, lured by the sunshine and crisp air characteristic of June, sat in open areas for minutes, maybe hours, allowing golden rays to seep through their skin pores.

Heaving from the weight of the two shopping bags Omo

unapologetically passed to her, Fiyin glanced at Omo, shook her head in admonishment. 'Hmm, Omo, you can't begin to imagine how lucky we are to have the kind of climate we do back home,' she said, recounting the first time she experienced winter…

Deaf to her parents' explanation about the notoriety of London's weather in December, fifteen-year-old Fiyin had insisted on accompanying her mother to a seminar in Leicester. A day after their arrival, Mrs Taylor left for her meeting after giving instructions to her daughter on what to have for breakfast and how to keep herself company until 3:00pm, when she returned.

Minutes after her mother left, Fiyin had scampered out of bed, checked all the windows to confirm they were all shut. After she lined the bottom of the entrance door with a duvet to stop the wicked claws of winter from sneaking through, she crawled back into bed and did not move for another hour or two. Fiyin woke up with a start, tried to reach for the mobile phone, only to realise her fingers were numb from the chill. Her toes too; despite being cocooned in three pairs of socks! The dam broke. She wailed for her mummy and her home.

At twenty-five minutes past three, Bree walked through the door. One look at her teenage daughter's puffy eyes, and she pinched herself to keep from bursting into uncontrollable laughter. The words, 'Didn't we tell you so!' wrestled hard to escape her pursed lips but lost in the end. The benefit of hindsight, they say, makes a sage of all; only absolute necessity now compels Fiyin to visit any country during such a savage season.

Once the ladies walked into the reception, Bill, the front desk staff, straightened up. He liked the ladies and would often chat with them, lapping up stories of Nigeria and their idiosyncrasies. Today, his forehead wrinkled at the sight of them. He attempted a light-hearted giggle but failed woefully. Running the tip of his tongue over his lips, he rearranged the papers on his desk for the second time in four seconds as he said, 'Um… I have some information for you, Miss Fee-yean.' Fiyin looked from Bill to Omo and back to Bill.

'It's Claudia, the uh… lady in apartment 412. She says she would be most appreciative if you… uh… controlled your… your footfalls. She complains it is most bothersome, Miss Fee-yean,' Bill said.

'What!' Omo pulled her lips into a crooked 'n'. 'Madam Postmistress again? What is wrong with her? Why can't people learn to tolerate other people? Or maybe I should say, why can't people tolerate those with a darker skin tone?' Fiyin gave Omo what she hoped was an inconspicuous nudge, for her to censor her thoughts before giving them voice.

'She is of a darker skin tone… Jamaican, to be exact,' Bill said almost under his breath. Omo had the dignity to hang her head but only for a moment. They thanked Bill and went on their way with Omo thinking, *Thank God we'll be leaving soon. She can eat the entire block.*

━◦

In Fiyin's last week at Greyburtons, Donald and Bree called their child at least twice every day. Something told them Fiyin needed a little more attention. 'You sound so distant and preoccupied these days,' Bree had prodded. 'Is anything the matter, baby? You know you can always talk to Mummy.' After Bree's conversation with Fiyin, an argument between Mr and Mrs Taylor followed.

'Now you are worried. Weren't you the one beating down on the poor child to produce a non-existent suitor? Of course, she is distant. The dread of facing her mother without the "ultimate prize" is more than the girl can face.' Oh, how Bree tried to swallow her retort. But try as she did, the words spilled.

'Are you aware of how self-absorbed you sound, Donald? You should accept your folly in holding her too close, making her too comfortable in her belief that every man should be like… like you.' Bree paused to change the tone of her voice and the expression on her face to one of mockery. 'Mr Goody Two Shoes! Kind, soft-spoken, understanding. O ti ya, it is time! Produce the "you" your daughter will marry!' she hissed, walking off and slamming the door shut behind her. Donald decided to let his wife be. Bree was in one of those moods where she blamed the silly pen for writing something wrong. He allowed thirty minutes before he went in search of her.

Two balls of tissue paper on the floor by the bed where Bree lay and her still-quaking shoulders told Donald what his wife had been busy doing.

'Darling,' Donald began as he sat on her bed, his tone conciliatory, 'I think you misunderstood my words. Or maybe I failed to give them proper expression. When we get to St Petersburg, let's allow her time to decompress… Fifi is young, beautiful and talented. In time, if she so wishes, her man will whisk her off her podium. Hmm?' he finished, squeezing her shoulders.

Turning towards her husband, Bree took her bawling three notches higher. 'This is the problem! Where will Fifi find a man who would understand her, especially when she is being unreasonable? Tell me where? How?' Not quite prepared for the response he received, Donald blinked back his surprise and gathered his wife in his arms. He spent the next fifteen minutes cooing his apologies for being himself.

⌒

Friday came in a hurry. Fiyin's last day at Greyburtons dragged on, one painful clock tick after the other. With most of her friends from her previous course gone, this set of new ones did not appear keen on saying goodbye. All they had been doing since 8:00am was cooking, eating, signing their scrapbooks, exchanging home addresses for possible visits, and giving lengthy speeches about one another. Mark, their course coordinator, said they would be free to go from 4:00pm, after they had received their certificates. 'In the meantime, you are all free to monkey around,' he said.

'Fiyin Taylor, you have guests at the reception,' Mark said before retreating to his office.

Mum and Dad! These guys! Why did they not tell me they were coming in today? Fiyin half walked, half ran to the reception.

Her steps faltered, like a toddler unsure of her next step. The smile which had begun to form around her mouth vanished. But for the 'tick-tock' coming from the wall clock, eloquent silence bounced on and off the white walls of Greyburtons' reception area. Every muscle on his face warred for supremacy; those responsible for smiling and those in control of puzzled frowns.

'Jide?' Fiyin's voice was scratchy, rasping.

One stride after the next brought Jide before the object of his three-month-old torture. Mr and Mrs Taylor gawked as the six-foot-three-inch stranger who had, like them, been sitting in one of the reception chairs, took the face of their only child in his hands. Donald's nose flared and his forehead wrinkled as Jide lowered his head to Fiyin's face. The kiss lasted about ten heartbeats. *Who is this rascal?*

Jide stepped back, tucked his hands in his denim pockets and said, in a hoarse whisper, 'Why, Fifi? What happened?' Jide's eyes darted around her face as though he might find his answer on it. The fizz in his eyes made Fiyin's barrage of 'whats', 'hows' and 'whys' content with floating around in her head, refusing to be echoed. Only the 'ahem' from Mr Taylor broke their gaze.

As Fiyin would later explain to Jide, wiping her mouth as she walked to her parents, who were still glued to their seats, was an unconscious act. Bree battled with which expression to project – surprise, curiosity or parental reprimand.

'Mummy! Daddy! You didn't tell me you were coming in today,' Fiyin said, an unsure smile playing around her lipstick-smudged mouth. Nothing prepared Jide for the sudden dearth of oxygen his windpipe experienced as only one thought crossed his mind, *Kai! Jide, you are an absolute dickhead!*

Donald drew his daughter into his arms. Bree gave her a quick hug and said into her right ear, 'Ta ni yen?', 'Who is he?', darting a quick look at Jide who now stood no more than six feet away, hands slammed deep in his denim back pockets, looking everywhere but at the couple; the couple he never suspected he would need to say anything else to, besides 'goodbye'.

Taking a few steps away and glancing from her parents to Jide and back to her parents, Fiyin made the introductions. 'Ahem, Mummy, Daddy, this is Jide... my... uh... a friend.' And angling towards Jide, she said, 'You've guessed right, these are my folks, Mr and Mrs Taylor.'

For some reason, Mr and Mrs Taylor found Jide's frown-tainted smile, as he walked towards them and genuflected with an inch-deep bow, both endearing and amusing.

'Omo dada! Bawo ni?' Bree asked Jide how he was doing in Yoruba dialect.

'Uh, Mummy, he is not Yoruba, he is Igbo,' Fiyin said. *No need to kick the can down the road.* Bree's smile wavered but at once slid back to complement her still-smiling husband, whose next words made Fiyin's eyes form two near-perfect circles.

'Nna, kedu?' Mr Taylor said, greeting Jide in the way Igbo men did only when addressing a younger man to whom they were favourably disposed. But in response to Jide's starstruck face, he clarified, his tone undulating with humour, 'Oh no! That's about all I can say in your language.'

Light-hearted giggles replacing the initial awkwardness in the room made Fiyin, with eyes darting from father to mother, start to believe her recent introductions and the 'assault' with which Jide plagued her lips mere moments ago were only fantasises playing themselves out in her head.

'Wait, I have another one... daalu. Goodbye... right?'

'You mean naagbo, sir. Daalu means thank you,' said Jide to Donald. By now, the tightening around Jide's chest had begun a gentle easing. Bolstered by the incipient cheery air, Fiyin no longer entertained her prior apprehension about the embarrassing meeting between Jide and her folks. She went back to class to receive her certificate and say her goodbyes.

At night as they lay in bed, Bree said to her husband, 'Do you think it's serious?'

'Yes, I think it is beyond serious... why?' Bree let out a long sigh, and propping herself to get a better view of her husband blurted, 'What do you mean "why"? You know why, Donald!' Yes, Donald only feigned ignorance and he admitted it by patting his wife's head as he said, 'Be at rest, my dear. Nobody takes note of these things anymore.' Bree leaned into her husband's left shoulder, hoping by heaven he was right.

⌒⌒

With no more than three days to spare before the Taylors' flight to St Petersburg, Jide refused to play peekaboo with serendipity. A pocketbook of home addresses and phone numbers served as his guarantee.

'If ever a certain lady, by some uncanny stroke of bad luck, needs tracking, I will be in no doubt of where to go or who to call.' Jide's self-assured smile as he made his announcement sent a warmth to Fiyin's belly. She ambled about, sliding him glances at intervals, as he cleared his apartment of his personal effects; he wanted Sina, his agent, to relist it on the short-let market.

'Omo must now be convinced I am a nutter. Tell me, what did she say when you told her how I came charging into Greyburtons?'

'Let's play rock, paper, scissors,' Fiyin said.

'You have no intention of telling me, do you?'

'Nope!'

Jide laughed, making a mental note to have the button art shipped to Fiyin. Twice, Fiyin caught him staring at her. After rock, paper, scissors, Jide suggested, with a curious sense of urgency, a workout at the gym downstairs in his apartment block, and they did — rowing, cycling and training on the elliptical. But when Jide suggested crowning their gym activities with some weights, Fiyin opted to play the role of his cheerleader, applauding him and prodding him.

In the changing room, Fiyin's phone rang.

'We are replanning, baby. Russia has threatened to attack Ukraine.'

'What!'

'Yes, we didn't think their squabbles would degenerate... and so fast. As we speak, Daddy is cancelling our flight and hotel bookings. He fears what may follow. Now he is suggesting Italy, but I'm thinking Dubai. What do you—'

'Du-what! Mummy, do you want us to turn to toast on arrival?'

'Ah, you're right. Maybe we should do Italy, then.'

'Hawaii?'

'O-ka-y! Hawaii sounds good, o. Hold on a minute.' Bree held the phone away from her mouth, conferred with her husband and returned to the call.

'Seems like we have a plan. Ehen, when are you available for dinner? Let's have a proper meeting with your... uh, friend. Tonight or tomorrow... whichever works for him.'

Back at the gym area, when Jide returned, his hair glistening with moisture, Fiyin told him about their change in travel plans and her mother's invitation. Jide whipped out his phone. It was true, Russia was roaring, and it could degenerate fast; Zelenskyy was no pushover. This could mean war. Jide's insides clenched. Wars had a way of being destructive on a global scale. One way or the other, important nations would become involved. Less important ones would suffer the fallouts; scarcities and price hikes. Wars were no good.

'So your folks want to assess me?'

'Come on! They don't bite!' Fiyin giggled as she gave him a light jab in the chest.

Jide caught her hand, and with a small smile tugging at his mouth, he said in a gruff whisper, 'Of course, they do not. I only worry about their first impression about me… I made an absolute mess of our first meeting, remember? I am not certain about what they think of me… of us.'

'Yes, you were a rascal,' said Fiyin, her eyes sliding away from his face to skirt around the space beside his left shoulder.

'Now I wonder what in heaven's name came over me… coming at you the way I did. Hmm. You, Miss Taylor, have a most peculiar effect on me. Come, let us go to your place.' Curious eyes followed them as Jide pulled a chuckling Fiyin out of the gym, into the fast-darkening evening. With only days before Fiyin and Jide went their separate ways again, they wanted to spend as much time together as time permitted.

⌐───◦

'For the one hundred billionth time, Jide, I will keep in touch. I promise! Besides, you forced me to hand you the numbers and home addresses of everyone within my immediate circle: my parents, Omo, Ifeatu. Or do you want our pastor's too?'

'Yes! What an unforgiveable oversight! Can I have it, please?' Their giggles rang through Fiyin's almost bare flat. It looked different from the last time Jide remembered. Other than an overnight bag with her toothbrush, make-up, night wear and a few clothes, all her personal effects were with her parents at Novotel, to be freighted to Nigeria.

'Forgive my trust issues, sweet pea. It might have a thing or more to do with how fast you dropped me... like a hot pot the minute I left London,' said Jide with measured light-heartedness.

Still smarting from self-reprimand since she learnt about his encounter days after he returned to Nigeria, Fiyin tried, again, to blame her actions on her rather colourful imagination; one borne out of her predisposition to place all life's problems on an Excel spreadsheet.

Fiyin had struck a foolish pose, with her mouth forming a small 'o', when Jide told her the reason behind his radio silence. Two days after his arrival at Abuja, he travelled to Lagos for a court hearing. On adjournment of the case, Jide, in high spirits, as the case appeared to be going as the Williams had hoped, decided to visit an old friend. Horns blaring from vehicle drivers, their contorted faces, and occasional outbursts at fellow road users, indicative of their urgency to reach wherever they were headed, drew a smile from Jide's parched lips. He lowered his guard. The sight of a young man hawking bottled water heightened Jide's thirst, and he wound down his window to buy a bottle.

'How much?' he said to the man hawking bottles of water.

'Fifty-fifty Naira.'

Jide interpreted the hawker's darting eyes as his desperation to close out his current transaction as fast as possible because he wanted to hurry off to another prospective customer.

'Give me two bottles,' Jide said, taking out a 500 Naira bill from his wallet, only to freeze at the sight he met when he lifted his eyes. A once droopy-eyed and sweaty hawker now glared at Jide with bloodshot eyes. And in a voice like a cross between the deep-throated growl of a bear and metal grating against metal, the hawker said, 'Oga, you better koprate if you no wan die for hia today. Oya, gimme all ya phone and moni now, now!' But for the cold steel nuzzle now pressed against his left ear, Jide would have needed more coercion to be cooperative. And like an obedient student handing in his homework to his teacher, Jide gave the robber his two phones and all the physical cash on him.

'So, you see, sweet pea, you read me wrong. I stopped calling only because the water-selling thief swore to bury a bullet in my skull if I asked him, one more time, to let me extract an important telephone number. I did not ignore you because I went spinning with the next lady who caught my fancy,' he had finished.

'And I happen to be running out of options of what I can say… or do… to wipe this off my slate… our slate.' Fiyin cocked her head to the left in that adorable way only she did.

'I could give you a clue or two,' Jide said, his eyes glistening. And before he could slide from his side of the sofa to hers, Fiyin took off, starting a game of 'catch me if you can'.

⁓

For the first time, minutes before Jide arrived for their short walk to Novotel, Omo received a tongue-lash from Fiyin. Her eyes had pooled with tears when Fiyin mentioned how disappointed her parents would be about Ben's absence at dinner. This new Omo did not quite fit Fiyin's idea of her friend.

'Omo, why are you crying? This is so not you!' As much as she tried, Fiyin was doing an awful job at hiding her impatience, as sliding in and out of sombre moods now played a major part in Omo's every day. Clear as the skies after the rains, she wanted a life of love and balance, but her adamantine decision to allow certain details to rob her of a chance at such a life defied Fiyin's reasoning.

'Yeah,' Omo said, sniffing and wiping a lone tear trickling from her right eye, 'but I think it's best we go our separate ways. Once I get back to Nigeria, it will be same dirty dish in the washer. The fights, the shame, and my mother drawing all the emotional energy she can out of me. London provided an escape from my truth.'

'All right, makes sense, and my heart breaks for you. But how does this relate to your refusal to speak to Ben?' Fiyin asked. She puckered her lips and twisted them to the left to keep from laughing at her friend's logic. Omo did not doubt Ben's intentions for her, but she feared his disappointment when she was stripped to her raw form; deprived, vulnerable, unsuitable. 'It would be a confirmation of whatever skewed information he has gathered about Africans,' she ended, her tears now flowing unfettered.

'Are you for real, Omo? Since when did watching or reading millions of Western horror movies or stories justify the belief that the streets and air space of London mill with zombies and witches zapping about on their brooms?' Omo's raised eyebrows and quickening breath made her look somewhat vulnerable and a lot confused.

Fiyin went on to make a solid case for Ben, insisting he was a gentleman on every level and did not strike her as one to hinge his judgments on the realities surrounding a person's existence alone. 'As far as I am concerned, the Ben I am familiar with would want to trace an inference from the choices such a person decides to either make or not make,' she said with a note of finality.

'So, your point is?' Omo asked, walking around the living room of her flat, as though to escape the jagged edges of Fiyin's words.

The scowl on Omo's face complemented the quick pace and movement of her legs and hands. They sent an unalloyed message: Fiyin's name on her friends' list was begging for the stroke of a Tipexx brush. Bent on tunnelling through her friend's mass of doubt, Fiyin carried on. 'My point is, until you stop poring over the pages of other people's stories, comparing notes with the prologue of yours, you will never, I repeat never ever, go on to the important parts of yours. Of course, learn from related books to gain better perspective in writing yours. It will help you better appreciate the beauty embedded within every chapter of your own life's book but move on to your own book for heaven's sake, Omoni!' Omo stopped pacing. She settled on her sofa, arms folded to her chest, to wait for Jide. Her eyes rested on Fiyin who idled away with poring over her phone. An epiphanic light crept into Omo's eyes. Fiyin was an ancient soul trapped in a young body.

~

'I'll drive. I am most certainly not interested in making myself a target, brandishing two gorgeous ladies at night,' he said with humour. *Perhaps he is anxious to meet her parents or is he nervous?* Omo mused, playing mind games with herself. Anything but think about Ben, whose face and voice now slid at will into her thoughts. Not in this lifetime did she believe a day would come when she would pine for the approval of another human being besides her father. And lit with night's cheery lights, Praed Street melted past as Jide sped off to Novotel.

Dinner went well, and besides Omo's occasional retreat into herself and the more than obvious non-reference to Ben, everyone had an excellent evening.

~

At last, the party broke up; Fiyin off to experience snorkelling and to indulge in the farm-to-table cuisines on the famous beaches of Maui, Hawaii; Jide off to Abuja to resume business as usual, and

Omo to Lagos to begin a new and perhaps important chapter in her life's story, each sad in a happy sort of way. But not one of them questioned if they would see each other again. For forged in the belly of London's winter and summer was a friendship with a promise to last a lifetime and back.

SEVEN

*ESCAPING FROM THE FOWLER'S SNARE
CALLS FOR A VICTORY DANCE INDEED*

For most people, the weight of tribulation is colossal and cannot be endured. For a few, the burden should be ridden on if mobile, or held fiercely unto if motionless. Dr Somadina Williams and his family held fast to their mulish, mammoth-sized tribulation. Left to Somadina, Jide, unlike his sister Kaira, never should have been drawn into the quagmire they swam in.

Although only a forty-five-minute flight separated Abuja from the coal city of Enugu, Afulenu and Somadina strived to insulate their daughter and her family from the mess they waddled in. So, Kaira stayed away from Abuja, making whatever news her folks decided to distil to her, and sometimes the media, her sole source of information. Deep in her heart, she suspected Kene hoarded details he believed would ruffle her dovecot; her husband of eight years had developed a strong bond with her folks and spoke to them often, but he never let on much.

Being a full-time mom spared Kaira the monotonicity of the nine-to-five grind. But on rare occasions, Kaira permitted herself to dispel the thick cloud of protection swaddled around her. These days, Kaira loathed the chosen lifestyle which, besides affording her ample time to dote on her family, also robbed her of any distraction from worry. Of course, there were the little spots of grey when she volunteered at the Enugu State Library. Where she let herself float away into the world of fiction and sometimes self-help books. Those were the only times Kaira thought not about her folks, husband or three children, but of worlds where she existed only in delightful oblivion.

Today, after she had kissed her husband goodbye and dropped Nicole, Nathaniel and Noah at school, Kaira made the eight-minute drive from Shalom-Ville private school to the library. Minutes after setting up her computer for the day's work and fusing into the world of underwater life in the land of 'Poiraqura', her phone began to buzz. *Mummy?* Kaira's brows furrowed as she snatched her phone off the desk before she drew more attention from the already curious heads turning towards her desk. In the kitchenette, Kaira breathed into the phone, for fear of being overheard, 'Mummy, good morning. O nwee?' she said, asking her mother, in Igbo, if all was well.

Since the shutdown of their hospitals and countless petitions, her parents rationed their calls to her. Most times, they sent handwritten letters through the drivers at 'Glory to God Transport' – for her protection, they had said. It therefore took Dr Afulenu Williams a few blinks to recall the last time she spoke to her daughter; five weeks ago. In some ways, she deserved the question, 'O nwe, is anything the matter?'

'It's done! Kaira nnwa mo! Our angels were on assignment the entire time! We will not be punished beyond our due! Olisa bi n'igwe, our God in heaven, is alive and well!' If Kaira did not pull her mother's reins, Afulenu would soliloquise into next week.

'Hold on, Mummy. What did our angels do? What is done?' Kaira's heart thumped with a knowing. For almost four years, only one issue had featured as the central theme of their prayers. And when the words came, they were a harmonious note to her ears.

In truth, she did not miss the telling pointers to the shift of the tides, but never did Kaira imagine how fast, how much in their favour and to what degree their tides would shift.

All three Soma-Williams hospitals had been reopened. While compensation for damages, as their lawyer had pushed for, did not grace the victory stand, all outstanding payments owed to them by the federal government were to be paid. When? Only the elements of the universe possessed such information. Kaira wondered if the media would publicise this news like they did the less favourable ones, such as the countless shameful appearances at the courts, the innuendos of the various 'courts of public opinion' and the brazen vengeful mud splashes by her parents' detractors and competitions. *How like the media to suddenly lose their verve*, she mused.

Now certain the loud drumming of her heart thudded all the way to the reading hall, she moved to the end of the kitchenette, near the refrigerator, hoping the dum-dum of her heart would drown in the hum from the appliance. Once her mother's call ended, Kaira dialled Kene.

'Honey bear, Mummy just called. The hospitals' licences! They've all been reinstated!' Kaira almost cracked from the sheer strain of shrinking her squeal into a whisper.

'I know, I know! Jide just called me! I tried to call you immediately, but your line was engaged! Awesome! Incredible! I still can't believe we are all not in one high-fever dream!' Kene's excitement sent tremors through Kaira's mobile phone, drawing a tear-jerking grin from her face. *Imagine Jide calling Kene before me. Hmm!* Kaira offered to fill a few blanks in her husband's narration of the court hearing. Of course, Kene held the longer end of the stick in certain areas too. Their battle for supremacy for the custodian of more information about the day's event only made him more excited and her smile a lot wider.

In the evening of the same day, they hopped from foot to foot, wanting to glean more details of the recent victory to feed their bottomless cup of curiosity, but no Williams phone line connected. Anyone would have thought all telecommunications companies got the memo from the media, to douse their victory in every way possible. After several hours, the 'siege' lifted. First, Kene spoke to Somadina, but his curiosity fell short of satisfaction so, he called Afulenu.

'Mum, please, is Jide close by? His phone is not connecting.'

'I think he is on the phone... let me see... uh... yes, he is, and with the way he is curled up in that chair, I doubt he has plans for anything else!' Kene's shoulders shook in silent humour at the bafflement in his mother-in-law's voice. *Am I still the only one with this tea?*

The days following the Williams' victory were filled with frenzied revisits of all the fine print Kaira had always suspected her husband hid from her. A deeper leaning towards the 'God Who Can Do All Things', as Kene now referred to the creator of the universe, formed the new compass for the Williams and their core circle. In Kene's opinion, which the Williams also shared, this recent tidal shift could not for a moment be downsized to a stroke of luck; in unmistakable splendour, divine intervention sat on their pinnacle of victory.

Six Saturdays after the court ruling, the announcement of the much-anticipated thanksgiving ceremony buzzed. Everyone familiar with the just-smoothened turf of the Williams not only expected one, but expected a loud one. Kene glued himself to the planning wheels, persuading everyone into pushing the event forward by another three weeks. In three weeks, his children would be on their term-end long break, making redundant the question of who would stay back in Enugu with the kids. Moreover, the Williams were his second family and whatever gladdened or grieved them, delighted or distressed him. But Kaira struggled with which took precedence as the reason for her almost giddy happiness: an opportunity for a getaway or the chance for a reunion-type visit to her folks.

The past few years and its ancillaries had foisted on Kene and Kaira an overt sense of self-preservation, or maybe caution. 'You cannot afford any summer trips during this period. Our enemies are countless, sometimes faceless, and shameless. They will swing as high or as low as possible,' Somadina had told his daughter over the phone.

'But Jide can go to London!' Kaira had whined almost with the same petulance as Noah her youngest child.

'An obstetrician hiding away in London and executing tasks deemed basic for interns? Kaira, that hardly sounds like a choice he made.'

Unlike her neighbour and friend Sochi, Kaira was not a make-up junkie, recognisable only when buried under layers of foundation and face powders. But today, although they were almost behind time for their flight to Abuja, she insisted on a light dust of powder here and a faint smear of lipstick there. It made so little difference in her husband's opinion. A smile pulled at Kene's mouth as Kaira redefined her flawlessly arched brows with her eye pencil. 'What? They accentuate my round eyes,' she said, her eyes crinkling at the sides. Each time Kaira smiled, both her cheeks dimpled, and her narrow nose widened ever so slightly.

'You don't need all these extras... you are easily the most beautiful woman I know,' Kene said, dashing off to attend to Noah who screamed loud enough for the neighbours, three streets away to hear, 'I – want – to – poo!'

'Exactly! You don't know many women,' Kaira called after him, chuckling. Kaira's insistence on applying make-up was, according to Kene, unnecessary and ill-timed. But he did not fuss today. While waiting for Noah to announce, with his customary applause, indicating he was done on his potty, Kene still did not fuss, but winced each time the longest arm of his wristwatch moved by another tick. His only regret? No one would be there to share in his humour when the humid air and heat of Enugu state's Akanu Ibiam Airport gave his wife's face a good wash. But Kaira paid no mind to her husband's subtle disapproval or inferred preference. Since the day she found a picture of his old flame on the internet, Kaira vowed never to listen to his theory of 'less is best'. Kene's ex-girlfriend's face resembled a mannequin's.

Nnamdi Azikiwe International airport looked nothing like Akanu Ibiam and its small rectangular tiles, faded and chipped at conspicuous points. Huge squares of burnished floor tiles, bouncing light off its surface, graced the grounds of the local wing of Nnamdi Azikiwe. Industrial air-conditioning fittings, powerful enough to subdue the angry waves of the July heat synonymous to Northern Nigeria, draped the flock of guests with a welcome so warm it caused Kaira's blood to begin to simmer. 'Enugu Airport is such a disgrace... tufiakwa.' Kaira pursed her lips at her husband's quizzical crumpling of the brows at her cursing. *Every year, we will refurbish, we will refurbish. When will they refurbish? We are our own worst enemies... tufiakwa!*

~

Right thumb and index finger pulling at her ear lobule, to emphasise the gravity of the issue about to be discussed, Kaira said to her oldest child, Nicole, 'What did I say? Do not look at or talk to anybody.' The six-year-old promptly shut her eyes and pursed her lips.

Are we relocating? What did she pack? Kene asked himself, a few heads away from his family and pulling two boxes big enough to each contain two sizeable goats. The weight of fourteen-month-old Noah, strapped on the baby carrier over his shoulders, made Kene huff and puff as he ambled towards his wife. Grappling with the task of explaining to Nicole, something she suspected her daughter did not require an explanation for, Kaira looked most displeased. Nicole decided to interpret her mother's instruction not to talk to or look at strangers as shutting her eyes and bumping into people and objects.

'But you said I should not look at anyone, Mummy!' Nicole said after a threat of a good hiding if she did not stop humming her words and gesticulating. Only when Kaira relaxed her squared shoulders, took two deep breaths, patted her child's braided hair, and said in a near whisper, 'Cutie, strangers may harm you here, just don't talk to anyone besides Daddy and me,' did Nicole agree to be cooperative.

'Mummy! I want to wee!' All entreaties by Kaira for four-year-old Nathaniel to hold in his wee until she located the restrooms were like throwing a brand-new basketball on a concrete surface. 'Nooooo! I want to wee now!' A few heads swung in their direction at Nathaniel's announcement. Kene stood some feet away from the exit with Nicole, two large boxes, burning shoulders, and Kaira's huge hand luggage, waiting for his wife and child to return from finding and using the restroom. The officer at the door, a man perhaps in his late fifties, looked upset at something. *His job?* Kene wondered as he sighted a now-placated Nathaniel returning with Kaira. As soon as they reached the exit, an instant grin slid over angry officer's face. 'Oga, welcome, o!' he said, not giving Kaira a second look. 'Big girl! Boss boy!' Officer smiled at Nicole and Nathaniel. When only blank expressions met his crooked smile, Officer collected the boarding stubs from Kene's stretched hand, his eyes darting from his hands to the boxes. Still holding on to the stubs, he bared his teeth at Kene. 'My Oga, anything for your boy?' Kene grimaced. *A fifty-something-year-old man has become my boy because of my perceived financial advantage.*

'Nothing today. Next time.' But Kaira caught the hardening in Officer's eyes and with the speed of lightening, dug her hand into her handbag in search of a NGN500 bill, which she handed to Kene. Not left with much choice, Kene shoved the bill into Officer's waiting hand. At once, a crooked-incisor-revealing grin replaced the initial scowl on Officer's face. He handed the boarding pass stubs to Kene. 'Ah my Oga! Thank you, o!' he called after them.

Kaira wondered since when she had become invisible, but she contended with more pressing issues.

'Where in heaven's name is Wilfred hiding? I can't stand this heat!' Kaira scanned the sea of people for her father's driver. Kene wanted to ask his wife why she insisted on tipping someone who did not acknowledge her presence. But he did not bother. He already guessed her response; *this is not a teaching moment, Kene.* And in a way, he knew she would be right. Plotting a learning curve for Officer would have made him more diligent in exercising his duties. Officer Crooked Incisor would have sifted through every item in their boxes, 'to make certain they had not managed to outsmart the infrared scanners'.

As Wilfred ate up the miles between the airport and her parents' home, Kaira wondered about the airport officer and his like. *Can things ever change in this country?* The utter lack of dignity in labour exhibited by most public officers, who were on the early and middle rungs of their career ladders, both irked and distressed her no end.

'But Daddy! Why is the doorman acting like a beggar!' Kaira had asked with a puzzled glare so many years ago, on her way out of a snack bar with her father. For starters, little Kaira had no patience for hunger pangs and already nursed a growing irritation, noting every detail within

her line of sight; the little kids begging for alms at the car park, the doorman's dirt-lined shirt sleeves and dusty gaping shoes. Never mind the shoe prints on the floor tiles of the eatery. On their way out, the man at the door revealed his yellow teeth to Dr Somadina in a smile.

'Happy Sunday, sir!' The doorman shifted his weight from one foot to the other, the expectant glint in his eyes unmistakable. Understanding at once, Kaira's father had dipped his hands in his pocket, in search of a few Naira bills for the doorman who waited patiently for 'Oga' to produce the object of his search.

It may never change; Kaira sighed, turning her attention away from the window to Nathaniel as he played Rail Rush on his iPad. The memory of when her first son could not understand why the avatar never made six seconds on the rail pulled a smile from her mouth. *This boy has become such a pro!*

~

Emotions warred as excitement met with nostalgia. For Afulenu, having her two children under her roof, for no matter how short a time, reminded her of how one never appreciated a possession until one lost it. She recalled, with regret, how her children used to trail her around the house, from the sitting room, into the kitchen, to the bedroom and sometimes to the bathroom, all to snatch their self-allotted shares of her attention. These days, they seldom carved any slot on their schedule for her. But her grandchildren were another matter. They always talked about 'Grandma in Abuja', wanting to visit, to speak with her, not wanting her to end the call, the few times she called. Two days with them, and Somadina and Afulenu were already in no doubt about how age featured as a pivotal factor in exuberance or the lack of it.

'I want Abuja soda! I want Abuja soda!' For several frustrating moments, Abigail the housekeeper scratched her head in puzzlement at what Nathaniel meant. *Which one is Abuja soda?* By Abuja soda, Nathaniel meant Fanta. Since tasting this bottle of sweetness, anyone would have mistaken the little plastic bottles of natural fruit juice, which Kaira bought for her children from Reetah stores in Enugu, for quinine.

Nicole and Nathaniel gawked in absolute delight the first time the heaven-crafted drink graced their tongues; such incomparable decadence. As you would have guessed already, everyone within the walls of Dr Williams' house suffered the consequence of indulging the most adorable six-year-old and four-year-old. Thankfully, Noah, the crown prince of chaos, was not yet old enough to partake of the deliciousness of Fanta; it would have been utter mayhem.

Thanksgiving service day fell short by only three nights and the frenzy in the Williams' home rattled even the two potted royal palm plants in the sitting room. Everybody wanted to attend, including the mother of Dr Somadina's cousin's neighbour. In truth, Afulenu did not care if the whole of Ifite-mmili village attended. The only crisis, if any, would lie in the emerging reality of her six-bedroom home not having enough space for the number of heads it would soon accommodate.

'Must he come with the entire village?' Afulenu asked her husband, her chest heaving with suppressed rage. One of the character traits Afulenu considered hair-pulling-infuriating about Nwafor, her husband's brother, included his sense of entitlement. Announcing his intended arrival with his wife and three cousins on the Friday preceding the Thanksgiving Sunday made all the tubes in Afulenu's gut twist in protest.

When managing his brother's excesses, Dr Somadina did not wield the same expertise he did with his surgical blade. Nwafor was, quite simply, a pain in the legendary neck. In Nwafor's view, his little brother owed him through this lifetime and two more for forgoing his own education to fend for him – a six-year-old – after their parents died in the civil war. And on days when he almost forgot the magnitude of his sacrifice for Somadina, his wife Agatha provided him with striking clarity. Agatha held fast her notion of 'rich Somadina and domineering Afulenu', with the tenacity of a starving man, grasping the one slice of bread he just found.

An episode still vivid in Agatha's mind's eye dates as old as twelve years. Her father had died, and custom required her husband to perform the traditional burial rites for his father-in-law. That did not pose such a complicated concept to understand. But the only unhinged bolt rested in the fine prints of those burial rites. Two robust cows, ten bags of rice and a hired dance troupe to perform for three straight days were required for the burial. One week after, still experiencing heart palpitations from the thought of raising the required funds, Nwafor received an additional list of items: ten rolls of made-in-Holland wrappers, twenty-five tubers of yam, and a complete renovation of the dead man's dilapidated house – one befitting of an accomplished man.

At once, Nwafor had besieged his brother with calls, text messages and emissaries for 'SUPPORT'. Somadina thought it ridiculous to place such a heavy burden on his brother, all to impress observers who had no modicum of care for the bereaved or their loved ones.

'What impression are you trying to create by meeting all these requirements... assuming you can? Brother, even after you provide all those things, the people watching still know you are a struggling man who cannot afford such extravagance. They will assume you begged or borrowed, just to appease their expectations, and my heart hurts as I say they will be correct,' Somadina had told his older brother in a most displeased tone.

The telephone conversation stretched for more than nine minutes.

'If you had given me the NGN7,000,000 I begged you to start the palm wine bottling company, nobody would have still been looking at me like a struggling man!' Nwafor's self-entitlement had reached through the phone speakers to move Somadina's head from one side to the other in utter disappointment. To have given Nwafor that money would have made it Somadina's sixth stab at setting his brother up in business. It did not matter that at the time of Nwafor's asking, his younger brother swam in the throes of financial hard times and therefore did not have as much money as anyone would have liked to believe. As would be imagined, their conversation did not go as either Nwafor or his wife had hoped it would.

'Please, leave him. Did I not tell you? Afulenu is using remote control for your brother!' Agatha's distant voice had floated through Somadina's earpiece; it could corrode a seven-pound block of steel.

⌇

Abuzz with activities, nobody missed Jide until half past eight, when Kene told everyone at the dinner table to carry on without him. 'He's gone out. Won't be back till later,' he said, chewing on a giant steamed carrot. Afulenu's eyes darted from Kene to her husband, to Kaira and back to Kene. Her head took a decisive bend over her plate of jollof rice, stewed assorted meat and steamed vegetables, her mind heavy on her soon-to-arrive guests.

Much to her relief, Nwafor and Agatha decided to push their journey to Saturday, and without the promised entourage too. To whatever or whoever made this welcome change possible, the Williams owed their deep gratitude. It would have been an excruciating ordeal of walking on broken glass, careful not to send 'a wrong impression' to their not-wholly-welcome guests. In Afulenu's opinion, an atmosphere devoid of Nwafor and Agatha translated to an atmosphere devoid of nuisance and anger.

With relish, Fiyin chewed, one piece at a time, on the spicy decadence in the gaping foil wrapping on their table.

'I told you! You cannot boast to have eaten good suya if you have not visited Suya village,' Jide said, his eyes glassy and crinkling at the sides. Between stabbing another piece of fire-roasted ram meat with a toothpick and nodding in assent, Fiyin gave Jide a thumbs-up. Rather than engage her mouth in the mindless exercise of talking, Omo crouched over her own foil wrapping. But she agreed with their host. The thin sheets of fire-roasted spicy meat were arguably the tastiest she had ever eaten.

Every now and again, Jide would slide his hand over Fiyin's idle hand, boring into her face with his eyes, as though to tunnel through her flawlessness to discover her imperfection. In a way, he believed finding a blemish would make him more deserving of her. Content on munching and sipping, Omo said nothing to her two companions. *These two should just shift, abeg!* Omo took a gulp from her glass of Chapman.

Although it came as a pleasant surprise to Jide when Omo agreed to accompany Fiyin to Abuja, each new crease on her face convinced him of her reluctance to make the journey.

Word had gone round of the lady who sold fabulous imported female wears and who was also skilled at making a facsimile of any which fell short of, or went beyond, a client's body size. Soon, the garage of Omo's rented two-bedroom bungalow became a fashion hub, buzzing with insatiable and avid clients. Thanks to Fiyin's prodding, Omo concluded the recruitment of two staff members before the thanksgiving, stripping her of the perfect excuse to miss the thanksgiving. She would have loved to remain buried in her four-month-old soaring fashion business and still smarted from being railroaded by Fiyin. She missed the hell out of Ben. 'Why will he not fight for me?' she often wailed into her tear-soaked pillow on the many nights she allowed herself the luxury of feeling.

Swigs of chilled Chapman travelled down their throats, abating the fury of the yaji spice on their tongues and lips. Jide explained why the suya makers doused their thin sheets of meat in the unique spice.

'The spice is crafted with a cocktail of specific herbs, which shrouds the flaming effect of the yaji until the zing clings to your tongue, mouth and throat! You would have eaten a significant pile of meat before you realise what nas hit you... and of course, your discomfort secures steady sales for their drinks,' he said between sips.

And once they returned to the hotel, Omo all but ran to the room she shared with Fiyin to relieve her bursting bladder of some of her three mugs of Chapman.

Now alone, Fiyin turned to Jide, her brows drawn to the middle.

'She looks forlorn. It's Ben, I am sure of it. This girl will self-destruct if she is not rescued from herself.'

'Mm-hmm.' Jide's eyes were distant as he idled with Fiyin's hands at the hotel lobby.

A warmth travelled from Fiyin's chest down to her belly at his reluctance to leave. Still, it did not matter how much pressure, coaxing or emotional blackmail Jide applied, Fiyin remained adamant.

'Please, sweet pea. Just a quick dash in, dash out?' said Jide.

'Nope.'

'Fiyin!'

'Nope.'

'I beg, nau!'

Now this drew a giggle from Fiyin. 'Please, please, please, stop, Jide! Nigerian pidgin doesn't suit you one bit!' she said, but soon slid back her serious countenance. 'I didn't plan to see your folks today, Jide. I need… you know… some time to get into character. Tomorrow is a better day for me… please. Besides, it's late, nau!' With the way Fiyin's eyes darted, fighting her utmost to hide her anxiety and also the fast-throbbing pulse at the base of her neck, Jide reckoned Fiyin needed time indeed.

So, still holding both of Fiyin's hands, he asked when he should come for her.

'Tomorrow? Breakfast? Brunch? Lunch?' The slight dip of his head to the right, as though in earnest appeal, goaded Fiyin's naughty double.

'Whatever happened to dinner?' she asked. A shadow slid over Jide's expectant face, his smile wavering. His gallant attempt at recovery from his disappointment pulled Fiyin's lips to an upward curve. But being placed under his parents' scrutiny made her nervous, and she wished for an infinite postponement of her meeting with them. However, one look at the deepening horizontal ridges on Jide's forehead had Fiyin deciding to be a little bolder for his sake.

'All right, I guess lunchtime would be fine.'

In bed, as the two friends yawned in readiness for sleep, Omo admitted she may have made a mistake with Ben. 'He probably never cared about me.' When Fiyin asked why she did not simply place a call to him or send him an email, Omo said, 'Me, call him? Have you never seen the words in the Holy Bible, he who finds a wife, finds a good thing? Babe, the man is supposed to do the chase!'

'Omo, for us Nigerians, telling a guy "no" means "I'm thinking about it", "impress me a little more", or "I am scared". But people like Ben are wired differently. For Ben, "yes" means "yes" and "no" means "no". O'tan. Finish.'

As far as Omo was concerned, having one feather on one's relationship quilt did not qualify anyone as an expert on heart matters, and she told Fiyin so.

'Well, you have a point there, but for naïve me, I don't believe in all that cat-and-mouse chase. Once a girl can establish a guy's love for her, she shouldn't be afraid to express her love. Wholly, fiercely, clearly. Moreover, the Bible verse you quoted said, he who finds a wife... *wife*, Omo. Get perspective!' Fiyin's voice and face reminded Omo of her elementary school mathematics teacher.

<hr />

When, at 8:45am, Somadina's phone began to ring, a gleam crept into his eyes. *Maybe they can no longer make the journey.* On his own, Nwafor was not much of a bother. But his wife, Agatha, was an entire chapter of dramatic conflicts. But a crease soon marred Somadina's forehead, casting a shadow on his initial glint.

'I hope they are fine. It's Brother Nwafor.' Afulenu straightened from tucking away the Bible they had just used for their morning prayers. Renewed devotion to God, borne out of their many persecutions from their once-upon-a-time big-named friends, expressed itself in their new enthusiasm for, in the words of their Reverend, feeding the spirit man.

'I'm sure they are all right. Answer the call,' Afulenu said, balling her hands into fists and placing them on her hips. She struck the pose of a mother hen, daring the eagle to come near her young. In truth, Somadina and Afulenu cared what happened to Nwafor. All they had ever done was show them some tough love in the hope that they would, someday, decide to grow into the potential they possessed.

'We are here!' Nwafor's voice boomed at the sound of his brother's tentative 'Hello?'

'Here where?' Somadina's eyes grew to three times their size when he learnt that Nwafor and Agatha were waiting at Wuse Park to be chauffeured to his home. *How did they get here so early? Why did they not call throughout the seven or eight hours of their journey?*

'We used night bus,' Nwafor filled the silence with the answer to Somadina's unspoken question. Afulenu gave up ever figuring out her brother-in-law and his family. *These people act like aliens*, she mused, shaking her head in disbelief.

Wilfred took the day off; toothache, he said. So, a rather displeased Jide inherited the task of going to pick up his uncle and auntie from the park. Before he left last night, Jide had coerced, begged and thrown in a dash of emotional blackmail, for Fiyin to let him pick her up at half past ten in the morning. He wanted her to meet his parents before the bustle became explosive. Now this. But to assure a level of bearability, he conscripted Kene to escort him. On their way to the motor park, he dialled Fiyin's mobile phone.

'I must be the only one without the faintest clue of the pivotal role my uncle and auntie dearest would be playing!' Jide was boiling.

Fiyin let out a soft chuckle and told him about her zealous guardian angels.

'They are particular about my comfort and are ready to shift anything for me to have my way. Guess who now has more time to prepare to meet your folks?' she said. When Jide would not stop his whining, Fiyin reminded him of the people caught in the Ukraine-Russia conflict. People with real problems. People grappling with starvation, cold, the uncertainty of their next breath; problems nowhere near the bandwidth of a one- or two-hour shift in personal schedules. 'Not to mention those of them living the painful reality of losing loved ones forever! Abeg, sink your teeth in a cool cucumber, joor! I'll see you when you see me.'

Jide shook his head. 'True, she got her way in the end,' he said glancing at Kene.

There existed between the two men a bond of sibling love and friendship. Jide and Kene did not have the average 'in-law' relationship foisted upon people by cultural expectation. They liked each other. Through Fiyin's voice filtering through the car phone speakers, Kene remained as still as a painting, taking note of, and memorising, every expression, quality or personality nuance a phone conversation would permit. But now, he burst into a long and nerve-scratching laughter. His shoulders still shook as he pointed out the salient points in Fiyin's terse lecture.

'Summary? You throw tantrums like Noah, your view is impaired; imperceptive to the trees responsible for the forest, and your perspective of life, or the lack of it, is not appreciated by cerebral beings. Damn. I like Fiyin already.'

Jide's grip on the steering tightened; he flexed his knuckles.

'Guy, abeg, don't run us off the road, o! My wife and children are expecting me back in the same condition I left,' Kene said, still revelling in his execution of a jab at Jide. Once an opportunity for a jab surfaced, Kene took it with flawless precision. Those opportunities were as frequent as total solar eclipses; Jide's head almost never left his shoulders.

Indeed, Jide looked like he held a mouthful of lime juice in his mouth as he blazed past tall buildings, exotic cars, and not-so-luxury cars. For a moment, the speedometer reading distracted Jide from his seething. He recalled the last time he visited Lagos and how he almost went berserk with the choked roads. Most of the roads or streets he plied resembled roads milling with unmanned vehicles in motion. He wondered if the roads should have been built wider, like the ones in Abuja. His thoughts remained on the Lagos roads, which were replete with wooden kiosks. Kiosks so miniature they barely housed the goods intended for them, providing them with the perfect excuse to encroach on the roads. Kaira's mantra, 'What's wrong with our country is a lack of consequences', echoed in Jide's mind; he sighed. He agreed with his sister and decided to pick, with utmost prudence, road-shuttle times, locations of business interests, and leisure choices in the cosmopolitan city of Lagos. Until proper consequences were developed and deployed.

The older Mr and Mrs Williams stuck their tongues to the roofs of their mouths as Jide drove them back home. At calculated intervals, Kene turned to ask Uncle Nwafor and Agatha if their legs had enough room. Minutes later, he announced that they would soon arrive; the awkwardness gnawed at his insides. As for Jide, he could not be bothered. Once they returned to the house, he, and Kene, like the two fine gentlemen they were raised to be, took out all the luggage from the boot. Jide asked the guard to send the gallon of oil, unripe plantains, and tubers of coco yam to the kitchen from the back. And almost as soon as they deposited the bags of their just-arrived guests in the visitors' room downstairs, Jide left with Kene.

'So?' Kene half turned to Jide.

An otherwise innocent question managed to crumple Jide's forehead into a scowl.

'So what?' said Jide, his eyes glued to the road as he ate the distance between him and Ross-hills hotel.

'Have you?' Kene said, purposely ignoring the growing scowl on the face of his brother-in-law and friend.

'No!' On some other occasion, regarding a matter less sensitive, Kene would have pestered Jide a touch more. But not on this occasion. He would let Jide brood in peace. And why not? Not too long ago, he had walked the same line himself.

EIGHT

HOLD DEAR THAT FRIEND WHO DANCES TO YOUR HAPPY TUNE

Sounds from a chuckling child, of a mother's reprimand, and from an upset toddler pulled at Afulenu's mouth, forcing it into a wistful smile. With Abigail off to the market with the caterers to serve as her madam's eyes, Afulenu lapped greedily at the bubbles of happiness floating towards her from her sitting room as she busied herself with lunch. Kaira reminded her much of herself. In the not-quite-distant past, her voice and those of her two children used to ring all the way to four houses away. Nostalgia washed over Afulenu; she had once said to them, 'With all this yelling, our neighbours must think a madwoman lives in this house. One day, they will whisk your mummy off to the asylum.' And Afulenu's cunning threat set a leash on their attention-seeking tantrums, if only for a while.

'Hei! Ewoo! You are still cooking?' Afulenu often wondered at people who asked questions with obvious answers. What else best described someone, spoon in hand, hovering over and stirring a pot on a lit burner?

'Yes, I'm still cooking.'

Agatha peered into the pot of vegetable soup. 'Eehh? What are you cooking?'

Three deep breaths lowered the heat under Afulenu's simmering rage as she turned away to start dicing fingers of unripe plantain; one of the meals approved by Nwafor's doctor since recently being diagnosed with 'type 2 diabetes mellitus'. It did not help much that Agatha waited until Afulenu was done preparing pounded yam, from scratch, before providing such an important piece of information. Nwafor's disdain for 'the lazy woman's poison' – poundo yam – puzzled Somadina and Afulenu. All efforts to convince Nwafor of the similarity between pounded yam tubers and poundo yam flour, which when rolled in a pot of boiling water gained the same consistency as actual pounded yam, met with obstinate scoffing. Afulenu had boiled and pounded fresh yams with a mortar and pestle, only for Agatha to express her gratitude with, 'Haa! No-oo! Doc said ordinary yam is not good for Nna'm Nwafor. But he can manage unripe planti.'

⌐━━⌐

Fiyin started to walk towards Jide and Kene the moment she spotted them at the reception area. In preparation for the famed fashionable wait, Kene had insisted on placing drink orders, hoping only for an acceptable delay before the ladies appeared. Kene's raised brows did not elude Jide.

'I told you so. The girl has nothing to prove to anyone.' Jide's self-assured smile highlighted his declaration.

'Mm-hmm, you're right.' Kene's furrowed brows made him look contemplative. Once Fiyin reached them, the two men stood. 'I am most pleased to have met you at last,' said Kene, taking her stretched hand in greeting.

A giggle accompanied her smile as she said, 'Same here.' Jide touched his mouth to Fiyin's temple in a silent kiss before she took the seat beside him.

'Is everyone around you always this formal in speech?' Fiyin asked Jide in amused whisper.

'No, only the guys… and only when they are around the ladies they find intriguing.'

Fiyin giggled like a teenage girl on her first date as she leaned away from Jide.

'Omo will be with us in a minute. Had to take a call,' she said, declining Kene's offer to order a drink for her. She thought no one, besides Omo, sensed how meeting Jide's folks petrified her, but it shone through her eyes with the same brightness as the midday sun. At last, Omo emerged from the bend beside the elevator sporting a bright scowl. Kene's forehead creased. Disapproval pulled Fiyin's mouth into a downward curve. *Hmm! I can tell this one is not used to waiting around for women.*

For Fiyin, the road to Maitama appeared to have folded, but Jide's right foot strained from maintaining an acceptable angle on the accelerator. He pulled into his parents' driveway, his heart thudding. Fiyin took in her surroundings and decided a visual illustrator could not have done a better job; Jide's family home fitted the exact description she gleaned from him. The grey stone-walled building with square black window frames sent shudders down Omo's spine. *Weird home for a regular guy like Jide*, she thought, taking decisively bold steps behind Fiyin into the house. But once inside the gothic-looking house, her budding dread fast evolved into something else as her jaw dropped a fraction in sheer awe. Brilliant white walls and ceilings, interspersed with exquisite paintings and spotlights, enveloped her.

'Daddy!' In reckless delight, Nicole and Nathaniel rumbled past Jide, Fiyin and Omo to Kene. He scooped up both his kids, placing them on his left and right sides.

'Now, like the nice children you are, say hello to your uncle and these two nice ladies,' Kene said.

'Hello uncs, hello ladies!' Nathaniel and Nicole said, both chuckling. Kaira got on her feet, balancing Noah on her waist. Jide did the introductions and pulled Fiyin away as soon as he learnt, from his sister, where their mother was. At the dining area, right before they reached the kitchen door, Jide stopped and whispered into Fiyin's ears. She stepped back, staring at Jide's rumpled brows for about four heartbeats. The sound of her giggling as she said, 'I... I... well... maybe,' drew Kaira, Omo, and Kene's fleeting attention.

Nothing from all the information she gathered about Afulenu warned Fiyin about the wave of warmth now floating towards her. As soon as Dr Afulenu Williams set eyes on them, she said, her face aglow, 'At last!' She wiped her hands and arms with her apron to wrap them around a wide-eyed but relieved Fiyin. Although she never questioned Jide's mum's charming persona; choosing to believe all he told her about his mother, Fiyin did well to leave her receptacle of expectations empty and available for a good filling of disappointment.

'Come, come. Sit right here with me. Jide, your dad says he wants to speak with you once you return,' Afulenu said, leading Fiyin to one of the three high stools tucked under the kitchen island.

Half questioning, half assuring Fiyin with a slight frown, an angled and shallow dip of the head, Jide went off in answer to his father's supposed call. The protest of cooking spoon against condiments, coming from the boiling pot of plantain pottage, joined forces with the delicious wafts pervading the seven-by-seven-feet kitchen in reminding Fiyin of her folly in skipping breakfast; she had woken up with her insides in tiny knots, anxious about her meeting with the Williams.

In no time, Afulenu loosened all Fiyin's knots. Determined to bridge a portion of the chasm between the southeast and the southwest, however small, she asked about Fiyin's family, what her name meant, how many uncles and aunties she had, and so on.

'What's your signature dish? I hear you impress even your most brutal detractors with your cooking skills.'

'And I doubt Jide would have been as brazen with his assertion a few months before Greyburtons,' Fiyin said, flashing her teeth in a smile. A battle ensued between Afulenu's normally sceptical, wary, measured self and her acutely emotional subconscious. She liked Fiyin months before she met her and now fought the sudden urge to hold her close, to beg her not to hurt her son.

With the number of times Jide said Fiyin's name over the past couple of months, his eyes turning glassy as he did, Afulenu entertained no doubt about her son falling into pieces if Fiyin turned out to be 'not the one'. But in the end, logical Afulenu saved the day.

'Come, come. Tell me what you think,' she said instead, motioning her head for Fiyin to come over to the burner. Fiyin smiled when Afulenu, for all her finesse, stirred the pot of boiling plantain pottage, tapped the neck of the cooking spoon on the pot's rim just enough to shake off the food while retaining some of the pottage juice and held it away from the heat. With no further prompting required, Fiyin stretched her hand in readiness for a dab from the back of Afulenu's ladle. As soon as tongue touched palm, hunger pangs which, before now, had exhibited decorum in expressing their frustration, let sense or reason run wild. Superhuman abilities were not summoned for Afulenu to read her young guest, and soon, a plate of steaming deliciousness became the object of Fiyin's undivided attention.

⌒

Because Kene's parents were in Abuja for their in-laws' party, he passed on joining Jide on his 9:00pm commute to Ross-hills hotel. Fearing his mother would develop a stroke over the 'abomination' posed by his initial idea of waiting until church service tomorrow to say his hellos to Uncle I.G, he decided to endure an excruciating hour of 'face time' with Uncle I.G at his Asokoro home.

'I wish your parents could damn this man for once! They should have just stayed at a hotel for crying out loud! Why do they put up with his poor behaviour anyway?' Kaira did not like her husband's uncle. His excesses were far too many, in her opinion. Kene tutted at his wife.

'You, my dear wife, have an interesting way of expressing gratitude to my uncle for all his benevolence to your current and future generation.' Kaira burst into a short-lived laughter.

I.G's claims of influencing the Williams' recent victory in court had now become a delightful family comic tale.

'The guy is beyond irritating. Tufiakwa! No wonder his poor wife escaped to Australia after only six years of being married to him. Are they even finally divorced?' said Kaira.

'For where? The man refused to sign. I know he'll die first before setting her free. Rumour has it that she has been in an undeclared affair for almost ten years. My uncle knows the man makes her happy, so he is holding her to ransom.'

'So he's fine with his wife being the sole custodian of their two children?'

'Three. They have three children. All mid- and late teens who can't stand their father,' Kene said.

'But to be honest, Kene, you guys indulge this man a tad too much!'

Kene heaved and shrugged his shoulders. Shaking his head in fatigued resignation, he snatched the keys to Afulenu's car; they used it whenever they visited. In truth, but for his parents, Kene would have been beyond pleased to tell Uncle I.G to go suck on an unripe cashew fruit. The man derived immense satisfaction from dumping down everyone else. Some say he possesses an intimidating mien; others call him manipulative. Many find power-infused wealth culpable, fewer suggest sorcery, and those tilting closer to Kene's theory say he is only trying to atone for his inferiority complex. But in Kene's uncut opinion, Uncle I.G, being the eldest of his father's siblings, is simply a poorly behaved pot-bellied boy who grew tall.

By evening, as Jide drove the ladies back to their hotel, a taut tranquillity pervaded the car space, everyone wrapped in their own unique cocoon of a thoughts-roller coaster. Jide thought of one thing alone; Omo, of Ben and her two new staff; while three issues plagued Fiyin's peace; the cause of the edginess seeping through Jide's fingers as they linked and held hers tight, the budding void which grew arms and legs since playing with Nicole and Nathaniel, and the reason her friend's distress refused to go away.

〜

A throng of activities jarred the Williams out of their beds at quarter past five in the morning. Thankfully, most of the chaos occurred outside the main building, on the grounds at the back, with professional caterers cutting, washing, and frying well-seasoned beef cuts, chicken laps and turkey wings. Four boys, not past their teenage years, hovered over a pile of yam tubers, each working with sharp knives, stripping them of their peel. A middle-aged woman, one of the hired cooks, holding out a jute sack, appealed to one of the yam peelers. 'My pikin... wey wear yellow shirt, abeg put the yam peeling inside this bag for me.'

A single vertical line appeared between the lad's brows. It indicated his preference for peeling as many yam tubers as possible to make his day's wage than running errands for entitled middle-aged ladies. Nevertheless, he took the couple of steps between the yam peelers and the meat fryers, and without as much as a look in her direction, snatched the bag from the woman and returned to his crew. Lifting his yellow shirt, he wiped the beads of sweat on his face and hunched over the pile to resume peeling, the vertical line on his forehead magically gone with his early morning sweat.

Rhythmic sounds of pounding lured the sun farther out of the clouds. A smaller group fussed over three giant-sized pots, parboiling, and washing rice, while another busied themselves with dicing carrots, peas, cabbages, onions and yellow peppers. Someone asked, wanting to measure the scope of their task, 'Na we go do salad?'

Someone else said, 'No, o. No be we.'

No longer able to wish away the chaos happening outside her house, Afulenu dragged herself out of bed, leaving a not-in-the-least-perturbed-about-his-environment Somadina to snore some more. She wished for night to ride backwards on eagles' wings. Her house coat strings were in place by the time she reached the landing of the stairs, to find Abigail, hands wringing and pacing back and forth. On seeing her, Afulenu needed no interpreter to transcribe the demeanour of her most trusted and longest serving staff. Something had gone awfully wrong.

'Abigail, what is it?' Afulenu asked, a sense of foreboding settling over her. The housekeeper's breathing sounded laboured. She wiped her sweaty palms on her behind, pursed her lips, as though in pain, before blurting, 'Savouries called me some minutes ago, ma. They cannot make today's appointment… The first lady's cousin moved her Monday dinner party to a Sunday Lunch. So, ehm… so they decided to drop us.'

A sudden itch in Afulenu's underarm announced panic-sweat. Abigail stared at her madam as she went back up the stairs without as much as a word, but she did not allow herself to be fooled by Afulenu's composure. It often underscored chaos.

Three taps on the door made Jide tap the 'mute' icon on his phone. He wanted to find out who bothered his peace so early in the morning.

'Come in.'

Kaira resembled a cat in search of all her ten kittens. In as few words as she could manage, namely about three hundred and five, she explained their current impasse. Fiyin waited with thinning patience for Jide to return to her call and started to dish out a lecture on 'the dangers of poor behaviour' when his words shoved hers back into her throat.

'I may need to call you back, my love. Some emergency came up... it is about the party.' But Fiyin would not let him off the call without a clear explanation. And once he did, she shifted to overdrive. It was her turn to tell Jide she would call back.

Fifteen minutes after, Afulenu, Somadina and Kaira had exhausted their individual lists of dessert places. Everyone had a party in Abuja that Sunday afternoon. But Fiyin did as she promised. She called back.

⌐⟳

'I think the universe is on our side,' said Jide to his lounge-sitting and listless-looking family. Kaira sprang to her feet to turn on the lights which, before now, were off, in silent camaraderie with the Williams. With growing anticipation, they lapped at Jide's every word. His friends, Fiyin and Omo, managed to arrange, with the restaurant in Ross-hills, for two hundred servings of salad and cheesecake. Jide would skip to the supermarket where he would buy bowls of ice cream, strawberries, granola, cherries, bespoke dessert cups and spoons. Fiyin would wave her wand at the ice cream and later join Omo, Kene, Kaira and Jide to double as guests and service hands.

Everyone started to talk at once. Who came up with this idea? What type of salad: Caesar, chicken, beef, tossed, garden? Could anyone vouch for the hotel's quality? The stream of questions flowed unending. At last, when Jide was able to interject, he provided the answers. Fiyin and Omo came up with the idea. Chicken and Caesar salads. And no, nobody had died, yet, from food poisoning at the hotel, but their salads and desserts were 'to die for'.

'Revival Cathedral Of Our Saviour' milled with attendees, an appreciable number of them being first-time attenders who came to celebrate with Dr and Dr Mrs Williams. The cathedral's one-hectare-sized gravel-covered parking lot strained under the weight of an assortment of vehicles, from average saloon cars to luxury sports utility vehicles, and everything between. A space once considered most impressive, now struggled with the sheer number of congregants. Nothing in all its hosting history would have prepared Revival Cathedral for the challenge it now grappled with – to provide seating positions for all its visitors. But thanks to the central cooling system and split air-conditioning units, each punctuating every sixth row of pews, the ambience remained most favourable. Adding a hot and humid atmosphere to the table would have been a most unpleasant side dish for the guests. With the number of people in attendance, one would think all other churches in the Federal Capital Territory of Nigeria had shut their doors in solidarity with the Williams.

A little after the processional hymn, Jide walked in, with Fiyin and Omo on his tail. Ross-hills hotel sat a considerable distance away from the church, and Omo, who must always fire on all four cylinders when it came down to her appearance, did not help time move slower. 'Maybe my Prince Charming will discover me today,' she had said. Fiyin, after only seconds inside the church, realised the marked difference between her concept of 'church' in comparison to Jide's family church. A less-than-friendly tug from an elderly woman, perhaps in her sixties, jolted Omo out of her awestruck observation of the church's beauty. Without a word, the woman handed Omo a new white handkerchief. Omo pouted, snatched the handkerchief, and made a meal of unfolding and placing it on her shiny baby curls, all the while wondering why the woman's headscarf almost touched her eyebrows. A quick sweep, with her eyes, of Omo's pew, and three more after it, convinced the stiff-lipped woman to move on to other pews in search of more blundering ladies.

From five pew rows away, Kaira tilted her head sideways, giving Omo and Fiyin a conciliatory look; an apology for not giving them prior warning about how to dress up to her family church. Keeping all three of her children in check was proving more distracting than she would have liked. Only minutes ago, Noah, while munching on a cookie, demanded water at the top of his voice and soon after, became fascinated by the almost ten-inch-high scarf on the head of the lady sitting in front of them. He nearly pulled it off the poor lady's head. Fiyin blew Jide's sister a kiss, and Omo smiled.

Another woman in a big white dress, from under the hem of which a purple skirt peeked and across whose shoulders hung a matching purple tippet, floated down the blue-rugged aisles. With eyes darting from one female worshipper to the next, she shoved multicoloured shawls into the unwilling hands of ladies who were sitting in front pews and whose knees were visible. She also extended the same favour to ladies whose necklines dipped too far from the clavicle. The purple-tippeted deaconess looked set to start giving each erring lady hard knocks on the head at any moment. It was a good thing she waddled away before turning herself into a distraction; but not before serving Kaira a pointed look. A look commanding her to control her children or take them outside.

Solemnity laved over and through the white edifice of the Revival Cathedral Of Our Saviour as hymns were sung and prayers muttered by worshippers. Fiyin caught the handkerchief-shoving lady in time before she did heaven knows what to Omo who thought a quick nap during all the tedium made for better use of her time. Although rattled, Omo offered Fiyin a thankful smile for the knee nudge.

The house of worship came alive at the announcement for the thanksgiving procession to begin. Somadina and Afulenu, accompanied by their friends and family, filed out of the church to converge at the entrance, from where they would dance in with their cash offerings, in gratitude for the divine intervention responsible for their victory over their 'adversaries'. Although unsure of how many of the enthusiastic waves, toothy smiles, and back-tapping-accompanied hugs came from a place of sincere love and friendship, Afulenu and Somadina responded in like fervour.

Amidst chants of *HE has given me victory, I will lift HIM higher*, the thankful worshippers floated in, swaying, shuffling their feet, and some turning around to engage the person behind them in a duet dance worship. In rhythm to drums, guitars, piano and voices, each worshipper tendered an envelope-encased cash or cheque offering.

Bright with face-splitting grins, the four-man clergy added more glitz to the Cathedral's dazzling incandescence. In Omo's opinion, the offering bags, almost bursting with white envelopes, took all the credit for the thrill their eyes exuded.

~

While Afulenu, or any other Williams, did not expect more flattering conduct from Agatha, the glee, and utter disregard for opinions, with which she ate everything bearing the most remote semblance of food, without as much as a flicker of interest in offering to help with anything, made everyone thankful for the insignificant number of people to whom she had been introduced as a member of the family.

'Chima! Chima! Give me malt, biko!'

Agatha's persistence on favouring the first, rather than the second half of Chimakaira's name, wounded Kaira's femaleness. As a child, Kaira had asked, her chest heaving from indignation, 'Why do you call me Chima and not Kaira, like everyone else? Chima is a boy's name.' And Agatha had said, 'Both of them are in your name, and it is my mouth. I shall call you the one my mouth likes.'

'Ehh? Then I shall hear the one my ears like too,' Kaira had said, clicking her tongue and stalking off like an angry peacock. True to Kaira's words, today, she neither acknowledged her uncle's wife's call, nor displayed any emotion akin to displeasure at being called a masculine name. In the end Agatha wobbled her 102kg mass to the cooling van to demand two bottles of malt drink. One for herself and one for her husband. But only moments later, recalling their doctor's warning about Nwafor's diet, Agatha guzzled the two malt drinks before ambling back to the van to ask for a bottle of club soda for her husband.

For the one millionth time, Omo said, with embellished passion, 'How I wish Timi made it for this party!' Of Jide's two bosom friends – Timi and Nnamdi – Omo preferred Timilehin and wished he had found a way to avoid the conference also responsible for Nnamdi's absence. Under her breath, Kaira asked Jide, 'Hope she knows about Teni?' Jide assured his sister of Omo's harmless affinity for Timi.

'Nothing to fear here. Omo is all right,' he said.

At first, Fiyin struggled with Omo's utter dislike for Nnamdi, but soon, Nnamdi's cheekiness and insipid, sometimes pungent, jokes grew more mind-numbing and cutting for her to bear. Not only Jide thought his second friend's absence served some purpose in easing Omo's countenance.

Numbed with fatigue from serving salads, plates of gourmet ice cream and cakes, Jide and his crew sat, feet-hanging on stools, in the sitting room when Fiyin spotted Nicole and Nathaniel peeking from the foot of the stairs.

'Hi guys!' she called.

'Come say hi,' their daddy said. The duo came out of hiding, their eyes twinkling with mischief. Nathaniel threw a 'hello!' and went to sit on his daddy's lap from where he stole side glances at Fiyin.

'Good evening, everybody!' Nicole said and went to whisper to her mummy. Kaira's long bout of uncontrollable laughter chased Nicole all the way up the stairs.

Everyone wanted the details of what Nicole had said, but Kaira promised to tell them as soon as blue whales began to lay eggs. Out of nowhere and to everyone's amusement, Nathaniel blurted, 'You are so cute!'

'Who?' Kene asked.

'Her!' Nathaniel was pointing at Fiyin with a smile he seemed reluctant to share with an audience.

At that, Fiyin got to her feet, curtsied, and said, 'Thank you, kind sir!' The room filled with laughter and Nathaniel buried his face in his father's chest. Moments later, Abigail came for him.

'Nathaniel, time to shower!' With the way Abigail kept up with her chores, juggling minding her madam's grandchildren with clearing up the kitchen, one would think the woman ran on stress rather than blood.

At 7:45pm, a service staff went to rouse Agatha from under the canopy, where she was nodding off and snoring; they wanted to take down the canopies and pack up their chairs. Agatha knuckle-rubbed her eyes, let out a loud and long yawn. The four-man clergy sauntered to their cars with their bulging brown envelopes, each lost in their own merry thoughts. They paid no mind to the large woman under the canopy who just expelled a loud fart. Outings like these often guaranteed immense financial rewards. Who cared about a little accidental discharge?

After their late dinner, everyone disagreed with Fiyin and Omo's bright idea, and soon, the two ladies started to buckle in their resolve to return to the hotel.

'But this is such a waste... we already paid for the room!' Omo's last effort earned her an incredulous stare from Somadina. With the way Jide refused to meet Fiyin's eyes as everyone prevailed on the two ladies to spend the night, she suspected 'her beloved' did not entertain any thoughts of driving her anywhere. How accurate her suspicions were! For as Jide sipped on his iced tea, he said to himself, *Even if she falls on her knees before me in worship, I will not drive anywhere this night.* For all Jide cared, if Fiyin still believed he had to prove his love for her by abdicating his logical thinking, a rethink about their amorous affair would be well in order.

In the end, reason won the tussle. And although the extra room upstairs, which Jide insisted on setting up by himself, offered all the comfort required of it, Fiyin spent most of the night in the lounge with Jide.

Kaira squirmed at the touch of her husband's face to her neck.

'Ooh, Kene! This cleanser will dry up if you don't let me clean my face in peace,' she said, giggling.

'Well, not if you tell me what Nicole told you,' he said against her neck.

So, in her best impression of her child, Kaira said, 'Daddy has you, Grandpa has Grandma and Uncle Jide has Auntie Fiyin, but where is Auntie Omo's own?'

When Kene's shoulders stopped shaking, he asked his wife, 'Auntie Omo's own what?'

'Maybe I should call her so we can find out?' said Kaira, her eyes glistening with humour.

'Don't you dare!' Kene pulled his wife up from her chair to claim her lips in a kiss, his eyes glistening with something Kaira recognised.

~~~

On their flight back to Lagos, Fiyin stared fixedly at nothing and Omo, hand on chin, crossed and uncrossed her legs at the ankles. A male flight attendant rolled a trolley to their seat. 'What would you like, please?'

Fiyin did not hear him; Omo took one look at the film-wrapped sandwiches, crackers, and packet juices and said, 'Nothing. Thanks.'

Fifteen minutes before landing, and unable to keep the clamp on the lid any longer, the two friends began to speak in unison.

'All right, you first,' Fiyin said.

'Ben... Ben is coming to Nigeria. He called yesterday... that time you were in the lounge with Jide. Fifi, he is really coming... my God, he is coming!' Omo's eyes shone with a thin film of tears. It did not matter that they were in an aircraft packed with over sixty travellers, Fiyin flung her arms around her friend in one moment of unfettered affection. No questions asked, her friend's days of torture were finally over!

Once the plane landed, Omo switched her phone on. 'He may have sent a text,' she said, sitting up in her seat and resting her back again, her excitement clear as spring. Crinkled eyes and upturned lips gave every indication of Fiyin's happiness for her friend. And as the airport taxi sped down Third Mainland Bridge, Omo sped through the details of her almost two-hour telephone conversation with Ben the night before. And to flesh the meat of the gist to the bone, they went past Lekki Phase 1, all the way to Omo's Agungi residence. Omo told Fiyin about Ben's defining declaration: I have lived the true definition of torture since you left, Omo.

Dabbing at the newly formed tear in her friend's right eye, Fiyin swallowed a lump. *Aww! My sweet friend is just as much of a softie as I am!*

'And you, you don't want to spill what you and Jide spent the better part of last night doing, *abi*? You this girl! You don spoil!' Omo said with a glint in her eyes as the taxi driver made to engage his gear to begin his twenty-minute drive back to Lekki Phase 1, where Fiyin lived with her folks.

'Jide asked me to marry him!'

Omo's weekend travel bag landed with a thud. Her mouth hung open. Fiyin stuck her head out of the window of the moving taxi, her eyes sparkling with unshed tears. The night's air carried her words to Omo; 'I said YES!'

She nestled back into the car to relive the sight of Omo doing the cabbage dance on the sidewalk beside her gate and smiled as the taxi driver's right cheek moved in what looked like a grin.

NINE

IF SOMETHING LOOKS TOO GOOD TO BE TRUE,
IT IS OFTEN PRUDENT TO LOOK AGAIN

No degree of explanation was convincing Afulenu. A basket of fruits and five cartons of choice wine; the only requirements for a South-Western marriage introductory visit? *Never!* 'A di'm eje ije ifele, I cannot go on a disgraceful errand,' she had told her husband.

But for Somadina's insistence on Nwafor and Agatha being part of his delegation for the introductory rites between Jide and Fiyin, that part of the string of ceremonies; introductory visit, payment of the bride price, traditional wedding, and white wedding, would have been settled two and a half months ago.

'How can I take a step of this magnitude alone when I have a living sibling? Ah, Afi, let's not overdo things!' Afulenu clicked her tongue at her husband. She recognised Somadina's all-so-familiar voice; one which often made her experience the frustration of a bound giant being feather-tickled in the nose by a bunch of impish children.

By 'not overdoing things', Somadina meant not doing things to upset or dishevel the existing tradition of involving family in all of one's private affairs, not minding one's conviction of the disruption such an involvement would provoke. A long time ago, Afulenu realised the futility in pointing out Nwafor's penchant for sculpting problems out of well-thought-through solutions.

Nwafor and his wife arrived in Lagos before Somadina and Afulenu's flight departed Abuja. And demonstrating the impropriety of the goat with no need of an invitation to enter a yam barn, they landed at the Williams' Ikoyi home where they, as soon as their bags were taken to the guest room, ordered Nsikan, the live-in cook, to prepare fried rice and peppered goat meat for them. The coming three days promised to try the patience of even a nun. Afulenu wished her daughter were with her. For some reason, with Kaira, Agatha often applied a measure of caution to her proclivities. But Jide never concerned himself with fripperies like the temperaments of others.

'I am only responsible for how I represent myself. If Uncle and his wife decide to be thick heads at every opportunity, they have my best wishes… I recommend you do the same,' he once said to his mother.

Friday sped past with Jide and his parents busy at their Lagos hospital. For most of the day, Jide wore a half-smile. When he was not consulting with patients, he was ambling into Timilehin's office to tell him how much he looked forward to tomorrow. Nnamdi was off duty, but everyone now knew how he spent his off-duty days.

At first, the thought of their friend maintaining an extra practice, alongside his stop-gap job at the Abuja teaching Hospital, in one of the unsettling parts of town tolled alarm bells for Jide and Timilehin. Worse still when he would not quit this extra practice, even after he and Timilehin resigned their jobs at the teaching hospital to return to the reinstated Soma-Williams hospital. But when Somadina later learnt, and shared with them, how much Nnamdi received as salary from this extra practice, they realised certain waters indeed ran deep. Nnamdi spent his days off work at Holy Cross Infant Hospital, Abulegba, a neonatal hospital on the mainland.

With his salary from the near run-down hospital, and most times a painful pinch of his savings, Nnamdi purchased ABDEK drops, which he offered as parting gifts to discharged babies.

Nnamdi promised to arrive at Timilehin's before nine o'clock the next morning, in time for the formal introduction of the Williams to the Taylors. In the evening, husband and wife returned to their Ikoyi home and Timilehin faced the infamous Lekki traffic to meet his heartthrob at Peaches and Plums salon. But Jide remained on Victoria Island. A little over a year ago, on one fine summer evening, in an almost-empty Chilfort Yards flat, a pact was made. Jide and Fiyin agreed on two weeks as the upper limit for the time allowed in reverence to their long-distance relationship. They were already two days overdue. Now on her second glass of virgin-mint-daiquiri at their favourite spot, Fiyin beamed as her date walked in.

Nothing topped spicy lamb chops and dead-cold drinks on a bed of decent jazz music. But long after the lamb chops and drinks were gone, Jide and Fiyin remained; holding hands, savouring the growing anticipation as tomorrow tiptoed nearer, one clock tick after another. And when at midnight Fiyin turned off her bedside lamp in submission to sleep's call, she convinced herself, *tomorrow… My heart is skipping beats because of tomorrow.*

~

'So, our would-be in-laws are not expecting us, eh?' Agatha sounded like a queen, annoyed at the sight of a stain on her favourite white linen. Somadina explained why the security officials insisted on clearance from the Taylors about the exact number of guests they were expecting. 'This is standard protocol for most estates,' he said. But the gulley now between Agatha's eyebrows refused to be filled. Everyone else – Somadina, Afulenu, Nkechi, Jide and his two friends – accommodated the pedantry imposed on them; different estates were entitled to their own rules, never mind how mindless.

With high-rise shopping malls, banks and filling stations sprouting from any patch of land with the faintest hint of viability, countless entrance and exit routes emerged. Lekki Phase 1 had been invaded. And to maintain the past glory of this once-exclusive residential cocoon, estate developers and home owners developed a brilliant plan – erecting walls or installing entrance and exit gates to serve a collection of homes. These sub communities were subsequently fitted with shared facility instruments like power, environmental management, and security, to live up to their rebranding attempt. Lekki Phase 1 was, once again, in a sense, considered somewhat exclusive.

⌒

Now boiling with impatience, Nwafor clenched his teeth as his nephew signed the security register which was to grant them access. The guards' insistence on observing security protocol irritated the sore of waiting for Nkechi, Afulenu's sister, to conclude her make-up. *If only Afulenu had allowed the cook to give me the yam pottage I wanted for breakfast. Brown bread like chaff and half-fried egg! Hah!*

Agatha sat in the passenger's seat of the vehicle behind, shifting from one butt cheek to the other as Somadina, Afulenu and Nkechi spoke in low tones. Nwafor thought his wife looked regal in the front seat of his brother's SUV. He sometimes wished his choices delivered more favourable outcomes, if only to empower him enough to give his wife the niceties of life. Nwafor's irritation maintained a steady climb. He wondered why his nephew's friends laughed so loud and into the back of his head. *All these spoilt youths!*

A short drive from the entrance gate brought them to a T-junction. Jide took a left and Somadina's driver, Manasseh, followed. Two blocks of terrace buildings, six one-storey units in each, flanked the road leading to another T-junction, at the end of which Jide turned right. Now, tall palms obscured the mid-morning sun from the right. Timilehin imagined the inhabitants of the twin duplexes on the left side of the road never bothered about the sun's glare. 'Men! This place is not bad at all! So away from all the Lekki madness,' Nnamdi said, looking around.

'Now you agree, there can be an eye in Lekki's storm,' Jide said, a smug smile pulling his mouth and brows. Timilehin nodded his agreement.

Now utter in their oblivion of the older man riding with them, the young men lost themselves in wild chatter about the cut-throat cost of land plots in Lagos. Nwafor mused over how his life's journey dipped a different tangent because he chose the apprenticeship job which was to oversee Somadina's schooling. The all-so-familiar taste of regret spread over his tongue. *To think I rejected Mazi Nnkwonta's offer! I should have followed him to Ibadan. Mazi would have sent me to secondary school.* But Nwafor did not go to Ibadan. *Who would have cared for Somadina?* He decided not to abandon his six-year-old brother in the village with Ibiliachi, their grand-auntie, to pursue his own dreams. Before Mama Nwafor bowed to the gangrene from her gunshot wounds, she had extricated a promise from her elder son. To nurture, protect and defend his little brother.

⌒⌒

Giddy with giggling and high-pitched chatting, Ifeatu and Omo met the guests outside. Although her face glowed, Ifeatu looked more fragile than her usual self. Yes, like you may have already guessed, she won. Her wedding took place in Lagos. And yes, nearly one thousand five hundred guests were in attendance. All her friends joked about how her husband retaliated by wasting no time in embossing his 'seal of ownership' on her. Ifeatu's corset was yet to dry from her sweating on her wedding party dance floor when the plastic stick she purchased from the pharmacy shone bright with two red lines.

Only standalone duplexes occupied this part of the estate. Mr and Mrs Taylor's home sat on a decent 550 square metres of land.

'Pregnancy becomes you,' said Jide as Ifeatu gave him the customary side hug. She did the same to Timilehin and Nnamdi. Her auntie's warning rang clear in her head as soon as Nwafor drew closer to her. *Old village men exchange the blooming lives of unborn children for their withering ones. They drink their blood, be careful when you meet them!* Placing a protective left arm over her bump, Ifeatu offered the old man her right hand. From a safe distance of a foot away, she moved her lips in faint whisper, 'The blood of Jesus,' like Auntie Onuwa advised, before she said, 'Nno, welcome sir.'

Manasseh parked behind Jide's car and the delegation, led by Omo and the young woman with the small baby bump, filed into 42, Pearl Alley, Waterpark Estate, Lekki.

As expected, Fiyin was conspicuously absent. For though tribes may differ, most traditions shook hands where cultural paths crossed. Brides-to-be always waited for a prompting before making their entrance. Soon after the pleasantries, a man sitting beside Mr Taylor and who looked like an older, less sophisticated version of him stood to address the gathering of twelve.

'Welcome friends and family. My name is Dele Taylor. I am the immediate elder brother of Dapo Taylor. When we learnt we were expecting guests from such a faraway place… all the way from across the Niger… we became excited but also curious. We wondered at the magnitude of the issue which has made these people want to travel such a distance. Nevertheless, we are famed for our warmth and so welcome you with open hearts and ears.'

From the doorway, Bree beckoned on her husband who, after a 'two-aside' with his wife, said something into the ears of a grey-haired man. Moments after, the man with grey hair said, 'Let us pray.'

After the choroused 'Amen', Agatha asked her husband, in what she tried to make a whisper, 'Who is Dapo Taylor?'

In response, Dele said, 'Oh, sorry. I am not used to his English name. Donald... Donald Taylor here is my younger brother.' A few awkward seconds after, Auntie Nkechi took the reins, to run through the age-long script of 'the beautiful flower in their hosts' garden which they sought to pluck'. On cue, the gifts meant to shine the beams in the dark corners of the garden, during their search, were presented: five cartons of choice wine, yards of lavishly sequinned laces, a hand-crafted box of perfumes and two baskets of exotic fruits. *Whatever happened to bananas and oranges?* Bree thought.

Since matters of this sort often required a bit of drama, three ladies and a fourth, with a baby bump, filed out from behind a door. As they entered, Dele asked, his eyes alight with embellished expectation, 'This one?' Their faces, montages of rainbow-coloured eyeshadows, applied with the precision of furious splashes of war paint, and their out-of-proportion damask head ties notwithstanding, the delegation was not fooled. They shook their heads in exaggerated rejection of their hosts' playful presentation of alternatives. They knew the exact 'flower' they had come to 'pluck'. And as soon as Fiyin emerged from the doorway, calls and nods of approval filled the Taylors' large sitting room.

Again, Auntie Nkechi took the wheels, raving about the freshness and fragrance of the 'flower'. One handshake after another, and with a somewhat tentative smile pulling at the corners of her mouth, Fiyin played the part of the soon-to-be bride welcoming her guests. Comfortable, with a healthy dose of amity, best described the ambience in Donald and Bree's sitting room. It was a good thing Donald listened when Bree discouraged him from his planned quick stop at the store to buy an ice fan. No need to acquire a new piece of appliance that would become useless after only one day.

When Uncle Dele announced the fruitfulness of their journey, applause filled the room. Soon after, Bree and her cousin, Auntie Folake, withdrew to the kitchen, from where sumptuousness and its accomplices emerged, to be unleashed on the visitors from the east, in welcome merriment.

Evening had begun leaning into night when the Williams, and their delegates, began their own leaning towards home. And like exiting the estate did not pose as much hassle as when they sought entrance, dropping Auntie Nkechi at her Oniru home did not either; nobody required the services of a make-up artist to return to their own home.

While Jide spent the better part of his workout time on the treadmill, talking with you-know-who, Somadina and Afulenu shared the rest of the night with Nwafor and Agatha. In easy chatter, they relived the success of the day's event. For too long, the two couples had been incapable of stringing a conversation together without any hint of strain. One toe tip after another, Afulenu began to dip her feet into the water of this welcome version of her relationship with her in-laws. A sudden thermal induction occurred, forcing all her toes out to safety. Awkward silence filled the lounge following Nwafor's question. To stress his need for an answer, he asked again, 'I said, who did the "Iju ase"?'

For a moment, Afulenu wondered if her husband, like herself, toyed with the tempting idea of feigning ignorance of the age-long Igbo tradition, 'Iju ase'; a tradition which required someone from a man's clan to go on an information quest in the land of their intended bride. On most occasions, this tradition served as a mere cultural observance since nothing of great weight often came out of such quests. But for the rare occasions where the queried families spotted a case of incest, suicide, rape, madness or frighteningly domineering women, most families would have tossed the 'Iju ase' tradition all together.

'Ah, this one two of you are not talking, let it not be what I am thinking, o,' said Agatha, sitting up in her chair like someone stirred by the start of an interesting TV programme.

Alarm bells began pealing in Afulenu's head, Nwafor's forehead formed craters to match his flared nostrils, and Somadina's palms grew sticky with sweat; nothing irked Somadina more than being placed in a vulnerable position for his brother's derision. Raised voices dragged Jide towards the lounge. Before the last turn from the hallway, which would have placed him in full glare, he stopped, to make meaning of the animated air.

'What a pity. You have siphoned all your brain and sold it for a cowrie,' Nwafor said, his face twisted in a way sure to exacerbate the condition of a convulsing child.

And to add more voltage to the already charged air, Agatha said, pushing wind out of her throat, 'Ihiee! A whole "Iju ase"!'

Her exclamation pricked Afulenu in different places. She garnered the full weight of her self-restraint to keep from pulling out the woman's hair.

'Nwafor, I will not have you speak to me in such a manner. If in the frenzy of all the excitement, a little part in the process hit my blind spot, I expect you to understand and address the issue as an oversight! Name-calling and undue criticism are utter in their needlessness!' And to underscore her husband's recent outburst and exit, Afulenu stormed out. Blinded by rage, Somadina missed his son's retreating figure.

On most Sundays, there were fewer cars than joggers – most of them women. Silence floated through the royal palm-flanked road of Ali Salami, Ikoyi. None of the early morning athletes exhibited any exertion since the tall tree branches broke the rays of the morning sun. One of the joggers aroused Jide's interest as he idled away, his arms resting on the balcony rail outside his bedroom. Every step manoeuvred her body into motion. She stopped, Jide believed, to catch her breath. Legs apart and hands akimbo, she took a couple of huffs and puffs, unzipped her waist bag. A bubble of laughter escaped Jide's lips as the object of his morning's curiosity infused her exercise-racked body with what looked like a bar of chocolate. How anyone managed to work towards a goal with the same determination as to cancel any progress achieved on the same goal in question, made no sense to Jide.

Timilehin once argued about self-harm being therapeutic to certain people. Although at the time, Jide disagreed with his friend's theory, terming it cognitive dissonance, today had him pulling into tactical retreat.

Engrossed, almost into oblivion, Jide did not hear the soft rap on his door, nor did he hear it creak open until Afulenu's presence startled him.

'Good morning, Mum.'

As usual, Afulenu flashed her son a smile.

'Morning, Son.' But today, right on the tail of her smile were pursed lips and a cracking of her finger knuckles. Jide walked back into the room with her to sit on the bed; the only other furniture besides the table and chair by the balcony door. Out of consideration for his parents, Jide had agreed to delay moving to his own place. But when, only months ago, Somadina and Afulenu learnt their son took a mortgage for a house, it came as no surprise.

Knee to knee they sat.

'Sleep well, Mum?'

'Mm-hm, I did.' With her eyes, Afulenu drew random patterns

from the floor to the wall, to her toes, and back to the floor. Jide's brows pulled together. He worried about his mother.

'Is anything the matter, Mum? You have bags.' Afulenu started to say something, but she stopped herself. To fill the awkward silence, Jide began to talk about his move. In four months, he would be in his own space.

'Oh, I almost forgot. Okwadu March? March, right?'

'Yes.'

And like a child would, after failing all her sums again, Afulenu pushed down her disappointment. If only Jide took a house in Abuja, his move would have been less wounding, or so Afulenu convinced herself.

They were going to miss him, and nothing in Jide's untidy but earnest explanations softened the blow of his looming move.

'Look at it this way,' he said with an ear-to-ear grin, 'I can always relocate… if only the bustle of Lagos did not hold as much appeal! But do not forget, you need a good screw to keep Nnamdi and Timilehin in place. You yourself said they were a horrible combination when left to their own devices.'

But Jide fooled no one. His sudden interest in Lagos drew life from a certain five-foot-six-inch female. A female who lived in Lagos and who now ran an internship programme in Lagos's iconic Hotel Royale.

At the door, on her way out, Afulenu hesitated, trying in vain to tame the words bent on escaping her pursed lips.

'Is anything about Fiyin's family worth mentioning? Anything pungent enough to raise brows?' she asked, half turning to Jide, a frown pulling at her brows.

Jide let out a soft chuckle and told his mother of something peculiar he learnt about Fiyin's great-grandfather. 'During his lifetime, on every full moon,' he said, his mouth quivering, fighting to conceal his humour, 'he used to turn into a tiger before wandering into the forest… to hunt for meat which his family would eat.' A visible loosening of the strings in Afulenu's shoulders eased Jide's own concern. Of course, Jide concealed how worried and fearful he had been since the night before. He would not tell her he overheard a substantial part of their argument, nor would he, on any account, disclose his immediate engagement of the services of a private investigator; an investigator whose feedback he expected within two weeks. In the unfortunate eventuality of any surprises, Jideofor Williams wanted the honour of first audience.

Soon after Manasseh, the grounds manager-cum-driver loaded and slammed the boot, Nwafor and Agatha walked out, every inch unperturbed by Somadina's drawn face as he escorted them to the car. Still sore from the night's banter, Afulenu did not bother with coming downstairs to bid them journey mercies. With a face-splitting grin, Nwafor promised to return with feedback on the 'Iju ase'.

'I will call you with my findings in three weeks… maybe earlier. Forget the cost. Consider it my own contribution to Jideofor's happiness,' he said.

Managing something between a smile and a sneer, Somadina thanked his brother, wished his departing guests a safe journey home and rushed back in. He had a flight to catch.

⌇

A mop of hair clung to Chef Flavio's sweaty forehead. He threw an impatient glance at Fiyin as she hovered over the saucepan on the burner.

'Dinner in forty-five! Can you set on tray in time?'

When Fiyin gave, again, the reason she now battled with time in her promise to wow their guests with cassoulet, an already flustered Flavio said, 'True, true,' wiping his forehead with the heels of his hands. 'Dorothy! She shop in a-slow motion… but if only you use the meat available… perfect in freezer! This will not have ha-ppen! But no! Not little Miss Goody No Shoes! Dorothy must stop everything and go to ram market. She must wait for ram fur to be burnt, as you or-dered. Why fur must be burnt, not scraped? Why no hot water scrape ram meat, mio Dio! Time, poof! Time, Fiyin!' he said, his face glowing a bright red.

'Two, Chef. It's Goody Two Shoes,' said Fiyin, peering through the oven glass, willing the crust to form around the baking plates, unperturbed by Chef Flavio's outburst. Other more important issues worried Fiyin. Today was Ifeatu's baby shower and the ice-cream cake could not arrive one minute late. Chef Flavio held his head with both hands, threaded his fingers through his thick, black, curly hair and let out an animated 'Mio Dio'. A few of the new staff bustling around the hotel's mammoth-sized kitchen exchanged startled glances but most others, like Fiyin and Dorothy, the grocery controller, who had grown used to his animated persona, carried on with their various activities.

'Don't lose any sweat, it comes with the territory,' Fiyin said to her rattled colleagues.

'Eccellente! Fantastica!' Chef Flavio, beaming like the sun through raindrops, planted a loud peck on Fiyin's forehead. Cassoulet graced the buffet spread in record time. And if the way Chef Flavio, on tasting the dish, closed his eyes in mock surrender offered any indication, Fiyin did a darn good job. A good helping sat in the flask now resting on the floor mat of the front seat; it would be sacrilege not to give Ifeatu and Omo a morsel of this paradise.

Friday traffic could not have picked the worst time with everyone in a rush to or from wherever. Fiyin threw frantic glances at the cake in the seat of her twenty-first birthday gift from her parents. Two battery-powered electric fans strapped to both back door handles boosted her waning belief in her promise to Ifeatu of the cake's prompt and safe arrival.

Fun did not come better parcelled. All knotted up by the week's work stress, hinges came undone for the girls as musical notes resonated. The full import of a baby shower did not elude Chike, Ifeatu's husband. He promised, in a grand gesture of chivalry, to tuck himself in his room upstairs, away from view – like he had any say in the matter. The entire ground floor of Ifeatu's one-storey building was a kaleidoscope of white, red and pink lights, balloons and ribbons, sparkling all the way from the ante room through the sitting room, to the guest room and kitchen. Even the stairway, leading upstairs, partook in the evening action.

One after another, friends of the soon-to-be mum arrived, each parking their cars inside their hostess's compound. The two guests to arrive last, Jessica and Akunna, had to park outside the gates, flushing as closely as possible to the perimeter fence. Of course, Naira bills exchanged hands, to guarantee Ifeatu's security guard's surveillance over the cars of his madam's visitors. The girls, all fourteen of them, dazzled in white outfits. Some donned themselves in linen tops and bottoms, others wore dresses in tune with the party decorations, which complemented the black plush leather sofas, white walls, grey dotted black centre rug, and grey curtains of Ifeatu's home. Gift bags and parcels huddled in a corner, away from the mounting bustle. The biggest parcel, Jessica's, sat apart from the rest, like its bearer. Not many of Ifeatu's friends liked Jessica. Sometimes, Fiyin wondered if her repellent personality had anything to do with her profession as a blogger or, in Omo's words, PG – Professional Gossip.

White spotlights bathed the house in radiance. Excitement bubbled through the entire ground floor, threatening to steal its way upstairs as high-pitched laughter, banter, music and cutlery clinking on glass plates fused into one merry ball. Defenceless to the allure of the evening's gaiety, Susan, Ifeatu's housekeeper, floated around with a sleepy smile, carrying out her duty of clearing and washing up with almost the same speed with which the mess arrived. For a lady in her mid-forties, Ifeatu thought of her housekeeper of seven months, who worked between 7am and 6pm, as a blessing and as a lady who possessed good propriety.

Susan lived with her sister miles away from her workplace but offered to stay the night today. To help with the mess, she said. But Ifeatu feigned ignorance of Susan's supplementary motivation for staying back; most of the leftover food would never make it to her fridge, not that Ifeatu minded. Besides applying efficiency in performing her duties, Susan also proved to be a delightful companion.

'Time to cut the cake!' said Ugomma, and on cue, Susan wiped her hands from washing the dishes to bring in the cake. It was the mould of a baby's dress with a pair of boyish trainers. Ifeatu wanted the gender of her baby to remain a surprise. In the guest room, Thelma and Fiyin brainstormed on the questions for the 'baby crib' game, where they would form a circle and, while they danced, pass round the bowl of folded papers. When the music stopped, the player with the bowl was to draw a question. Anyone unable to answer the question on her paper must remove a clothing or jewellery item. With Chike upstairs, pressure weighed a tonne on everyone to pick 'light' questions. Privy to the kind of questions in the bowl, Thelma and Fiyin hoped they did not drown in their own mischief.

The chant of 'B-A-B-Y!' preceded the cutting of the cake and while everyone dug in, Ifeatu carved an appreciable slice with which to placate her husband. As she wobbled up the stairs, Njide said, 'Weight watching can go on recess today. This cake is pure bliss, mehn!' Ifeatu wrapped her fingers around the stairs' railing to steady herself from giggling. And while the ladies continued in their chaotic fun, as they waited for their hostess to join them again, Chike treated his wife to a much-needed foot and back rub.

Besides the rule of consequences, only one other rule governed the 'baby crib' game: speak only the truth or risk being 'blessed' with sextuplets on your planned last conception. Susan volunteered to serve as disc jockey and performed her duty with absolute passion, turning her back to the ladies to avoid bias.

By forty-seven minutes past eight, bracelets, shoes, wristwatches, wigs, earrings, cycle shorts, anklets, girdles, rings, pantyhoses, waist beads and glasses lay in one heap.

'When and from whom did you last have an orgasm?'

Open-mouthed, Fiyin gaped at the paper in her hand, questioning the fairness of the party fairies. She recalled snickering when a premonition told her she would be the one to pick the paper she now gawked at. Omo began her signature cabbage dance in anticipation of her bestie's downfall. Fiyin ran a cursory assessment of all twenty-six eyes piercing through her forehead. Ifeatu cupped her right eye in mock embarrassment. With Susan on a quick break from her disc-jockey duty, to send some food and drinks to Abu, Ifeatu's security guard, the question did not pose such a hassle to answer, if tackled without delay.

'Yesterday at 10:45pm.' Scattered chants of 'From whom? From whom? How? Are you cheating on Jide?' rang through the room. And Fiyinfunoluwa Taylor, in one moment of glibness, perhaps induced by her many glasses of cocktail, blurted, between giggles, 'From staying in touch with my sensuality!' Raucous laughter and scattered applause filled the room as Chelsea ran off to Susan's workstation to hover over the playlist. 'Senza Una Donna' by Zucchero and Paul Young soon filtered through the speakers. Omo's face almost split from grinning. Ifeatu's mouth hung open in shock. 'It must be the wine,' she said out loud.

'This chick is tipsy!' someone else said with a giggle. They were having crazy fun! But an almost indiscernible shadow slid past Jessica's flawless face.

Chike had sent his fifth text message, asking Ifeatu if his torture would end any time soon; they were all unread. The last agenda, 'rattle the bun', had just begun when the buzz on Omo's upper thigh from her phone startled her. Mrs Bamiloye, one of her steady clients, had a wedding for the following day and sent her niece to pick up her dress from the shop. Omo expected feedback from her client as soon as she received and tried on her outfit. So, amid all the fun, Omo constrained her mind from straying too far away from her phone. Eh? Darting her eyes across to Fiyin, Omo scampered away, safe from the centre of chaos. Placing a finger over one ear, she blocked off the music.

'Jide is here,' said Omo, pulling Fiyin by the arm. Desperation forced him to call Omo's mobile. Fiyin reclaimed her arm and dived for her bag in search of her phone. Jeezzzz! *Thirteen missed calls?* The two ladies scurried out, unnoticed by the bunch of ladies making Ifeatu sweat on the dance floor. The 'bun' sure would be rattled tonight. After moments of deliberations, Ifeatu, Omo and Fiyin decided. It would be a case of 'Don't ask, don't tell'. Mr and Mrs Taylor did not need to be involved in the slight tweak in their daughter's initial plan to sleep at Ifeatu's house.

~

'No bra?' Jide's hands skated idly over Fiyin's shoulders as he tore through the night's air. She liked to lean into the crook of his right arm when they rode together under night's covering. Something made Fiyin agree to leave with Jide. Something about the way he bore a hole in her head when he said, 'Sweet pea, I need you to come with me... to my place. We need to talk... please.' His words came with an ominous calm, further defined by his unruffled composure. His countless unanswered calls to Fiyin, Omo and Ifeatu should have ruffled him, if only a little. Why was Jide not ruffled? He should not be this calm. This was too controlled.

At twenty-seven minutes past nine, traffic out of Victoria Island still held fast with teeth-gnashing tenacity. A young lad, perhaps in his twenties, rushed to their side. Fiyin reached for the windshield wiper knob but not before the lad squished some soapy liquid on the windshield and proceeded to wipe it with a rag which Fiyin believed crawled with maggots. The wipers were defenceless against the ferocious cleansing of the rag. Determined to earn his handout by wiping with all his might, the lad expertly avoided the angry swishes of the wipers. And right before the gridlock eased out, he said, 'Bros, abeg, find me something. Your guy never chop since morning.' Against Fiyin's not-too-subtle caution, Jide handed him a five hundred Naira bill.

'You can't have forgotten so soon what happened to you! What if he had a knife, or worse, a gun? Me, I never engage with all these people at night… some of them can be savage,' she said, her eyes darting around. Jide agreed with Fiyin but feared the youngster's sunken eyes would haunt his dreams if he did not offer him anything.

Nightlife faded as Jide's tail lights bade Victoria Island goodbye. 'I lost it in the "baby crib" game… my bra.' The rest of their journey to Jide's home drowned in the fine print of, not the baby crib game alone, but the entire party, with Jide punctuating with, 'No way! That girl is crazy!', 'Mehhnnn! You said what?', 'Wait, you are an impostor. What did you do to my Fifi!', 'You realise you can never unsay what has been said, right? Please tell me Ifeatu's blogger cousin did not attend this party?' and 'Now, this is the part where you tell me you have been pulling my legs the entire time!'

                                             —

With all the sumptuous spread at the baby shower, a spoon or sip of anything held no appeal for Fiyin. So, Jide ate alone, smacking his lips in emphasis of what Fiyin missed by not acceding to his entreaties to join in his late-night meal of catfish pepper soup and roasted sweet potatoes. In fairness to Nsikan, with the flavours wafting across the entire sitting room, she suspected Jide's lip-smacking was no embellishment.

Now showered, Fiyin donned her nightwear and a shirt she borrowed from Jide. When she packed for the party, she had not thought her night would end anywhere outside Ifeatu's guest room. She curled up in the lounge, pensive about what Jide considered too grave to discuss over the phone from Abuja. With her two hands, she pulled at the front ends of the shirt, gave the hem a determined tuck in between her thighs. Into the three-seater sofa she leaned, folding her feet under her bottom. Her pose drew a lopsided smile from Jide. He thought she looked like a scared kitten in a sack and told her so.

'It's not that… it's… well, it's my nightie… my nightie is a little too much.'

For the first time, Fiyin doubted the sensibility in her getaway. She was saving herself for 'the one' and made it clear to Jide at the start of their relationship. As she sat waiting for him to begin talking, his words to her months ago came floating back to her.

Sweet pea, I am neither a villain nor a saint, but until your daddy takes that long solemn walk with you, your sash stays on. I will not have you ever doubt the reason you persist on this mad ride with me. Ever!' Visible strain, on not his face alone, accompanied those words and from that, Fiyin drew comfort; her man's manly vigour was not in question.

This night, a different kind of strain was etched on only one part of Jide's anatomy: his face. Black joggers under a black fitted T-shirt complemented young Dr Williams' demeanour. Crackling his finger knuckles, he left his seat to join Fiyin, and took her hands in his.

'Fifi, the private investigator I told you about came back to me on Wednesday.'

TEN

CASUALTIES OF ACCIDENTS OF HISTORY

In utter silence, Fiyin lapped up every word in the report. And for what seemed like an eon, the tears would not stop coursing down her face. Jide's continued squeezing of both her hands did nothing to ease the pressure building from her chest upwards, all the way to her head. Dry eyes piercing like laser needles tore through her tear-soaked ones.

'This means nothing, my love. Do you understand what I am saying, Fiyin? This changes nothing. We cannot tell anyone about this.' To Fiyin, Jide's words were more like questions than her much-needed answers, and her abating tears returned with renewed intensity.

At the ring of her mobile phone, Fiyin's eyes fluttered open. An 87kg mass of bones and muscles in the lone chair beside the bed where she passed her turbulent night greeted her. Jide's eyes were bloodshot. On the fourth ring, Fiyin willed her hands towards her phone to answer her mother's 8.20am call.

'How did the party go, baby?'

'Fine! But I am at Jide's place now. I'll give you all the details later… when I return.' Fiyin's artful circumvention of the exact time 'now' started almost made Jide forget the severity of last night.

'Sleep well, sweet pea?' Jide asked after the call. Wary of leaving her by herself after her silent tears gave way to deep-throated sobbing, Jide sat by, watching her until sleep's soothing arms engulfed them both.

⌐──⌐

Back in Abuja, for Jide, work dragged on with encumbered resilience. Each time a nurse tapped on his door, his heart skipped a beat, dreading the words, 'CMD needs your attention, sir.' But after five days with nobody saying those feared words, Jide dared to hope. Perhaps they found nothing. He began to exhale and asked Fiyin to do the same.

'I think we are all right, sweet pea. What we must now do is move as fast as we can before anyone starts to have zealous ideas.' Fiyin agreed. The sooner they moved, the better. But 'sooner' underestimated fate's speed, for only days later, Nwafor called.

'Somadina, nsogbu di, there is trouble.'

'Ogini? What happened? How is Agatha?'

After a long pause, Nwafor said, 'The "iju ase" o, Somadina. The "Iju ase" adabaro. It was not successful. The marriage will not work. Jide must find another wife.'

For the significant part of their relationship, Afulenu seldom had any reason to dissent from her husband's plans. On almost all occasions, he would have combed through his decision with a fine-toothed comb. In addition, Somadina would have tested such a plan in a blue-flamed furnace after sieving it through a muslin cloth, before presentation. Today, Afulenu faced a terrain alien to her; one with the strange footprints of a brash, emotional, and one-dimensionally reached decision. Even before he said them, Somadina's words lurked in the corners of her mind, stoking the flames of her dismay. 'I don't think we can go on with Jide's marriage plans.'

Afulenu's words came in a whisper. 'Just like that, Soma?' Their eyes held for the most fleeting of moments before Somadina explained the implications associated with touching 'those people' with a pole.

'Just like that? We surrender the reins of our son's chance at true happiness… our type of happiness?' Afulenu said again. The disappointment in her voice rang with eloquent precision. Somadina's shoulders sagged.

'What will you have me do? To play with Osu caste system, is like roasting chicken inside a house of hay. Any compromise will break all the legs of any relationship we have.'

'You're correct, but what if we beg Nwafor to keep silent? This thing is a fast-waning tradition… many people consider it outdated and go on to inter- marry, downright ignoring the demonic custom!' Afulenu's eyes sparkling with renewed hope caused Somadina's to shimmer with the tears he so fought to contain.

~

'You do not understand. He… he is… Doctor, nothing is wrong with him.'

'Oh! He has taken tests?'

'No, Doctor.'

'I am afraid I no longer understand.'

'He is from a long lineage of potent men and fertile women. My… my own mother suffered barrenness for six years before her first child.'

Jide gaped at his two o'clock appointment. 'You are a mechanical engineer,' he eventually said, skimming through the open file on his desk. 'Ma'am… I have no better way to explain this… for any meaningful intervention, your husband must visit our unit… for investigative tests, potent lineage or not.' The strain from the effort of not sounding condescending almost made Jide wince. 'All your fertility tests came back favourable; the next logical step would be to investigate the other piece of the puzzle.'

'He will not come...'

'Why not?'

'He is... he is not a very humble man.'

'All right. Have you considered adoption?'

'Doctor, my husband believes our own children will come when God decides they will come... he believes God does not need human assistance or intellect to fulfil HIS will...'

In response to her pooling eyes, Dorothy Coker's nose began to flare, and Jide perceived an imminent emotional breakdown. As fast as his fingers allowed him, he dialled his nursing assistant.

'Have a word with Mrs Coker if you may, Loretta.' Within seconds, a nurse walked into Jide's office. One look at the woman now dabbing with quick movements at a rogue tear, and a lump began to grow in Nurse Loretta's throat; the kind which often accompanied restrained rage. *I tire for these men, shaa. Somehow, women bear the monopoly of blame when the babies do not come,* she hissed in her head and led Dorothy to the adjoining treatment room for one of those 'calming' exercises.

With only minutes left until the end of his shift, Jide willed the tear-filled eyes of his last patient away from his mind's eye. It unsettled him, how desperation shone through them. He made a note to find out what Fiyin thought about infertility and adoption. He did not want any surprises. She must understand his priorities. Her first, babies second; adopted or otherwise.

Intent on finding the object of his search, Jide checked the many packs of coloured popcorn in the snack aisle of 'Grocer's Delight'.

'Ah, at last! Sweet confetti!' he said, his mouth curving in a smile and watering in delicious anticipation of the scrumptiousness about to be unleashed on it.

At the first checkout counter, three customers waited their turn to pay, their trolleys nearly spilling with rolls of tissue, tins of powdered milk, noodles, insecticide, bin bags, sausages and whatever else. Jide scanned the length of the checkout tills. *I need a more workable queue... Yes! Thank God!* Through the mangle of customers, Jide meandered to the just-opened checkout counter. But not before a man, in his mid-forties perhaps, planted his left foot a few odd inches ahead of himself. Stepping back, Jide allowed 'left foot' to pay for his half-eaten gala sausage roll and almost empty bottle of Kongo bitters. Brilliant white lights from the sky-high ceiling of the store glowed on 'left foot's greasy head, outlining specks of grey hair and tiny beads of sweat.

Jide paid for his five packs of popcorn and once back in his car, tore open a pack as he pulled out into the lit street.

For some reason, the tear-filled eyes of his last patient slid in and out of his thoughts. Reprieve came when his phone's ringtone floated through his car speakers. *Fifi!* A small smile began to tug at his mouth. But it disappeared when he glanced at his dashboard for the caller identification. 'Cassandra Android Homes'. Fifteen seconds after, the car fell silent. But Cassandra called again. This went on for about three cycles.

When Jide first expressed concerns about the repossession clause in the 'deed of assignment' for his house allocation, his friends had tried to allay his fears. With tones a little louder than usual, slamming their hands in and out of their pockets and paying attention to everywhere but Jide's face, they had offered assurances.

'Come on, na! A one- or two-week delay in payment can't be enough reason for them to repossess or reassign your unit,' Timilehin had said.

'This thing is no biggie,' Nnamdi had lent his own support, reminding Jide that they would always 'chip in' and, most importantly, that the loan shark guys were always ready to come through. 'Remember you can borrow from them... to deal with stuff... and pay back, as soon as you can.'

'You mean pay back within a month or start piling the back-breaking interests, right? Something tells me I am on a nose-dive back to square zero,' Jide had said with a bridge between a smile and a smirk.

An unsettling crept up Jide's chest at the sight of four cars parked within the grounds of his family home. The popcorn in his mouth now tasted like cottonwool. He ran his tongue over his suddenly dry lips, noting the metal-like taste of the air that invaded his lungs. Who were these? One tired foot followed the other out of his car. By the house, towards the back, Afulenu stood waiting for Jide. A sob threatened to escape her pursed lips any instant. Alarm flaming in her eyes, she beckoned him.

'What happened to your phone? I've been calling you. Come, come. Osiso, quick!' Jide shut his door and took brisk steps after his mother, his shoulders tensing like the muscles in his chest. Afulenu's shallow breathing worried Jide. Why did they have to go into the house through the kitchen door at the back?

'Your dad's relatives are having a meeting about you and Fiyin.' Afulenu searched her son's face as she spoke, her breaths short and shallow. Her tone bristly. A crease formed on Jide's forehead. He asked who the relatives were, his heart mimicking the conga; dum,

dum, dum. The pulse at the base of Afulenu's neck pushed against her skin in quick throbs as guilt lanced through her chest. *I should have told him about Nwafor's call! I should have!*

'Who else but Nwafor and his cohorts,' Afulenu said, grating the words under her clenched teeth. In one moment of desperate improvisation, Abigail, no longer able to play invisible, decided to dispose of the dustbin; she all but ran out of the kitchen with only a quarter-full rubbish bag.

Within thirty-five seconds, Jide gleaned all the details about their evening guests. Uncle Nwafor and I.G, Kene's uncle, came with three other men who Afulenu said were their kinsmen. Not unlike his nephew, Afulenu loathed the floor I.G trod. 'I can stomach why Nwafor may have anything to say about you and Fiyin. What I can't understand is what gives I.G the impetus to invite himself into my family's affair!' Afulenu said, pacing the length of her kitchen. 'Can you believe the fool! Telling me to give them a moment to confer? Hah! In my own house!'

'The attention, Mum, is what fuels Mr I.G's impetus. And he is bloated from it,' said Jide, his hands akimbo. Exhaustion pulled his head into a slight bow. Afulenu stopped her pacing for Jide's next words to plant their feet in her brain.

'I fear something is wrong, Mum. The Taylors… they are… they say…' Afulenu's piercing gaze at her son wavered, fluttered sideways.

He's found out! My God, he already knows! But how? Jide recognised his mother's fluttering sideways glances. Often a reflection of her effort to cloak unsavoury realities.

'I apologise, Mum. I found out a little while ago but thought not to give life to a hopefully dying tradition… maybe I hoped it would go away. How foolhardy of me.'

Afulenu wanted to be certain. 'What did you find out, Jide?'

But Jide shook his head. 'Later, Mum. Dusk has already befallen this black goat.' A wry smile tugged at Jide's mouth as he regarded his mother. He kissed her somewhere between her left cheek and her temple and, with long strides, left the kitchen for the sitting room. Afulenu's fear was confirmed; the evening's drama just added bells and feathers to its already ridiculous costume. She followed.

Six men, propping forward in their seats, stopped their hushed conversation when Jide walked in.

'Good evening, Dad… sirs,' he said, nodding in the general direction of the men.

'Mm-hm, evening,' the men said in response, shifting and straightening in their seats. Somadina cast a quick glance at and away from his son and wife. Everyone in the room, but Uncle I.G, looked perturbed by Jide's arrival. At an ordinary gathering of guests, spicy peanut butter, garden eggs or fried beef and drinks would often adorn the side stools of the Williams' sitting room. But the gathering of men who now threw glances at Jide and his mother, was not ordinary. One of the men stared at Jide like a zookeeper who was wondering if the tigers were aware that their cage was missing a latch.

'It is a good thing you are back,' I.G said, looking Jide dead in the eye. His Samanja-style moustache moved as he spoke, distracting Jide from the pounding in his chest, the clenching of his insides. 'Please come closer. Your father has something of great importance to tell you.' I.G picked up a glass of water and leaned back into his chair to take a loud sip. The meeting ended faster than anyone anticipated. It went from BAD to WORST in one breath.

⸻

Abigail had just squeezed a piece of paper that held twenty crisp five-hundred-naira notes into the left hand of I.G's driver and was fast retreating to the kitchen, through the back door, as the long squeak from the front entrance door startled the night. On sighting his boss, Alfonso pushed down, further into his pocket, the money Abigail asked him to deliver to Joseph and jumped out of the car to hold the car door open, as had been outlined as an intrinsic part of his job description.

'Will you close that door, my friend! Have I finished talking? Buffoon!'

Alfonso scurried back into the car.

I.G said a few more words to Somadina and a minute later, three urgent taps on the car had I.G's driver scurrying out to, once again, hold the door open.

Alfonso waited for exactly seven minutes into the drive before he dared to cough. With a slight quiver in his voice, he said, 'I am sorry, sir... but I please want to beg you for something, sir. Please, sir, if you can give me advance payment for half salary for next month... is my daughter, sir. They say she must to buy three textbook if she want to pass for university. Is NGN28,000 for the three, sir, but I have only NGN17,000. Please, sir, is her final year. If you ca—'

'Alfonso, do you think money grows on trees? Look, things are tough for now. You can borrow from someone and pay back at the end of the month when you receive your salary. Now move faster, I must not miss today's match,' I.G said, casting an angry glance out of the window. Alfonso heaved. He would ask Joseph for a loan. *Maybe 5k?* Joseph was Abigail's brother. He was also I.G's cook.

❦

As Somadina started to drift off in sleep, with the hope of putting distance between himself and the events of the evening, his mobile phone started to ring. He tapped the 'answer' icon, held the phone to his ear and in a tired voice said, 'Hello?'

'Bia Doc, this one you are sounding like this, I hope you understand the seriousness of this matter. You can't allow your son to jeopardise our family ties, o. Better explain to him that if you people go on with that abominable association, your daughter will be in a terrible spot. And remember, you have my connection to thank for the way things went between you and the government. Let Jideofor fly up an iroko tree and smash himself to the ground, it will change nothing! I have made a few phone calls. Ah, ah? A branch cannot outgrow its tree, nau! No! Mbanu! Not while I am alive!' I.G's voice filtered through the phone line. The hum from the air-conditioning unit cowered under the sound of Somadina's laboured breathing as he begged I.G to give him some time. Time for Jide to assimilate the new information.

I.G responded with a cynicism-laced chuckle. 'Children of these days. Small school and they think they are now the custodians of wisdom and knowledge... running off with the first thing that catches their fancy. Well, I will wait for you to talk some sense into him. But let's be clear, I will not sit by with folded arms. Hia! Outcasts!' The call lasted a little less than two minutes.

'I.G again?' asked Afulenu, her fury reawakening. What's this supposed to mean, eh, Somadina... calling you at odd hours? Anyway, I don't blame him. It is your jobless brother I blame. But for—'

Somadina asked his wife to stop hurling names. 'Afi, let's not be petty. I think Nwafor only panicked and acted out of concern. We must tread with caution. Don't forget, friction with I.G's family can affect Kaira.'

'Are you listening to yourself, Somadina? You talk as if Jide's happiness is of no consequence to you... Is Kaira the only one with something to lose? Please tell everyone to step back. And stop allowing these people to push you around!'

For a moment, Somadina felt like a pupil whom a headmistress caught climbing a mango tree during lessons.

'Nobody is pushing me around.'

'Are you for real, Soma? Not from where I'm standing!' said Afulenu.

'You mean down-side-up? Afulenu, calm down!'

'You still cannot manage it, can you?'

'What?'

'From day one, Kaira has always been the jewel! Ked'ife Jide melu gi? What did that boy ever do to you? Your preference is blinding!'

A scowl began to form on Somadina's face; his breathing became measured.

'So, now I prefer Kaira, eh? I will hold back from dignifying such an absurd allusion with a response.'

'Because you have none!' Afulenu yanked the duvet off the bed, climbed into bed and pulled it over herself, turning her back to her husband.

'No! Guess what? I won't let this slide. Afulenu, has it ever occurred to you why Jide has turned out the way he has? A man? Independent? Purposeful? Level-headed and the archetype of masculinity?'

'Meaning?'

'Meaning, but for my parenting style that provided the required balance, our golden son would have been a caricature of a man; the types we see milling around these days, many of whom are yet to be weaned of breastmilk – entitled, spoilt and absolute in their ignorance of the portrait of manliness!'

'Did you ever question the way I parented him?'

'My point, Afulenu. That balance was needed. My parenting was intentional. I refused to flow with the tide of paternal instincts!'

Afulenu looked lost.

'I don't understand what we are even arguing about anymore. How does this your exposé help Jide's case?'

'It doesn't. Jide's stakes are lower… The world is tipped in his favour. Why can you not understand this?'

'Soma! You of all people know that narrative is a ruse manufactured by men to give them a false sense of superiority! Jide is first human and will suffer as much as a woman if deprived of true love.'

'Look, I won't lean into that talk right now. Afi, Kaira is already in an established home and is more vulnerable. You will appreciate my stance once you descend from your sky-high narrative of father-daughter favouritism.'

Afulenu started to dish an equal measure of acrid remark in response to her husband, but Somadina's extra zing clamped her lips.

'For the benefit of your obvious ignorance, let me explain I.G's call. If Jide becomes associated with an Osu by marriage, we all, according to the caste system, become Osu. My dear wife, our daughter will be trapped in a bad place. She is married to I.G's nephew and would, in I.G's words, contaminate his lineage too. His tentacles may not be long enough to reach the corridors of Aso Rock, but I don't underestimate the man. If he is anything close to his reputation, he will do everything to make life difficult for us and our daughter in more ways than we can count. Are you not tired of swimming in troubled waters? My cloak still drips, and I'm in no hurry for a re-enactment of the past four years of our lives!'

For a fleeting moment, Afulenu questioned her most defining decision. Why did she marry this man with whom she fell hopelessly in love? Flinching at the slam of the door on Somadina's way out, Afulenu swallowed the pain of her newly discovered folly.

⌐——⌐

Much like every other day, breath-sapping disorderliness saturated the air in Hotel Royale's kitchen. Shouts of, 'Too much salt!', 'Burnt,

burnt, burnt! This crepe is burnt!', 'Order fifteen is due!', 'Hello! Yes, hello! Dorothy, where are you? Traffic?', 'I need pans. All the pans are dirty.', 'Who took my chopped onions?', 'This deep fryer is not working.' and, 'Two platters, please!' bounced around the kitchen. Amidst all the bustle, Fiyin lay on one of the two couches in the kitchen's briefing room, her eyes pinned to the ceiling.

Vanilla freshness often preceded Anita's arrival and announced her presence before her slim fingers tapped Fiyin on the shoulders.

'Girlie, what's going on with you? You've been so glum these past days.' Crouched by the couch, to keep eye level, Anita's perfect brows came together at the centre. For a lady in her mid-thirties, she must have her gene pool to thank for her late-teenage years look. Fiyin admired her colleague's impeccable grooming. Where did all that money come from?

Once, after work, when Fiyin's car would not start, Anita had offered her a lift home in her luxury SUV. And to Fiyin's comments about her love for luxury, Anita had responded, 'Girlie, are you not familiar with the saying, dress the way you want to be addressed? Plus, the state of Lagos roads has made owning an SUV a necessity rather than a luxury… What you save from not buying one, you lose from incessant trips to the mechanic's workshop to fix the shocks, bearings, and bushings of your low-traction car.' An argument followed about who should assume responsibility for infrastructure construction and maintenance. The ladies went back and forth on jurisdictions bordering federal roads and state roads and the function of the office of the local government chairman. One thread held their argument: the acknowledgment of the elected officials, and not the electorate, as the party responsible for the provision of a fair environment for citizens. Laughter filled the car when Anita gave the analogy of the national cake. 'In the past,' she said, 'politicians used to slice the national cake with table knives. Through the years, they graduated to tablespoons and cooking spoons. Today, they go armed with shovels!'

Their laughter had suffered an immediate halt when Fiyin asked, 'What will happen if the electorate begins to vote based on grounded information on competent and willing politicians? If we snub an underperforming ruling party or the ones who share petty cash a few months and weeks before elections?' Anita's continued silence had made Fiyin further ask, 'And by the way, why do the so-called elites not exercise their voting rights? For instance, did you vote in the last elections?' In answer to her passenger, Anita had relieved herself of a long loud yawn and turned up the volume of Onyeka Onwenu's 'One Love'.

'Nothing. Only man trouble,' Fiyin said. A tear slid down the side of her right eye and Anita broke its course with the tip of her thumb.

'Whenever you need a shoulder, girl, I'll be right here... they are not worth the trouble, believe me,' she said, straightening up to grab her bag from her locker. And as she headed for the bathroom to shower and rid herself of her work uniform, she cast another glance at Fiyin. Thanks to the dual shift policy of the hotel, her duty ended in minutes. Some of Anita's endearing qualities included her intuition; she was able to tell when someone else suffered. But most appealing were her empathy and ability to sense and retreat once she started flirting with invasion.

⌐━━⌐

After two failed attempts to set the evening's strawberry pudding and a burnt blueberry pie, everyone received a tacit memorandum to allow Fiyin some room to breathe. Last night's call from Somadina did not settle well with anyone in Donald Taylor's three-man family.

'We will be coming to Lagos on Friday to discuss the marriage intention,' he had said. What, about the traditional wedding plans, defied a telephone conversation? But they did not wonder for too long. Jide's phone call, afterwards, sent whirling sounds to Fiyin's ears.

'What now?' she had asked in a small voice, her chest tightening.

Early this morning, Fiyin made the two clarifications Jide asked of her. Since after the investigator's report, Fiyin had evaded confronting her parents for answers; but not anymore. Today, at about four o'clock in the morning, she asked her parents how, in Mother nature's green earth, she had roots in Igbo land, when all her life, she was made to believe she was of pure Yoruba stock. The second question: would they give their blessings without Jide's parents?

'My ancestral line dates back to a woman called Urenmma, born many generations ago.'

For close to an hour, Bree's words came in rasping whispers, her eyes glistening with unshed tears. Her child would be a casualty of a past even her grandmother was not a player in. It was not fair. For whatever reason, Bree never reckoned her child would cross paths, and fall in love, with an easterner. She always assumed, perhaps hoped, that *like* would always attract *like*.

And no. If Jide's parents did not consider their ancestral line pristine enough for their son, they would not throw their child at them.

ELEVEN

AND SO THE YUMMY COOKIE CRUMBLES

Donald called the security gate and all four of his visitors were granted access. Bree's stomach clenched a little tighter when she saw neither Afulenu nor Jide among the people in her sitting room. After light refreshments of drinks and diced peppered goat meat, a man whom Bree and Donald did not recognise indicated his readiness to speak by coughing and shifting in his seat. From behind the door leading to the corridor, through the open hinge, Fiyin peered at her unwelcome guests, pressing her phone to the door. And as soon as the man started to speak, she pushed the 'record' button, the sound of her own heartbeat threatening to burst her eardrums. Jide had begged Fiyin to record the meeting – in case his people spoke in Igbo.

When Donald asked his guests to explain what they meant by, 'the "Iju ase" exercise came back unfavourable', the words he and Bree feared the most rained on them with impenitent brutality.

'In summary, your wife, and by association, you and your daughter belong to the Osu-outcast clan. For Ndi Igbo, this is a mountain in the centre of the road... it dates all the way back to when the sun existed as only a small spark of fire.'

Somadina avoided the unflinching glower from Donald and Bree. In response to the man they were both meeting for the first time, Bree pulled her mouth down, forming a skewed and flaccid 'n'. Donald's heart ached at the sound of his wife breathing; the last time he remembered Bree wheezing was twelve years ago, during their Dubai desert safari adventure.

'So,' he said, his eyes still on Somadina, 'because of an ancestral lineage, far down an infinite number of years, one alien to even my wife's grandmother's grandmother, a mountain has magically landed in the centre of our road?' Silence filled the room, save for the persistent hum from the air-conditioning unit.

In response to the awkwardness, which now threatened to slip into absurdity, Somadina began to speak, but because he sounded like someone on trial, Nwafor cut in. Propping himself, to lean forward from his chair, he squeezed his knees as he expressed their regrets at the turn in events, admitting how silly it may all sound, given the abstract nature of the 'issue'. How else could the discovery of a lineage, so removed from a person, have the power to obstruct a once-upon-a-time smooth journey? A lineage tainted by a woman whose only abominable crime was fleeing into the wilds, away from her assaulters.

For the first time, Bree, who before now had appeared content with leaning into her chair with her arms folded, grimacing and shaking her legs which were also folded at the ankles, spoke. 'Let me be certain I understand. So, my daughter and your son are going to be punished for an intangible problem they didn't create?' Somadina began to apologise and, again, Nwafor cut in.

'Is tangible, o! The problem is very, very tangible. If you don't believe us, ask any freeborn who ignored culture to marry Osu. The women suffer barrenness, and even when they cheat nature by forming children inside bottles, they don't last; they die like chickens suffering from bird flu! Kinsmen they acquired by marriage or even business, cut themselves off from them and they become complete outcasts. The men nko? In their old age, when they should be enjoying life, they start suffering strange things. The latest one is the one where tears will just be flowing from their eyes for no reason. Biko… please, we cannot be infected with Osu curse. The marriage proposal is cancelled.'

The meeting was over. The group got up to leave. Donald recoiled, Bree's unshed tears began to flow, and Somadina pinned his eyes to the floor, his hands folded to his back. But the lady behind the door experienced a blend of novel emotions: panic, hysteria, anger, and pain, all in one short breath.

Pushing the red button on her phone to end the voice recording, quick strides led Fiyin back to her bedroom. With Omo at the airport to receive Ben, Fiyin did not want to shroud her friend's current sunshine with her own gloom; the exact reason she refrained from telling Omo about the visit in the first instance. Her phone began to ring.

'Sweet pea, what happened?'

'I'll call you back.' Fiyin ended the call, scrolled down to another number.

'Hi Anita. Where are you?' Pause. 'No worries, I'm coming to you. See you in a bit.' Fiyin grabbed her car keys and as she walked to the door, she answered her parents' unspoken question.

'I need to run an errand.' Donald and Bree did not try to stop her. They both knew she needed time to confront her new reality. The pain in their chests pulled back the words they so wanted to say to their child.

⌒

Unable to see clearly through the dim lights and fog from cigarette smoke, Fiyin left the techno music-thumping room to both fill her lungs with clean air and have some semblance of tranquillity.

She still did not want to speak to Jide. *He should have come for the meeting.* Moreover, with the quantity of alcohol Fiyin now swam in, she doubted her ability to make any meaningful conversation. Forty-five missed calls; eight from Omo, the rest from Jide. Twelve text messages; three from Omo, eight from Jide. There was one from her dad, *'Where are you, baby? We love you.'*

'Mind if I join you?'

Oh, gosh! Not now! A few minutes before this intrusion, Fiyin basked in the peace the garden provided, willing it to last a lifetime. She forced her eyes to focus on the unwelcome companion now sitting in the empty space beside her. A hairless head, lush black beard, and an almost impossibly straight nose; one with the exact required hint of a dorsal hump, crowned a narrow frame. From the way Companion's words exuded a tinge of subtlety, Fiyin suspected his origin lay in the Northern parts of Nigeria. And that he arrived his mother's birth-bed, brandishing two platinum spoons too.

'Wow. Didn't a visit to the club mean a longing to dance the night away? Yet here we are… hiding out,' he said. A bizarre force drove Fiyin to turn towards her companion, to give him her full attention. Twenty-three decent inches separated them, but with each second ticking after the other, the space between them seemed to shrink. Companion's invasion twisted her insides in a welcome, warming way. Fiyin liked the garden better now. It was a great idea to have escaped from the mayhem unleashing itself within the walls of the club, after all.

'My name is Ah-lee Dansule. Please tell me you are here with either a girlfriend or a loser.' Fiyin liked the way he pronounced his name, the way he accentuated the first letter, like the sound one would make after drinking a sweating glass of water on a hot day.

Their night chat did well for Fiyin but soon, although this stranger almost tricked her into forgetting why she was at a downtown club on a Friday night, rather than in her bed, she stood to leave.

'Of course!' Ali got on his feet. 'Shoot!' he said. 'Look how easily we killed an hour!' He also quipped about her alluring personality robbing him of his flawless sense of timing.

A white floodlight now washed over them, and Fiyin angled her neck upward, to better acquaint herself with her new 'friend'.

'The former... I'm here with my home girl,' she said between alcohol-triggered giggles as she sauntered back into the club.

Anita was not smiling as she weaved her way from the dance floor to Fiyin, who now sat on a bar stool, glass in hand. 'Girlie! Where have you been? You got me mad worried,' she said, pulling a chair.

She burst into uncontrollable laughter when Fiyin replied with, 'Yeah, so worried you were, rocking and gyrating on the dance floor. Eh?' Anita snatched Fiyin's glass for a swig, shoved it back to her.

'What's this?'

Anyone would have thought Fiyin had been sipping on a glass of concentrated vinegar mixed with rotten lime juice. Anita ordered a drink for herself.

'One dirty strawberry mojito, please!' A blend of whisky, mint, rum, strawberry, and coconut milk, by far, outranked Fiyin's glass of lime-infused water on ice rocks.

On their way home, Anita asked again, 'But girlie, where were you? For real, on the dance floor, I kept scanning the room, looking for you. I won't lie, I was having a great time. But remember I can work and chew gum, nau!' In a few phrases, Fiyin filled the blank spaces. 'Wait... do you mean *the* Ali Dansule, as in *Ali Dan-Su-Le?*' Anita's eyes looked like they would pop. It made less than little sense to her; Ali Dansule, the son of the two-time petroleum minister of Nigeria, should live, rent free, in any sane single lady's conscious and subconscious!

Anita insisted. 'You must come in… grab a glass of water, at least. It's not like you are in such a rush to go back home,' she said, pulling Fiyin along.

Regardless of the growing popularity of new-age real-estate developers along the Lekki peninsula, who adopted building styles with the sole aim of stacking residents like sardines in a can, Anita made excellent use of her two-bedroom flat. With her split-unit air conditioner and 32-inch television hanging on the black wall, the only other adornments in her sitting room were a palm plant in a long, slender grey vase standing in a corner, and two cream leather sitting poufs on her black fluffy rug. Within mere minutes, the tour ended. Only the bedroom, with its silver-speckled black walls, offered a hint of cheer; even her kitchen and bathroom tiles were black. Fiyin's brows pulled into a frown.

'Why so much black?'

'Black represents my mood… joking! I think it's different, attention-grabbing too,' Anita said.

'I thought you said your siblings lived with you?'

'Yep.'

'Where are they?'

'My brother travelled to see my folks… my mum had a medical emergency… her second one in four months.'

'Oh, my! Anita, you should have said something!' Fiyin almost pinched herself for bemoaning her issues to someone with a lot more to deal with.

'Mm-hmm.' Anita shrugged her shoulders. She didn't want pity and from where she stood, Fiyin had nothing else to give.

'How about your two sisters?'

'They're out… earning a living.'

Fiyin did not understand. She cocked her head to the left, raised her brows a fraction.

'I thought you said your sisters were in Yabatech?'

'Eh-he? People wey dey go school no fit work? They need to help themselves too. Sister Anita cannot come and die for them, abeg!' Fiyin sensed her friend's growing irritation and decided to stop her quest for clarification.

'How about that glass of water you promised?'

'Now you are talking! I have Baileys, o!'

'You are not serious. Please, I'm driving!' And their laughter eased the tense air of before.

An intended five-minute dash-in stretched into an hour, but neither Anita nor Fiyin minded. For Fiyin, going home only meant a discussion with her parents.

The two days following the visit from Jide's folks tore chunk after chunk off Fiyin's heart, while Jide waddled in a sludge of emotions. First, Fiyin would not pick up Jide's calls. Plus, Donald asked him to stay away for a while. 'Give her room to process this new development and your actions or inactions for that matter,' he had said. Then Omo's clueless responses and Ifeatu's less-than-civil reception. *Whoever said girls are their own worst enemies*, Jide thought as he packed a travel case, tossing, with needless force, toothpaste, toothbrush, boxers, and clippers. If only the poor travel case and items played any role in his current frustrations.

⌐⌐⌐

At the hotel reception, waiting for Fiyin's shift to end, Ben and Omo sipped from their glasses of 'something pink'. Amused, yet goaded by how the sea of eyes, at varied intervals, first glanced their way, next skirted around an object near them, and then snatched another quick peek before returning to their own spaces, they decided to rattle them a little more. Ben stopped twirling Omo's new natural locks. He shifted for her to further lean into him, and much to the disapproval of their audience, began to plant soft pecks all over her hair, all the while stealing quick glances, to assess the wide-ranging shifts in dispositions. Some remained adamant in their displeasure, a few became amused. But many now seemed to decide they were not the regular pair of an expatriate and his 'Nigerian plaything'.

When their glasses became empty, Omo would not let Ben place another order. Not with her plans to assault his palate at the hangout they would be whisking Fiyin to. She had it all arranged. For three weeks, her planned string of activities guaranteed the time of her life with her bestie and her heart-throb. Yes, her heart-throb. Sometimes, the only element lacking in a seemingly impossible relationship is spotless candour.

Everything now made perfect sense.

'I love you even more for trusting me with your fault lines. Such a long and treacherous one… this walk called life leaves you with deep blisters,' Ben had said during their Skype chat two weeks ago. At first, the words resisted the flow but when Omo started to talk, only exhaustion was able to dam them. Halfway into Omo's revelation of her family dynamics, tears began to flow on both sides of the Atlantic. She exhumed her painful childhood memories, her non-existent relationship with her father. How her mother's cousin, Uncle Felix, showed her, at the unripe age of nine, under the staircase of her father's house, the meaning of womanhood. How for eight years afterwards, she dwelt under the tutelage of Auntie Cynthia, the only other person besides Fiyin and now Ben, in whom she confided. Auntie Cynthia tutored Omo on how to hone her feminine powers, how never to forget, and when best to serve vengeance. So when, at the age of nineteen, Omo sparked an official but secret relationship with Uncle Felix, her lifelong mission to destroy him tiptoed a few inches closer to reality than she ever hoped for.

Mr Felix Oseh worked as a lecturer in the same university Omo attended.

'How much should I charge this one? She had a "D" and wants a "B",' Felix would often ask Omo while skimming through his students' examination answer scripts. Most times, what to charge each student for a grade swap stopped on Omo's desk. So, during a planned crackdown on corrupt lecturers, Omo volunteered her services to the university board. With audio and video recordings of his trade by barter with students, Felix stood defenceless before the board. Days after, his lifeless body, hanging from his balcony, concluded Omo's lifelong mission. A conclusion made even more bearable by her uncle's forever pact with bachelorhood.

A thin film of guilt settled on Omo as she admitted her satisfaction at the disreputable death of her uncle. But deep in the recesses of her heart, she held herself, alone, accountable for her long and shameful journey down the lane of immorality.

'Sometimes, I'm repulsed by myself... gosh, I feel so dirty!' Omo had wailed on that emotion-laden night.

'You cannot do this to yourself, my love! Why? Why are you taking this route? Why would you hurt yourself with more self-loathing than when you walked the path of your past? You were but a victim of unfortunate exposures, Omo... Fight the lies your mind keeps telling, Omo. You should be proud of how far you've come, my love.' Although not certain if Ben's words poured cold cream or hot spice on her gaping wound, Omo reined in. And had laughed a little when Ben alluded to karma applying a needless measure of leniency in dealing with her uncle. 'Paedo Felix's injustice fell a few inches shy from being squared,' he had said, his nose flaring in quick response to his reddening face.

⌒

'See my people!' Breathless from her quick steps, Fiyin half walked, half jogged to them. Ben broke into a smile as big as the reception area as he got on his feet to hold her in embrace. 'Sorry I kept you guys waiting for so long. I ruined the dessert and had to make another batch... I am so, so sorry,' she said.

'Hello, stranger,' said Omo with a weak smile. She still did not understand why Fiyin chose the company of an ordinary colleague over hers on a day as defining as last Friday.

'So, Ben, how did you find the largest city in West Africa? Not unlike this one to whisk you off on a road trip barely two days after you landed in Naija!' Fiyin said, giving Omo a playful grimace. Since two days after Ben's arrival Fiyin still would not pick up her calls, Omo sent a text message informing her about an impromptu contract she landed.

I'll be leaving for Ibadan with Ben for this gig. We'll be there the whole week. Should be back by Friday-ish.' Imagine Omo's perplexity and anguish when, on Tuesday, Fiyin called her with all the details of the past days. But for the monetary and brand visibility gains she anticipated from the Ibadan job, Omo would have taken the next bus back to Lagos.

Fiyin stepped back to immerse herself in the moment. Ben in Nigeria rang a surreal note in her head. Her heart brimmed with joy for them. But her joy was akin to a mother's happiness on her child's first day at school. And, without warning, her eyes brimmed with tears. While Ben thought, *Her eyes are sunken*, Omo forced herself to ignore Fiyin's jutting collar bones.

'So where are we headed?' Fiyin sought to fill the silence.

'Hanger's Lounge! You'll ride with us... you can come back for your car afterwards.' Actual stars danced in Omo's eyes as she sang, rather than spoke, her words. When Fiyin's forehead crumpled with the inaudible question about when Omo had bought a car, Ben explained. They have been making use of hired vehicles for the days their myriad of movements stretched into the night.

'Oh!' Fiyin said.

'Remember, we don't have ransom money to pay if you-know-what happens. We'd rather not make headlines that touch the heart,' Omo said giggling as they walked out of the lobby, down the short flight of stairs and into the car park. Of the three, only Ben considered his girlfriend's remarks an insipid attempt at humour as his eyes darted around, half expecting *unknown gunmen*, an alias for kidnappers, to jump out any minute.

⌒

With the way Omo bent over, giving her unalloyed attention to her Isi Ewu – the little mortar piled with boiled goat head rolled in palm oil and spicy aromatic leaves – anyone would think it held a tapestry of innovative fashion designs. At well-paced intervals, she looked up to sip from her sweating glass of cranberry juice. Ben's equally sweating face as he wolfed down his catfish pepper soup and boiled ripe plantains made her chuckle. Fiyin nursed her less dramatic meal of spicy chicken wings and buttery naan bread, chipping in every now and again, 'Careful with the bones, Ben. They are vicious, please be mindful.' Ben dabbed his cream-coloured face-towel on his bright-pink face, to control the liquid running down his forehead, eyes, and nose. By the ticking seconds, it became harder to tell where one liquid ended and the other started.

'Damn, Ben,' said Omo between mouthfuls of goat head, 'there is something infinitely cute about the confused look on your face! Oh, my cute, cute honey bear!' Omo punctuated her remark with a slurp of her drink. An assessment of Omo's statement caused

Fiyin to throw her head back in loud laughter. Ben indeed looked flummoxed, in a way suggestive of the spices in his soup jarring the components of his skull.

Mild conversation flowed with their meals. They talked about Ben's privileged life. Being able to take time off work to, in his words, clear his head after his gramps' passing. Ben talked a little about his gramps, how much he still missed him, how inheriting his dog, Chloe, cloaked and sometimes bared his absence.

'So where is Chloe now?' Fiyin asked.

'With my parents. And I am told she is having a ball!' An unsettling atmosphere invaded the air when Fiyin asked Ben if he considered relying on his parents at every hiccup an indication of maturity or its antonym.

'I mean, your gramps' death is sad. Life's mastery of the art of throwing dirt at even the most noble is applaudable. But you chose to inherit Chloe. You offered her solace and succour. Yet at the first opportunity you get, bam! You jet off to Nigeria without the least consideration about how your actions would impact her!'

'But she is being cared for... my pare—'

'Ah! We've circled back to parents! I almost forgot about them. They are always there for when our seams come apart, aren't they?' Omo shifted in her seat. Always one who lived for the details, the rise and fall at the base of Fiyin's neck did not elude her.

Utter in his unawareness of the fast-thinning air, Ben said, his eyes twinkling with humour, 'I guess it is a major component of their job description, right?'

'No, Ben. I think it is reflective of sheer self-centredness and the highest degree of irresponsibility! When your gramps died, you should have left Chloe alone, allowed someone else to take her... care for her. Someone who will not leave her at the first sign of a hurdle, hoping she will be fine in the end. But of course not! You wouldn't dare pass off the thrilling opportunity to take on the novel project of caring for a helpless chihuahua!' With the rapid rising and falling of Fiyin's chest, it was certain she would begin sobbing any minute. Ben's mouth hung open in complete shock. He cast a quick glance at Omo and back to Fiyin. A quietness settled over him at the realisation of the metaphoric conversation he had just engaged in.

The effect of the clashing spices in Ben's soup paled in direct comparison to his worry as he racked his head for a way to correct the course of their evening. Acutely aware of Omo's hand kneading his left knee beneath the table, Ben battled and won the urge to point Fiyin in the actual direction of her frustration. Why would she not speak to Jide, to listen to his defence if nothing else!

'Yes, you are indeed right, Fifi. I never thought about it from your perspective.' Ben's tone sounded like a transistor radio in need of new batteries. Naked as the skies on a clear day, Fiyin's pain dazzled, untainted by clouds of reason. She ached from hurt, and not her alone knew the one person with the elixir to make it all go away. Ben fiddled with his phone and moments after, Omo received a text message from him. It read, *Sweetheart, you've got to talk to Jide. This is teetering on the edge of absurdity.* For the first time in a week, Omo agreed to her hopeless romantic's entreaties to mediate.

'Guess who got the gig to make Chief Igweike's daughter's traditional wedding attires?' Omo said, pointing both thumbs to herself and doing a little dance in her seat. 'She's going to have five appearances!' she further announced.

'And with the light in your eyes, my dearest, I imagine Chief Ig-wee-kay is one of your wealthy politicians. Now, isn't this the perfect timing for a professional to manage the affairs of your growing fashion enterprise?' Ben said, his lips widening into a smile, willing Fiyin out of her dark waters.

'Come on, babes! Be happy for me! Your girl is finally moving up the ladder,' said Omo, pulling at Fiyin's arm in that playful way.

Fiyin's eyes, formerly as cold as fish, warmed as a smile broke through her pursed lips. Ben joked about relocating to Nigeria, naturalising, and running for political office. Fiyin gave him an exaggerated glare before, amidst chuckles, she said, 'Remind me to buy you a drum of tanning lotion for starters.' Soon, talks about Fiyin and her own plans took centre stage, with her talking about how properties for her catering outfit were sliding miles beyond her reach.

'At this rate, I hope I am still able to acquire one. If I cannot, I may begin to explore other options… but renting a property will not be one of them.' Omo agreed. She believed rent, third to governmental bottlenecks and the abysmal public power supply, constituted a major component of the predatory cocktail currently plaguing Nigerian businesses.

'I would never have survived without my garage,' she said.

But Ben did not think so. 'Ladies, you are forgetting about grants, bank loans and angel investors,' he said. The two ladies exchanged glances and, on cue, shook their heads in mock surrender to the tourist's idealistic views.

'But I serve a God of impossibilities! My economy is not of this world, so, I shall profess what I want. I'll buy a property, hire a pro to run it for a while, and when I am certain I can, I'll take the wheels,' Fiyin said. On and on she went, unaware of the mounting diffidence and exchange of glances between the two lovebirds.

A salvaged night, which only moments before, had ridden on the wings of fun and laughter, now hovered on a cliff overlooking the ragged teeth of gloom. Fiyin snatched her hand from Ben. 'If my non-existent relationship is what you both want to cap the night with, then it's home o'clock for me,' she said in answer to Ben when he said, without any warning, 'Won't you at least take his call, Fifi?'

'Or better still, see him,' Omo added, her eyes imploring. Heads turned in their direction, in response to the scraping sound from Fiyin's chair as she excused herself from their table.

'All honest people should be getting set for bed,' she said, stalking off.

Fiyin waited for Omo and Ben to settle the bill and take her back to the hotel, for her car. In an unconscious attempt to shield herself from the gloom disguised in the night's warm air, she ran her hands over her goosebump-covered arms. Although Fiyin's mobile phone now reeled from an assault by a litany of text messages and missed calls from Jide, she battled with who else to blame for the existing state of her heart. But did they have a point? Then, recalling how her friend's eyes shone with new light each time she talked about Ben, Fiyin scoffed. *When romanticism speaks, logical thinking sleeps!* Omo's 180-degree spin in her perspective of relationship dynamics made Fiyin woozy. Maybe if Omo still ached from Ben's aloofness, she would have given her friend's new disposition more thought. Maybe if Afulenu's phone number had slid into Fiyin's long list of missed calls, her stance would have been less rigid. Perhaps if she had been privy to her mother's curt text message to Afulenu, she might have been more yielding; the message Bree sent after she ignored countless calls from Afulenu, telling her, in radiantly coloured language, where to shove Jide's marriage proposal. Bree directed Afulenu to shove her son's proposal into the part of the human anatomy responsible for expelling solid waste.

⌒

Something about their mien, where they chose to mount their checkpoint, and the almost furtive glances that two of the three police officers threw around, was alarming. Ready to reel out her customary, 'Officers, una well done, o! We dey see una good hand work', by way of blarney, Fiyin started to slow down. A sudden wave of premonition washed over her, and she descended on her accelerator, shooting into the night. The policemen were too stunned to react in good time.

Fiyin regretted rejecting Omo's invitation to join her and Ben for a gospel concert. If only she had not said, 'Tomorrow is a busy day for me, I have no clothes, nothing. I need to go home.' Why did she not agree to go to the concert, call her mum, and borrow Omo's clothes? Why did she choose the likelihood of harm over spending time with friends in an atmosphere she often promoted to Omo as the panacea for life's chaos? The real reason jeered at her. Her car's air-conditioning vent now blew hot air. *I filled this thing with AC gas only this morning*, she thought, winding down her windows a tiny fraction. An odour filled her car. *Burning?* She did not swerve in good time and dived into a pothole large enough to sit two adults. 'It will never be well with the ministry for works! Ah! Ko ni da fun won!' Fiyin cursed out loud. A hissing sound, a crackling. Gosh. But she maintained her speed needle on 110km/hr.

Although twilight had since leaned into darkness, the men gave no indication of noticing. One sipped on his brandy, one on water, and the other chewed on his upper lip, drawing air through his clenched teeth at intervals. Even when the warm air started to rise to meet them, they made no move to retreat into Jide's hotel suite.

'Guy, you may need to let this one go,' Timilehin said at last.

'Hmm,' Jide acquiesced, getting on his feet with a start. He leaned over the balcony railing, eight floors above ground level, as though to peer at something of grave importance. As much as Jide prided himself on his logical streak, the way out of his current labyrinth proved impossible to navigate.

A scowl now marred Jide's usually appealing facial features. Nnamdi's rant about him not going to Fiyin's parents' a few days before his family had gone, did little to ease his current turmoil. Nor did his advice for Jide to either plant his 'oat' on Fiyin's 'soil' or elope with her offer any meaningful recourse. But Jide did not agree with Timilehin's allusion either; the Taylors were not unclean. 'Let's be rational,' Timilehin said, pausing for theatrical emphasis. Planting his feet a few inches apart to gesticulate with his hands, he continued. 'Even the history of her ancestry sounds spooky. A human camping out with a three-legged she-goat cannot be dismissed with a wave of the hand. It all sounds demonic!'

'What is demonic? Abeg, it's no biggie! Why must everything be spiritual for you? And by the way, it was a one-legged she-goat. Onuku!' Nnamdi said, baring his teeth in a sneer.

'Same to you... whatever "Onuku" means!' Timilehin threw back.

Nnamdi shrugged, turning towards Jide. 'Dude, don't listen to Timi and start doubting yourself. I am Igbo. Timi is not, and I can tell you that Osu caste system is pure cultural bullshit!'

'So culture is now bullshit, abi?' said Timilehin.

'Yes. Hot, smelly, fly-swarming, maggot-infested bullshit! At least the ones that no longer serve humanity.'

'So, culture and tradition should now be cherry-picked? Nnamdi listen to yourself for once!'

'Again, yes! Timilehin, yes! Culture and tradition can and should be cherry-picked. Or else, thanks to sister Slessor, we should have still been flinging twin babies into the evil forest. Why did they change that? And before you come at me with "that example is weak given that it had to do with human lives", can I ask why the whole of Nigeria is currently clamouring for a change in constitution? I mean the constitution is our culture and tradition, why change it? Right? I didn't think so.' Timilehin opened his mouth, but no words came. He swallowed air and shoved his hands into the pockets of his deep-blue denim shorts.

For the better part of their adult lives, the three men bound their friendship with a common career path and an acceptance-fortified fiducial chord, the foundation of which, since inception, has suffered intense trauma but once. A well-guarded secret, encrypted within the fortress of Nnamdi's shame-stitched heart, reared its indecorous head years ago. Claiming to have a meeting with one of his uncles, Nnamdi had taken a rain check on an invitation from his friends to explore Obudu cattle ranch during their annual leave. Not wanting to enjoy the famous scenic beauty of Calabar without the third musketeer, they decided to cancel, opting for something less adventurous instead. But shock and disgust swept over Jide and Timilehin when they bumped into their friend at a resort in the outskirts of town, arm around waist, with socialite Benedicta Thomas.

Till this day, of the two reasons his friends fussed about his relationship with Benedicta, Nnamdi agreed with only one. He regretted dating a married woman but refused to bow to the narrative of the reprehensible nature of a relationship between a man and a much older woman. A trade of words had followed Nnamdi's question about the number of people who ever batted their lids over a relationship between a lady and a man who was twice, maybe three times, her age.

'Oga, stop calling a spade a garden fork, common na! You are not dating Benedicta. You guys are having bloody sex, plain and simple!' Timilehin had said, looking like he swallowed a cup of raw eggs.

'Ehh? Oya sue me!' shouted Nnamdi, his lips thinning, his breath quickening, and his eyes glistening. He reminded Timilehin that he did not live on 'Sainthood Lane' himself. 'Yet, Saint Timilehin stands against me in judgement... and I don't remember anyone crucifying him for raping Teniayo!'

'I was tipsy... we were tipsy, asshole!' Timilehin had said with a snarl.

Through it all, Jide had said only three words: 'How long? Why?' None of Nnamdi's explanations made it any more palatable for Jide. Not his profession of his love for Benedicta Thomas, not how the fifty-eight-year-old woman's husband trolled university campuses, exploring the niceties of young femininity, and not how she often spotted a black patch around her eye each time she confronted her husband. Not one of those enlightenments made the truth sit any better on Jide's frontal lobes. Imagine their absolute delight when, weeks later, Nnamdi announced his break-off with Granny, as they called Benedicta Thomas. To this day, Jide and Timilehin still wonder how their friend came out of such a furnace unscathed.

Of the three friends, Jide had always been the one with his head better screwed on, the one who seldom needed guidance, the one who possessed the uncanny ability to sidestep trouble, and the one who always found creative ways to detangle seemingly irreparably mangled paths. But today, his head lay someplace far away from his neck. Jide now wandered, headless, in a maze and would pay whatever it cost for an extra pair of hands and a good head to help straighten out the path before him. For the first time, Jide admitted an undisputable reality; he needed guidance. *I am not the enemy, Fifi!* he screamed in his head as he stared into the night at the hotel guests sitting around the swimming pool area. A handful of the guests sat alone, nursing a glass of something. *Are they waiting for their dates to arrive?* Three or more tables were cluttered with guests. *Discussing important stuff? Perhaps they are just having a good time.*

The bickering behind Jide had ended a while ago, and in its place now was smouldering silence. He drew in a sharp breath. 'I am going to look for her. I'll go to her house, her office… her church, anywhere,' he said through clenched teeth, leaving the balcony to walk back into his room, his strides filled with intention.

'Mehn! But it will be a serious shame if they don't end up together, shaa. After all their waiting-till-marriage philosophy. What if the marriage never happens?'

Timilehin was still subdued by Nnamdi's last lecture, so he constrained himself from responding with what his mouth so ached to say. Moreover, Nnamdi's tone projected genuine concern. Or so Timilehin convinced himself. So instead, he settled for, 'You really need a spiritual epiphany. Your only worry is their celibacy. Did Jide complain to you? Follow Jesus Christ. I have told you; His teachings are not restrictive. They are only a guide to help us lead happy and wholesome lives.'

Nnamdi muffled a loud ball of laughter, 'Follower of Jesus! Did Jesus teach you to drink alcohol?' When Timilehin argued that Jesus never said not to, Nnamdi asked, 'Did he say you should rape women, then?'

Timilehin walked away with his glass of brandy to join the saner of his two friends; the friend whose present facial expression should ordinarily be sending him to his car, or at least in the opposite direction.

'Auntie Nkechi, thank you. I appreciate your good intentions, but I would be most grateful if we did not discuss this… I am not in any mood to talk about this with anybody. Not now, or any other time.' His tone had risen an octave higher by the end of his phone conversation with his auntie. Her advice to him, to let sore dogs lick their own wounds in peace, only pushed him further down the tunnel which Somadina feared his son now plunged through.

Timilehin stood for moments, regarding Jide, who still sat in the bed and still held his phone, as though contemplating whether to make a call. He placed a firm hand over Jide's right shoulder. *Kai! If only he didn't love her this hard.* 'Guy, keep your head up. If it will be, it will be. Remember what I always do.' Yes, Jide remembered what Timilehin always did; he always asked God to do what was best, and to soothe him when their 'bests' did not align. Jide could not trust himself to say such a prayer.

'Timi, I love this girl,' he said, his eyes darkening with contained pain. Timilehin let out air through half-sealed lips. If anyone else would understand and validate Jide's warring emotions, it had to be him. He loved Teni so hard it almost hurt.

TWELVE

ALONG COMES A KNIGHT IN SHINING SPANNER

His ringtone drew his eyes away from the road for a moment. Without any strategy besides hitting 'redial' each time his call to Fiyin timed out, Jide had driven from the end of Bar Beach's Ahmadu Bello Way to the foot of Marina Bridge two times already, and had just made the roundabout, to begin his third drive through. *It had better not be Auntie Nkechi.* But Auntie Nkechi understood Jide the first time. Like the lights of an impressive show of fireworks, Omo's name dazzled on Jide's phone display, quickening his heart rate.

Since Ben and Omo wanted front seats at the concert, their hang-out lasted only twenty-five minutes. But in the short time they spent together, Jide discovered kindred spirit in Ben.

'Correct me if I am mistaken, but the whole concept makes as much sense as attempting to open a file link in Notepad. Some ancestor ran to some shrine for help and... boom! Everyone within the radius of such a lineage is accursed! What's more, if you as much as touch a descendant of such an ancestor with a ten-metre pole, you grow horns, fangs and a tail too?' For the first time in hours, Jide managed a smile. *This guy should be a creative writer,* he thought, now chuckling at Ben's sweeping representation of the matter responsible for his many sleepless nights.

'I only wonder, Ben. The absurdity of the entire charade shocks my boots off me,' Jide said.

'Sweetie, I think this is a tad out of your league,' Omo said, cocking her head to the left, raising her brows a fraction to serve Ben a stare. Jide swallowed a painful lump in his throat. Why did such a small gesture make him feel so alone?

'Even the so-called western worlds have their own deal breakers... some far-left wingers will rather die of starvation than break bread with conservatives, and vice versa,' she said.

So-called? Jide wondered if Ben was privy to Omo's stance on world map nomenclature.

She believed that those responsible for the categorisation of western and eastern worlds did so out of disdain. Omo questioned why the imaginary longitude splicing the world into West and East, has Africa and Europe sitting on the same side, yet the world chooses to name Europe West but not her southern neighbour. Fiyin, on the other hand, would argue about skin colour nomenclature; why Americans and Europeans are referred to as whites, while Africans have been christened blacks. 'Snow is white, and coal is black,' she once said.

Omo continued, 'You cannot treat these kinds of complex issues with such light-heartedness. As much as I don't agree with generations a million years down the line being burdened with the debt acquired from the actions or misfortunes of one person – be it seeking refuge in the bosom of a goddess, being a product of incest, grappling with schizophrenia, mental health challenges, albinism or whatever else they failed to understand in those days – I reckon certain unsavoury consequences occurred with forming alliances with the so-called outcasts. So, while judging the proponents of this tradition, let's not forget how fear, perhaps needless, may be playing a major role in their pushback.' The two men exchanged brow-raised glances, and cynical amusement spread through Omo at their audacious admiration of her ability to place emotions and logical thinking apart.

⌒

'Auntie, you want injector cleaner?' the fuel attendant asked as he sold petrol to Fiyin. She squinted at the print on the small can of liquid. The product promised to atone for the wreckage caused by the corruption in the downstream sector of the petroleum industry. A sector responsible for ruining thousands of car fuel pumps with adulterated petrol. Fumes from the disgust bubbling in Fiyin's chest began to spread all the way to her tongue; disgust for the corrupt system. She wondered at the hypocrisy. Who was to be held accountable for the corruption? The government? Or the people? Who was the government and who were the people? Were they not both slices from the same pie?

Anita once said she believed sole distributors of imported products ensured they remained relevant to the market by greasing the palms of people in government, to frustrate the efforts of local producers and manufacturers. At first, Fiyin argued her claims were unsubstantiated, that she was simply one of those unpatriotic citizens who never saw any good in the government. But after an indigenous tomato paste factory ran into the ground, leaving local tomato farmers with no other major marketing channel, and complaints devolved into protests of *BRING BACK OUR FACTORY,* and the chief executive officer cited the prohibitive cost of providing their own alternative electric power supply as the major reason they decided to close shop, Fiyin began to rethink her stance. When a celebrated textile company accused the government of multiple taxation and ran away to set up in Ghana, spewing hundreds of workers back into the labour market, Fiyin started to make observations. When poultry farmers began to lose countless numbers of birds because the local pharmaceutical companies, which produced Viraclean, Neoxyvita Forte and Growvit A, shut down without warning, Fiyin began to draw conclusions. And, finally, when a major toothpick manufacturing company went up in flames, Fiyin embraced Anita's theory – spirit, body, and soul.

'No, next time. Thank you,' said Fiyin.

'Eeh? But Auntie, e be like say something dey burn for this your car. Abi you go check am?' Fiyin told the petrol attendant not to worry.

'I'll go to my mechanic tomorrow,' she said. In truth, Fiyin's car did not require a petrol refill. She would have much preferred to race on home, but she needed an immediate break from the adrenalin rush caused by her recent car race. With grand humility, when her car would not start after the refill, Fiyin held open her bonnet for the attendant and his colleague as they peered.

'Kai! And our mechanic don close for today. Wetin we go come do now?' the attendant said, scratching his head and peering into the night.

Fiyin suspected her car trouble may not be half as bad as the attendants wanted her to believe. She noted, with disdain, the glint in their eyes as soon as she asked them to try the injector cleaning tonic and anything else they believed might help. At 10:15pm, the petrol station, which now ran on a lean staff, had but the two attendants on duty. One fiddled with wires in her bonnet and the other fed her car a good dose of fuel injector cleaning liquid. 'Try am again,' the one at the bonnet said. Fiyin turned the key in the ignition, but her engine did not as much as cough. A car drove in and parked by one of the six pumps. The injector cleaning attendant rushed off to serve the just-arrived luxury SUV. *Tinted glasses. Must be these government fellas*, Fiyin hissed in her head.

So far, manoeuvring wires and gorging her car with fuel injector cleaning fluid had not been of any help. And after another failed attempt at cranking her engine Fiyin came out to stand by her open bonnet, hands akimbo, looking like a lost mouse, until his voice came floating towards her from the SUV with the tinted glasses.

'Well, if this isn't my lucky night!'

Fiyin's eyes grew large. *Ali Dansule?*

Ali sprang out of his car. He hovered over Fiyin's bonnet for a few seconds and went back in search of his toolbox. It took a bit of searching in his boot to find it. A simple tightening of her battery terminals, and Fiyin's car roared back to life. Gratitude, relief, and joy made her smile stretch wider and last longer. She flushed by the station's perimeter fence, close to the exit driveway, to walk back to her 'knight in shining spanner' to better express her appreciation. Ali, already back behind his wheels, wound down his window. Chrome grills, tinted glasses, alloyed rims, and rich-black leather pulled at Fiyin's vanity. *So much luxury in one equipment!* And to place further emphasis, he layered it with his built-to-perfection frame and features. 'Pheephee, you really should start on your way. All honest ladies should be in bed at this time.' The way he rolled her name off his tongue, with his eyes crinkling at the sides made Fiyin catch her breath. *Ali Dansule was a fine specimen of masculinity.*

'Here… my card. Please call me… now you owe me,' he said, flashing his teeth. A bubble of laughter began to escape Fiyin's lips before her eyes caught a shadow behind Ali, on the other side.

Not wanting to appear obvious, Fiyin, lowering her eyelids, cast a sideways glance at the young lady almost melting into her seat. Ali introduced the lady, 'Oh, sorry, that's Talatu… a… uh family friend.'

'Hi,' Fiyin said, seizing the opportunity to take a better look at the lady in the back seat of Ali's car.

'Hello,' said Talatu in a small voice, flashing a set of incredibly white and uniform teeth. A model? A dancer? Maybe someone who did not like to eat. Fiyin could not quite decide.

'My mother will curl into a knot if I let her go home by herself; I dare not have an opinion in the matter.' Ali bared his teeth in a smile. Fiyin joined Ali in courteous laughter, but nothing relaxed Talatu's visibly tense shoulders.

⌐──◞

'Please, sweetheart, pick up. I am in Lagos, Fifi. Talk to me, please.' Fiyin scrolled through to Jide's tenth text message for the day as she approached her estate gate. A car parked outside by the fence caught her attention. She recognised the number plate and parked. A blanket of guilt clung to her skin the way silk would to a wet body as she peered at Jide, fast asleep in his reclined seat. He was absolute in his oblivion to the portentous dangers of the night. Fiyin shook her head. She wondered if the estate guards took any notice of his presence. Startled by her gentle tap on his window, Jide sat up, ran his palms over his face and mouth. He looked embarrassed.

'How long have you been here?'

Jide moved his mouth and eyebrows with a shallow and tired grimace as he said, 'Fiyin, you sure are a piece of work.' Thankfulness for the opportunity to see her at last denied Jide the luxury of a decent annoyance.

'Drive behind me, let's go inside,' Fiyin said.

Fiyin pulled into the driveway and waited for Jide to park his car behind her. Soon after he slid into her car, she called her mum. 'Hello, Mummy... Yes, I am fine... No, it didn't stop. I'm in front of the house now... with... with Jide.'

Then came the long pause.

'No. Mmhh… at the estate gate.' Fiyin's voice was now an octave lower, as though to prevent her audience from following her side of the dialogue. 'Yes, Mummy. I won't be long.'

The way Jide pushed the chair back and angled himself gave him a good view of her.

'Why, Fifi?'

This might as well pass for his tag line, Fiyin thought fleetingly.

'Why?' Jide asked again. He took her right hand in both of his, his eyes searching, imploring. 'This is not your fight alone. Fifi, the battle is ours to fight.' The inflection in his voice when he said 'ours' pulled at Fiyin's heartstrings. He looked at least five years older.

Inside the house, Donald stared at his wife, a slight frown emerging between his brows.

'For how long, Bridget?'

Bree shrugged.

'I can't say… Fiyin told me less than twenty minutes ago after she met him at the estate gate.' She made to walk past her husband, hoping he would not do what she suspected he would. Donald's eyes widened to nearly twice their circumference.

'Less than twenty mi… I am going to invite him in,' he said.

Bree rushed back, planted herself in front of their bedroom door, arms akimbo. 'No, Donald! You will not give the entire Williams community an extra reason to come here accusing us of contaminating their lineage… The audience Fifi is granting him is bad enough!' Without as much as a word, Donald put his arms through the hoops of his wife's arms and lifted her off the floor, away from the door, muttering something about not allowing himself to be sucked into the emotional impracticality of a scorned woman. Bree's five-feet-three-inch frame did not stand a chance. Her husband towered over her.

At the end of the concert, Atlantic Point Resort milled with people and cars. When Ben first told Omo about the concert, she did not leap in excitement. Although now more in tune with God, the universe, and the invisible string which linked her to them, Omo's perception about those who pointed out those linking strings remained adamant in its scepticism. 'Unlike most pastors in Nigeria, *oyinbo* pastors mix their preaching with a considerable helping of respect,' she had once told Fiyin. And when Fiyin argued that God did not require respect to convey his commands to man, Omo said, 'The pastors are not God. If they claim to be God's representatives, let them walk on water, turn water into wine and truly make dead people live again!' Fiyin raised a white flag.

Through the ride back to Ben's hotel and the few seconds up the elevator to his floor, Omo talked non-stop about her epiphany. 'We are like characters in a script written by God. If we stick to His script, most of our journeys will be seamless. And guess what? When we deviate, which often happens, He can rewrite the plot... perhaps with consequences, perhaps without, the prerogative is His, right? Why I never understood this until lately still beats my imagi—'

'Then I suggest you mind the kind of pastors you listen to,' Ben said with a chuckle as he inserted his key card to let them in. Besides when he said, 'I am glad you are enjoying yourself,' he appeared content drinking in Omo's enthusiasm through the concert and afterwards. But for Omo's merry heart and the cloak of the night's darkness, Ben would have improvised an explanation for his brimming eyes.

At past midnight, though questioning the wisdom in it, chivalry compelled Ben to ask Omo to spend the night. 'No, sugar bear. Bad idea... we've discussed this,' Omo said. Backing up to the door, she told Ben they would talk in the morning, about their plans to visit her mum in Benin. 'I'm off. Sweet dreams, sugar.'

'What? No goodnight kiss? Was I such an awful date?' The

door held her firmly in place as she obliged. And in that moment, her arms around Ben's waist, his hands cradling her face ever so tenderly, Omo wanted it – the total essence of Benjamin Edward Wright. The fullness of the warmth, kindness, self-control, truth and gallantry he exuded. Omo wanted to crawl under and into it. Nurture and live it.

'Goodnight, my love.' Ben's voice suggested an element of urgency. *Jeesuuuu! This British boy!* Omo groaned in her head as she willed her arms to unclasp Ben's waist, to begin her homebound journey. Ayomide, the car rental driver, rubbed his sleep-tugged eyes with his forefinger and thumb. He began his ten-minute drive to drop off his last client for the day. Or was it his first?

Mr Taylor's tone left no room for an argument. His viscous baritone boomed into the quiet night. 'Good evening, Jide. I suggest you both come in. Whatever is being discussed can't lose its importance if taken into the house,' he said in answer to Jide's uncertain, 'Good evening, sir.'

Propelled by Donald's censorious glare, Bree's reluctant feet pulled her to the sitting room to offer Jide some dinner and a place to rest his head till the morning.

'Good evening, ma'am,' Jide said, still on his feet, searching desperately for that twinkle in Bree's eyes. The twinkle which always seemed to say, 'I am about to draw a grin from you.' But all Jide saw was a coldness that chilled his bones to cracking. She might as well have been talking to the door behind him.

However politely executed, rejecting her offer of dinner did not promise a favourable outcome. But Jide could not find the courage to dine at the table of someone who, not too long ago, was informed by his family of how horrendous associating with them had become. His shoulders relaxed when Fiyin said, 'Mummy, Jide will have his dinner in the guest room.'

With conscientious intentionality from Jide and excruciating patience from Fiyin, they walked through the events running up to the, in Jide's words, poignant visit. Every now and again, their eyes skirted over the open plate of fried rice, carelessly adorned with a piece of fried chicken drumstick. A drumstick which highlighted a solid representation of the now familiar term – outcast.

'I was confused, angry... and frustrated... and... and stupid. Not speaking with your parents before my family's invasion of a meeting wins the award for the most thoughtless decision of the decade.'

The lid over Fiyin's boiling anger shifted a fraction, letting part of the steam escape. She smacked her lips, parted them to blow air through her still-clenched teeth. 'It's all right, Jide. To be honest, I am no longer sure of what your speaking with them would have achieved. But with the benefit of hindsight, sitting in Abuja and asking me to record the meeting was a lousy addition to the list of options. I realised the degree of its senselessness when I said it out loud to Omo. Hah! Recording the meeting. To serve what purpose?' Jide kneaded his temples with both forefingers as he let out a self-mocking chuckle.

'Yes... I still do not believe I asked you to do it... made you do it. Sweet pea, I am sorry... for being such an ass.'

Of all Jide's names for her, 'sweet pea' took the crown. Sometimes she attributed her fondness for the endearment to its rarity of use. Other times, the inflection in his voice when he said it pulled at all the right strings. This night, she leaned into 'sweet pea' because it covered her in warmth. Made her safe, much like a warm cup of coffee, or maybe cocoa, on a cold night, wielding a shield against the still-present chill. And when Jide begged for assurances; for her to be waiting for him on the other side of the battlefield, Fiyin was jolted by a knowing. She would be there waiting; head, heart, and all.

One hour limped past the other as they talked into the wee hours of the morning. And not because Bree had attained a degree of 'new age' sophistication, but because of the muffled voices she heard every time she pressed her ear to the guest room door, she left the young lovers alone.

~

'Please, ma'am, may I have it "to go"?' Jide said, referring to the toast Bree offered him for breakfast. All three Taylors were ready for work, and being the only one out of the four people seated in the dining area yet to take a shower, he reckoned his intrusion would appear less obvious the sooner he left. With the almost genial smile on Bree's face as she scurried to the kitchen to wrap the toast, Jide dared to hope his brief but earnest speech had succeeded in soothing some sore spots.

'Thank you, sir... ma'am, for letting me in your home after everything... I love your daughter as I am certain my folks do too. Please find it in your hearts to excuse... I mean forgive their... my reaction. I um... it is bewildering how even the best of us can lose our sense of better judgement in the face of fear. I cannot claim to know a lot about the caste system, but I do know that no one should be called unclean, what God has called clean. And while it rings somewhat logical to acknowledge the insensibility of holding on to one person, against all seeming hurdles, in a planet of over seven billion people, my desperate willingness to jump those hurdles, scrape my knees, maybe break a limb or two, in complete disinterest of the seeming options I have in the seven billion, tells me I have been blessed with the fortune of stumbling on the kind of love only explored in wild dreams... and one does not relinquish such a fortune... not for anything... and... and by God, I pray Fiyin

still agrees with me. My intentions towards Fiyin will not and cannot change, and if you give me the opportunity... again... I will owe you my gratitude through this lifetime and back... please.' Only the sound of Jide's unsteady breathing echoed in the room.

Wafts of deliciousness filled his car. His foil-wrapped toast looked more like a club sandwich for two. Jide waved back as Bree and Donald, on their way to work, drove away from their driveway. Dressed in a pair of black slacks, which flared above her ankles, and a matching black fitted cold-shoulder top, the belts at the end of its high collar holding themselves in a bow at the back of her neck, Fiyin completed perfection with her hair bunched up in the centre. Jide's breath caught in his throat. Fiyinfunoluwa made nonsense of the mutual exclusivity of vulnerability and vigour. The thought of the rest of his life without her in it made Jide's insides experience the chaos much like what happens when 'Robert the robot' of *Justin's House* hits the panic button. And when she mouthed, 'I love you' to him as he pulled away, he managed a slow blink; the painful tightness in his throat stole his breath – again.

~

'Professor Taylor... I mean, your dad... didn't say which of the two properties you were more inclined towards. Should we arrange a skip over... a look around... to help you decide, Miss Taylor?' Mrs Alexis Azike Smith did not sound anything like Fiyin expected. For her outstanding success in the real estate and events management space, the American held the title of 'tree-bark tough'. Her marriage to Mr Onyeka Azike made the news as the sweetest match ever. But when stories about her relationship with her husband's relatives began to slide into tabloids and social media platforms, the much-loved 'oyinbo' started to court the wrath of the people.

For most of her life, Alexis grew up in Washington DC, but

on one of her vacations to England, to spend time with her Aunt Delphine, she met and fell in love with Onyeka, a third-year major in health information management at Oxford University. A two-year affair ensued, and soon, Onyeka returned to Nigeria with his Alexis.

Fiyin snatched herself out of her daydream. 'Uh. Yes, ma'am. We should. Would next weekend be fine… ma'am?'

'Ahhh! Let me run through my schedule and give you a call, if that's all right.'

'That's fine, ma… I mean, ma'am. Thank you so much for your call.'

'No worries! I'm always giddy with excitement when I meet young ladies who are willing to dare industry norms. We'll decide on a specific date during the week. I hope you find one of them to your liking.'

'Thanks a lot, ma'am.'

Anita's sudden and unannounced presence startled Fiyin. She wondered how much of her phone conversation had not been private. No need to wonder for too long as Anita, without any prelude said, 'Girlie, I will miss you, o!'

'Haba! I still dey, nau,' Fiyin said, assuring her colleague. 'Besides, wherever I decide to set up cannot be outside Victoria Island or Ikoyi. So, we'll always connect. I also need six months or more to set up, so…'

'Abeg, when you blow, don't forget our discussion, o. Your girl can be of good use to you,' Anita said, referring to her pitch for the position of kitchen manager in Fiyin's catering outfit. It reminded Fiyin about one of Anita's many rants. 'This country na scam! In the corporate world, what matters is your connection. Then we wonder why the streets are filled with sound but jobless graduates. Why won't crime be on the rise?' she would rave. Her most recent tirade happened as long ago as yesterday, when her brother called to inform her of another 'we regret to inform you' letter from another job interviewer.

'Blow?' Fiyin chuckled.

'Of course, nau! You won't only survive in the business, you will thrive, girlfriend! No be Alexis Azike go sell property give you? By the time she channels all her power clients to you for catering events… mehhnnn! Me thinks you don't understand the gold mine you're sitting on!' A small smile pulled at Fiyin's mouth; her sometimes-cheery-sometimes-moody colleague-cum-friend had already plotted the success graph of her catering business.

Anita asked, 'How is she though?'

'Who?' said Fiyin.

'Mrs Azike. What's she like? People say she's one tough cookie.' Anita's eyes twinkled like Tom's would when about to snatch Jerry's last cracker.

'I haven't yet met her in person, but she sounds pleasant on the phone,' Fiyin said.

Word around town portrayed Alexis Azike as the devil in high heels.

'People say she doesn't encourage her husband to help his people,' Anita said.

'It's because of that story *People's Chronicles* carried. The one with the gist of her husband's cousins who showed up at their Oniru house in search of jobs in Lagos merely one week after their wedding.'

'Exactly! They said the woman gave them their transport fares back to the village where they came from. I think that was mean, shaa.'

But narratives varied. Another version purports that barely months after they settled in Nigeria, her husband's uncle began to hound his nephew with telephone calls, asking for a one million Naira loan to start a catfish business. When Mr Azike asked for a draft of his business plan and a proposed repayment schedule, the man's phone calls stopped. Afterwards, phrases like 'ajo nwanyi', bad woman, and 'amosu ocha', white witch, became popular pronouns for the lady. But no matter what version soared, in the workplace, Alexis made no room for mediocrity. Her motto –'the utmost best or nothing'– left nobody in any doubt of what Alexis Azike symbolised.

As usual, Anita and Fiyin sat together during lunchtime. 'Ehe, I forgot to tell you, madam manager said a phone call came for you,' Anita said between mouthfuls of pasta and sauce. Fiyin's brows rose.

'Me? From who?'

Anita set down her fork and began to tap her narrow fingers, mimicking a drum roll.

'Ali Dansule!' Anita ignored Fiyin's discomfiture and continued, 'Correct gentleman! Can you believe he didn't ask for your phone number? Only said to tell you he'll call again… around 3:00pm, I think.' When Fiyin willed her brain back to normal functioning, she kicked herself for succumbing to her profuse gratitude after he rescued her at the petrol station, when he fixed her battery terminals. Because of her overwhelming thankfulness, Fiyin had volunteered her work address.

THIRTEEN

WHEN BULLS LOCK HORNS, NOTHING SUFFERS.
THEY ARE BUT A SPECTACLE

Under ideal circumstances, apart from during break time, staff at the hotel neither asked for, nor received, time off work at the hotel. Especially not when such a time off selected the hotel lobby as its place of observance. But a visit by Ali Dansule and an ideal circumstance did not quite fit in the same frame. Protocols were broken, rules ignored, and norms bent to suit individuals of Ali Dansule's pedigree. So, Fiyin's unease shone through her eyes as they darted around, with the hope of catching the eyes of a few of her co-workers as they carried on with their duties. They did not have the luxury of having someone important request a sit-out with them. On company time! However, the impressive piece of work called Ali appeared to be at absolute peace with his environment.

'Come on, have something to drink,' Ali said.

This guy is not serious at all. I should have something to drink, Fiyin scoffed.

'I'm sorry, would you rather be holed away... sweating over pots and pans,' Ali said, sitting up to set his glass of mocktail on the little stool between their chairs and leaning back again to rest his eyes on her.

The lobby did not buzz with the usual chatter typical of Tuesday afternoons. By 2:45pm, lunch buffet should have been well underway. But save for a sprinkle of guests trickling through the hotel's revolving doors, either heading for the elevator or to the hotel restaurant a few strides ahead, the lobby was empty. The emptiness was made starker by the brilliance of the area's many chandelier lights and cold blasting from air-conditioning units. Fiyin bared her teeth as she assured Ali of her intense delight at sitting to have a chat with him. And why not? Mrs Deneri already asked her to burn as much company time as she liked at the lobby; Fiyin reckoned finding her guest's company delightful now featured as a key performance indicator on her appraisal sheet.

'He is Chairman's son's friend. I don't want any complaints,' Mrs Deneri, the hotel manager had said.

Startled by her own mobile phone's ringtone, Fiyin apologised as her eyes registered the caller. *Jide?* She ended the call. She let her eyes wander from the maroon leather seat beside Ali to the narrow strip of black rug behind him; it ran from the revolving entrance doors and stopped a few inches before the elevator gates. A man and a lady walked through the doors. They caught Fiyin's attention. *Oh, what a mismatch!* When they reached the elevator, everything checked out. Although executed with such skill, Fiyin did not miss the eye exchange between the two. Whatever cryptic message they exchanged caused the lady to step back and wait for the next elevator trip. *Ahh! Aristo!* Fiyin concluded, referring to the concept of young girls who, to maintain their lavish lifestyles, offered their companionships to older and fiscally stable men. The distaste in Fiyin's mouth spilled and splattered all over her face.

'This is poor timing on my part, I think,' Ali said. The stretching silence managed to have crawled beneath his skin. And although

Fiyin shook her head in vehement denial, Ali was not to be fooled.

'The question should be if you would like to chill with me... Fiyin,' he said, with the galling self-assuredness often associated with men who were used to females falling over themselves for a slice of their attention. Her brain began to improvise for a soothing excuse to discourage further companionship with Ali when her phone began to ring again.

'Go on, take your call. The fellow is mighty insistent,' Ali said, adding with humour, 'Who wouldn't be?'

Fiyin took her call. 'Hi.'

Jide huffed and puffed, like someone would after a sprint. 'Fifi... hi. I have... not been able to reach you... all afternoon. When do you finish work today? I am just stepping into the lobby.'

Fyin's eyes grew large with surprise.

'Uh... which lobby?' Ali did not miss the tremor in her giggle.

'The lobby at the hotel... where you work... you are at work, are you not?' Jide said, walking through the hotel entrance. Fiyin pulled her left drooping sleeve over her gaping shoulder. She made to stand but forced herself back into her seat, pressing her back into it. Ali followed her eyeline, turning towards the revolving door to find the source of his companion's disquiet.

'Ah, the boyfriend?' he asked. And to her non-verbal assent, he said, flashing his teeth in an ear-to-ear grin, 'Didn't fool myself into assuming the non-existence of one.'

Hands locked in a firm handshake. 'I am Ali... Dansule.' After a nanosecond of waiting for Jide's brows to rise in recognition, Ali relaxed his grip and sank back in his seat. He expected raised brows during introductions; one of the perks of being a Dansule. But Jide's brows did not rise in the faintest flicker of an acknowledgment, and rather than offer his name in reciprocity, Jide offered a curt hello and sank into the seat beside a somewhat tense Fiyin. He reached for her right hand and, for a moment, became oblivious to anyone else as he planted a soft kiss in it.

A text message from Mrs Deneri buzzed Fiyin's mobile phone, breaking the moment.

'*Is your discussion with Mr Dansule over?*' the message said.

'*No, ma'am.*'

'*Is the other man sitting with you his guest, then?*'

'*No, ma'am.*'

'*You cannot be wasting company time on your private guests. Dismiss him and focus on Mr Dansule. Which part of "he is Chairman's son's friend" did you not understand? Maybe I should have added "very, very good friend".*'

Fiyin placed her phone, face down, on the empty space on her seat. *Can you imagine! I'm only an intern, not a staff at your mercy! Jaga-jaga woman.* She snarled in her head.

A porter walked up to their corner. 'Sir,' he said, addressing Jide, 'I am sorry for the disturb. Security say please you should come and repark your car, sir... please.' The porter shifted from one foot to the other, his voice quavering. He hated being saddled with the task of inconveniencing a prospective 'happy customer'. Inconveniencing customers often whittled down the chances of any tips exchanging hands.

Once Jide excused himself, Ali's eyes twinkled. He angled his head in a manner suggestive of something Fiyin struggled to find a word for. 'You haven't done anything wrong, you know? At least not yet.'

Fiyin's eyes fluttered in confusion. She battled with the best response to Ali's wobbly subliminal messages and settled for, 'I do not sweat over pots and pans. I craft food so lovely you would want to postpone eating it but, in the end, be glad you succumbed to its alluring sumptuousness.'

Ali's brows lifted.

'What an ingenious description of your vocation. Now your cooking shall haunt me until I am convinced you didn't just blow hot air down my backside.' And though Ali's humour did not arrive in the most exquisite of parcels, how dare he refer to Fiyin's career as a vocation, the air around them lost a fraction of its tension. But once Fiyin began talking about her plans for a catering school, Jide walked through the doors.

'Maybe we should do this some other time… soon?' Ali said.

'Yes, maybe.'

'Let's exchange numbers,' he said, reaching for his mobile phone from beside his now empty glass. Ali's smile lingered until Jide sat back down.

Fiyin's phone began to ring and with a wide grin, Ali said, 'That's me.'

Jide resembled a child with a big morsel of fufu stuck in his throat.

'It would have been a pleasure to chat a little longer with you, Pheephee. And… uh… not sure I caught your name,' Ali said, turning to Jide in what Jide perceived as mock modesty.

'Oh! It was a pleasure to have made your acquaintance!' Jide's grin made an expert cocktail of sarcasm and humour. 'My name is Jideofor… Jideofor Williams.' Jide got on his feet to take Ali's hand, to lock eyes with him. And a moment passed. A fleeting moment when Jide waited for Ali's brows to rise in recognition.

Two pairs of eyes followed Ali to the door, and once they were alone, Jide turned towards Fiyin. 'Forgive my barging in on you this way. I tried to reach you, but I guess you were… busy.' The inflection on 'busy' did not escape Fiyin.

He is jealous. Hmmm! Like I suspected! She wondered if this fresh realisation did not present a new weapon for her to wield.

'Cheekiness? How unbecoming of you, my darling,' Fiyin said, squinting with a chuckle and pulling her nose up at Jide. His brows formed a near-flat line, expressing a mischief-embossed cluelessness.

With the way Jide sat back in his chair, applying a remarkable measure of idleness in twiddling his car keys, feasting his eyes on the many people now in the lobby, Fiyin concluded, *Whatever made him drive through the rush hour traffic of Victoria Island would not have turned into a catastrophe had he waited till the evening.*

'Would you like something to eat?' she asked.

'No, thank you.'

'Something to drink, then.' Fiyin's tone gave no room for further negotiations.

'You win, but later,' Jide said with a smile. Half tilting towards her and clutching his left knee – something he often did to relieve anxiety. He spent some moments feeding his amusement at the diverse calibre of guests milling around.

'I have an idea… and I understand why you may be alarmed at first but I think, with some thought… maybe…' Jide stopped talking when Anita walked up to their corner. Her eyes started twinkling once they rested on her colleague's guest, like the sole custodian of an information of utmost discretion.

'Hi,' she cooed, regarding Jide from under her lashes before bending over to whisper to Fiyin, 'Only you, girlfriend? Two full servings of fine wine! I beg, drink one and toss the other down my drain. Mrs Deneri wants you back.'

'Like now?'

'Like yesterday,' Anita said, bending lower, her low-cut blouse struggling to contain everything stuffed in it.

'Of course, she does.'

Anyone would have thought Fiyin had bitten down on an unripe cashew fruit. The oddity in her voice drew a quizzical glance from Jide as Anita sashayed off, throwing one last look Jide's way. Of all the emotions sprung on Fiyin in the past week, her incipient loathing for Anita never once struck her as something to expect. And Fiyin's belief that Jide's eyes lingered for those three extra seconds — when Anita's buttocks moved, each independent of the other, as though they did not both belong to the same waist — did nothing to quell her rising annoyance.

'Let's talk after I finish work,' she said rising. 'I have a sense Chef Jose will soon be sending out a search party. Plus, my manager will order my head on a platter any moment from now.'

Jide meant the tentative pull on Fiyin's right index finger as an appeal.

'Please stay a while longer,' he said, his eyes persuading, imploring. Most times, all Fiyin needed to have her skipping back to Jide's side lay in his eyes, when they rose in childlike plea and hope. *Vulnerability suites him.* Fiyin sat back down, but only to give Jide's wrist a soft squeeze, to explain why the hotel manager liked her better when Ali was her guest.

The muscles around Jide's forehead and temple relaxed.

'In Ali's defence, though, one cannot be held wholly accountable for the fame or notoriety of one's family.' When Fiyin raised her brows in mock surprise, he added, 'I would also pick him over me if the health of my business depended on my choice.'

'Yeah, right, Dr Ji-de-ofor! I'm off. Will be back in an hour,' Fiyin said, a smile playing around her lips as she hurried back to the kitchen. Jide's wisecracking did not distract her; Fiyin suspected Ali had unsettled her self-assured doctor lover, if only a tiny bit. She liked it. Yes, Fiyin liked it a little too much.

⁓

Afulenu's eyes smarted from both the tears she shed before and the ones still trapped in them. Jide's current impasse did not stand in isolation as the possible culprit of Afulenu's despondence. On occasion, light shone through a crack in her mind, on the second possible reason. Perhaps the new closeness between her husband and his brother bore the blame for the progressive tightening in her chest?

Many years ago, on one of the days Afulenu begged for his blessings over her choice for a husband, her father had said, 'This short boy you are running after will choose his family over you. They always do. Ndi mba amaro anu nwayi. Outsiders treat their wives with disdain, mark me!' It did not matter that her husband was not a short man. They both shared the same height. Average. Five feet, six inches was average in Afulenu's family, short in her father's lexicon.

Today, the more her father's words jeered at her, the tighter the invisible hand squeezed Afulenu's chest.

Not once in Afulenu's thirty-two years of knowing Somadina had he spoken to her with disrespect. Yet today, she lay in her bed, staring at her husband, trying to make meaning of the words he had just said.

'Eh, Afulenu? So, you no longer care whether I eat or not?' he said again. Only this time, the words were an octave higher than before and rolled out of a mouth now shaped in an 'n' with a skewed tilt to the right.

'Somadina, today is the last Thursday of the quarter, and on the last Thursday of the quarter, you go for your alumni meeting, where you eat,' Afulenu said in a near-whisper. She often dropped her tone to a whisper to register her intense disappointment in her husband. Somadina began to say something, but realising his dearth of a superior riposte, stopped with an almost comical abruptness. He looked around their white-walled bedroom, mumbled something Afulenu could not quite decipher and stomped off.

A sigh escaped her throat in gratitude for her retrieved solitude. Still, Afulenu did not like her husband's new skill of skirting around vital information regarding work. She did not like his often-grumbling self; he seldom laughed these days. But most of all, she did not like how every now and again, he dialled Agatha's mobile number to say, 'I only called to find out how you people are doing.'

The first and only time she challenged him about calling Agatha, and not Nwafor, her husband had answered in a voice she almost did not recognise. 'Is she not my in-law? I guess your majesty also does not understand the cultural requirement of maintaining relationships with family.' Afulenu suspected emotional blackmail as the reason behind her husband's new leaning into his clan. Somadina wanted her to bear the weight of operating in the minority. What surprised Afulenu most was that no matter how absurd the opinions of her husband's new alliances were, he still placed them above his own good judgement.

'What a shame your father chooses to defer to Nwafor and his witch in such an intimate matter! Such a private matter! Tufiakwa.' Afulenu had said to Kaira yesterday, the tears stinging her eyes. After her phone conversation with Kaira, Afulenu questioned in whose camp her daughter belonged.

'Mummy, don't overstress yourself. In the end, Jide will do the right thing... he always does,' Kaira had said. What did her daughter's words mean? Through the rest of her day, Afulenu went about like someone with a heavy bag of sand on her chest.

⌒

Because Somadina served his nursing officer a blank stare, she repeated her question.

'I would like to confirm if Dr Jide will be coming in tomorrow, sir.'

'Um... why? Any issues?' Something about the way Nurse Anyammili held his gaze, almost in reprimand, unnerved the chief medical director.

'We have a C-section scheduled for Mrs Usman tomorrow... Friday, sir... Mrs Usman...' Nurse Anyammili paused for emphasis, 'Senator Danladi Abubakar's daughter. She requested for Dr Jide, in particular, to handle her procedure and we agreed… in writing.'

Somadina swallowed a gulp of air, scratching the thumb-sized patch of grey hair in the centre of his head. The more Somadina swivelled in his black ergonomic chair, the tighter Nurse Anyammili's teeth clenched and the wider her nose flared. She remained unmoving, waiting for a response. She was now tempted to place her hand on her hip and begin to tap her foot.

Since their three-week-old talk, Jide exercised intentionality in avoiding any form of conflict with his father, and his approach did not preclude staying out of Somadina's line of sight. But whatever existing hopes Somadina nursed about his wife and son realising the ephemeral nature of their own concept of the Osu caste system, soon suffered an obliterating blow.

'I will handle this whole thing, don't worry,' I.G had promised Somadina only a few days ago. In truth, Somadina wondered how his daughter's father-in-law's brother would settle the chaos responsible for placing his masculinity and cultural awareness under scrutiny, but he dared to hope. The justification Nwafor presented for further involving the man whom fewer than a handful of people liked, went along the lines of, 'He has connections. The man washes his hands in the same bowl with big, big men. I think he can force those Yoruba people to restrain their daughter from making our son bring disgrace and bad luck to us. Let us not be swimming in water and allow soap to enter our eyes.'

'But Nwafor, tell me the truth, do you think this thing is as serious as I.G is making it sound? I have been carrying out my own enquiries, and not many people seem truly interested in it anymore,' Somadina had said.

'Eh, call me back, my credit has finished,' Nwafor had said, ending the call – as he often did when an immediate answer eluded him. He needed to confer with his wife.

Nurse Anyammili shuffled her feet to emphasise her need for

a response; she did not look like she planned to leave without one.

'Should I persuade her to settle for Dr Zildina, sir?'

Somadina rolled his tongue in his mouth, shut his eyes for a moment and fluttered them open again. The hospital's Matron must have run an assessment of the consequence of shoving an expatriate doctor down their client's throat before escalating to him. Before now, he relied on his wife and son for matters like this; a simple phone call to Jide would have settled this matter. But last night, after I.G shared the details of his so-called intervention, Somadina feared his son would cut all ties with him.

'Call Mrs Usman. Tell her I will be handling her surgery... due to circumstances beyond the hospital's control.' Because she did not trust herself to speak, Roseline responded with a nod and began to leave. 'Matron,' Somadina called when she reached the door, 'apologise to her on my... um... our behalf,' he finished. His eyes dropped to his desk, resting on the miniature decorative model of the earth.

'Hmm.' The nurse scurried off with a grunt. 'Beyond the hospital's control, my foot!' she murmured. Every hallway, room and ward in the hospital hummed with the real reason behind young Dr Williams' absence; he wanted to marry an Osu, an outcast, and his father said no. The hospital also hummed with varying assumptions of what 'Chief' would do when he found out the cultural status of his trusted matron. What would the CMD do when he found out that his trusted matron of many years also belonged to the loathed caste system.

But at eight o'clock in the morning of the following day, curious eyes tailed a grinning Jide as he walked through the doors of the Soma-Williams hospital headquarters.

'Lagos air must be good for him, considering all the stress the poor guy has been going through,' Sylvia purred, her voice dripping embroidered pity.

'Say the one doing you,' Uncle Nosa, the maintenance manager, threw at her with the requisite measure of chuckle which he hoped would make his crass comment still pass for a joke. The sheer size of Nurse Sylvia's crush on Jide Williams put a blue whale to shame.

Roseline's relief spanned the entire city; Mrs Usman's threat of a media smear on Soma-Williams Hospital no longer worried her.

⌐—⌐

Like every other day, Donald Taylor walked into his office at 7:45am. With the year gliding towards its end, the air around Acme University flowed with welcome ease. A significant cut in workload allowed Professor Donald Taylor, Senior Registrar of Acme University, to resume at 10:00am if he fancied, but Donald was yet to master the art of contending with his own character.

He asked his secretary for a mug of coffee to go with his wife's toast, and was about to dive under his pile of emails when the image of a blinking envelope on his computer screen drew his eyes. A twelve o'clock meeting invite for an audit review. *Why should I be in this meeting? This must be a mistake*, he thought, placing a call to his executive assistant. The office line rang out. Donald reached for his mobile phone, to dial Toke on her private line. 'She is late again. I wonder if her nanny has resigned again or maybe her driver this time,' he said to himself, hitting the dial button. Solomon walked in carrying a tray with a mug of steaming water, a can of coffee granules, a teaspoon, a bottle of honey, and a tin of liquid milk. 'Thank you, Solomon,' Donald said. Toke's private phone rang out.

Donald returned to the mail inviting him for the audit. Although puzzled by the invitation itself, the list of attendees baffled him even more. Why was he the only invitee? *Anyway, whatever this is about, I'll find out at twelve noon*, he said to himself, settling to enjoy his breakfast.

'This will take only a few minutes, Professor. We are here about a loan you took from the Federal Scholarship Board twenty-seven years ago.'

Donald, sitting before what he now recognised as a panel, supressed the sudden urge to undo his tie. *Why Kunle? Why?* Donald told himself to control his intake and release of air. *No cause to worry*, a voice in his head said. *Besides, you paid back every kobo*, the voice added. But had Donald taken a legitimate loan, this meeting would have been unnecessary.

For five years, Professor Udenkwo waited, prowling, licking his wounds, and biding his time for the opportunity to serve Donald a befitting revenge. With glee, he accepted the task of presiding over this meeting. Eyes gleaming in anticipation, he salivated as Donald scanned the eight pairs of eyes in the room, shifting in his chair, as though to dodge the rain of their reprimanding stares. Udenkwo never forgave Donald for not signing in his favour after being accused of student-lecturer misconduct. And although Donald's signature did not matter in the end, not every grudge accepted the atonement of time.

Further emboldened by the menacing hum from the two-horsepower air-conditioning unit, the silence danced around the room, provoking the pores in Donald's underarms to release beads of sweat.

Two and a half hours never flew by any faster. Donald spotted Toke through her glass door. The woman started to turn towards him, but snatched her head back to her desk, in obvious avoidance of a visual confrontation. Donald said, 'Hello,' but did not wait to find out if she acknowledged his greeting or not.

'Good afternoo... I mean welcome, sir,' said Solomon. His voice gave off a croak-like quality. Donald managed a smile.

It took a little over an hour and a half for Donald to clear out his office, make the drive back home, and begin an introductory explanation to his wife, of not only why he held a suspension letter, but also why the university tribunal currently held a case against him.

Bree struggled to make sense of her husband's explanation.

A horn blared in the distance, and she let out a long hiss. 'I wonder why people toot their horns in a gated community! Hah, so much noise!'

~

Nine years may sound short for anyone considering the age of a child, but it is excruciatingly long for anybody hoping or praying for one. Bree sped through one fellowship after another.

'Be fruitful!'

'Receive it!'

'Your time is now!' were a few of the take-home assurances from countless pastors, apostles, reverends, and bishops. Some went as far as asking her to sow cash seeds, by way of offerings, to *lock in* her answer from heaven. But nothing jarred Donald like the day he came back from the office to meet his wife cooing over the latest addition to their bedroom – a prophet asked her to purchase a baby crib. 'Faith without works is dead. Act with confidence... like you already have what you are praying for,' he had said. After that, Donald decided to begin to think outside the allegorical box.

In vitro fertilisation presented a most welcome option. Mr and Mrs Taylor embraced the not-so-popular-in-Nigeria medical intervention. But the requisite cash for tickets, accommodation, and the actual procedure, ran into thousands of pounds sterling. They needed help. Donald ran to his office cooperative for financial aid, while Bree sought help of any kind from her pastor.

'What you are applying for is the entire cooperative's savings for the year. If we grant this loan, the purse will be empty and questions will start to fly about,' said Alfonso the chairperson of the cooperative which most of the senior staff at the university belonged to. When Bree recounted her discussion with their pastor, Donald blamed her for thrusting too many details at the clergy.

'Sister, why are you placing your trust in horses and chariots?' Pastor Oduah had asked, disappointment etched all over his face. With every passing day, Bree sat, arms tied, twiddling her fingers, and praying for divine intervention as her ova sped down fossil lane.

Indeed, heaven responded! With Kunle's influence, Donald secured a loan. And the best part? An option to stagger the repayment. While Bree sang in worship to God, her heart floating in gratitude, Donald cringed with guilt. Should he explain to his dear wife that, in one moment of desperation, fuelled by not only societal pressure but her fast-dwindling self-worth, he took an unauthorised loan from the State Scholarship Board? Kunle Osunde, his friend of years too many to count, assured him of his discretion.

'This begins and ends with you and me,' he had said. And it did, until the Minister of State for Education summoned him for a chat with respect to financial management during his tenure as Director of the State scholarship board. 'This case is under wraps and has undergone a rigorous probe. So, tell me in fine detail, what happened. If you do, you and everything you represent will be preserved.' When Kunle parted his lips to begin a fierce denial, the Minister stopped him with a raised hand, 'I suggest you apply caution in choosing your words, Mr Osunde… remember your son's budding political career.' Kunle pursed his lips and leaned back into his chair.

⌐━⌐

The cry of a newborn often drew smiles from all ordinary people.

But the cries from twins stretched the smiles twice as wide. Still numb and groggy from spinal anaesthesia and sedation, Mrs Usman managed a smile. 'Thank you, Jide. I never questioned your skilled hands.'

Jide smiled at his classmate from secondary school. 'I only let God guide my hands, Zainab.'

'Well done, son… and thank you,' Somadina said. Jide grunted his response at the retreating figure of his father.

Later, in Jide's office, Somadina sat opposite his son, waiting for his answer. 'Yes, Dad. I will come home after work.' A light flashed in Somadina's eyes. Perhaps the rumours about Jide seeking to float his own practice were only rumours. *I am in no need for further drama*, Somadina said to himself. But nobody anticipated the myriad of disorderliness that would follow Fiyin's phone call to Jide while the Williams sat having dinner as a family. It ended in a shouting session between father and son. Somadina demanded an apology from Jide for likening his alliance with I.G to a dog rolling in its vomit.

'Apology! You are unbelievable! Do you realise what that man has done? The Taylors' careers are ruined! All three of them!'

'Well, if they were as virtuous as you projected, they wouldn't have been in such a mess to begin with!'

'Wow, Dad! Did you learn nothing from these past years?' Jide's words came out hushed; they exuded an element of utter disappointment – akin to the tone an elder would employ in admonishing an errant child. Afulenu sat alone at the dining table watching, through tear-blurred eyes, as her perfect dinner lay to waste. In the morning, she woke up to her phone's ringtone. Jide called to wish her a good morning – from the airport.

'I will be in Lagos for a while… I am sorry, Mother… I cannot bear to look at him.'

FOURTEEN

MIND: THE THIEF OF SERENITY, THE ROGUE OF TRANQUILLITY

What an adult sees while sitting remains hidden, even to a child hoisted on the tallest of trees. So goes an African adage. At half past one in the morning, a phone call from Kaira roused Afulenu and Somadina. This call brought 'the object' under scrutiny closer to the child. At first a stream of incoherent words, layered over muffled sobs, tumbled through Somadina's mobile phone. And not until Afulenu snatched the phone from her husband to say, 'Will you pull yourself together and speak, Chimakaira!' did Kaira's words begin a leaning into any meaning.

'Kene's people met yesterday... they... they gave me an ultimatum. If Jide goes ahead with his marriage plans to Fiyin, they'll have nothing more to do with me... they are saying... they are threatening to take the children from me and—'

'Trailer load of rubbish! Not while I'm still alive!' Afulenu said, sucking her teeth.

'Was Kene's uncle part of this meeting?' Somadina asked, his voice weary.

'Daddy, he was the meeting convener!' Still sobbing, Kaira

repeated I.G's parting words to her after the meeting. 'Chimakaira, you will fight for the custody of your children, but your fight will be long, bitter, and an effort in futility.'

Somadina's greatest fear had come upon him. He had not thought I.G would live out his threat… at least not this soon. In the quietness of the room, Afulenu stared at her husband.

'Soma, how long have you known about this… this demonic blackmail?'

'Long enough.'

For the remaining hours of the night, Afulenu snuggled a little tighter to her husband, fearful of the raging war ahead but girding herself in readiness, nonetheless.

⌒

Anita's call formed a scowl on Fiyin's face.

'I sent you a text message. Check the link and call me back.' Not fast enough in rewarding her friend with a lashing for waking her up at three in the morning to read a text message before the line went dead, the little envelope dancing on her phone screen earned itself a long and loud hiss.

'Your friend, Ifeatu, is a devil. Open this link.'

Cold crawled up Fiyin's spine the moment she clicked on the link; it directed her to Jessica's blog site. Between the article publication on 'The Hush Vine' and the comments it generated, Fiyin battled with which contributed more to her current rage bank. Wait, what? 2,022 comments?

didiflo-

'These New Age lovers think they knows everything. Throwing away our cultures and traditions, all in the name of love.'

suzzyq-

@didiflo 'Please, go and sit on a dump! First off... THEY KNOW (the pronoun 'they' must be used with the verb – know). The relationship between your pronouns and verbs need a hell of fixing. Your bad belle is letting your illiteracy shine so bright. Jealousy! Go and beg God to give you the kind of love worth fighting for.'

Kokobabes-

'If only this girl had just settled for one fine Yoruba boy, this thing would not have gone this way.'

Adababy-

@kokobabes 'How will she? Your response alone says it all. She will be settling if she goes for a Yoruba guy. Do they *care for* their wives? When it comes to maintaining women, Igbo guys are too much! Abeg, leave the girl. She followed her heart.'

MrYarn-

'Sorry oo. Since when did women "morph" into appliances in need of maintenance?'

Yoursintippex

'Hi guys. I have one creed I spread when I troll blogs... ONLY SMALL MINDS DISCUSS PEOPLE... And @suzzyq, RELATIONSHIP NEEDS not NEED! At least, power-scrub your grammar before conferring the title of ILLITERATE on anyone (not cool from any angle). Don't burn me, please. I am only contributing my quota to humanity, one Tippex stroke at a time. CIAO!'

Shineloading-

@Adababy 'Which heart did she follow? Goat! Igbo ritual killers, 419, kidnappers, cannibals!!!'

Adababy-

@Shineloading 'YOU AND YOUR GENERATION ARE THE GOATS! Yoruba demon! Do I blame you? All you need for your wedding is your suit. Your bride's family will practically fund the entire wedding.'

Firefirechamp-

'Na who chop belleful dey fall in love.'

Selfie123-

@Adababy 'Wedding, not marriage, right? Let your small brain decide which is more important. Mumu!'

SirRalph-

'What's all this nonsense? This is one thing I hate about social media. Now we have left the issue on ground and started talking rubbish. Anyway, I don't blame anybody here. I blame our corrupt politicians. If they created enough job opportunities, we wouldn't have had the time to be crawling all over social media. I come in peace... We are one. No Yoruba, Hausa, Igbo, Efik, Tiv or Urhobo.'

Adababy-

'God forbid bad thing! We are not one and will never be one. PS Those of you cursing me, may you offend your helpers!'

Kukumena-

'From this post, it's obvious that the girl is a fortune hunter! Someone who knows her told me that the only reason she is following the boy, like bee to nectar, is because he's a millionaire, working in one of these IOCs.'

Firefirechamp-

'Anybody here want to make cool cash, visit www.sharpsharp coolcashfire.com and let's end poverty in Nigeria, forever! 30% of your investment every month and you receive your capital within 48 hours of requesting.'

Checkers2005-

'Fact check!! The boy is a doctor based in Saudi Arabia…!'

Nenendia-

@Adababy 'My auntie has been the major provider since her wedding day, and we are Igbo. Your theory of Igbo men "maintaining" their wives is pure BS! Responsibility, not tribe, is the required currency for running a home.'

Suzzyq-
'Oh God, when! Please, when will my own oil boy locate me?'
@Yoursintippex, 'Ah ahn! We dey fight? Thanks for correcting my honest typo though.'
'PS Some of us only use this medium for entertainment… We are not small minds!'

Freshboy-

'Please does he have a sister? I need a bride in mega cash.'

SamOgene-

@Freshboy 'Animal! Don't go and find work. Sit down and be waiting for rich BAE.'

Mallamcoolaid-

'The girl must be using black magic from her caste system to control the guy.'

Firefirechamp-

'Invest NGN50,000 and make NGN300,000 in one week. Visit www.sharpsharpcoolcashfire.com.'

TejiriUSA-

@Mallamcoolaid 'Are you sure it's not the other way round? Maybe it's the guy holding the girl down. Otherwise, with all the pain their relationship is causing her family, why can't she let go already?'

Omogepoison-

'You never can tell. This may be workings of the famous backyard magic. And Mr @firefirechamp, no work for here. Go find mugu for your papa backyard. Olodo! FRAUDSTER!'

Adababy-

'Dear 'my auntie is the breadwinner', please cross-check your lineage well. You are not Igbo.'

Nenendia-

@Adababy 'Your ignorance deserves a Nobel prize.' @Yoursintippex 'Nice one!'

Firefirechamp-

@Omogepoison 'The thunder wey go fire your mouth still dey do press up. Last, last, I go still chop your money. If I no chop your money, na poison go kill you. Oya, say Amen. Ode!'

Suzzyq-

@Omogepoison 'Which other backyard magic abeg?'

Covenantkid-

'If you are reading this, Jesus loves you. Repent!' @Yoursintippex 'God bless you.'

Omogepoison-

@Suzzyq 'Ah, ahn, you don't know? The one down South – famous for the downfall of great men. Wink, wink.'

MissAkpan-

'Rubbish! Is there gold in her own? Abeg! I think there is more to this thing than the so-called backyard magic.'

Nenendia-

'Or maybe they are just helplessly in love. Believe me, when love hits, the membrane between your heart and brain becomes porous.

Moreover, are we just going to ignore how hypocritical all this is? We will be the first to scream racism when we travel to the abroad, yet here we are, two people from the same country, both melanin popping! Kai!'

MissAkpan-

'She is a witch. Let her remove her fangs, and let us, less complicated babes, try our luck.'

Selfie123-

'Fact-checking the fact-checker... the guy is based in Naija, o!'

Eastmeetswest-

@Covenantkid 'Hallelujah.'

Mallamcoolaid-

'Word around the area says the girl is a bean-flicking virgin.'

SamOgene-

@Mallamcoolaid 'How do you know? Did you go visiting?'

Sheer shock at the plethora of cutting comments tore through Fiyin. A throbbing in the back of her head added rhythm to the reverberating words from the many people without faces, robbing Fiyin of any hope of more sleep. *Kaai! Ifeatu why?*

She slid her phone into her bedside drawer. Renewed regret washed over her, she should not have agreed to meet Jide and his folks.

The following hours wrapped Fiyin in a quicksand of emotions. Only good manners and consideration for Chike, Ifeatu's husband, stopped her from calling before seven in the morning. Chike answered on the first ring.

'How dare you, Ifeatu?' Nostrils flaring and heart rate racing, Fiyin held on, with all her might, to her last string of decorum. 'Of all the things to share... my private issues, and with Jessica of all peop—'

'Good morning, Fiyin. Ifeatu is still asleep.' Five and a half odd seconds of silence slid by before Fiyin collected herself enough to apologise to Chike.

'No worries at all. I'll ask her to ring you back once she's up.'

'Chike, I am so sorry for—'

'No worries. My three sisters are on a higher echelon of expression,' he said and hung up, his voice dripping with the humour only he acknowledged.

⌒

Waves of melancholy rode with the evening breeze, washing over Afulenu. And as though reprimanding herself for indulging in the luxury of self-pity, she cleaned, in one angry swipe, the stray tear on her left cheek. She crossed her arms over her chest, running her palms over them to ward off the chill. Moreover, she did not want her husband to sense her hopelessness. Afulenu often feared for Somadina's health. During the trials of the past years, Somadina suffered a blood pressure spike and had since been on Coveram 5/5 mg.

Of all the marriage tips buried in Afulenu's trove, one from her mother occupied a prized spot. 'When fighting with your husband, maintain back-to-back formation. Never forget you're on the same team. Never turn on him.'

With the events of these past months, Afulenu's marriage had gathered speed on a southbound destination, and with a crippling sense of foreboding, she envisaged the looming repercussions. So, one rainy night, while Somadina lay on the couch in his study – his new-found sanctuary since I.G's intervention, Afulenu arrived at a decision.

'Against my maternal instincts, although at war with myself, I am willing to defer to your leading, Soma… Nothing is worth placing our health in the balance. And with our recent endeavours, one of us may soon have serious health complications. I only pray our son doesn't live his marital days in regret, wishing he fought harder.' Afulenu's decision was bathed in her tears, but her voice gave not the faintest clue of a quiver. That night, her words nudged Somadina towards a new path around the mountain in the centre of their child's road to happiness. Afulenu agreed with her husband's resulting proposal but wondered, in private, if a path littered with possible pain for I.G would not serve a more fulfilling purpose.

In silence and unseeing, husband and wife stared over their balcony at the mass of nothing floating above the gate of their Ikoyi home. Somadina and Afulenu agreed on the absurdity of Nwafor's suggestion. Although they suspected their counter plan may meet with fierce rebuff, they believed Nwafor's was more atrocious.

'Do you think she will agree? Won't she believe we have gone quite mad? Did you speak to her afterwards?'

'We can only try. Stop worrying, my dear. Besides, the dinner isn't until two days time.' Let's save all our worrying until then.' But the rapid flutter of Afulenu's eyes betrayed the uncertainty beneath the unflinching confidence of her voice. Should she tell Somadina that, since accepting their invite, Fiyin had stopped picking up Jide's calls? In her heart, Afulenu understood Fiyin's reaction. Perhaps a short time of reflection was responsible for the rays now beaming on her folly. Her folly in attempting any form of cordiality with them.

Afulenu's phone ringtone caused a brief distraction from their thoughts.

'Mum, I may not be home in time for dinner. I am driving to her. I will park at her gate if I must.'

'Hello, hello. Hold on. I can't hear you.' Afulenu swung her phone left and right, scurrying back to the bedroom, in search of a better mobile signal; a mobile signal that was never lost.

'What do you mean, drive to her? How will you gain entrance to their estate without a call from a resident? Why not try her a few more times?' she said once she escaped her husband's questioning eyes.

But Jide did not want to keep trying. He wanted to be able to read every crease in Fiyin's face. Every wavering of her brow. Every quivering in her mouth, Jide wanted to read them all. Since the events after their introductory visit, a thick fog had engulfed Jide's certainty.

'Oh, I see!' Afulenu said. But Afulenu did not really see. She did not believe in the brilliance of her son's plan, but she reckoned any plan by far outranked 'no plan'.

⁓

Wafts of cigar smoke unfurled into the night air. Every breath reminded Fiyin of her childhood, on those Saturday evenings, when she visited Ikoyi club with her parents. Nostalgia pulled at her mood, which Anita was not helping to make any lighter.

'Certain people in your life only pretend to care for you because they want your gist, first-hand.' With so much on their minds, going into the club did not pose the usual attraction.

On Fridays, the club, ever ablaze with guests, often provided a cleansing arena for corporate Lagos to exorcise their hamster-wheel demons. Guests fewer than a normal person's fingers speckled the sit-out area, chatting in hushed tones.

For Fiyin and Anita, sitting outside under the night's cloud, inhaling a mix of rich cottony ocean breeze cocooned in the mild floral scents from the beds of the Queen of the Night, offered a better promise of reflective solitude. Once white, the marble benches they sat on now looked more grey than white from years of persevering through sun and rain.

'Maybe Ifeatu didn't expect her cousin to make merchandise of my misery,' Fiyin said in her friend's defence.

'Mmhh? How so? Abegi!' Anita was not buying it. She had easily become one of Fiyin's favourite companions since the visit from Jide's folks. With Omo's head far into the clouds over Ben and her new leaning towards spiritual emergence, Fiyin saved herself the disappointment which every so often tailed expectations. Else, why was Omo not returning her phone calls or text messages after sending her one-line text message announcement about her planned journey to Benin… with Ben?

Anita nursed her cocktail, swishing her drink around in her mouth as she stared at her only friend.

Once, Fiyin had asked Anita how her salary from the hotel funded her classy lifestyle. With a glint in her eyes, she had confided in Fiyin, about her 'escort services' side hustle.

'You offer escort services?'

'Yep.'

'Oh.'

In one breath, frost had replaced the glint in Anita's eyes when Fiyin began to highlight the gaping hole in her moral fabric.

'Until you do, Fiyin, you have no right to judge me.'

'But we are friends. Can't I be honest with my opinion? At lea—'

Shutters slid over Anita's frosted eyes, and within a fraction of that moment, the baseline and boundaries of their friendship were set.

Anita slurped a mouthful of her drink, leaned back into her seat to regard Fiyin from under her lashes.

'Why do people like to play around with food they can't eat, while the one they can enjoy without fear of indigestion goes to waste?'

'Please, don't start with this Ali matter.'

People, food, and indigestion. Fiyin understood Anita's analogy. Short of kneeling before Ali, in blatant supplication for his attention, Anita had tried everything.

'As rich and influential as the guy is, you are forming attitude. Na wah for you, Fiyin. You worry, o.'

'As pathetic as this may sound, I have no more room in my heart. Jide lives here,' Fiyin said, patting her left breast and sporting a smile, miles away from her eyes.

'Pa-the-tic,' sang Anita into the fast-deepening night.

Two feet away, a couple mistook the club's sit-out arena for their room and began to make unwholesome noises. Fiyin thought they grunted like three he-goats, attempting to push a wheelbarrow full of yams. It made her stomach churn in disgust.

'This your friend, is he coming or not? I'm legit sick of this place,' Fiyin said, pushing away her still-full-but-no-longer-chilled glass of Chapman.

A call came through Anita's mobile, and in a clipped tone, she said, 'Yes. No wahala… see you soon.'

Reaching for her handbag, Fiyin said, 'Look, it's getting quite late, and I hate night driving. Besides, my parents will soon start calli—'

'Girlie, Ali is on his way. I told him abou…' An instant furrow formed between Fiyin's brow, stopping Anita's flow of words.

'Wait… Ali is the friend we've been waiting for?' With blooming impatience, Fiyin endured Anita's explanation. How, since the abrupt end of her internship at the hotel, Ali had stopped by daily. Cajoling, begging, and bribing her, with irresistible gifts, to make her convince Fiyin to pick up his calls. How Ali shunned her flirting efforts; 'I'm a trophy hunter. I hunt harder when my preys elude me,' he had said. Anita also talked about Ali's dejection last week, after another refusal from her to arrange an 'accidental' meeting between himself and Fiyin.

'Ali Dansule's shoulders sagged! How much can a sister bear… I mean, we are talking about THE Ali, girlfriend!' Anita's tone was conciliatory.

Too late. Fiyin could not get away fast enough.

'Please, don't run. I promise, I won't bite… won't even scratch.' That infinitely annoying cockiness reserved only for the likes of Ali Dansule! Eyes darting between Ali and the car park, Fiyin measured how much time Ali needed to reach her if she ran. *His legs are too long*, she thought, giving Anita the eye. Anita's sudden preoccupation with something inside her phone infused a shot of amusement into Fiyin's anger.

'Do you believe I spoke to a PR friend of mine earlier today? We explored the option of putting out a public notice… in search of the most gorgeous five-foot-six female alive.' A smile played around Fiyin's mouth.

'That bad?'

'Desperation makes a man do the outrageous.' Ali's cocky smile was on recess. 'Can we see tomorrow? Please?'

Fiyin obliged, and almost as though it never left, Ali's smugness returned. With only a few meetings between them, Fiyin now squinted, in search of the line separating Ali's conceit from his more acceptable courteous confidence.

Fiyin did not return Anita's limp wave. She gave her the eye as she wove her way out of the club's crammed parking lot, into the less safe, yet more familiar night. And through her rear-view mirror, she saw Ali and Anita walking back, towards the club's entrance door.

The next day, Anita visited bearing a parcel.

'What is this?' Fiyin said, giving the box a cautious shake.

Anita smiled. She not only took note of Fiyin's peculiar frown, but also found that almost imperceptible rise in her left brow white-bunny cute.

'Open it first,' Anita said with a chuckle.

'No, nau! You shouldn't have! I'm no longer angry, nau! Now, I'll look horrible if I reject it!' Growing excitement made Fiyin struggle with the ribbons on the wrapped box. It was a globe-shaped night light, preloaded with the Serenquillity application – audio Bible verses on a bed of soft piano tunes. Fiyin had heard about the app. It arrived in the software market only weeks ago and still hung far beyond reach for the financially weary.

'Anita, nooo!' *Wait. A note?*

'*Hope you like.*

Serene and tranquil thots,

Alee.'

An inner voice told Fiyin to reject the gift, to snap out of her lull from logic, to get her feet off her adventure roller skates, but she did not. In, at first, little waves, and later bigger waves, a tingling started spreading from Fiyin's chest to her stomach, all the way to her toes. It lingered long after she bade Anita goodbye. Long after her dinner, and right before Ali's name danced on her phone screen. She tapped the answer icon to hear him ask, 'Who did Cain marry?'

'What?'

'In the book of Genesis, after Cain cancelled his bro, Abel, and wandered away, who did he hitch in the land of Nod?'

'Ali, are you reading the Bible?' The disbelief in Fiyin's voice reached through the phone line to draw a smile from Ali's mouth.

'Should I not?'

'I don't mean... I... I mean, it sounds—'

'Sounds implausible?'

'Sort of.'

'Cos I'm Muslim?' Ali's tone exuded a quaint blend of markers; light and strained. Larky and sombre.

Is this guy laughing? Does he think this is funny? This was one of the two subjects Fiyin dreaded discussing or dissenting with people she generally liked, people with whom she did not intend to cut ties with: religion and politics. Fiyin did not understand why Ali was reading the Bible, so she asked him.

'I'll tell you tomorrow if you agree to have lunch with me.'

'Sorry, I have a meeting with Mrs Azike.'

'Oh yeah! The famous Mrs Azike!'

'You bet!'

'Can I ask a favour?'

'What?'

'Please don't drive. Let me take you. I promise not to be in your way. I'll drop you off for your meeting, go about being up to no good as usual, and return to pick you up once you are ready.'

'Oh, shoot!'

'What? What's the matter?'

'I have dinner to attend at... with my—'

'You have a date with your man?'

'Not exactly. Uh... with his folks. For a discussion, chat... I'm not sure...'

'You're all right, Pheephee. But you still haven't told me who Mr Cain married... or are you as clueless as the rest of us?' The quality of amusement in Ali's voice goaded Fiyin into providing an answer.

'Introspective. Not clueless. I plan on confirming when I arrive at the pearly gates... among other things like the existence of an alternate universe. Don't think I should develop a migraine over issues of such little consequence... on this side of reality.'

'And I'm cool with your self-preserving mode. So about tomorrow, I pick you up after your meeting, we have a quick lunch, and I drive you back in time for your date, I mean discussion... with Jideofor's parents.'

Lady Intuition's warning about the suspicious simplicity of Ali's itinerary met with Fiyin sticking out her tongue at her.

FIFTEEN

A SOFT ANSWER TURNETH AWAY WRATH

For the best part of twenty years, Ifeatu Osita and Fiyinfunoluwa Taylor had shared their lives; the ups, the downs and the sideways. They moved within the same circle of acquaintances. Sometimes, a new friend came along but seldom survived the grafting process. For many of those friends, Fiyin broke no sweat, but not so for Jessica, Ifeatu's cousin; Fiyin loathed sharing air space with her. So, finding herself and Jessica in the anteroom attached to the private ward of Oasis Hospital proved an arduous task to execute. Ifeatu once chided Fiyin years ago when she and Jessica bared their fangs at each other.

'She is family, Fifi! Jessica is my cousin! Family functions will always feature her. Abeg, learn to ignore her, biko!'

Sometimes, Fiyin allowed herself to recall the one time she questioned the authenticity of the righteous indignation Jessica's presence often evoked in her. Years ago, on Ifeatu's father's sixtieth birthday, as usual, Jessica made her entry almost two hours into the party, her recently acquired car crunching its tyres on the gravel-covered grounds of Chief Osita's home. And not until Ifeatu scampered to the car, to ask her to turn down the music blaring from her car speakers, did Jessica decide to tone down her arrival. Femi, Fiyin's classmate asked, 'Fiyin, who's the babe?'

'Jessica… Ifeatu's cousin.' Fiyin's mouth bent into a left and downward tilt. Ann's mouth formed a space between her lips.

'Wow! Sweet ride!' she said.

'I tell you!' Femi said, slow bobbing his head at his girlfriend who went on, 'Oh boy! The ride fit the chick die!'

Bile spread over Fiyin's tongue. The reason for all the cooing and heroine-worship eluded her.

'The model is notorious for its unreliability. Soon, the raining season will unleash. One puddle and it's gone. Look. It's already leaking.' she said, pointing under the car, in what she thought to be an arcane manner.

'That's AC water,' said Femi and Ann in unison, and a wet cloak of mortification settled on Fiyin for the remaining part of the party. Through the gaiety and the twisty turns on the dance floor, Fiyin's dripping cloak of shame clung fast to her skin; it still flashes in her mind's eye every now and again.

Other than the gentle hum from the air-conditioning unit, the room remained silent. With Fiyin's gaze decisively fixed on her phone, Jessica's attempts to strike eye contact, let alone a conversation, yielded nothing.

'Fifi, who told you?'

'What?' Anyone would have assumed Fiyin was talking to someone inside her phone.

'About Ifeatu… the bleeding.' Jessica applied intentionality in her disregard of her companion's aloofness.

'This morning… I called for… for something else when Chike told me.' Fiyin's eyes held fast to her phone's screen. A soft self-loathing nudged at her heart; she had not known her friend was not merely avoiding her calls.

On a different occasion of less severity, Jessica would have made a snide remark about Fiyin's gruff tone, but she subdued the urge.

'Mehn! Ify gave us a scare yesterday, I swear. You need to have seen Chike. The guy was shaking,' she said instead.

The full weight of what Ifeatu's state portended rested on Fiyin, and she sent out a silent prayer for mother and child to be safe.

After almost an eon, a round-faced nurse with kind eyes tucked her head through the door. 'You can go in now.' Jessica and Fiyin sprang to their feet. At Fiyin's ensuing hesitance, the kind-eyed nurse added that Ifeatu wanted them to come in together, before shutting the door. At once, Jessica sauntered away from the room with Fiyin forcing her feet to follow.

'Nwanyi, how far!' Ifeatu smiled at her cousin's customary greeting. A moment passed with Fiyin shifting from one foot to the other, watching as Jessica dropped her bag on the lone chair to hurry to her cousin's bedside. She pinched Ifeatu's cheeks. 'Hmm! Some colour at last!'

'Uh… I… came as soon as I learnt.' Fiyin's eyes were searching, somewhat conciliatory as she stood by the door, for the first time, the third person in the room.

'Yes. Chike told me about your call. Come, sit,' Ifeatu said, tapping the space next to herself on the bed. Jessica walked back to the table by the door, peering into her cousin's food flask before walking off to settle in the only chair in the room. After Ifeatu's lunch of boiled unripe plantains and smoked fish with pumpkin leaves, she explained what landed her at the hospital. 'Placenta previa. The doctors say I must retreat into hibernation and, while at it, eat like a starving horse… to keep my placenta nourished. Fare thee well to my hopes of snapping back after the push! Fifi, if you open that fridge, you'll weep for your friend. Hah! In the name of obeying doctor's orders, Chike and his supporters rammed a festival feast into it!' But Fiyin thought Ifeatu's distress over her failing plan to regain her slim figure after childbirth sat at the bottom rung on the ladder of pressing issues.

Jessica let out a loud yawn. She placed her right leg over the left and let it down again to cross her trainers clad feet at the ankles. The 'kin-kin' and intermittent popping of her chewing gum, pulling at the taut tranquillity, poked at Fiyin's every nerve. And mere seconds after she started to embrace the comfort of her budding indifference, the bedside telephone gave a shrill ring.

'Your auntie is here, ma.'

'Let her in.' Ifeatu set down the receiver, heaved herself from the bed to go to the bathroom. 'I'm coming. These days, I pee like a punctured city water reservoir,' she said.

Auntie Onuwa let herself in. On seeing Fiyin sitting on her niece's hospital bed, her next words came in rasped breaths. 'Blood of Jesus! Where is Ifeatu?' The woman angled her head towards the other half of the room, her dread for Fiyin and the space near her apparent.

'Bathroom… Pop!' rang Jessica's answer. A scared squirrel would have exhibited better comportment. Auntie Onuwa's steps faltered. She pressed her back into the door, mumbling unintelligible words. Soon, Ifeatu returned and did not require elucidation on the reason for the taut air in the room. Still, she courted normalcy.

'Auntie, you remem—'

'I don't need any introduction. So, Ifeatu, after everything I told you, wisdom is still far. I am coming. Let me go and call your mother. If anything happens to you or your baby, aka'm n'ukwu'm adirokwa ya. I will not be held responsible. I have done what I should have done. I brought your dinner. When she goes, call me.' Auntie Onuwa pulled out a food flask from her nylon bag, took four indecisive steps towards the bed, to set it on the overbed table. She snatched the flask with the remnants of her niece's lunch and marched out of the room without another word.

'Na wa, o.' Jessica said, expelling the breath she had held without much success. At least now she could breathe. She still did not understand why Ifeatu's auntie never used perfumes, never used make-up products, always wore oversized skirts and blouses, and never found the right cream that would not leave her knuckles and ankles blackened.

A tear escaped Fiyin's right eye, in response to her now quivering lower lip.

'Fifi, I am so sorry. My mother's sister is such a loudmouth.' Ifeatu cast a tentative glance Fiyin's way, willing her to understand, to forgive her less-than-tactful auntie. Fiyin swiped an angry hand at her tear-stained face.

'Do I blame her? What do you expect when people can neither protect delicate matters entrusted to them nor mind their business when they happen on such matters?' Fiyin said to the room.

A glance, almost too quick for the untrained eye, passed between Ifeatu and her cousin. Jessica shifted in her chair. 'I'll be leaving soon… I have a meeting with a client who will go bonkers if I come one minute later than we agr—'

'Another client. What a pity.' Fiyin's voice rang an octave higher than she intended.

Pop! went Jessica's chewing gum in response. Pasting something best described as a hybrid of a smile and a scowl on her face, Ifeatu sat back in bed, grimacing at the vicious kick in her belly. Fiyin shifted from one butt to the other and let out a low cough. The growing silence now choking, Ifeatu buckled. 'Would you ladies…uh… like anything… from the fridge?' Since she received no response besides more silence, she asked Fiyin about Omo.

'She is not in town,' said Fiyin in a clipped tone.

'My parents are coming to spend time with me, once they return from the U.S.' Ifeatu was clawing about for normalcy.

'Nice,' Fiyin said.

'You know what? I've never fancied splashing around the point. So, I'm no longer going to pretend you and Jessi—'

'Ifeatu, wait!' Jessica set her handbag on the desk by her chair and leaned forward. 'Fiyin,' the slight quiver in Jessica's voice denied the confidence her perfectly arched brows and unflinching gaze fought, with all vigour to exude, 'look, I'm not gonna feign ignorance on how much you despise me, nor will I feign ignorance of the reason why—'

'Choose one.'

'I beg your pardon?' Jessica's eyes fluttered at Fiyin in confusion.

'Either you use "reason" or you use "why". You can't say both.'

Ifeatu's mouth muscles began to quiver. This was no time for humour; she pulled her lips into her mouth, so the tip of her tongue touched them.

'Well, most Americans say both, and I am not writing. Moreover, the point of what I was saying is tha—'

But Fiyin robbed Jessica of her attempt at a dignified defence.

'You are neither an American citizen nor a resident! And for a person skilled in posting not only improper but fake news about people, the least you can do is speak authentic English.' Ifeatu took one look at her friend whose chest still heaved from her gust of words and burst into rib-hurting laughter.

'Are you ladies sure you don't want some of the decadent ice cream in my fridge?' Her shoulders still shook with ill-controlled laughter.

'I am sorry, Fiyin.'

For a moment, the room fell silent. The simple art of breathing now required mastery, like walking on a line across a gorge. And when only four eyes fixed on her forehead promised to be the only response her words would draw, Jessica said, 'I realised, a tad too late…what I did was unfair. What started as a naughty poke spiralled out of my control, and all my attempts to claw back yielded nothing.'

As hard as Fiyin held on to her hurt, reason won in the end. The rapid-waterfalls-like rushing of her blood and rumba-type beating of her heart started to slow down.

'All the clawing you need is to take the damn post down!' Fiyin's words squeezed themselves through her teeth.

'My exact thought!' At last, Ifeatu found her voice and continued, 'Nothing good is coming out of your post! I even heard there have been protest resignations in some government parastatals... by people who... who... '

'By fellow Osus, you mean,' Fiyin said, her face looking as though a bad odour had filled the room and somehow overpowered the appealing smell of bleach mixed with lemon-fragranced floor cleaner.

'True,' said Jessica, 'but are you reading all the comments the post is evoking? People are talking, Fiyin! Something we don't do enough of these days. Granted, a bunch of loafers started the discourse, as is often the case, but somewhere within the chaos, the embargo on sensibility lifted. And check this, I control the narrative of your story if I hold the reins. You will shudder at the other possibilities lurking in the crannies of the blogging industry.'

Fiyin shook her head in urgent jerks, in dissent. She sprang off the bed to begin pacing, her hands gripping her waist.

'No, no, no, no, no. I'm not having any of that, Jessica. There is nothing positive about people losing their means of livelihood, stoking unnecessary tensions and bitterness. All avoidable stuff! Why didn't you check with me... before publishing anything? Why did you run off with the gist from Ifeatu?'

'But I didn't tell her anything... Jessica, tell her!' Ifeatu's nose flared as her tone took a downward inflection. Her eyes were beginning to shimmer with unshed tears.

'So, who did? Unless you want me to believe your cousin dearest is clairvoyant... or are you?' A sharp retort slid to the tip of Jessica's tongue, but the emerging sheen in Fiyin's eyes pushed it back down her throat.

'My source forced me to sign a non-disclosure... but on everything I live for, Ifeatu didn't tell me anything,' Jessica said, instead.

Ifeatu splayed her hands upwards, proclaiming her innocence.

'Non-disclosure my ass! Who gave you my story?'

'I can't tell you that, it's unethical!'

'YOU are unethical! Ifeatu, tell your cousin to name her source.'

'Jessica, tell us, nau. Who gave you the gist? You can see Fifi is pained.'

'I cannot tell you!'

Back and forth, side to side, in and out they went for almost fifteen minutes, but Jessica refused to give a name.

'Guess what? I am no longer bothered. I hope you and your informant are now swimming in ecstasy. My romance with the Williams is over, finished, dead... You guys can concoct and write whatever. Jessica, bask in your conquest. Do what you do best. Go ahead! Trample on people, as long as you arrive wherever the hell you think you are headed.'

Ifeatu shook her head at Fiyin, as a mother would at her tantrum-throwing toddler.

A hush swaddled the room the moment Jessica said she would take down the post.

'Yes, take down the post and experience your first swipe at decency... believe me when I say it's a worthwhile and extensively liberating endeavour.' Jessica's tongue barricaded her own retort.

Ifeatu took a lungful of air. 'So, all is settled! We, at least, agree on one thing... publishing the post was a mistake,' she said, heaving herself up to hold her waist, towards her back, with both hands. As she stretched her legs and began wriggling her toes, a frown fell over Fiyin's face.

'Ify, you sure you're good?'

'Well, yes… before you robbed me of a significant portion of my lifespan, mediating between you and Jessica.' Fiyin's unwilling lips moved in a small smile.

Jessica looked up from her phone, let out a short giggle before she said, 'Done… the post is down. Fiyin, for what it's worth, I'm sorry.'

'I'll live.'

The slight shrug from Fiyin reminded Ifeatu of the parable of the broken raw egg. And to lighten the thick air, she said again, 'Does anyone want some ice cream? I have chocolate chip, cookie cream dough, and peanut butter party flavours!'

'I'm in! I want!' Jessica said.

A buzz from her phone made Fiyin nearly jump. She whipped it out from her handbag, swiped up. *Damn! Twelve missed calls and four text messages from Jide.*

'I forgot! I am supposed to meet with… Jide… and his parents.'

For the third time, the room fell silent. 'Maybe they want to formally apologise for… for… whatever,' she said by way of clarification, her tone a scale higher, battling to dwarf the silence stomping about. To wrestle to subjugation the glare from the four eyes which now threatened to char her, Fiyin tapped a button on her phone and walked out to the anteroom.

⁓

For Fiyin, Ikoyi often inspired a sense of something elusive. Sometimes, the ambience of Lagos's pride and joy of dated wealth evoked in her a vague longing for inclusiveness. Today, the looming silence hovering over the streets made Fiyin clutch her steering wheel. And for good measure, she imagined the royal palm trees lining the street to the right and bending away from the strong evening wind were, indeed, deriding her with their obeisance. Like a messenger leading the town's jester to the palace, to be either applauded by a delighted royal or executed by a displeased noble, Jide drove ahead of Fiyin. A dinner in honour of Somadina's sixtieth birthday was quite in order. But extending an invitation to her and following up with calls to ensure her attendance caused a keen unsettling in Fiyin's stomach. *Maybe they want to absolve themselves from the reason Mum and Dad lost their jobs... or is it to cut the last thread between Jide and me? It must be something along the lines of, 'God has a better plan for you, dear.' Or maybe they want to suggest a way fo... no, mscheww! Who am I kidding?* The short drive saved Fiyin from beating herself sore with her own thoughts.

As soon as Jide called to say, 'We are close,' Afulenu planted herself by the awning. 'My darling!' She all but ran to the car, wrapping Fiyin in an embrace once she stepped out of her car. 'Hope we didn't drag you away from anything important?' Afulenu took a step away but did not release Fiyin's hands.

With a nervous giggle, Fiyin said, 'No, ma.' Jide sat back in his car, his eyes trailing them as, hand in hand, they walked into the house. A force pulled his heart to the bottom of his belly. He feared who would emerge afterwards... his future wife or his ex-fiancée.

Kaira made the trip down to Lagos, but her children stayed back in Enugu with Kene. The last time Fiyin and Kaira chatted was over the phone, months ago, when Kaira told Fiyin to pay her husband's uncle no mind. 'Nobody can stop you guys from getting married. No one wields that much power,' she had said. But Kaira had since stopped responding to Fiyin's calls or text messages.

'It may be family life taking its toll. I will call her... this is not typical of Kaira,' Jide would often skip to his sister's defence each time Fiyin worried.

Today, Kaira pasted a prudish smile, refusing to meet Fiyin's eyes, even when Fiyin followed her to the kitchen to help with taking the food out to the dining table.

Afulenu regarded her son for a few moments. He had not said two words all evening. 'You're not enjoying the food?'

'The food is perfect... I may have stuffed myself at lunch.' Shoving a forkful of broccoli into his mouth, Jide underscored his excuse.

'You must be bursting from food to ignore the chicken,' said his mother with a mischievous smile. She went on to recount an age-long delightful family anecdote. This appeared to ease, to a marked degree, the burden of whatever bothered Kaira, because for the first time since Fiyin's arrival, she laughed. According to Afulenu, as a child, Jide's 'frequent' headaches showed a remarkable level of reverence for cinnamon-flavoured roasted drumsticks. Since he loathed school assignments, he always feigned a headache any time one surfaced. Not once did little Jide imagine how much advantage adulthood offered his mother who soon discovered the magic stick with the power to rid him of his headaches. 'J-boy!' Afulenu would often call to a 'shivering' Jide, 'Drumsticks!' Out, Jide would spring from his bed, his headache and fever abandoned under his sheets. Suffice it to say, Jide always had his schoolwork done. Today, not only did Jide's head ache, but his heart did too. Nsikan's new improved cinnamon-flavoured chicken roast tried but failed to cajole these aches back to Jide's room, under his sheets. *What if she says no? What if she thinks I am no longer worth the trouble? I am sure she...*

'Hope you like the food, Fifi?' A hint of a smile formed creases around Somadina's eyes.

'Yes, sir. A lot.'

'Nsikan had it prepared... uh... more peppered snails?' Afulenu's fawning flowed unfettered, and a wrinkle appeared on

Fiyin's forehead; at how heavy the words, 'We are sorry, but it is for the best if you both went your separate ways', would be on the woman's lips when she, at last, spoke them. Incipient contempt for the man who once filled her world with colourful bubbles pushed against her insides.

'I am full. Thank you, ma. It was really delicious.'

On the few occasions Fiyin visited the Williams' home, it often wrapped her in a warm welcome. But today was different. Today, as she trailed Afulenu to her room for a chat, the marble floor felt like snow under her feet, the white walls glared at her, and the off-whitewood-trimmed marble stairs bade her come, as though to a guillotine.

SIXTEEN

KNOWING ME, KNOWING YOU

'One-day-old Jide. The boy almost tore me to shreds with his big head... This one is his first day at school. He cried so hard. Jide hated leaving home. These days he can't wait to leave... His tenth birthday! The girls had begun to swoon. I remember his first crush. Hah, Jide! You need to see the cute oyinbo girl! Ah! Boarding school! Look at his long neck. I wept so hard when he returned for his first holiday, and after only two terms, I enrolled him in the day school he graduated from.' From one page of the album to the next, Afulenu fed Fiyin delightful morsels of Jide's childhood. But once Afulenu closed the photo album, her eyes lost their previous light. Her voice settled into a low hum.

'Darling, I need not cut your hearts open. The love you both share is in plain view. Jide's dad and I have been searching for any solution to correct the course of this journey. Everything somewhat spiralled out of our control.' Afulenu let out a long breath and Fiyin sucked a short one at the older woman's next words. 'The reason I wanted to talk to you is to... Fiyin, my husband and I discussed this at length and agreed to ask you if—' Afulenu's phone started to ring. 'One moment, love. I must take this call.' Afulenu left her room through another door.

Strength and sweetness were qualities Fiyin admired in Dr Afulenu Williams. But those same qualities brandished the jagged edges responsible for making futile all Fiyin's efforts to fit Jide's mother onto a shelf. A shelf Fiyin built with painstaking precision. A bespoke shelf for entitled mothers who thought little of trashing all obstacles obstructing their dear sons' utmost comfort and satisfaction, harsh consequences regardless. Another album beckoned Fiyin, but she lost her chance at a quick peek because the door creaked open.

'Oh! You are here? Where is my mum?' Kaira's feigned surprise at seeing Fiyin in her mother's room shone with stunning clarity. Fiyin jerked her head towards the door leading out to the balcony from Afulenu's bedroom.

'Outside… call.'

~

Fiyin walked in front of Afulenu, out of the bedroom and down the stairs. At the foot of the stairs, leaning against the wall, Jide pinned his eyes on Fiyin's bare feet, waiting for her to walk past before he raised his half-closed eyes. Spine straightened, shoulders rolled backwards, Fiyin walked on. A lacklustre painting in a gallery would most assuredly have received a glance, but not Jide.

'What did she say?' Jide's whisper to his mum floated towards Fiyin. Her legs did not carry her fast enough for her ears to evade those laboured but urgent words. Every syllable of Jide's enquiry, made taunting by their crispiness, fell like sharp pines on Fiyin's back.

'She would not let me get to it. I went to the balcony to take a call, and when I returned, she looked like a chick under the shadow of a hovering hawk. Next thing I know, she grabs her bag and…' Breathless, Afulenu scurried past her son.

With the way Somadina grinned at her, Fiyin no longer doubted if there were two little horns buried inside the man's moderate afro. *How dare he smile at me? Spineless hypocrite. Sending your child to… to do your filthy laundry!*

'Leaving?' His brows rose.

'Yes, sir.'

'We will see you again… before we return to Abuja.'

Not sure if Somadina was asking or telling, Fiyin said, 'Mmhh.' Confusion and concern drew a furrow above the bridge of Afulenu's nose, pulling her lips like a baby not quite certain if it should cry or try to be brave.

As fast as her legs allowed, while fighting to retain composure, Fiyin fled to her car, the voice in her head screaming, *It is over! Over! I am never having anything to do with Jide. Never! Never again! And to think I cancelled my meeting with Mrs Azike and Ali for this!* Fast pooling, her eyes smarted. Cold air from her car vents licked the tear streaks off her cheeks. These past weeks had startled her with a growing awareness; deep in her heart, Fiyin feared she would crawl on hot coal if it guaranteed a life with Jide. Therein lay her undoing. And long after every happy, content, honest and normal person had floated off into sleep's cocoon, she stared, unseeing, at her ceiling, listening to Jide's voice note.

'My sweet pea, something strange happened in my mother's room, of that I am certain. But I am begging you to trust me enough to tell me what. I would be unarmed if you do not. In this whirlwind I am prepared to ride out, all I need is your trust. Help me, Fifi. I wanted to do this on my own, but I guess the fear of failure crippled me. So here I am, nose to nose with my folly… again. One more chance is all I ask, my love. Afterwards, I will let fate decide. This is all I ask. Fiyinfunoluwa, I am in love with you, and the worst part is, I cannot be anything else… anyhow else with you.'

After the thirteenth play, Fiyin hit 'delete'. To hell with the Williams and their untainted bloodline.

Fiyin called the gate to grant Ali access, took one last look at herself in the mirror before she began to stuff her purse with face tissue, her driver's licence, her ATM card, and some petty cash; for if she became angry and decided to abandon her date. On her way to the door, Fiyin half hoped she did not look underdressed. She wondered if her three-inch-heeled silver pumps and white chiffon top on zebra-patterned bottoms would match whatever casual class Ali would brandish.

'Now, who's she trying to impress, Mrs Azike or little old me?' Ali's eyes crinkling at the sides as soon as Fiyin reached his car pulled a giggle from her. Comforted but in no way fooled by the veiled modesty of Ali's matching white linen top on trousers and brown leather slippers, Fiyin slid in beside him, intent on having as much fun as the occasional violent tug at her heart would permit.

With one tap of his finger, Ali peeled back the roof of his car, allowing both the mid-morning breeze and curious eyes better access. Tunes from 'Busta Rhymes' filtered through the car speakers, and wide-eyed amusement spread across Fiyin's face as the lyrics from *Dangerous* and *Make It Clap* rolled off Ali's enthusiastic tongue. The drive to Mrs Azike's Banana Island residence pulled Fiyin up a learning curve – grown men enjoyed rap music.

Not too long after Fiyin walked through the gates for her meeting with Mrs Azike, she dialled Ali's mobile.

'Wow. This wins the award for the shortest business meeting, ever,' he said, beaming the moment Fiyin closed the door after herself.

For the one millionth time, Ali asked Fiyin, 'What was your appointment about?' Maybe because the weight of the disappointment threatened to crush her, or perhaps because she hoped for some truth in the saying, 'a problem shared is a problem halved', or maybe because the urge to release the sobs bubbling deep in her chest was too powerful to overcome, but this time, Fiyin told him. She came to cancel, in person, a request her father had made on her behalf. Fiyin came to inform Mrs Azike of her change in plans. She would not be purchasing a property any longer. When red-faced, the lady asked why, Fiyin said she was ill-prepared to take the dive into open waters but believed another year of internship would do her much good.

'All right, so I'm hoping you'll tell me the real reason you cancelled.' Ali gave Fiyin a tissue with which to dab at her tears. She began to deny the existence of any other when Ali's short and mirthless laughter stopped her.

'People don't cry when they make changes in their career decisions, Pheephee... not in the absence of an underlying cause. Why did you cancel, Pheephee? Cash issues?'

'No!' Fiyin tucked her hair behind her ears to stare, unseeing, at the zapping scenery on her side of the car. 'Can you put back the roof of your car, please? I think it attracts attention... in a childish way.' Fiyin's words came in short bursts. She blamed herself for being a crystal glass.

'Oh! Cash issues, then.' Ali drove in circles until Fiyin asked if they were no longer going for their planned lunch.

'Sure! I'm only waiting your scowl out... don't want my fans thinking I forced the most gorgeous lady alive to lunch.' His bland face, combined with his response, tickled Fiyin's mouth into a smile. Fiyin aimed only to give a conciliatory rub on the back of Ali's hand, but he held her hand, touched her knuckles to his pursed lips as his eyes locked with hers. Everything happened within split seconds, but Fiyin's heart drummed like one straight off a marathon. Busta Rhymes' voice filled the air, saving them from the torture of the awkwardness of the next few minutes.

For Fiyin, valet services were not a common fixture in Lagos, but with the seamless exchange of greetings and handover of car keys between visitors and staff, she suspected the clientele of 'The Clove' did not share in her inference; they trod on familiar turf. From the sublime lighting to the benign chatter, and the seemingly floaty movement of the service staff on the three-inch-thick black rugged floor of 'The Clove', nothing of the food Mecca mimicked ordinary. Ali had taken Fiyin on a lunch date to a place where only a miniscule fraction of the privileged one per cent of Lagos residents dared to tread.

From the corner where they sat, away from the centre of things, the gentle hum of discussion still reached them, and Fiyin wondered how many ordinary people like herself were in the building. How many, if any, mustered the effrontery to contribute to the gentle hum of conversation. Fiyin tried but failed in stimulating her thinking faculty. In the end, she ordered the same meal Ali ordered for himself – the house's special – and jumped at his suggestion to try a drink called 'Dry Waterfalls' too. Any time Fiyin allowed herself some respite from trying to decipher what her meal comprised, she stole the opportunity to appreciate the well-looking waiters and waitresses – she suppressed the urge to ask Ali what they were called. Certainly not waiters and waitresses! They looked like mid-level bank executives.

Ali broke his silence during their dessert of 'Chocolate Mess': a wafer-cave-surrounded mound of pistachio, vanilla, and hazelnut ice cream with a lava of dark chocolate oozing from its centre. How they were able to achieve such a clash of temperatures registered itself as a source of torturous research for Fiyin in the weeks following her outing.

'So, let's talk about Jesus.' With the tip of his tongue, Ali wiped off a streak of dark chocolate from the side of his lower lip, pinning Fiyin with an amused twinkling stare.

'About Jesus… the Christ?' Fiyin's eyes grew in circumference, her brows rumpling.

'Yes, the Christ. How can you guys believe he is the son of God and also God?'

'He said so. As a Christian, I believe in the divinity of Jesus

Chri… but wait… why are you so interested in Christianity? The other day, it was Caine. Now it's Jesus. Are you growing dissatisfied with your own religion?' Ali did not believe anybody held the monopoly of beliefs, who should or should not share in which of them, and he told Fiyin so. Still, Ali expected more from Fiyin; he expected an educated answer. One not drenched in the pool of dogma. In his opinion, many religious enthusiasts were lazy, and fierce in their aversion to any notion contrary to their indoctrination. So, he gave her one more opportunity to redeem herself.

'What gives you the conviction of the Trinity, God the Father, God the Son, and God the Holy Spirit? If they are one, how come Jesus Christ kept referring to God as 'My Father' and 'He who sent me'? How come He admitted only God the Father holds the timetable of His return? If they are the same, who did He cry out to on the cross of Calvary? And why, Pheephee, why did He promise to send the Holy Spirit after his ascension?'

'Look, Ali, the Bible I believe in says my God is three in one. By faith, I believe every scripture of the Bible. Now, if you believe my faith to be foolishness, permit me to remind you of my entitlement to exercise my foolishness to the full extent of my liking!' Ali's eyes lost their initial sparkle. He thought the three-pound matter encased in Fiyin's skull deserved better representation.

The cosy chatter of conversation now distant and the awkwardness around them now distinct, Fiyin's eyes skirted everywhere but around Ali. At ill-timed intervals, she picked up her phone, scrolled through and set it down again by her glass. Sipped her drink, picked up her phone again, scrolled through. Sipped more of her drink, picked up her phone. On and on the cycle went, until Ali, almost breathless from enduring the steadily thinning air, sought to reinject some cheer back into their fast-waning afternoon.

'Well, I guess these grey areas exist to remind us of our mortality. Right, Pheephee?'

'Thank you for a most entertaining time,' Fiyin said at the entrance to her home.

'No worries, Pheephee… it's what I do.' *Cockiness becomes Ali… most times*, Fiyin decided. Ali reached for Fiyin's shoulders, turned her away from him and towards the door. He lowered his head a fraction and said to the back of her right ear, his voice a low buzz, 'In case this little piece of information somehow managed to elude you, I have money… scratch that. I have a shit load of money, and I love to share.'

'Well, I like to earn my own pay, kind sir! Good night, Ali.' Fiyin all but ran into her house.

Later at night, after a ten-minute-long phone conversation with Ali about her father's indefinite suspension and the current clamp on their finances, Ali promised to throw some weight around. 'I'll hook you up to earn your own pay, Pheephee,' was the last thing Ali said before he bade Fiyin sweet dreams. A little while after, Jide called Fiyin's mobile phone. It rang out. Twice. After Fiyin said her bedtime prayers and slid under her sheets, Ali's face flashed in her mind's eye. If her response about the divinity of Christ evoked such disappointment in him, she cringed at the monumental let-down the hosts of heaven must have suffered.

Please, God, explain this to me, because I too do not understand, she said in silent and involuntary supplication.

Devoid of the usual frenzy, the hours between five and eight o'clock in the morning now idled by in the home of the Taylors. Only days after Donald began his suspension, Bree received a recommendation, from her line manager, to tender her resignation. 'The order came from the top,' he had said.

Sunday, their driver, soon found himself without a job as well. And for the longest time, he would erroneously believe his street-fight of the week before bore the blame for the abrupt termination of his employment.

A week after Donald's suspension, he received a call from the police area command. Sunday had been arrested, and for the first time, Donald found himself within the walls of a police station. The deplorable condition of the building shook him to his core. A curious stench hung in the room. How dirty can a room with a wooden table, two plastic chairs and an unclad floor be? Red soil peeped through four broken portions of the cement-plastered floor of the reception; one at the entrance, two in the centre of the room, and another to the left, joining the wall where it met the floor. On the high desk, from behind which two scowling and red-eyed officers served him snide glances, Donald spotted a little mound of melted candle wax, and on cue, looked up at the ceiling, where he expected to see a light bulb, only to find a broken bulb holder, half ensconced in a nest of cobwebs. He sent out a silent prayer for a swift and scandal-free resolution of his case with the university tribunal; the thought of being confined within those grounds made the hair on the back of his neck stand.

A few minutes before two in the afternoon, Fiyin returned from her new job where she offered her service as masseuse to Ali's aunt for $750 per hour, three times a week. Something about the employment pack pulled at her caution strings, but she took the job. Bree met her at the door. 'Welcome, baby! How did it go? What is the work condition like? Hope she's a nice lady?'

Alhaja Aminat with the sonorous voice was a delight to work with. A tad chatty, but a delight, nonetheless. She wanted the details of Fiyin's friendship with her nephew.

'I think he is into you. I can tell from the way he goes on and on about you… we are quite close, so, best believe me when I tell you, this isn't one of his regular park adventures,' she said hours ago, while Fiyin kneaded away the countless knots in her shoulders.

At the end of the session, Alhaja charmed Fiyin into tea at the poolside where they shared gourmet cakes, sweets, and some tea of course; an occurrence Fiyin would learn to accept as standard practice each time she reported for duty. Bree breathed a sigh of relief. 'But the salary though,' she said, shaking her head, wondering how many oil blocks Ali's father awarded his sister.

Bree asked Donald if he wanted anything from the pharmacy. 'I'll stop by after fellowship.' She now attended daily prayer meetings at 'Restoration Christ Rock Ministries'.

'No, nothing.' Donald did not want anything… well, maybe a pill to wake him from the nightmare of being jobless and in the throes of a fraud scandal.

After Bree left instructions for lunch with Fiyin – rolled wheat flour with okra soup – she scurried out of the house. Although almost certain of his response, Fiyin asked her father still. 'Will you be going out, Daddy?'

'No.'

Fiyin planned a lock-away in her bathroom. She intended to soak in her tub for as long as the water remained warm. Donald sighed as she turned to leave. And not one to miss the undertone in her father's sighs, Fiyin's strides faltered.

'Come, sit,' he said.

Apprehension clutched at Fiyin's heart. *What now.* She slid into the chair beside her father. Donald's words came with great effort, like they were being pushed out, kicking and scratching from his throat. Or was it his chest?

Fiyin's meeting with Mrs Azike about cancelling the search for a property pained him.

'But you don't have the money any longer. Daddy, your bedroom walls are not soundproof, but you and Mummy often forget.' Donald heaved. He never intended for her to find out about the freeze on their accounts.

'I am your father, and my obligation to set you up has not been reviewed... My mistakes are mine to remedy, you shouldn't and will not pay for them... This new friend of yours and the job he found for you... Fifi, I'm not sure... Things are not as terrible as they appear. And... and I quite understand your current disposition, but don't lose faith in your parents... Not yet...'

Most times, a tremor in Donald's voice often only embodied deep emotion. But not so today. Today, Fiyin recognised the tremor in her father's voice as the clarion call for an adult male to burst into sobs; she clamped down on her retort about God working in mysterious ways.

Instead, she said, 'I am so sorry, Daddy. Now your perspective is clearer to me.' Fiyin's hurried steps away from the sitting room had not carried her far enough when the doorbell rang, pulling her back, past her father and to the door. *Mummy?* Bree did not look pleased.

'Ah, ahn, Fiyinfunoluwa! K'oda, nau. I taught you better!' Father and daughter's eyes widened in utter bemusement.

'If only for courtesy's sake, you should have at least picked up the boy's calls, haba!' Bree gave her daughter the eye as she plunged into the seat beside her husband, kicking off her shoes from her ankles. Every day since the past week, Jide parked, for two hours, outside Waterpark Estate, hoping for one of the cars driving in and out of the estate to be Fiyin's. Today, in a last-ditch effort, he called Bree and now drove towards their estate with the speed of a demented bull. Donald glared at the invisible horn in the centre of his daughter's head. Fiyin's lips pursed before turning downwards; her eyes and shoulders followed.

Spa-type music blended into soft lighting, mild chatter, and food aromas that teased tongues to wetness.

'Let's kill this thing, Jide.' Eyes shimmering with tears belied Fiyin's words. 'I am exhausted! The strain of defending our relationship, rather than having one… is… is draining me.' Fiyin did not wonder at Jide's refusal to break eye or hand contact with her. Almost as if such a break would make her disappear again. But she pondered on his reason for not asking her why she refused to take his calls or respond to his text messages and voice notes. It stretched her reasoning to its limit.

'But we do not have to defend anything, Fifi. We have a relationship. Ignore the blind bats, they do not get it. They will never get it.'

Fiyin leaned her back into Jide's chest. He made room for her, letting her cheek rest on the arm with which he held her close. One teardrop heralded a few more. Jide's sleeves were rolled up to about three inches below his elbows, and a dark patch now formed on the right sleeve where Fiyin's tears landed.

'Everyone we hold dear is hurting. Your folks, my folks, our friends… you… you thought I wouldn't find out, but didn't Timi and Nnamdi almost come to fists on our account? And Ifeatu! Jide, you won't believe Ifeatu's baby dedication is next month, and I am not attending.'

'Wait, what? Why?'

'Apparently, my "condition" is contagious and may contaminate her child… or at least, so her auntie believes.'

For many moments, Jide did nothing but stare at Fiyin. Of all the consequences of her relationship with Jide, its blow on her friendship with Ifeatu surprised her with the same sting a mother's first smack would surprise her favourite child. But Jide's utter ignorance of what his parents truly thought about her surprised Fiyin most of all. One finger at a time, she separated her hand from Jide's clasp as she sat up to turn towards him. She took his face in her hands, pressing them into his prickly cheeks, as if to assure herself of the tangibility of him. Jide's heart began to thud in ominous rhythm to her laboured breathing. A stream of tears, which she swiped away as fast as they emerged, accompanied her words.

'That day in your mother's room… when she left to take a call, Kaira came in and said… ho… horrible things to me.'

'What – did – Kaira – say to you?' Jide's tone dropped to a whisper.

'That I should release you. That you're a prisoner of your chivalry. That your parents were between two impossible choices because of me. How they were at the verge of losing friends, family, and influence… She also talked about her marriage, how she would lose her husband, her children, her life. That letting you go would be proof of any decency I may have. Two days after, I received an anonymous note at work… the second of such, with a one-liner. "Stay within your species or…".' Fiyin inhaled a lungful of air.

'Gosh, Kaira!'

For endless moments, Jide stared at Fiyin, his eyes searching. 'But Kaira would never go that far. That note has I.G stamped all over it,' he said.

'Well, until now, I thought your sister liked me. But I think you are right about Kene's uncle. I am afraid he is also behind the case against my father… We learnt the whistleblowing came from the top.' Fiyin sounded small.

'How? How can you bear to still look at me, with all the pain I have caused you, my love?' Jide made a hand signal for the bill.

'Fifi, Please, come with me.'

'Where?'

'Somewhere. Please, I need to speak to you in a place where... some place private. I need to talk to you, and I need you to hear me.'

⌐⌐⌐

'My plan was to make a proper meal of the surprise, but... here we are!' Fiyin's breath caught in her throat.

'Did you rent a duplex, Jide?'

'No. I did not rent a duplex, my love. I bought one. Almost cracked under the strain, but...' Jide said, a small smile tugging his lips to the right. Save for a Persian rug in the centre of the living room, the house lay bare.

'Oh, my goodness! White walls!'

'Because white is your favourite colour.'

Quick steps took Fiyin to the kitchen with Jide following.

'No kitchen cabinets?'

'And risk your wrath? "Happy wife, happy life", they say. You have unfettered authority here, sweetheart... if you will still have me.' Jide's voice exuded an element of huskiness which made his words sound more intense. Fiyin threw her head back in a stifled chuckle. Up the stairs, past a small lounge, to the bedrooms; only walls, floor tiles and more walls greeted Fiyin. But the bathroom attached to the master bedroom made Fiyin blink. Three large windows embellished the proportion of the already large bathroom, drawing Fiyin farther in.

'Ah! A hot tub! I love the play of white and peach. Honey, this is simply exqui—' Fiyin turned to look at Jide, but he had dropped to his knees. 'Why are... Jide, what... what are you doing?' Alarm rang in Fiyin's voice. He leaned towards her, held her around the waist, his face turned upwards.

'Fiyin, please! Please stick with me. Believe me, my parents did not send Kaira on her stupid rant mission. True, her marriage is under threat… which compelled me to speak to my folks… a gross error on my part, as I have come to realise. People do the most bizarre things when… I admit soliciting my mother's help… to convince you was not only an absurd idea, but one which should make me apologise for wanting to touch the concept of marriage with a ten-metre pole.'

With a half smile, Fiyin unclasped Jide's arms, making to pull him up. Jide let out a broken sigh and got on his feet, fighting for the words that refused to form in his brain. 'Fifi, my darling, my love, I have a thought.' His words came out bumpy. 'Please, sweetheart, think about what I am going to tell you… bef… before you certify me a lunatic. I want… let me… let us…'

A chuckle escaped Fiyin's pursed lips, her two-stepped gentle retreat, her half smile and wrinkled forehead indicative of puzzle-tainted amusement. 'Jide, what? Why are you…? We are not here to plan a heist, are we?'

Jide blew raspberries, let out a sigh.

'Your parents will never agree to us eloping. But if I… if we got into a situation, would they not be a little more amenable? You and I… we can go to some island. Leave all this behind.'

Eloping? Situation? Island? The deepening crease in Fiyin's forehead prompted further elucidation. Jide sighed. 'Your parents would never be able to bear the pain if… if we left without a plausible explanation. But if we… you… um… perhaps convinced them that in the throes of passion, we made a mistake, and I made you… and you became pregnant, they may be willi—'

'What? You want to make me… you want me to become… pregnant?' Fiyin's chest heaved, her nose flared, and her eyes narrowed. She moved further away from Jide. 'Jesus!'

'Fiyin, sweet pea…' Jide pulled in air into his mouth. 'I… do not mean… I am not going to… I mean, you will not become pregnant in the actual sense… but… but your folks do not need the extra detail.'

Fiyin shut her eyes, flung them open, squeezed them shut and snapped them open again. She cast a quick glance at the open bathroom door. 'Wait! Fiyin, please!' Jide started towards her, stopped himself. Stress lines pulled his forehead into horizontal ridges. Now close to the bathroom door, the anguish in Jide's voice made Fiyin stop. She turned towards him, her chest rising and falling in rapid succession. Jide took four strides to close the gap between them.

'What I am trying, and failing woefully, to articulate is… In our present circumstance, your options are many… You are a whole remarkable human being. You know it, I know it, your folks know it. But if we present them with a hopeless situation which appears to obliterate your options, they may not be as opposed to you and I relocating to some place safe… A location only a select few would be privy to. That way, Kaira would not have to pay for my problems.'

'Us is a problem?'

'Fifi! I did not mean that!' Jide's frustration was becoming harder for him to contain by every ticking second. He took a few steps away and began to pace the bathroom.

'Your parents… are they in on this? Did you… do they… are they aware of this… this fake pregnancy elopement plan?' Fiyin's words stilled Jide's feet, halting his pacing. His eyes drooped at the sides.

'But for this cultural roadblock, our parents already gave their blessings. And before God, nothing else legitimises any union… the rest is a string of formalities. So, doing what married loving couples do would not be a square moon. My folks understand this, so no. Their suggestion is for a real pregnancy. But we have our values, do we not? I… I reckoned a feigned pregnancy should present a more workable option… my mother offered to explain it to you in a way we all hoped you would understand.'

'In a way you ALL hoped I would understand.'

'Fifi! Please don't be like this!' In three long strides, Jide covered the gap between them again.

'Be like how? Your ground-breaking plan is to have me hide away from the rest of the world for the rest of my life! How the hell else do you want me to be? After asking me to not only lie to my parents but to abandon them?' Fiyin said, her tone brusque, her breathing laboured.

'Well, I... I do not know what else to do, Fifi! I beg you, meet me half way! The only alternative, which is not an option, is Uncle Nwafor's ludicrous sugge—'

'Uncle Nwafor too? He is also being consulted?'

'Fifi!'

A quick holding out of Fiyin's hands put an abrupt stop to Jide's attempt at a hug.

'Fifi, please... don't... don't push me away.'

Fiyin let out a mirthless giggle. 'Tell me, Jide. I'm curious, what's Uncle's bright idea?'

'I'd rather not,' Jide said, walking away to rest his back on the white-tiled wall of his bathroom, from where he stole micro-quick glances at Fiyin.

'Please do tell. I am certain your entire village would also have a thing or two to say about the love life of their darling son!'

'Now you are being hurtful.' Jide stuck his hands in his pockets, began to draw patterns on the floor with his eyes.

'I'm being hurtful.'

'Yes, you are, Fiyin. And since you insist, Uncle Nwafor suggested you and your parents go for a cleansing ritual in my village. To... rid yourselves of all the so-called gunk of the caste system.'

Fiyin shook her head in bewilderment. After a few moments of blinking and swallowing nothing, she asked Jide if he believed his bright idea would fool his sister's uncle-in-law. 'No, since you've got it all planned, tell me how MR.IGNATIUS would miss it when, in one flash, the buzz about us wanting to be married dies and not long after, we disappear?' Indeed, Jide had it all planned. Fiyin would feign a relationship with Ali, and he with Omo. The already mad blogger would go madder, and the news would, with any luck, spread like desert fire. As soon as Omo was ready to join Ben, he would disappear. Everyone would assume they left the country together. When the public moves on, she would join him at the destination of their choosing.

'I want to go home. Please take me home… now!' And so, what began as an evening of desperate romance, contoured by the cruel fingers of an impossible love, ended in a bizarre web of unease. Fiyin purposed to put an interminable gulf between herself and the Williams, this time for good.

⌐⌐⌐

An alarming number of missed calls and text messages blinked on Fiyin's mobile phone in the morning. Eight calls and five text messages from Jide.

I called you all night, but I quite understand why you would rather not speak to me. I had to return to Abuja this morning. An emergency. Salpingectomy. Just landed.

'Please, call me when you can. I love you.'

'Hi, sweet pea. I am still waiting for your call. About last night, please scratch everything I said.'

'Fiyin, I'll have you on your terms… whatever you propose. Please call me.'

'I do not have a plan B. Tell me when to come to you. I love you, Fiyin.'

Two missed calls and a text message from Ali.

'Hey, Pheephee. I have a nickname for King Solomon. SKS; Smooth King Solo! How did he manage to slide his letters into the most popular book of all time! I'm free to chat whenever you are.'

Without a thread of restraint, Fiyin sent her response: *'I'm free.'* And in two hours, they were in another one of Ali's cars, on their way to another exotic restaurant.

'It's a floating diner… first of its kind in Nigeria,' said Ali, every bit the proud host.

Later that night, the two friends each pondered over a different segment of their outing. Fiyin snuggled under her duvet, waiting for the gentle lull of sleep, as she relived the entire evening. The great food, alluring ambience, amiable banter, time spent listening to track after track from LL Cool J, filtering from Ali's car speakers, and picturesque scenery during the leisurely evening drive reminded her of what an amazing evening she had. But of all the highlights of the evening, one stood in sparkling splendour. Ali's exhaustive 'improvement' on certain sections of the book of 'The Song of Solomon' taunted Fiyin until she tottered on the precipice of squeamishness.

Ali, sitting on the balcony of his pent-floor flat in Ikoyi, relishing both the night breeze and the last few drags of his shisha, berated himself on end for not having an adequate retort for Fiyin's eventual explanation of the Holy Trinity. First, Fiyin referred to his quest for a broader view of the two most popular religions as 'a skittish affair' with his spirituality.

'Why do you devote your energy to questioning my faith, rather than concentrating on living and enjoying yours?' she had said. And, to her eventual summation about a certain peace, a certain settling which came with knowing that a person will, in due time, come to the knowledge of all things, Ali conferred on her the lifetime ambassador of laziness, complacency, and dogmatism; challenging her to question the divinity of Jesus Christ. Halfway through their fruit platter, Fiyin had asked him if he believed in the concept of God as creator of mankind and the three-dimensional nature of man – spirit, soul, and body.

'Yes, Allah is the all-knowing creator of all things. But we are two-dimensional beings, not three. I believe we occupy a body here on earth and when we die, our spirits are called to Jannah or Jahannam. Paradise or hell.'

'Oh, yeah? Then you don't dream, right?'

'What do you mean? I dream, silly! Ali needed no telling; the wheel of their conversation was fast slipping from his grasp.

'There you go, dear friend. The soul is the third dimension you forgot. If the body of a mere mortal can remain in bed, allowing its soul to float off in a dream to wherever while its spirit ensures life remains, how much more the immortal and invincible God? As a potent reminder of our mortality, I suppose we are limited to exploiting only two dimensions. I believe The Almighty God functions in all three dimensions. HE seats on HIS throne as God the Father, Jesus Christ operates as our advocate or redeemer as God the Son, while the life-giving enabler walks the earth as God the Holy Spirit! Kapish?'

Hours after their date, Ali tried in vain to shrug off the heaviness which Fiyin's simple, yet somewhat convincing concept of the Holy Trinity foisted on him. His want for an adequate comeback not only surprised him. It irked him.

The day after, Fiyin missed her usual phone banters with Ali, but Anita's visit did more than atone for her looming solitude. For hours, the ladies shuttled through cooking, eating, talking about work, bemoaning the state of infrastructure in the country, and regretting the depletion of family values. Values which they were certain would have ensured a steady supply of responsible marriage-worthy males, had they been inculcated in boys early — and to the requisite extent. As they washed plates, pans and pots, Anita ventured towards more sensitive subjects.

'So, how far with Jide?'

'Not far.'

'Ali, nko?'

'What about him?' By now Fiyin's shoulders threatened to snap. Anita turned off the tap, to give Fiyin her full attention.

'Which of them are you dating?'

'Does it matter?' Fiyin's brusque tone sent a note of caution to Anita who paused to draw deep breaths, examining how best to say what she needed to say. Should she tell Fiyin how meeting and befriending her had given her a reason to dare again? Would Fiyin understand how the values she held, the way she expressed them, had since applied araldite to her own broken moral compass? What would Fiyin think if she told her she drew strength and purpose from her? That she lived vicariously through her? Oh, how she wished Fiyin would remain the girl she first met, the one so unlike herself.

But Anita shrugged instead. And as she turned on the tap again, she said, 'And so my pristine friend joins the world of worldly-wise women!'

'Says the queen of them all. I'm only following your trail, Your Majesty.'

'Never judge a book you are yet to read,' Anita said.

'All right, can I borrow this book, please?'

'I'll think about it… maybe I'll read it to you, someday.' Anita's tone allowed tentative humour back into their almost ruined evening.

~

The window on the passenger's side of Anita's car slid down, and Fiyin leaned over to bid her friend goodbye. 'We should do this again… soon,' she said.

'Yeah.' Anita blew air out of her mouth and turned on the ignition. A while after, she turned the air-conditioner knob. 'I'm scratching around for money… for my mother's stem cell transplant, that's my "why". Don't ever change, Fiyin. Remain true to who you are… people like you are the only thread of hope people like me cling to.' With Anita's stick now in drive mode, Fiyin pulled away from the car, and Anita melted into the night, leaving her friend with a gully between her brows and a gap between her lips.

SEVENTEEN

ANSWERS ABOUND AT THE FOOT OF THE BRIDGE

For the best part of the night, and a few nights after, Anita's parting words kept Fiyin awake, questioning who she was becoming and why. One file at a time, she played back Jide's catalogue of voice notes, and one chunk after another, his voice gnawed at her mountain-high layer of defence. And only days after her solemn vow to have nothing more to do with him, Fiyin dialled Jide's number. 'How did the salpingectomy go?'

A few feet from the shoreline, waves sent tiny rays of water their way. Fiyin and Jide sat in a two-seater basket swing chair, licking their salty lips every now and again. Jide swallowed a mouthful of air, and after three heartbeats, exhaled. Like heat would melt wax, his words made a puddle of Fiyin's resolve.

Jide apologised for his aloofness to how his great plan would alter not only her life, but those of her parents. He admitted pushing his normally rational parents into a gorge of guilt for placing Kaira's happiness over his. 'Why else would folks as sensible as mine agree to such an absurdity?' Fiyin's heart drummed hard enough to reach her ears. Why was Jide evoking in her a sense of foreboding? Were these the introductory lines of his break-up speech? But soon, clasping to his now more urgent words, the drumming quietened. 'Sweet pea, several people are moving on from this "caste system" confusion. Kene's uncle is the only one poking the beehive... perhaps, he is the one to tackle.'

'Tackle I.G?'

'I am afraid so.'

'That man is a real principality and power!'

'Prince of Persia and Anambra.'

'No, ruler of darkness.'

'I am most certain the descriptive phrase you seek is, spiritual wickedness in high places... Wait, I got one. I got one!'

'What?' Fiyin was already chuckling in anticipation of whatever name Jide would manufacture.

'Igna-satan-us!'

Fiyin cast Jide a sharp glance, as though only now aware of his presence.

'Oh my God, Jideofor! I fear you may have missed your calling. You are a confirmed nomenclaturist!'

They burst into long and purposeful laughter. After they quietened, streaks of tears still in the corners of their eyes, the tremors from their recent exercise still tingling in their bellies, Fiyin asked what Jide meant by tackling I.G.

'But how do you mean, tackle him?'

⌐━━⌐

'Ji-de-o-for! I cannot go grovelling before that man!' How Jide came to such an absurd decision baffled Fiyin. A man whose name alone twisted his belly strings in knots. A man who would much prefer people with her impediment to migrate to Uranus.

'The man thinks I come from a long line of misfits... of, of unclean things! You... you loathe the man, nau!'

'I do… still do. Sweetheart… wait… please listen to me for a minute… please? From what I learnt from Kene, the man lives for attention. Maybe that is all he wants. If we give I.G what he wants and he agrees to drop this matter, perhaps even throw his weight behind us, no one else will bother us, ever again. But if he decides to continue to fight us, life can become ugly… especially for my sister. If grovelling will solve this, please let us grovel. I beg of you, Fifi.'

Near riotous voices in her head and the profound silence in her car competed for precedence as Fiyin drove home from the beach. Somewhere in between, Jide's words tormented her.

'If grovelling will solve this, please let us grovel.'

What will my parents think?

'If grovelling will solve this, please let us grovel.'

To go and explain to a man who considers my whole lineage a contaminant how we are not quite as diseased… ha! It doesn't make any sense. I will only confirm my desperation if I do.

'If grovelling will solve this, please let us grovel.'

Will this not set a precedent for my married life, deferring to whatever catches Mr I.G-THE-GREAT'S fancy?

'If grovelling will solve this, please let us grovel.'

What if he never stops reminding me of my heritage? Won't this shadow loom forever?

'If grovelling will solve this, please let us grovel.'

No, I cannot, I will not. Jide is not the only man in the world. I should not deal with this mess. I am Yoruba. I am not Igbo… But you are half Igbo… history says so.

Before her frayed nerves and darting thoughts began to yield to the little tranquillity the thought of sleep dangled, Fiyin decided to tell someone. Dad and Mum would never approve. Who else could she discuss this mad quest for approval with? To seek consent from someone of kindred spirit with the devil, as had been articulated to her, sounded both scary and beneath her. *Who else? Where in heaven's name is Omo? Ifeatu is not an option! Will Anita understand?*

~

'Have you suspended all logical thinking, Pheephee?' Incredulity grew Ali's eyes to almost the same size as the apples Fiyin served her Saturday afternoon guest. Yes, guest. Ali did not receive as much 'pushback' from Mr and Mrs Taylor as he had feared he would. Not once did Ali delude himself enough to expect the Taylors – devout Christians – to welcome a Muslim as their only child's male friend. But they did. And why not? The friend was Ali, the son of Professor Aminu-Dan-Dansule, the ex-minister of petroleum, whose influence made Donald's looming prosecution vanish; after only a minor settlement with what should have been the start-up funds for Fiyin's catering career.

'Easy! All I am considering is a visit to someone who may be able push back on a certain traditional obsolescence. I do not intend to... uh...'

'Fawn? Call the damn thing by its bloody name, Pheephee! You are going to the den of some conceited self-acclaimed lion to truckle, to kowtow to... to let yourself be trampled on. Who would have thought. How can you submit to the mercy of that dark-minded traditionalist. All because... because of... Pheephee, come on. You are too good for this.'

'Lower your voice!' Fiyin's eyes darted to the curtain-covered arch leading away from the sitting room to the corridor and stairway, from where she feared her mother played sleuth. 'Nobody is going to kowtow! This is a situation neither Jide nor I can control. Too many good people will suffer if... if we do nothing.' Fiyin's words were now almost inaudible. She got up with a start and rushed to the curtain, yanking it to the side in one quick move, ready to glare at her mother. Nobody. She sighed, her heart slowing its racing.

When she returned to Ali, his arms were folded across his chest. Fiyin chuckled. He struck the pose of an angry teenager confronting his errant parents. On the few occasions he visited, Ali requested one of her signature cookies, iced tea, or fresh fruits. She noted, with no surprise, how the two apples she served him still sat untouched. Pouting in comradery.

'Am I correct to presume the mastermind of this plan is your doctor—'

'Jide... Ali, his name is Jide.' Fiyin did not appreciate Ali's condescension.

'My apologies, Jide. I suppose Jide is the brains behind this brilliant idea?'

Ali pursed his lips, bowed his head in contemplation, and threatened to tell Fiyin's parents.

'You wouldn't dare!'

After a long pause, Ali proposed a compromise. 'All right, I won't. But please, don't go alone!'

'I am not going alone... Jide and I will—'

'No... someone else must go with you. Someone, besides your... somebody for whose spine we can both vouch.' Fiyin bit her lower lip.

'Omo is incommunicado, I'm now an outcast to Ifeatu, Anita can't afford to skip work, not for one day. Who else?'

'Me?'

'You? Very funny... you want to... to... go with...' Fiyin's eyes narrowed in puzzlement.

'Kidding! You shouldn't take me so seriously, Pheephee!' Ali's smile stopped right below his nose.

Before Fiyin reached the door, to walk Ali to his car, the door knocker rattled, taking both Fiyin and Ali by surprise.

'Expecting someone?' Ali's lips dipped in shallow disapproval.

'No. Most likely a neighbour.'

Not a neighbour but an estate guard.

'Anty, one Anty wey I dey por gate since long time. Me tell am make I call your pone, but I say I don lose am por im pone. Anty tell me make I call you. I say no, I say, a beg. I say no, I say a beg. Anty dey cry, cry, cry, say I don go another estate por una priend, say dem no let am enter. I dey beg me, dey beg me, dey cry, dey be...'

'No problem, oga. What is the auntie's name?' Fiyin asked, realising the guard would, if given continued audience, take them into next week with expressing the efficacy and stringency he applied in discharging his official duties. He never broke estate protocols, he never granted access to uncleared visitors – unless presented with a convincing incentive.

Forefinger to his lips, the security guard rumpled his face in thought. 'Ehmm... walahi, I don porget. I say Amu... abi na Uma... kai!'

It was too much. Ali erupted in the laughter he had been holding in for the longest time.

'No worries. I dey come for the gate. Thank you.' Fiyin did her utmost to match the guard's Hausa variant of Nigerian pidgin. She would come to the gate to see the aunty who lost her phone, who had gone to another estate where her friend lived, and was also turned back, and who was now back at the estate gate, crying and crying and crying.

After waiting a few moments for the retreating guard to be well beyond earshot, Fiyin, with a half-smile, reprimanded Ali. 'Ah, ahn, Ali! How rude and unfair can you be?'

'You cannot blame me for succumbing to your guard's irresistible humour!' Ali's shoulders still shook.

'I don't believe the poor guard is to blame. I often wonder at the chasm between the rich and poor northerners. You went to Harvard, yet another human being, a foot away from you, cannot afford to attend a proper school where he can learn the difference between the pronouns "she" and "I", or how and when to use the "f" and "p" consonants.'

'Don't try playing that self-righteous card with me, Pheephee.' Ali still fought his laughter. 'Till the end of time, the rich and the poor will always co-exist. Even your holy book says so.'

'Hmm, Reverend Ali! What chapter and what verse?'

'Jokes apart! I can't quite remember now, but I swear I've seen something like that.' Strolling to Ali's car, Fiyin wondered how many of them he had; this looked new. Well, all of Ali's cars looked straight off the lot. Fiyin slid in beside him for a ride to the gate. Chances were her night guest was Omo.

'Anyhow,' Ali went on, 'I'll tell you why I was laughing. Your estate guard's vocabulary is not the only culprit. Pheephee, the illusion projected by most estate developers is a complete insult to any clear-thinking individual, walahi! Rather than acquire the services of reputable security companies in the league of *Flash Securities* or *Borderline Limited*, they gather people who have zero-to-no training. People who, but for the want for bread on their tables, would be light years away from the industry, and who will, as a matter of statistics, flee at the slightest indication of a security breach. Your estate is not secure, Pheephee.'

'Whatever. Let us be. We'll be fine.' She imagined Ali in a white wig and a black robe. A keen awareness of her sudden exhaustion made her stifle a yawn as she squinted at the cars parked in the estate's buffer zone, in search of her visitor.

'Fifi!'

'Omo!'

⌒

Fiyin did not dare to blink as Omo replayed her ordeal like a movie blockbuster. Ben wanted to experience 'the country'. So, for their visit to Benin, he proposed a road trip. Everything spun in seamless synergy. Well, until they met with an unforeseen knot, about one hour after Órè town. At first, Ben thought they were in for another 'stretching leg break' as the bus driver referred to the stops he made. Most passengers anticipated those stops, to either shop from the swarm of hawkers or empty their bladders, or whatever else. But the sudden invasion of unease confirmed otherwise. This was not a 'stretching leg break'.

'Everybody, stay calm!' The AK-47-wielding robber's loud command, made worse by the hoodie and dark shades he wore, birthed a damp quietness. Dread seeped into every fibre of the vehicle.

'Dude! Hey. There are only six of them. If we pounce now, others will join us... we can bring them down.' Ben paced his breathing, expectant of a response, any response. None came. The man about whom Ben and Omo had been sharing private jokes about the veins and muscles straining on the back of his head did not flinch; he might as well have been deaf.

'Ben, are you mad?' Omo said, under her breath. There were no less than fifteen more of the robbers outside the bus. 'I beg you, in the name of God Almighty, Benjamin, hold your peace!' Through her urgent whispers, muscle-head did not as much as flinch.

One of the six, the one who spoke, began to walk down the aisle of the bus. Omo sank her nails into Ben's right palm. 'Lower your eyes!' Omo's heart was tumbling down to the bottom of her stomach. Wincing, Ben obeyed. A second robber followed, and they both planted themselves by the last seats in the bus. One of the remaining four at the front asked everyone to lift their hands.

'This is going to be a fast operation. We will be nice if you all behave. All we need is your cooperation. Only truth. No lies, and nobody will die here today... no rape.' This robber's English was clean. Within minutes, all the passengers were stripped of their phones, jewellery, tablets, and laptops.

'If you get your ATM card for here, hands up... I say hands up!' Another robber's voice jolted everyone into raising their hands.

'Oya, twenty, twenty K, three, three times! And if I catch you trying to be sharp, eeh!' said yet another robber whose teeth looked to be in fierce contention with his mouth. He passed POS machines to the terrified travellers, his eyes drawing web-like patterns inside the bus. His horrendous dentition would have offered Omo a nanosecond of entertainment had it not been for their perilous circumstance.

Within the longest twenty minutes in history, they were done. With their operation over, the thieves began to file out of the bus and the passengers started to exhale. But at the door, one of the robbers turned back.

'Oyinbo, come!' Ben broke into cold sweat.

'You deaf? I say follow me!' The robber's voice sent chills down the spine of the already shivering commuters. After his first two steps towards Ben and Omo, Ben sprang to his feet and started to float towards the armed robber with his eyes lowered.

One of the few survival tips Ben had learnt was to never stare at a criminal during an operation. Doing so would multiply any chance of the victim's survival by zero. Horrendous dentition asked, 'Na where be your country?'

'Liechtenstein.' Ben blinked at his own lie, another survival tip. As a foreign tourist or expatriate of a light skin tone, never divulge your real nationality. Claim a country less likely to pay a kidnap ransom.

'Leave him.'

Clean-English did not think Liechtenstein was worth the extra luggage. The other robbers began to mumble.

'True talk. Dis guy go be extra weight. And for wetin? Liechtenstein? Oyinbo wey dey travel by bus. Ordinary flight ticket, e no fit buy. Oya go back,' said the first robber, the one who made the introductions. Clean-English snapped his fingers, circled his index finger twice above his head, and with military precision, his accomplices filed out of the bus, back to their heavily tinted off-roaders.

For ten minutes, the bus driver sat motionless and so did his passengers. Not one person dared to take full breaths.

'Shall we return to Lagos?' Ben's face still shone a bright pink. Omo chuckled. The robbers were long gone, but Ben still whispered.

'Ben, how? By bus again? In less than fifteen minutes, we'll be in Benin, let's continue.'

'All right, but we must book our flight tickets back to Lagos the minute we arrive.'

Once at the bus terminal, Omo told Ben she needed a place to change into a dress.

'What, why?' Ben's eyes travelled down Omo's frame twice before they registered the reason for her need: a water map, the size of three adult palms, on Omo's light-brown trousers on her behind and spanning to her thighs in front.

'Oh, sweetheart! I am so sorry!' Without a moment's hesitation, Ben undid his long-sleeved shirt and gave it to her to sash around her waist. The large sweat maps in the underarms of his white T-shirt were by far less of an embarrassment in Ben's opinion.

❦

After dinner, the ladies retired to Fiyin's bedroom. Fiyin still did not understand why Omo did not contact her through their stay, and what kept them so long in Benin. 'I didn't commit your number to my memory. Plus, I don't carry around my SIM certificate like an ID card, and I needed it for SIM retrieval.'

'Oh dear! Na wah for these our telcoms, shaa.'

Fiyin's eyes dimmed in sadness when Omo explained what kept them back in Benin. Her father had found his faith and chose his first wife as the legitimate one. The others, he said, were husband thieves-cum-concubines. According to his pastor, the other women neither had a spot in his new life nor home. But for Omo's mother's thriving fabrics business, she would have considered a relocation to Lagos. It took more time than they planned to find a decent house and get her settled in. A quietness filled the room for several moments, and Fiyin blinked, to clear the annoying sheen in her eyes.

'Ah! What's this?' Omo ran her fingers over the globe on the bedside drawer.

'A night light, preloaded with the Serenquillity app.'

'Babes, wait, seren-what!' Omo knew the cost.

And so Fiyin gave her friend a summary of the events of the past weeks. Omo sitting still through a narration often typified intense disapproval. She was not applauding her friend's adventure.

'Babes, I think you are acting, not thinking.' Omo's forehead wrinkled.

'Because…?' A tinge of annoyance coloured Fiyin's response.

'Because of everything you have told me. Anyone would think you are leaving your options open.'

'When did Ben leave Nigeria?' Fiyin did not want to follow Omo's new path of conversation.

'Yesterday, after we went to your office and learnt, from your manager, about the abrupt end of your internship… only your option is no option at all!' Omo said, insisting on dragging Fiyin along her preferred path of conversation.

'When will Ben visit again? Or have the highway keepers succeeded in scarring him away for good? Why is Ali not an option?'

'Not at all. He'll come, and sometimes, I'll go… until we can't bear the distance any longer… Fiyin, for obvious reasons, Ali is not an option.'

'Obvious reasons which are…?'

'One, you are madly, doe-eyed, heart-flutteringly in love with Jide. Two, you have no spiritual connection with Ali. Three, strip Ali of his influence, wealth and good looks and you are left with a parcel of nothing. Four, by the time Ali takes his second, third and fourth wife, you will—'

'All right, all right... point made!' Fiyin said, fluffing her pillow with added vigour.

'Look, Fifi, I can relate. Sometimes, it's all right to indulge your sweet tooth, but babes, Ali is an unmistakable plaque-forming, tartar-stimulating, cavity-engendering, and abscess-spawning clump of refined sugar.'

'But I have an endless supply of toothpaste, nau,' Fiyin said, an impish smile forming around her mouth and eyes.

'I recommend a truckload of unadulterated activated charcoal.'

'I hear you. Goodnight!' Half smiling, Fiyin settled on her belly.

'And please, about your trip to meet with Igna-satan-us, don't involve anyone else... you and Jide alone should go.'

'I've heard, Omo. Goodnight,' Fiyin said again, flicking off the bedside switch and turning on the night light to fill the room with serenity.

⁓

After two and a half hours from Ikoyi, through Ikeja and Oshodi, enduring the freneticism synonymous with the city of Lagos – cross-drives that make nonsense of the expertise with which spiders spin their webs, car horns blaring their cacophonous orchestra, hawkers running after cars and buses and imploring commuters to buy plantains, wristwatches, bottled water, popcorn, wall paintings, broccoli or puppies; not to forget alms-seeking women with malnourished babies straddling their waists, and LASTMA officials, desperate in their search for erring car users to arrest or levy – the airport in the distance offered such welcome relief.

So far, the most trying part of the morning remained their bout with the Vehicle Inspection Officers, VIO.

A few metres ahead, a group of inspection officers signalled cars to veer off and park on the kerb. Jide had asked the Uber driver, 'Why are you stopping?' He was certain the official did not flag down their vehicle, as the official's eyes were everywhere but on their car when he made a sweeping arm movement towards the road shoulder.

Pulling his mouth into a frown, the driver wound down his car window. 'Morning, Officer.' A shift ever so slight in his cheek muscles accompanied his reluctant greeting.

'Morning.' A gush of cool air and rich fragrance floated towards the officer. His eyes twinkled as they darted around, noting well-looking passengers. 'Particulars!'

The driver clicked open the glove compartment and handed over a thick brown envelope, bursting with his car papers; vehicle license, change of ownership, third-party insurance, tint permit, and road worthiness permit. Officer took out the stack of papers, sifting through each sheet, twisting his wrist to squint at the back of some before shoving the stack back to him.

'Where is your C-caution and fire extinguisher?'

'But Oga officer, that is not your job, nau.' The driver's smile bent into a scowl.

'You say what?' Officer struck a pose with his hands in his pockets, drawing in air to fill his chest.

Jide suspected the driver did not have at least one of the two items. 'Officer, well done! Good morning!' he said from the captain's seat.

'Morning, sir.' The official slid his right hand out of his pocket as he ambled towards Jide, undecided on whether to smile or not.

Jide wound down his window. 'Officer, how you dey, nau!' Fiyin's brows rose of their own volition.

'My chairman, sir!' said the VIO Official, breaking into a smile.

'This sun hot, o! You suppose drink water.' To the untutored eye, only Jide's observation of the weather and suggestion for the officer to cool his supposed patched throat, not the surreptitious exchange of Naira notes, wielded the magic wand. At once, Officer waved and saluted as their car slid back on the main road, back on their way to the airport for their flight to Abuja. Not meeting I.G in Abuja today would mean waiting for another opportunity.

'Next tomorrow, he will travel to his village for their Ifejioku preparation meeting. Make sure you people don't miss him in Abuja,' Uncle Nwafor had said a day before.

For most people, the maxim, 'The night is darkest at the brink of dawn' holds true. But as Jide stared at his phone, he realised the interminable gulf between his current reality and this age-long saying. Why else would Uncle Nwafor call, only minutes after Fiyin and Jide's flight arrived in Abuja, to announce I.G's change in plans? Jide recognised the humour in Uncle Nwafor's voice and acknowledged his folly. Perhaps he should not have involved his father's brother. Why had he thought that incentivising Uncle Nwafor would truly buy him over? Was Uncle Nwafor revelling in his impasse, taking his opportunity to at last avenge his bruised ego for all the indifference and condescension Jide served him for so long? Large beads of sweat hung on his forehead, and his next words were painful to speak.

'I.G left for the East early this morning… and first thing the day after tomorrow, he leaves for Mauritius. I… I am… Damn. I do not know what to do.' Hands akimbo, Jide's eyes swept across the arrival hall, almost like the clues he sought would step out of the walls of the airport if he waited long enough. For some reason, Fiyin found the look of utter confusion and vulnerability on Jide most endearing.

'But I thought you said Uncle Nwafor was on top of this thing, that I.G was now more agreeable?'

'That was what he said… I am… hmmm… I–'

'Sweetheart, calm down. Here's what we'll do. Let's fly to Asaba and hire a car to your village. Hmm?' Jide wanted to lift Fiyin, throw her up, catch her and kiss her; his heart swelled with gratitude. Fiyin had just offered him what he feared to ask of her.

The Niger bridge, an image not more than the length of a tall man's leg, grew larger and longer as their taxi drew closer to it. Once they reached the head of the bridge and the cars began a slow traffic crawl over it, Fiyin snaked her arm around Jide's waist, digging her nails into his side.

'You need not worry, sweet pea… the bridge is solid,' Jide said, his mouth brushing against her ear in a smile. But the integrity of the bridge sat far down Fiyin's list of worries; for some uncanny reason, the air miles between Abuja and Asaba were no match for the chilling finality of crossing the River Niger. The trail of lies she left in the wake of her race towards an uncertain destination pulled at her conscience. To the best of the Taylors' knowledge, their only child chose to travel to Delta state with her friend Anita only because she did not want to be lonely while they were away in Ekiti to visit their oil palm plantation – a venture they now purposed to oversee with more diligence.

An eclectic line-up of hawkers chanting tag lines to charm customers into buying their wares, fishermen on their canoes, and the general difference in atmospheric tone almost distracted Fiyin from the sound of her fast-beating heart. A hawker announced his ware, 'Akwa Ogazi!' Someone from three cars ahead beckoned to the hawker and bought three packs. Of all the consumables being hawked – gala, boiled eggs, loaves of bread of varying shapes, biscuits, apples, egg rolls, and fried beef – Akwa Ogazi stuck out for Fiyin.

'What are those?' she asked Jide.

'Duck eggs… would you like to try?'

For the first time since negotiating and boarding the taxi, their bald driver spoke.

'Oga, na guinea fowl egg, no be duck egg… e no be the same tin with chicken egg, but e sweet well, well.'

Jide's brows rose in silent humour. 'Oh? Thank you for the… um… correction.' They bought four packs of guinea fowl eggs– six in each pack. At the foot of the bridge, as they entered Onitsha, the heart of old south-eastern Nigeria, a self-consciousness washed over Fiyin, one much like the morning after the night a damsel loses her hymen.

Through all five police checkpoints where, despite his pristine car particulars, he parted with NGN500, the taxi driver grumbled. Once he pulled up at their destination, a short muffled dialogue between Jide and Fiyin resulted in Fiyin handing him an extra, in addition to the agreed fare.

'Haa! My Oga, I dey too much grateful, o!' the driver sang, giving Jide an ear-to-ear grin and a deep bow, which Jide did not wait to acknowledge. Fiyin only smiled at the absurdity of the driver's gender-specific impaired vision.

'My father's ani-obi, his inherited land,' said Jide, pointing to a half-fenced compound in the distance. A creeper-plants-invaded massive blockwork building at its decking stage sat in the centre of it.

'It is abandoned!'

Fiyin's stating of the obvious earned her an explanation.

'The initial plan was supposed to accommodate the two brothers. At least in my father's thinking. But Uncle Nwafor came into some money and chose his independence… my father no longer saw need to finish.'

'So where do you guys stay when you come home?'

'We seldom come home… never do. On the few occasions my father visits, he lodges in a guest house at the edge of town… Century Hub. The reviews are sterling, so I am certain we will be comfortable.' Jide's words matched his brisk steps, leading them towards a large compound with a petite bungalow.

'Behold, Uncle Nwafor's palace!' Fiyin's shoulders shook with humour at the glint in Jide's eyes. A goat and four hens loitered around the red-earthed grounds of Uncle Nwafor's ani-obi. After they reached the front door, having navigated, with great expertise, the front yard, dodging the repercussions of raising free-range domestic animals in one's home, Jide clapped his hands five times to announce their presence. They turned towards a rustling by the side of the house. A little girl, not more than eight years old, peeped at them.

'Onye? Who?' Agatha came ambling out, wiping her hands with the wrapper around her waist.

'Ah, you have come. Welcome, o!' Agatha looked tired as she ushered them into the dark living room.

'Oche di, there is seat,' she said, making a sweeping gesture in the general direction of three brown sofas. She pulled back the worn flower-patterned curtains to allow some natural lighting. Dust from the curtains or the fabric of the not-so-sturdy sofas tickled Fiyin's nostrils. She stifled a cough.

About an hour later, Nwafor returned from Diokpa Akulue's house. His eyes glowed with delight at seeing Jide and Fiyin. A glow genuine enough in appearance for Fiyin's strained shoulders to relax.

'Agatha, have you offered our visitors something?'

'I will, after I finish pressing cassava for night food.' Her tone sounded angry. But when, moments later, Jide declined her dinner of fufu and bitter leaf soup and announced their plan to lodge at the guest house outside town, Agatha's tone grew even angrier.

'No problem. Our food is not good enough for you, our house is not good enough for you, I wonder how our help will manage to be good enough for—'

'Not at all ma!' Fiyin gave Jide a discreet nudge on the knee.

'Jide only means we ate too much nonsense on the way… and… we don't want to impose. But if you insist, we will be more than happy to stay.'

Jide thought he would explode with rage. The prospect of sleeping in his uncle's he-goat stench-infested house sent his heart rate into panic mode. For the first time since their arrival, Agatha gave them a warm smile.

'No problem. We will sleep together in my room. Jide can sleep with his uncle.' A bubble of laughter almost escaped Jide's pursed lips.

'Foot-in-mouth disease,' Fiyin sang under her breath.

'What?' said Uncle Nwafor.

Jide came to her defence. 'She said spending the night here makes her more at ease.' As an alternative to a proper meal, Agatha suggested garden eggs and local peanut butter. They bobbed their heads in enthusiasm.

'Garden egg is easy on the stomach and will not give you any MOUTH DISEASE,' she said as she left for the kitchen. Jide and Fiyin stiffened.

Jide offered to show Fiyin the grounds, but in truth, they only escaped to feast on their remaining Akwa Ogazi; hunger pangs threatened to demolish their stomach walls. Fiyin linked her right arm with Jide's left, leaving his right hand free to point his phone to the ground, for the mild lighting to guide their wary feet past chicken and goat droppings.

'I pray everything works out with I.G tomorrow,' she said.

'And will all not working out mean God's disapproval?'

'Well, God is more powerful than any other force, and something not happening should be indicative of His will or the lack of it, don't you think?'

Jide sucked in air through his teeth, exhaled through half-parted lips, and swallowed, trying to measure his next words.

'In a way, I do… but I also believe God, who spoke light

and animals and plants into being, could have as well thrown in aeroplanes, furniture, and electrical appliances. But He did not. Instead, He formed man with not only a brain to conceive inventions but also with the will to claw his way out of every valley of failure until he reaches the pinnacle of success.'

'Wow, Jide! Now, you're beginning to sound like Ali.'

Jide's nose flared in response. 'Yeah, Ali... your Hausa man friend.'

For the longest time, Fiyin wondered why Jide never kept any female friends. Not one. So today, she asked.

'I do not hang around a barber's shop except when I am in need of a haircut,' Jide said and planted a noisy kiss on Fiyin's lips. Fiyin tucked a stray braid behind her ear, casting a pitiful glance at Somadina's unfinished building as they walked past it, towards the main road.

'I think your dad should finish this structure... maybe not to the initial intended scale. You guys will come home for one thing or the other... like now, for instance. Each time I remember who my roomie for the night will be, my heart sinks a little further into my stomach.'

'Of what use would it be... building a home one would never inhabit?' came Jide's terse response.

'And what is so horrid about building a house in your village and inhabiting it, Jide?' Fiyin could not hide her bewilderment. Sometimes, Fiyin visited her hometown with her parents. Everything about keeping ties with one's roots made absolute sense to her.

'Why must one invest in a place with no investment in one? Building in a community a person's great-grandparents called home is overrated. Some choose to follow the footprints of their ancestors in perpetuity, no matter how constraining or straining. Others create, with the advantage of hindsight, new ancestral footprints for their coming bloodline to walk in... if they so choose.'

'A tight community, built over decades, overrated? No place like sweet home, my love.'

'Well, I am a stranger in my so-called home, so I will take a rain check. Abuja, Lagos, and even London are more of homes to me than this place will ever be.'

None of Fiyin's counter-defences stood to any reason, in Jide's opinion. Who made the rules? Where did one lineage end and another begin? By the Christian account of creation, all humans come from Papa Adam and Mama Eve. So how did different families, clans, towns, states, countries, or continents emerge? Jide gave his summation. 'People migrated, making homes in places they synched with. If my father does not synch with this place, he is within his right to choose someplace else... and so is anyone else.'

'Nigeria is a crucible of ethnic, political, and religious habitudes. What if a war erupts? Where will you seek refuge?'

Jide threw back his head in laughter. 'Darling, dust your history books! No corner of our dear motherland, however remote, will escape the desolation of any war intense enough to rattle Lagos and Abuja... where I synch with.'

'Well, maybe if you visited more, you would be able to synch with—'

'Why belabour a matter of such small consequence? Let us not make a brain tumour out of a simple headache, my love... more eggs?'

'Yes, please.' Fiyin's aching knuckle reminded her to wait for Jide's help in cracking the egg. No other food rivalled Akwa Ogazi in hardness. Perhaps walnuts?

'So, are you?' Jide said, stealing a quick glimpse at Fiyin as he gave her the peeled egg.

'Am I what?' A quickening in Fiyin's pulse accompanied her three words.

'In need of a haircut,' said Jide.

'Ali is just a go-to friend.'

'Hmm. Does he know that?'

'Can we go get a drink? My throat is parched,' Fiyin said, pointing to a store a few metres away and letting out a loud burp.

'The more delectable they are, the less decorum they exhibit,' Jide said to the night, shaking his head in embellished bafflement. He ran off towards the almost-closed store, in time to evade Fiyin's playful fist.

EIGHTEEN

A JOLT IN THE ATLANTIC

Besides Agatha's occasional loud expulsion of air through her nostrils with an accompanying heave or intermittent tap on Fiyin's back, to tell her, 'This is too bad! Go outside and mess if you want to mess,' Fiyin's night fared better than she anticipated. With any luck, they would be done with I.G in time for a dash to the airport. Not so for Jide, who endured Uncle Nwafor's loud snoring until, not able to take it any longer, he escaped to the sitting room where he sought refuge in the longest cushion available. The bug-bumps he acquired by the morning, two on his neck and five on his right arm, left him wondering at the sofa's possible original colour.

Uncle Nwafor fulfilled his promise, to accompany them to I.G's hometown, two towns away. Only to I.G's gate, no further.

Jide promised to call Uncle Nwafor with an update of their visit. Work commitments would not let them stay one more day. 'Once we are done, we will take the next flight back to Lagos,' he said.

A smile tugged at Uncle Nwafor's lips as he journeyed back to his home. At intervals, he tapped the bulging envelope in his pocket. *Jide can be a good boy when he wants to be,* he mused. He thought he might even now like him a little more. *Ife osu a elijuro afo, biko. This osu business is not that serious, please.*

A uniformed guard missing an incisor peered through the square cut in I.G's black gate. 'Who be dat!' he said in response to the ding-dong of the bell. Jide informed him of their appointment, and after a brief hesitation, perhaps to consult authority, he let them in.

'Stand there.' He pointed his baton at a lone African purple pear tree by the perimeter fence. The gravel-covered grounds, groaning under the assault of his black boots as he marched off towards the back of the red-roofed mansion, pulled tighter, the already tense air.

Jide linked his fingers with Fiyin's sweaty ones, then brought them to his lips. Fiyin looked up to find a pair of haunted eyes boring into hers and wondered, for the eleventh time, why she had not resorted to blackmailing Omo into coming with her.

The uniformed guard returned. After several seconds of standing a few feet away from them, chewing on heaven-knows-what, and running his eyes up and down their frames at least four times, he said, 'Oga is coming… wait.' As the guard marched off, he stuck his index finger into the side of his mouth. Fiyin almost gagged at the sound of him sucking and, most assuredly, swallowing the dislodged masticated food.

From the front door, a few meters away from Jide and Fiyin, I.G emerged. A young lady trailed him to the car port not too far away from the door.

'He is leaving?' Jide said, putting his right foot forward, but Fiyin tugged at his hand as I.G slid into his waiting car. At the gate, the driver wound down his window to beckon them.

'Oga dey call you.'

They scampered to I.G, at the owner's side of his sports utility vehicle. After close to fifteen seconds, he slid down his heavily tinted window.

To their harmonious, 'Good morning, sir,' I.G said, 'Jide, how are you?'

'Fine, sir.'

'Good. Ehhh… as you can see, I am on my way out for a meeting with the town's ruling council, and I won't return until late at night. I'm not sure if your uncle told you about my planned trip for first thing tomorrow. So, this should be quick.' I.G's passing glance at Fiyin almost convinced her of her kinship with the goat and chicken droppings in Uncle Nwafor's compound. She exchanged her weight distribution from one foot to the other.

'I never thought I would witness the day infatuation would make a football out of an eligible bachelor like you,' I.G said.

Jide swallowed.

'Look, from one successful man to another, this girl is not worth anything, Jide. But of course, the implication of messing with a tainted bloodline is a joke to you. Osu aburo obel'ife, Osu caste system is not a joke. Anyway, am not surprised! How will you understand our cultures and traditions when you, and your entire family, have boiling hatred for the East? Come for Christmas – Mba! New year – for what! Easter – how can! New yam festival – never! Look, Jideofor, too many things will spoil. And if you think I will stand by while you jeopardise a legacy of a pure heritage simply because of a girl who has desperation plastered all over her, you must be a mad clown, indeed. Tell this girl to leave you alone. Let her stay within her species. I am late for my meeting.'

Every syllable of I.G's words landed on Fiyin like the fists of a hundred angry men on a blindfolded convict. And several moments after the guard closed the gates behind his boss's car, the coolness of the morning breeze continued to spread, ever so gently, from the crown of her head, down to the tip of her toes. For Jide, their recent three-minute encounter was either a bad dream or an out-of-body experience.

By half past six in the evening, when they landed in Lagos, Fiyin had still not said a word to Jide. A contemplative Fiyin was one thing, but a detached Fiyin transported Jide to uncharted territories. Through their ride to the airport and flight back to Lagos, Fiyin kept company with her mobile phone. Jide blamed himself. For dragging Fiyin along this blistering path. For not doing his due diligence. For jumping at the faintest hint of a possibility.

His promise to 'fix it' made no difference. Jide got nothing from Fiyin. Not a raised brow, not a quickening in breathing. Nothing.

At the arrival lounge, Fiyin pulled away her hand from Jide's now desperate grip.

'I need to be alone,' she said.

Jide began to form the words. Those with which to persuade her to share some alone time with him, but the thought of being alone with Jide revolted Fiyin.

A young man Fiyin did not recognise walked up to them as soon as they exited the arrival area. He said something into her ear.

'Let's talk later,' she said to Jide and scampered after the man, towards a car parked by the curb a couple of feet away. At first, Jide strained to see past the heavy tint of the windows, but when the door swung open and Ali Dansule sprang out to grab Fiyin's overnight bag, his shoulders went slack.

'How did it go?' Ali's words broke the dam, and Fiyin flew into his ready arms. Mustafa kept his eyes glued to the road, pretending the loud sobbing from behind did not unsettle him. Nothing possessed the power to affect him after eight years of working as Ali's driver. From loud arguments between his boss and a score of scorned ladies, to light-hearted raunchiness between consenting adults, Mustafa weathered them all. But something about his boss's 'new project' pulled his attention. This was more than a project for his boss, he concluded as he stole a glance from his rear-view mirror.

Ali's cooing soon quietened Fiyin's sobs into occasional sniffs. When he offered to call his auntie to cancel her massage appointment, Fiyin declined.

'You can't work like this, Pheephee! Let me take you home... don't worry about your fee for today I'll...' Ali's words slid back into his throat at the sharp glance Fiyin cast him.

She took a deep breath. 'I can't not go. Your auntie looks forward to my visits... besides, spending time with her will help me clear the fog.'

As soon as the gate slid open in answer to Fiyin's bell buzz, and she walked in, Ali knuckle-tapped his window for Mustafa to drive away.

After an hour, Alhaja Aminat strolled with her masseuse-turned-junior friend to the door; she spotted her nephew standing outside his car at the foot of the driveway, a distance away from the front porch. Ali blew a kiss which Aminat caught with both hands, touched to her chest, and threw back to him. To see them play the way they did made Fiyin smile.

'Until next week, ma,' she said.

'Sure! I'll be expecting you.'

For a person of Alhaja Aminat's pedigree, Fiyin had not anticipated such intense mellowness. She therefore shilly-shallied on the best response before settling for a chuckle. And head held up, shoulders rolled back, arms swinging loosely, and leading with her moderately sized bosom, Fiyin strutted towards her ride home.

'Such a nice-looking girl!' Alhaja muttered as she went back in.

Much like most of her recent decisions, made with little or no thought of consequences, Fiyin accepted Ali's invitation to stop by his Victoria Island house. Maybe she enjoyed the distraction his company afforded her. Or she needed more time to prepare to confront her parents with the illusory details of her trip with Anita. Perhaps she liked the version of herself which Ali's company unearthed.

Within minutes, the sometimes-dim, sometimes-bright lights of central Victoria Island flowed into the harmonious soothing glow of high-end Eko Atlantic City.

'You didn't tell me your other house was at Eko Atlantic!' Fiyin said in accusatory whisper as they entered the imposing gates of the city, her eyes growing larger by each dazzlingly bright solar-powered street light they zapped past. Without Fiyin's permission, her body leaned farther into the leather seat of Ali's car.

'Last time I checked, Eko Atlantic was on V.I, not so?' Ali's mouth widened into a grin.

'No! Victoria Island is where the crème of the society lives, but Eko Atlantic is reserved only for the topping on the crème.'

'It's not such a big deal, Pheephee. Believe me.'

'Well, I don't. Ali, Eko Atlantic City is a big deal, and I suspect this piece of information is no news headline to you.' The tautness around Fiyin's shoulders started to ease, but as soon as Mustafa began the winding climb to Phoenix Peak's car park, it returned with intense savagery.

'Good night, Musty,' Ali said to his driver as he took Fiyin's hand for the elevator ride to the thirty-third floor.

All 2,845 square metres of Ali's penthouse apartment dripped with insane appeal. Five bedrooms, fitted with ensuite bathrooms, a master bedroom that exited into a large, heated swimming pool area. Ali's house overlooked a panoramic view of the city of Lagos: the marina, the Atlantic, the Commodore Channel, Tarkwa Bay and the Apapa port. A door to the right of the pool led back to the anteroom.

'Ali, this is be-au-ti-ful! You live alone?'

'Yep.'

'Who cleans for you?'

'Cleaning service.'

'Oh.'

A grand piano in the corner pulled Fiyin.

'You play?'

'Yep. I'll play something for you… if you like.'

Fiyin often pondered on the near-celestial exaltation of the grand piano above the upright piano and basked in the warmth of Ali's enlightenment.

'The finest materials – top-grade spruce, wool felt, expensive hard maple veneers, and all the components incorporated into its manufacture reflect on its musical output… they are, in fact, incomparable,' Ali said, running his hands over the musical equipment. Fiyin giggled and started towards the kitchen.

'Wow! This is lovely!' Languid steps pulled Ali after her.

'Hungry?' he asked, peering into his refrigerator. A compartment was bursting with a hodgepodge of labelled packed foods: braised king prawns, T-bone steak, steamed rice, mashed potatoes, steamed broccoli, sautéed cauliflower, grilled salmon quinoa salad, goat meat pepper soup, cream of shrimp. Fiyin marvelled at the sheer assortment.

'Is eating all you do!'

'No, I like to do other things.' At the smouldering in Ali's eyes, Fiyin stiffened.

He let out a strained chuckle.

'Before you sent your SOS, I had plans to host… someone.'

'Oh! I have been such a disruption! I am super-sorry. I never would ha—'

'To any conceivable degree, Pheephee, disrupt me at your every whim… I'd love nothing more. I crave nothing more.'

'Salad, mashed potatoes and maybe prawns,' Fiyin blurted, putting three feet between herself and Ali, to stare at the scenery of Tarkwa Bay from the kitchen window.

Dinner went on in soothing silence. And after loading the dishwasher with plates and cutlery, Ali offered to dazzle Fiyin with his piano skills.

'Ali. It's almost ten,' she said.

'Five minutes… please.' The look in Ali's eyes compelled Fiyin to throw in a few more minutes. Her eyes lit with amusement as he all but ran to the piano.

The hymn 'Be Thou My Vision' resonated with Fiyin's childhood and adulthood as a song but never as a piano rendition. At the end, Ali filled the blanks on Fiyin's face.

'Somewhere along the course of my grandfather's life, he converted to Christianity… two of his children followed his lead, but my mother remained true to Islam. On the many occasions I visited, I followed him to church… I used to be quite fond of him before he passed, nine years ago. That apart, I love the British Royal family, and for some weird reason, the hymn registers in my head, as their favourite.'

In the restroom, Fiyin dialled a number on her phone. She pressed the phone to her mouth.

'Omo, where are you?'

'V.I, but on my way home… why?'

'Please come and get me… I'll be at the petrol station opposite Empire Chinese. Please come. Now.'

The tremor in Fiyin's voice compelled Omo to contain her bubbling stream of questions.

'Oga, please turn back. I need to pick someone up on Samad Street,' she said to the cab driver.

Ali did not understand, but the calm finality in Fiyin's voice when she asked to be dropped at the filling station, where she would meet Omo, made him acquiesce. Parked a safe distance away, he waited until Omo's cab pulled up, and Fiyin boarded. After the tail lights of the taxi melted into the darkness, Ali started back home, keenly aware of a throbbing in his left temple.

The instant Fiyin slid in beside Omo and the taxi sped off from the Atlantic towards the peninsula, Fiyin sped through the events before her call to Omo. Through her recount, Omo pursed her lips; she figured a reprimand would only cause Fiyin more grief. But words like 'puerility' and 'presumption' bounced around in her head. With an intentional pacing of her action, she took out some face tissue from her bag for Fiyin to blow into.

'Let me go to him! Omo, I want to go to him!' But for the gravity of things, Omo would have laughed; Fiyin oozed desperation.

'Babe, you can't go to Ikoyi this night. Moreover, he could be anywhere. We can't tell if he is in his house or at the hospital. But why won't this guy pick up his calls, at least!' Omo said, dialling Jide's number for the fifth time. In the end, they agreed. Fiyin would spend the night at Omo's.

'Hello, Mummy. I'm back in Lagos, but I'm with Omo now.' Bree would have loved to chat, but she sensed her child would rather be asleep. So, she let her be.

'Goodnight, baby. Give my love to Omo.'

Before they turned in for the night, a long time after midnight, Omo stared at Fiyin's tear-stained face. 'But babes, what changed... between the airport and when you called me?' For several moments, Fiyin planted a blank stare at the door of Omo's bedroom. But right when Omo accepted that Fiyin must have thought her question was rhetorical, Fiyin told her what changed.

'For the first time, I saw a possibility of doing my life without Jide in it and I was terrified. Omo, I don't know what I would do if... if Jide decides to move on with his life.'

A fresh stream of tears began to course down Fiyin's face as she turned away to reach for her mobile phone, again.

⁓

Jide warred with conflicting emotions until half past one in the morning. No longer able to ignore Fiyin's phone calls, he picked up her twelfth call to say ten words. 'Fiyin… I get it… trust me. Now, I get it.'

'Jide, plea—' The line went dead. The rest of her attempts to reach Jide sent her to his voicemail.

'Hi, you have reached Dr Jide Williams. I cannot talk now, but you may leave a message.'

⁓

Nsikan popped his head out of the kitchen door. 'Manasseh! Oya, come and carry your breakfast.' In a flash, Manasseh tossed his gardening rake and half ran to the kitchen. He grabbed a bar stool, narrowing his eyes at Nsikan as he sat in front of his breakfast of pancakes, bacon strips, sunny side up and oats.

'Look, Nsikan, I don't have any spare cash to lend you, o! Things are tight until end of the month.'

Shaking his head, Nsikan pulled his lips down in a mirthless smile as he told Manasseh the real reason for his elaborate breakfast.

'Oga Jide refused his breakfast… like he rejected his dinner last night. So, you're more like a dustbin to me, not a bank.'

'Ah! In that case, I am happy to be a dustbin for a long time,' Manasseh said, giving his food his full attention.

'But on a serious note,' said Nsikan, 'he has not been his usual self for some time now, and I think it's about the stuff with Auntie Fiyin.'

'The one Abigail gisted you?'

'Yes. I wonder what will become of Abigail when they find out she is also an outcast,' Nsikan said, pulling the second bar stool closer to Manasseh.

'Hah, Nsikan! Abigail an outcast? How?'

'True to my God! She told me so herself!'

'So? Did she ask you to tell anyone? You better keep your mouth shut if you don't want the poor woman to lose her job. Didn't you say she is a widow?'

'She is.'

'Aha! Case dismissed. Nsikan, better shut your mou—' A knock. The kitchen door creaked open.

'Manasseh, come outside. Auntie Fiyin dey for gate. She wan see Oga Jide,' said Fidelis the security guard.

A quick glance at Nsikan, and Manasseh abandoned his meal, along with his initial gusto. Last night, Jide had left instructions; he did not want to be disturbed. And when Manasseh asked, 'What about auntie Fiyin?' Jide said over his shoulders, 'I do not want to be disturbed.'

At half past six in the evening, Jide plodded to the kitchen. He had spent the entire day in his bedroom and now wanted something to eat.

'What is available?' he asked Nsikan.

'Okra soup and vegetable soup… but I can make jollof rice if you give me forty-five minutes, sir.'

'Okra will do. Do we have oatmeal?'

'Yes, sir.'

'Right, I will have that.' Jide swung his right leg over the bar stool and sat. His light drumming, with the tips of his fingers, on the kitchen island unsettled Nsikan, who sighed at intervals of eight seconds.

'Is something the matter, Nsik—'

'Nothing, sir.'

Within minutes, Nsikan placed Jide's meal in front of him. 'Here, sir,' he said, almost knocking over Jide's glass of lemon-flavoured water. 'I'm sorry, sir.'

All was clearly not well with Nsikan, so Jide asked again, 'Are you all right, Nsikan?'

'I'm fine, sir... in short, no. I... you said you don't want anybody to disturb you, but I must tell you this. Auntie Fiyin has been at the gate since eight in the morning... sir.'

Panic gripped Jide's insides. He knocked over the stool as he sprang to his feet. By the time he reached the front door, he had broken into a trot.

Fidelis charged to the gate the instant he saw Jide.

Jide told him not to bother and eased himself out through the pedestrian gate.

She was in her car, parked by the fence, hunched over, and writing on a piece of paper. He had been watching her for over five seconds before she looked up. Fiyin put aside the paper and pen on the empty seat beside her and undid her car locks. Jide pulled open the door, but did not take any step towards her. The air conditioner blew warm air.

'Thank you, Manasseh. You may leave,' said Jide.

Sullen-faced, Manasseh peeled his back off the wall, from where he had been keeping unsolicited company with Fiyin and serving as water vendor when she asked. He returned to the compound without a word to anyone.

'What are you writing?' Jide asked when they were alone. His eyes were like iron bands, holding Fiyin's gaze in one firm grasp.

'A note to you... before leaving... to return again tomorrow.'

'Will you tell me what is in it?'

Half hesitant, Fiyin began in a small voice.

'Sweetheart, I panicked... please don't hate me.' Only seven words, and the fort of resentment that Jide had spent nearly two days in erecting crumbled without as much as a sound.

'Please move over.'

Left leg after the right, over her gear stick, into the passenger's seat, Fiyin yielded the wheels. After Fidelis shut the gate, he looked on, with puzzlement etched on his face, at the retreating figures of Jide and Fiyin walking into the house.

NINETEEN

*TIME SPENT ON THE DANCE FLOOR IS TIME ENOUGH
FOR ANOTHER TO TAKE YOUR SEAT*

Between morsels of his own meal, Jide pinned Fiyin with long stares. Fiyin's stomach walls did not churn with hunger, but she would have done about anything to atone; Jide only had to ask. So, she laboured through her goat meat pepper soup and cast Nsikan a contrite look as she pushed away her bowl, with two-thirds of the soup still in it. Jide took their used plates to the sink and returned to the stool to resume tunnelling through Fiyin's head with his eyes.

Like one pressed for a bathroom break, Nsikan tidied the kitchen and ran out, leaving Jide and Fiyin alone to enjoy the hum from the refrigerator.

'Why, Fiyin?'

Jide's voice did not radiate its element of calm assuredness today; it was scratchy and breathy, much like sounds from a larynx with heavily inflamed vocal folds.

'Jide, I am sorry.'

Fiyin tore her face from his gaze as two teardrops landed on the granite top of the kitchen island. She swiped at the streak they left in their wake.

'Let me tell you what breaks me, Fiyin. What breaks me is that I cannot delude myself into thinking I would be happier if you never found love again. I genuinely want you to be happy, whether that includes me or not. And guess what? Because we are survivors, if we do walk away, we will claw at everything thrown at us until we attain a semblance of happiness. I was ready to claw like hell, but you jumped ship. Why, Fiyin?'

'Ji-de-o-for, please... let me explain.'

Fiyin's tentative hand on the tips of Jide's three longest fingers sent a warmness down his arm. She waited for him to pull away and when he did not, she met his gaze, albeit fearful of what she might find. If Fiyin ever confronted Jide's resentment for her, she would never be able to unsee it.

'Come.' Jide got to his feet, waited for Fiyin to follow him upstairs, to the lounge.

Perhaps Fiyin expected – needed – Jide to join her on the three-seater sofa, like he always did, but on this occasion Jide required laser-sharp focus. He took the armchair opposite her, assuming the role of a professor in a viva examination.

'Why, Fifi? Why is your first reaction... your instinct... to throw me away at the feeblest hint of a hurdle? Why?'

'I'm immature, naïve, foolish... Jide, I'm foolish.'

'Is it the money?'

'No!'

'His looks? Security? Influence?'

'God, no! Jide, no! Please, stop.'

'So, what? For heaven's sake, Fiyinfunoluwa, tell me what I am missing?'

The frustration in Jide's voice, the anguish in his eyes, reached into Fiyin's chest to force a torrent of words from her mouth.

'He was... I defined Ali as a safe distraction. Omo is in love. Her... her thoughts are always across the Atlantic, and I don't begrudge her. Ifeatu is married. And with the current gulley between us, we no longer talk. Anita... Anita is dealing with so much already. I was alone. Jide, I was lonely, confused.' Fiyin gulped a mouthful of air and resumed. 'Our meeting with I.G stripped me of the last stitches of my dignity. I already thought I... I fell too hard, too fast for you. That I should have let you woo me a little longer—'

'What!' Jide's nose flared in disbelief.

'I'm no longer sure of what I'm saying. In retrospect, I think I was using Ali's attention as proof that I hadn't made you the centre of my world... I never sensed any... real threat... Ali felt like a stronger, more influential version of Omo unti—'

'Until what? Sweet pea... did that bastard touch you?' Jide's voice was the sound of terror. Fiyin burst into violent sobs. In three long strides, Jide reached and wrapped her in his arms. She buried her face in his chest and wailed into his shirt for a long four minutes. After she quietened, they sat, stretched out, on the sofa, in soothing silence.

Eyes closed, leaning her back into Jide's chest, Fiyin savoured the assuring rigidity of him, the scent of him. Jide's fingers patting her hair was lulling, but she managed to stay awake to drag him through everything; from the moment she went into Ali's car until he found her at his gate.

'Sweet pea, our hurdles are far from over. There will be days when you will wonder if I am still worth the trouble. Will I be in perpetual worry of you going off with the next shiny and influential male likeness of Omo?'

'No, Jide. Never!' Fiyin pulled away to turn towards Jide, folded her feet under her bottom, so her knees were between his.

'I don't want an "all right life" with anyone else... I want an amazing, inspiring, and resplendent life. Jide, I can't have that with anyone else. Only you.'

Jide pressed her palm to his right cheek, then to his lips. In one quick move, Fiyin leaned into him, to claim his lips in a long and hard kiss she never wanted to end. Between rasped breaths, Jide untangled himself from Fiyin. His heart raced with him to the balcony, where he dialled a phone number.

'Timi, I beg show... Fiyin is here and I... I think she plans to spend the night... I no wan fuck up, I beg.'

Within thirty minutes, Timilehin arrived at Jide's house with his overnight bag. He required no annotation for his friend's SOS.

⌁

Somadina endured I.G's three-minute call, his berating him for his ineptitude in running his household. Right after the call ended, Afulenu dialled Jide.

'If you had told me about this, I would have discouraged you.'

'Mother, I am dealing with this. One way or another, I will have this sorted.'

Afulenu took the cue. When Jide called her 'Mother', the case was almost always dismissed. After their past troubles, the hospital in Port-Harcourt needed resuscitating. Husband and wife gloved up for the work ahead, pushing I.G and his mischiefs as far away as the Treasure Base of the Nation permitted them.

⌁

'If you are open to my method, we may be able to ruffle I.G.'

A heavy weight slid off Jide's chest. Monday's words were a symphony to Jide's ears. When, only two days before, the private investigator outlined the complications constraining the 'management' of a man as wealthy and as influential as I.G, Jide feared he may have placed an undeserved amount of faith in an amateur.

'How hard can it be to distract a man long enough for others to go about with their lives?' Jide had asked Monday, kneading his temple with his thumb and forefinger. But with this new update, Jide dared to hope.

Monday merely exhumed a relic, his box of dirty tricks from his earlier days of practice.

'The job will be a clean cut, no debris. Won't take more than a week, and afterwards, the brute will be too busy wiping mud from his brow to pay you any attention.' The plan? Unearth a hidden crease in I.G's pristine sheets, one big enough to keep him busy with rebuilding his image, one ugly enough to rob him of his influence. Not once did Jide consider a total fabrication of a crease, but his options were fast whittling. And to reference Timilehin, 'Why play fair with a professional sludge slinger?'

Yes, I.G's slingshots of sludge crossed boundaries to reach their targets and did not mind smearing anything in their path.

⁓

'Unlike ladies, gentlemen seldom hold a grudge', is a notion still in contest. But for Timilehin and Nnamdi, nothing could be any truer. After three days of working in the same building and exchanging no more than a grunt every time their paths crossed, the men came to a tacit agreement about the absurdity of their behaviour.

'Guy, what's eating you up, sef? Since the day I almost tattooed my knuckles on your face, you've been licking your bruised ego,' Nnamdi said, strolling into Timilehin's office. He plopped into the single sofa across Timilehin's desk. After a short-lived glaring contest, the two friends burst into wild laughter.

'Olodo! Daft!' Timilehin said.

'Ekpelima! Area tout!' Nnamdi said with equal humour.

A shadow of solemnity slid past Timilehin's face.

'But Nnamdi, you just like to blab… no control.'

Nnamdi's weak smile and non-retort screamed his desperation for Timilehin, to yield to amity, to sheath the fabled sword.

Nothing had changed since their last argument. Timilehin maintained his stance; Jide should fly into every battle ring and fight for the life he wanted with Fiyin. Nnamdi, on the other hand, called his friends weak and people whose positions stemmed from naïveté. No babe was worth that kind of distress!

But Jide and Timilehin were not wholly taken by their friend's façade. Nnamdi only protected himself from the horror of vulnerability.

'What do you say, we chill out after our shift?' Timilehin said. Peace at last. Nnamdi pounced on the idea of drinks after work and was blithesome as he returned to his ward rounds.

⌒

Jide stared at Timilehin, a hunch told him that his trusted friend had just halved the solution to his problem by sharing it with their other trusted friend.

'You should not have told him. I mean, when has Nnamdi ever provided meaningful input with respect to real issues?'

'Jide, I didn't realise I couldn't talk about it with Nnamdi. Let's not kid each other… of the three of us, Nnamdi is the one who would identify the plot holes in this thing,' Timilehin said.

Jide slammed his hands in his pockets and looked away from Timilehin. Looking at him stoked the embers of his smouldering rage. Rage at himself for sharing Monday's 'method' with Timilehin, rage at Timilehin for assuming Nnamdi would, for once, keep his filters in place, rage at the situation responsible for his current impasse, and rage at Nnamdi for daring to be right for the first time in a long time.

'All right. I am sorry. But Jide, breathe for a bit. What he said makes sense, come on na!' Indeed, Nnamdi made sense. Any strategy comprising lies, blackmail and a third party sets up its players for doom and regret. More so if those players are beautiful hearts like Jide and Fiyin.

'I'll contract one of these babes to work I.G. It's a turf he trolls. We'll hang his ambassadorial aspiration on the recording and shut his trap forever about an obsolete tradition,' Monday had said, his eyes gleaming.

Before Jide's trip to Ajoafo to meet with I.G, he would have cringed at the thought of exploring such an abhorrent option. But the more he rolled this absurdity around in his head, the more it took on the likeness of absolute sense. I.G was no saint. In fact, he did not come close to anything decent. Taking such an obnoxious individual off a list of candidates aspiring to represent a country already flaying her arms in the swamp of disrepute should be considered an act of patriotism. *There are wrong ways to do the right things.* Jide did not see any other way. *Or else, I.G will never let me be.*

At the chime of the bell, Timilehin hurried off to the door, grateful for Nnamdi's arrival; the look of betrayal in Jide's eyes clawed at his conscience.

'Sorry guys. Unplanned delays at the mainland. Mr Husband refused to sign off for a caesarean to deliver his wife of their triplets.' Nnamdi closed his eyes briefly to knead his nape before he drew a dining chair to seat between his friends.

'Let me guess... you are paying for the surgery,' Timilehin said.

'And you, my friend, are a sage,' said Nnamdi, resting his elbows on the dining table and narrowing his eyes. 'Jide, your investigator is being crude with his so-called method. All he is doing is providing a quick fix and not giving a hoot about the fallouts... It won't take a rocket scientist to tie you to the blackmail. You think I.G climbed this high up the societal ladder by extending courtesies to those in his path? Hell, no! The guy is ruthless and will pulverise you and anything within your radius.'

Timilehin served Jide an 'I-told-you-so' look. Jide grimaced.

'You make sense, Nnamdi... plenty sense. But what do you recommend I do? Snooze? While another human being dictates how I ride out the rest of my life?' Jide said.

'A petition.'

'What?' Timilehin and Jide echoed, looking at Nnamdi like his neck just budded an extra head.

'Yes, a petition with over thirty thousand signatures. A demand for Ajoafo to implement the abolishment law, passed in 1956, by the Eastern Nigerian House of Assembly... the law abolishing the Osu caste system. A petition of that weight is sure to grab the attention of the Minister of Culture and Cohesion.'

Though hanging on Nnamdi's every word, Jide started to ask how they would ever reach such corridors when he slammed his mouth shut, his eyes fizzing with excitement. The Minister of Culture and Cohesion was Ifeatu's uncle... *Ifeatu, Fiyin's friend.*

Wonder coloured Timilehin's eyes, turning to Jide, he said, 'Let's call Fiyin.'

Jide held out his hand. 'Mba, mba, mba. Not this time. I am done flying into plans. This time, we will think through the entire process, the cost of compiling those signatures, how to lend weight to the petition... perhaps court the buy-in of the king...' He pushed a long gust of shaky air out of his half-sealed lips, as if to steady the tremors inside him. 'Until I have a clear path, we cannot involve Fiyin and Ifeatu and whoever else. Shame on me if I make the same mistake twice.' Yet with every word Jide spoke, his eyes glimmered with hope, his belly fluttered with anticipation. For in pursuit of his own happiness, the promise of an ultimate greater good waved in the distance.

~⌐⌐

Five weeks of trotting around Europe with Ben, did Omo more good than she anticipated. In Ben's opinion, they successfully squeezed Omo's six-month Schengen visa dry of every juice of its validity. From London to Paris, Istanbul, Milan, Vienna, and back to London, Omo was living out her fantasy. Besides Ben's hints about spending the coming Christmas in Nigeria, clinching the contract to style the bridesmaids for Teni and Timi's wedding made Omo's legs less heavy as she walked away from Ben to securities, through immigration, past the boarding gates and at last into the aircraft.

~⌐⌐

After Jide, the next person to break her big news to was Omo, and Fiyin itched with the excitement of telling her.

'Miracles still happen, Omo! Out of nowhere, Mrs Azike called me, said she wanted to invest in me... to sort of... give back to humanity—'

'Slow down, babes!' Omo said, pushing aside the little bags she had been stuffing with the holiday gifts she bought.

'What do you mean, invest in you?' Her eyes grew large as Fiyin narrated her surreal news. A duplex in the heart of Victoria Island, for Fiyin's catering outfit! With grounds large enough to fit an extra building, maybe a bungalow, for trainings when she wanted to start the catering school!

'For free?' Omo asked, shifting in her bed, her eyes fluttering with excitement.

'Not quite... she asked me to draw up a payment plan, which I can stretch for twenty-five years if I like. We were still reeling with my miracle when my dad's application for the federal government agricultural funding pulled through! Now, he is in the process of procuring a partnership with a Brazilian company as an outlet for the exportation of oil palm! Omo, this is a windfall! I still don't believe I won't wake up from this dream!'

Omo's eyes often did not need much inducement to water with tears, but this occasion more than justified a good cry. She blew a loud snort into a tissue. 'Who says angels don't exist?' she said, reaching for Fiyin and wrapping her in a tight hug.

'We should go out to celebrate... let's go to Crème Palace. My treat,' Fiyin said.

But Omo had a better idea. She got on her feet, and starting a slow cabbage dance said, 'Tomorrow will be a better day after I take delivery of my car,' giving Fiyin a double wink.

At once, Fiyin sprang to her feet to join in the cabbage dance. She stopped for a moment. 'What model, what model?' she asked, her eyes emitting unalloyed delight for her friend's new car.

'Rav, baby!' Omo said.

'Rav4! Yaaay!'

Omo fastened her gaze on the road, ignoring her itchy forehead and sweaty armpits. All the way to Crème Palace, Fiyin laughed at Omo.

'Chick! You don't need to hug your steering wheel to be careful. You never drove like this when you were learning with my own car, o!'

'Fiyin, I beg you in the name of God Almighty, stop distracting me.' Omo did not as much as cast Fiyin a sideward glance. Her jesting was not helping with Omo's mission of securing their safe arrival at Crème Palace.

They settled in their seats. Fiyin picked up the ice-cream menu but waited a while for her friend's breathing to ease. Parking proved tricky for Omo who now leaned over the ice-cream menu on her side of the table. She made a mental note to enrol with *Zoom Riders* for a one-week crash program to sharpen her driving skills.

'Two scoops of pistachio sorbet, one scoop of salted caramel and two crème cookies,' Omo said.

'Glass-wafer bowls or paper-wafer bowls?' the waiter said in a rich baritone.

'Paper-wafer.'

The waiter turned to Fiyin. 'Ma'am?'

Fiyin cleared her throat before she said, 'Same... I'll have the same.'

While they waited for the customary three to five minutes for their orders to arrive, Omo resumed her globe-trotting tales, from where she left off the day before. Ben's parents had gone with them to Turkey where they spent three days.

'I never knew the country sat on two continents. Ephesus is in—' Their orders arrived.

'Yeah, part of Turkey is in the south of Europe, the other part sits in the west of Asia,' Fiyin said closing her eyes briefly to savour the creaminess in her mouth.

'Ehe! Guess what! We almost visited the Virgin Mary's hou—' Omo stopped, sucked in a sharp breath. 'Fifi, don't look.' Omo's eyes narrowed to slits.

'What? Omo, what?' Fiyin said, stiffening, her voice an octave lower than normal.

'Turn slowly to your right... like you want to look at the entrance... the table in that corner... can you see?'

Fiyin turned. It took a while for her eyes to settle on what they were meant to find. Her breath stuck in her throat, forming a painful lump. Sitting in a corner, his back to them, was Jide with an undeniably attractive lady. After ice creams they had planned to stop by the hospital but cancelled when Jide said he would be in a meeting. A sheen formed in Fiyin's eyes. She snatched her eyes away from the side of Jide's head to stare into her bowl of ice cream. Omo sucked in air through her teeth.

'Guys though,' she said, shaking her head. Then, as though struck by a sudden bright idea, she said, 'Let's go.'

'Go where?'

'To them. Let's go and say hi. We can't sit here pretending like we aren't seeing what we are seeing. I swear to God, Fiyin, the guy will deny it if you don't confront him now. That's their S.O.P.' Omo's voice had become raspy.

'God forbid! I can't. Never! Abeg, let's leave this place.' Fiyin was tired.

'Wait, what? We should leave?'

'Look, Omo… I didn't want to say anything before. But after our last fight—'

'The one after Eko Atlantic?'

'Yes, that one. I sensed something in Jide. I'm not quite sure what, but I suspect Jide is withdrawing… I'll explain in the car. Let's go.'

'But… but nothing happened at Eko Atlantic. Right? I thought you guys were good,' Omo said with rumpled brows, grabbing their still-full ice-cream bowls, to follow Fiyin.

They did not speak until they drove into Omo's compound and Fiyin got into her own car, ready to head home. 'Jide invented this "space thing"; we remain committed to each other, but allow ourselves enough room to breathe — to be certain we are clear on what we want.'

'Crap. The dude is breaking up with you.'

'Maybe, but he is transmitting mixed messages. Still loving, only a bit distant. His latest gift is embossed with absolution… for hurting me in advance. Or why would Jide clean himself out to give me a cheque of NGN10,000,000 for the first instalment for the property from Mrs Azike? I didn't tell you about it yesterday because I still didn't know how to interpret such a gift.'

'Shit, Fifi. There's no other interpretation, nau. Jide has given you a farewell gift. Kai. Did you see that chick at Crème Palace? She fine die.'

Nothing rivalled a pair of goggles in providing a masking for a bruised heart. Fiyin reached for her dark designer fashion glasses; one of the gifts Omo got for her from Paris. She pasted a smile on her face as, donning them, she let herself into her house. In her bedroom, Fiyin pulled the last drawer on her dressing table, ran her fingers over the expensive piece of rectangular paper. No matter how hard her heart hurt, she planned to return Jide's gift. *If Jide has fallen out of love with me, I cannot force him to fall back in.* Her chest tightened, as though sealing her resolve. It hurt. Damn, it hurt.

TWENTY

SOMETIMES, LOVE IS HOLDING ON.
OTHER TIMES, IT IS LETTING GO

Weddings were often emotional for Fiyin, but Timilehin's wedding evoked a summons for acute distress. First, Jide's role as 'Best Man' came with consequences; they would not be attending as a pair. Ifeatu's persistent fever almost guaranteed she would not be attending either. Anita travelled to Port Harcourt to 'visit' one of her 'Chairmen'. Save for an occasional generic text message, to which Fiyin never replied, Ali and Fiyin honoured their tacit agreement to starve their friendship; Alhaji Aminat also seemed to have received the memo.

To further poke at an already sore muscle, Omo travelled to Benin. And although she promised to return early enough to attend the wedding, Fiyin feared she may not be able to finish with her mother's new house before the big day. After months of prayers and fasting, Omo's father received a spiritual prompting to buy houses for the other wives he sent away – his last obligation to them. Fiyin pondered on the misfortune of the women whose husbands did not experience the spiritual or moral nudge to compensate the wives they wooed, married, and kicked out in response to an awakening of their faith.

A shrill sound from Fiyin's phone startled her out of her musings. Yesterday, while waiting to meet with the brand agent for her catering outfit, she changed her phone's ringtone and still had not grown accustomed to its jolting invasion. *Jide?* She looked at her bedside clock. For half past eleven in the night, he sounded too alert, too light-spirited.

'Sweet pea, I am so sorry I did not call back like I promised. Too many issues to deal with. I will explain everything tomorrow.' But 'tomorrow' came and Jide called again to apologise. His parents were in Lagos for the wedding, and wanted ultraviolet printing done on the wedding souvenirs they brought with them.

'Once I am finished at the printer's, I will come for you,' Jide said. When Fiyin offered to drive to him, he dissuaded her with talks about the madness of Lagos traffic.

'I think not. Sweet pea, wait. The minute I am done, I will come to you.' But he did not. At midnight, he sent her a text message.

'My sweetheart, today has been a most hectic day. I love you more than you will ever fathom. See you at the wedding.'

An invisible hand pulled Fiyin's heart into the bottom of her stomach, pinning it, keeping it in place. And as hard as she fought to ignore the imaginary slamming of a door, it persisted; opening and slamming, opening, and slamming… opening… and slamming… opening and slamming… opening and slamming, until her eyes yielded to sleep.

By morning, Fiyin's heart came up to the base of her neck, beating violently against her soft skin. She knelt by her bed to say her morning prayers.

'Oh Lord, thank you for today. Thank you for loving me, in spite of me. Thank you for always carrying me. Please, Lord, show me the way to go, and help me walk in it. At the end of today, please, let me have

many reasons to say thank you again. In Jesus's name I pray. Amen.'

Right after her prayers, Fiyin's phone startled her again. It was Omo.

'Babes, I just landed. I'll go straight to my house to grab my things. I'll tell the cab man to wait and drive me back to you… so we ca—'

Omo's call made Fiyin's room a little brighter than before. But Fiyin had a different idea.

'No, chick, why don't I come to you, instead? Let's go to Timi's wedding in style!'

'In style? Oh, my car!'

'Of course! Mine is faithful… but it's old. So, we will go in your mint jeep. I'll dress up at your place. Ring me once you are on third mainland bridge, so I can start coming to you.'

⌒

Fiyin sought Jide's gaze as she and Omo walked the few metres from the parking area to the side of the church building, away from direct view. His face broke into a smile the moment their eyes met. But Fiyin foraged for something else; something less ephemeral, something more solid. Something familiar. The groomsmen, all four of them, were a swoon-worthy lot, in their coffee-brown suits, cream-coloured shirts and matching brown bow ties. Their cream pocket squares complemented their hickory-coloured brogues too. Except for their tuxedos, Jide and Timilehin matched the groomsmen's elegance.

'Wow! They look so good! At this rate, I'm no longer confident I'll deliver on my brand promise. Speaking of which, where are the bridesmaids?' Omo said under her breath.

'I almost didn't recognise you!' said Fiyin, serving Nnamdi an exaggerated look of appreciation. Nnamdi's eyes crinkled at the sides as he introduced the other three groomsmen to recover from his uncharacteristic but fleeting diffidence.

'Congratulations, Timi!' Omo said and went into a singing feat. Jide pulled Fiyin away from her 'Another One Bites the Dust' rendering friend.'You look amazing, my beautiful.' The sparkle in Jide's eyes lent more intensity to his hushed words. More intensity than Fiyin believed he meant for them to have.

He began to tell her about the events of yesterday when the bride's convoy arrived.

Timilehin's face broke into a grin large enough to cover the church grounds. 'She's here!' he said, his eyes fixed on the white limousine as it glided into St. Bartholomew's Catholic Church, making its way to the back, to park by the vestry.

'Of course, she's here. Did you think she would Maggie Carpenter you?' Nnamdi said, referring to the 1999 hit film, *Runaway Bride*.

One of the groomsmen, the one Nnamdi introduced as Hazman, asked if the ring bearer was with the bride's convoy or already in the church.

Jide reached for his phone. 'Yes, let me call Kaira. Nathaniel is supposed to do the march-in with the bride.'

In the frenzy and uncertainty of the past week, the prospect of meeting Kaira for the first time since the last time, had not registered in Fiyin's mind. Jide read the slight crease between her brows and told her to pay Kaira no mind; she was only being spoilt little Kaira.

'She owes you an apology, expect one,' Jide said, touching his lips to her forehead and walking away to dial his sister's number.

⌐⌐

The bridesmaids were breathtakingly un-eclipsed in their cute outfits – cream and gold French lace halter-neck tops flowing into champagne-coloured taffeta knee-length ball dresses. Yet, the groomsmen employed spirited bravery in matching their resplendence.

Kaira raked the pews, in search of Fiyin. When their eyes locked, she blew Fiyin a kiss with both hands, placed them on her chest, and mouthed, 'I am sorry.' Fiyin's face lit up with an involuntary smile, and she blew back a kiss. To stay mad at Kaira would be to yawn without your eyes squinting or watering, no matter how little. Kene gave Fiyin a discreet wave.

Somewhat now keener on enjoying the wedding, Kaira settled into her seat, adjusted Nicole's hair piece and Noah's bow tie.

The two siblings sat, contained between their parents, their backs against the hard wood of the pew. But the third sibling sat up front, thorough in his role as ring bearer and every bit enchanted by the sparse scattering of white stones on the beautiful bride's white lacy long-sleeved floor-sweeping wedding dress. Eight-year-old Nathaniel wondered if his own bride would like a tiara as shiny and a veil as long as auntie Teni's own.

The Reverend's spirited sermon lasted about thirty minutes and left the congregation animated afterwards. He charged the new couple to make their matrimony enjoyable and not endurable. Towards the end, he admonished the congregation.

'Forget the simpletons who promote a woman's ability to cook delicious meals as the magic potion for all marital issues... they must be living in a world where restaurants and hotels have gone extinct. Pay no mind to the shallow minds who dangle a man's financial success as the guarantee to a happy and lasting union... if they were right, the wives of two famous financial powerhouses, whose names I shall not mention, would have remained in their marriages, regardless of their husbands' philandering. The fundamental requirement? Make Jesus Christ the bedrock of your marriage. Any other approach is like crossing the expressway with a blindfold and hoping to arrive on the other side unscathed. Truth be told, even the most careful of pedestrians may be knocked over. But wouldn't you agree that crossing without a blindfold offers you a better chance at safety? Regardless of all I have said, I will leave you with this… a well-baked cake with frosting often looks more appealing, and is most times sweeter than one without. Therefore, Timilehin, make sure you make money… lots of money. And Teniayo, cook scrumptious dishes for your husband… add frosting to your marriage. May our good Lord bless and keep your union.' And the congregation gave a resounding 'Amen!' amidst short-lived laughter and chattering.

During the photo shoot outside the church, photographers clicked at batches of wedding guests.

'Couple with bridesmaids!'

'Couple with groomsmen!'

'Bride's family!'

'Groom's family!'

'Friends of the bride!'

'Friends of the groom!' The list was endless.

Teni was nursing a scowl; her chief bridesmaid deemed chatting with Haz-man, a more rewarding endeavour than ensuring she did not sweat. But Timi stole the scowl with something he said into her neck. As they waited for the couple to endure their endless photo shoot, Jide's breath fanned Fiyin's ears. 'I will deny this before Teni, but you are the most beautiful girl here.' Fiyin giggled. The tightness in her belly started to loosen. Perhaps she was dealing with a bout of paranoia, after all. She pulled away, going in search of his folks.

'My darling! You look gorgeous!' Afulenu said, beaming as she hugged Fiyin with both arms.

Cream and gold artificial flowers punctuated the large white-walled and wood-grain-floored reception hall. The seating arrangements of no more than five per table emphasised the spacing. A harmonious play of white and warm lighting created an ethereal but pleasing ambience. Less, indeed, is best. Before the couple and their train marched in, Jide told Fiyin to wait till the end of the reception.

'We have been a thousand years apart, sweetheart,' he said. Fiyin revised her plans; she would ride with Jide after the reception. After she told Omo, and they went to find Jide's car, to transfer Fiyin's overnight bag to it, they went back into the hall and found a table for themselves – beside Kaira and Kene's table.

Nicole and Nathaniel sent endless imploring glances to their parents; they wanted to switch tables. In the end, Kaira nodded her approval, and they scampered away to Fiyin and Omo's. And why not? Fiyin and Omo dazzled with the easy mien often associated with most fun aunties. The music, compère, food, and service bore testament to the properness of the head on the wedding planner's shoulders. Noah demanded chips and ketchup. He did not want fried rice. After a little convincing, he settled for bread rolls and jam. For his sake, his parents shared from the little wicker basket on Omo and Fiyin's table, leaving the young lad to do what he pleased with the full basket of bread rolls on their own table.

'The bridesmaids look so beautiful!' Nicole said. Omo asked what she liked best about them, suspecting she would say their cream feather hair pieces or their three-inch-heeled tortilla-coloured rhinestone slingback pumps.

'Their dresses! They look like princesses,' Nicole said, without hesitation.

'Guess who the designer is?' said Omo, beaming.

'Ow-my-God! Oh, my God, oh, my God, oh, my God! You! You designed the dresses!' A disconcerting number of heads swinging in their direction inspired 'the eye' from Kaira to her daughter; Nicole was reminded to use her indoor voice. Her next words caused a momentary uneasiness.

'Auntie Fiyin, can I be a bridesmaid at you and Uncle Jide's wedding? Please, please, pretty please with cherry on top?'

Her hands clasped, her eyes squeezed shut, and her body leaning towards Fiyin, imploring, infused some humour into the awkward moment, and the adults on the two tables shared a moment giggling away the awkwardness.

The compère nominated Kaira for the role of 'observer' for the couple's cake-cutting exercise.

After Kaira left, to execute her observatory assignment, Omo lowered her head to Nicole. 'You're still too young to be Auntie Fifi's bridesmaid, but I promise, I will style the outfits for your own bridesmaids, and they will look even more amazing!'

'Wait, what! Like my own bridesmaids... meaning I'll be the bride?'

'Of course!' Omo's face was breaking into a grin, anticipating Nicole's next reaction.

'Eww!' Nicole shrieked, sticking out her chin in utter disgust.

The compère selected Kaira as the one of the five observers to relay her findings about the couple's first joint assignment. She said, 'Teni held the knife first and Timi's hand covered hers. This means Timi is indeed the protector, the covering. But with Teni gripping the knife, nobody should be in any doubt about who dictates where the knife goes.' The hall broke into riotous applause.

When she returned, Kene, with crinkles at the sides of his eyes, announced his new commitment to triple-check before going ahead with any decision he thought he may have made. A waiter rolled a trolley to their table with little saucers of meat.

'What's this?' Omo asked.

'Asun, ma.' He offered a saucer to the adults on the two tables.

'Me? No, thanks. I don't eat goat meat,' Fiyin said, wrinkling her nose.

With the first dance and gift presentations long done, the hall did not look half as full as before. Minutes after Kene and Kaira left, Omo said, 'I better start heading home. Make darkness no catch me for here... let me gather small confidence in my driving first.' Only a few steps out of the hall with Omo, and Fiyin saw them. She faltered in mid-stride.

'Omo... is that not the chick from the other day? The one with Jide at Crème Palace?' Omo swung her head to see Jide speaking to the cleavage-popping, perfectly sculpted lady. Her eyes narrowed.

'She's the one.' Omo's affirmation was a monotone.

'Keep walking. Let's leave this place,' Fiyin said, picking up pace.

'But... but what about your stuff in his car?' Matching her friend's fleeing pace, Omo split her attention; Fiyin's face, the walkway ahead, back to Fiyin's face.

'You're right. Let's go back.' Fiyin's words were coming in angry bursts. A few feet away from Jide and his mystery lady, Fiyin almost changed her mind again. Too late! Jide saw them already, but the burgeoning grin on his face first wobbled before disappearing altogether. Omo slid into a seat, leaving Fiyin alone, to confront her lover and rival.

'Sweet pea I would like to introduce Cassa—'

'I'd like to take my bag... I'm leaving with Omo.'

'Why? I thought we—'

'I want to leave now!' Fiyin constrained herself from underpinning her announcement with an angry stamp of her foot. Rapid shallow breathing, thin film of tears forming in her eyes, and Jide understood at once what Fiyin was thinking, what she was fighting. He turned to the lady.

'May I be excused? The love of my life is in obvious distress, and whatever it is needs to be addressed at once.'

Without waiting to witness the lady's knowing smile, Jide linked his fingers through Fiyin's stiff ones and took deliberate strides, past

Omo, to the car park. For moments, Omo sat still, contemplating on what to say to the lady who was now walking towards Nnamdi. *She's even chummed up with his friends! Ozuo!* Omo screamed in her head.

The departure of the new couple reminded Omo to go to the car park in search of Fiyin. She saw her, deep in conversation with Jide in his car.

It took a bit of coaxing for Jide to convince Fiyin to sit with him, if only for two minutes. Fiyin did not see why Jide insisted on stringing her along. Her hands were flaying, her voice quivering, her eyes brimming.

'Don't make this any harder for me, Jide. Please, release me with whatever is left of my dignity, I beg you! I have always adored you for your consistent approach towards relationships... friendships. But I don't expect you to... wait... wait around until God-knows-when for God-knows-what, but I would apprecia—' Jide caught her still-flaying right hand, placed it on his chest. This slow and wordless act dammed Fiyin's words.

'Can you not feel it, sweet pea?'

'What?'

'My heart... you must. My heart says your name, non-stop, my love. I told you before, and I am telling you again, I am impertinently in love with you, Fiyinfunoluwa Taylor... I do not know how else or what else to be with you.'

Jide took Fiyin's face in his hands and with his thumbs, brushed away the steady stream of tears mixed with mascara and brown powder still rolling down her face.

'What are you doing to me, Ji-de-ofor! What are you doing!'

'I am fighting for life to happen for us, not to us. I am fighting to hold on to you with my broken nails and fingers. Sweet pea, I am fighting for us.'

Omo watched the inaudible pantomime from a distance, as Jide told Fiyin about the petition and Ifeatu's pivotal role in its final execution, how the lady in the hall was a lawyer – Nnamdi's friend – helping to put together the petition.

'After many modifications and countless second guesses, she came to the wedding with the document… we are ready. Fifi, I have no plan that does not feature you.' Jide's eyes were two glistening balls of emotion.

Over the phone, before Fiyin fused into her bed in surrender to the day's fatigue, she voiced her surprise to Jide about Nnamdi being the one to come up with such a brilliant solution.

'Nnamdi is dealing with a backlog of childhood trauma, but that aside, he is an incredible guy… when he decides to try.' They both laughed long and hard.

⌒⌒

'And we've got ourselves a leak-proof plan! My uncle says many Igbo communities are beginning to embrace the abolition law. All he needs is the Igwe's support, and we're on!' Ifeatu's words came in bursts of excitement; this would seal her reconciliation with her best friend. Fiyin sped through her mental glossary of Igbo words and came out blank.

'Igwe?' she asked.

'Igwe. King,' said Ifeatu.

'Oh, I thought… so what is Eze?' At this rate, Fiyin did not see how she would win Nnamdi's NGN200,000. He had wagered she would still not be able to hold a three-minute conversation in Igbo language by Christmas. The prospect of Nnamdi stuffing his foot in his own mouth sounded like the most fun Fiyin would have in the year.

'No worries, I'll tell Jide about the Igwe's signature,' Fiyin said.

'And… and a royal letter-headed note… something short, to lend creden– arrgghhh!'

'What? Ify, what happened?' Fiyin strained to hear what was happening on the other side of the telephone line.

'This boy wants to bite off my nipple! I swear, I will wean him at nine months! Hah! Two more months. God help me!'

'Please feed my boy, biko! Sebi he was chilling in heaven, jeje, when you and Chike went to drag him down.'

The carefree humour in Fiyin's voice made Ifeatu's lips curl in a smile. Much like old times, though now flavoured with more life-defining conversations, the two friends were back to being friends, talking three times, sometimes four times, before the end of every day.

~

Executing the plan called for laser-precision timing. After a myriad of phone calls, visits to offices, sometimes residences, and trips to Ajoafo, where free medical services were promised, money exchanged hands and an assortment of foodstuff and provisions were gifted, 33,363 citizens of Ajoafo town signed a petition demanding the implementation of the abolishment law for the Osu caste system in Ajoafo. They will no longer recognise the Osu Caste System... All men would be reborn. All men would be pure.

Only last week, the secretary to the crown called with the good news: the crown approved their 'gift'. A new car for the Igwe, funds for the renovation of the shopping mall in the centre of town, and primary school scholarships to be awarded to ten children – in the name of the Igwe, were all the inducements required to facilitate the crown's signature and letter to the Minister of Culture and Cohesion. Without the anonymous secret funding, set up and solicited for, by Nnamdi, Timilehin and Jide, the entire endeavour would never have been a success.

As they made their descent into Asaba International Airport, Jide's heart plummeted into his belly, but Nnamdi believed he worried over nothing.

'By the time we get this elixir of a letter and the all-mighty signature, you'll remember how to smile!' he said, bumping Jide in the shoulder with his fist, but Jide's facial muscles snubbed Nnamdi's efforts at humour. Professor Nwanta, a prominent native of Ajoafo, volunteered to attend their meeting with the Igwe, but his presence did little to dispel the sense of foreboding that threatened to engulf Jide.

Professor Nwanta's driver suffered a flat tyre on his way to the airport, so he called to inform them he would need another thirty minutes. They settled in a restaurant at the airport lounge to wait for him. Nnamdi ordered peppered snails and fried beef.

'Do you have freshly squeezed juice?' he asked the waiter.

'No, sir. But we have soft drinks and beer. Sir… beer is wonderful with the meat.'

The men opted for water. Jide took a piece of beef, which he chewed with the enthusiasm of a snail invited to a speed test. Nnamdi gave Jide a quizzical stare.

'Come on, Jide! We've done everything. We struck while the iron was hot. We've begged and bribed. You've prayed and persuaded… wetin remain again? No need to fret, nau!' But only when, at the entrance to the Igwe's palace, Professor Nwanta placed his hand on Jide's shoulder and said, 'Breathe, Jide. It all ends today,' did Jide allow the tension in his shoulders to begin to fall away.

Fifteen minutes after they were ushered to the palace reception, a lady came in with a tray of drinks and saucers of garden eggs. She placed them on the centre table and left without saying anything. Moments later, Mazi Okechukwu, the secretary to the crown, joined them, a genial smile playing on his face.

'Welcome! Ahh, Prof! We were not expecting you, o! Nno

nu, welcome!' he said. The men exchanged pleasantries and, as a mark of courtesy, obliged when Mazi Okechukwu invited them to feast on the drinks and garden eggs. Nnamdi gave Mazi a brown envelope. Mazi flipped it open, peered; it contained a cheque for NGN10,000,000. 'Igwe will be pleased! The letter is ready, no problem at all! Hope you brought the petition for his signature,' Mazi said, turning to Jide. Jide nodded.

'And this one is for you,' Nnamdi said, slipping Mazi a bundle of NGN500 notes. A young man came in, whispered to Mazi, and the nascent beam on his face dried up.

'Ehm. Ahem. I am coming. Please, excuse me,' Mazi said, scurrying out like one treading on hot coal.

It took everything for Jide to retain his composure when, about an hour after Mazi Okechukwu left them, he cast an idle glance towards the door to see I.G and four severe-looking men walk past with Mazi in their wake. At the sound of car doors slamming and tyres screeching away, Jide's voice hovered between laughing and crying. 'We may have come all this way for nothing,' he said. The young man from before, the one who whispered to Mazi, came in to tell Professor Nwanta that the Igwe wanted a brief meeting.

'Only Prof,' he said, when Jide and Nnamdi got on their feet to follow.

Large beads of sweat started to form on Jide's forehead, while Nnamdi rolled out an unending string of expletives. 'How can anyone say all sins are the same? That fool will lay hell's foundation! He will wrong his helpers and calamity will clothe him like skin… Bagger! Nincompoop! Who the fuck does he think he is?'

Mazi's re-entrance clogged Nnamdi's tirade. He handed back the brown envelope to Nnamdi, his face a blanket of distress.

'I'm confused… I don't know how this happened. Chief was in America… he was supposed to be there for three months… I… I just don't know. Somebody leaked it. Somebody leaked this thing to him. And with the way he was smiling and talking to himself just now, I don't think Igwe will give you people that letter again. Ehm… for the other one you gave me… let me send somebody to the house to go and bring it back… I already—'

Without lifting his head, Jide said, 'No need. We already gave it to you. It's only money, sir. Rapuba, do not worry.'

Mazi exhaled, mumbled something indistinct and scurried off again.

Nnamdi placed both hands behind his head, clasping his fingers. He squeezed his eyes shut for a moment and unclasped his hands to run them over his face, pulling his lower lip with his two index fingers before hunching to place his hands on his knees. Jide fought his tears. If only he had a moment to gather himself. But he did not. At the touch of Nnamdi's hand on his shoulder, his eyes started to shimmer. He tried. Oh, how Jide tried! But his well of emotions had no more room, so his rapid blinking, rather than dispelling his tears, caused them to flow hot, fast, unfettered.

Professor Nwanta came back to the waiting room, his shoulders slack, and his face curiously expressionless. Their worst fears were confirmed. The king would no longer be involved.

'In Igwe's words, I.G holds the yam and the knife. He is disappointed that an elder like me would be involved in signature forgery,' Professor Nwanta said. His eyes exuded empathy and fatigue; the young men did what they had to do. He did not know, but he did not blame them. The drive back to Asaba and the flight back to Lagos suffered intense silence among the men.

Nnamdi planned to stay with Jide till the morning, but Fiyin arrived, so his plans changed. When two hours earlier, Jide had sent her a one-liner text message, 'Back in Lagos… it did not work', Fiyin's reply was a one-liner of her own. 'I'm coming over'.

Still reeling from a mass of emotions after their child's account of the gruelling happenings of the past months, Bree and Donald feigned ignorance when Fiyin sought their permission to go to Ifeatu's house, to spend the night.

Before Nnamdi left, he took Fiyin's hands. 'I love Jide like my own brother, and I don't even like people. He is the most sensible guy I have had the fortune of sharing a corner with. And if he is going the distance for you… with you… it means you must make a lot of sense. This night, I'll do something I haven't done in a while. I will pray… for Jide… for you. Abeg, Fiyin… I take God beg you, stick around for my guy… abeg.'

Fiyin employed her age-long technique of closing and opening her eyes in rapid succession both to shun her fast-forming tears and to welcome the novelty of the retreating figure of this emotive and reflective Nnamdi.

⌐───᠎⌐

Jide and Fiyin took quick shallow breaths as their friend pitched their case.

'Uncle, they already have more than thirty thousand signatures on the petition! Only the letter is remaining, but the Igwe is no longer ready to provide it!'

A few seconds ticked by with Ifeatu listening to her uncle.

'I understand, Uncle, but the man has no real point. People have been inter-marrying since… no, the Igwe cancelled the meeting with them.'

More silence.

'Uncle, but… yes, Uncle… thank you, I'll tell them.'

Only a few of the Minister's words reached their ears after Ifeatu tapped the speaker icon on her phone, '…bad for them, but I cannot override the King's office. Moreover, your friends shouldn't have forged that man's signature… they shouldn't have crossed that line. Culture is culture and must be respected. And let me tell you,

Ify, there is a silent majority of influential people who believe there is merit in exercising caution in dealing with those people… I wish your friends well.'

'Thank you, Uncle.' Ifeatu set down her phone on the space beside her. She did not understand the sense of it. Why customary beliefs, a factor meant to unify so wholly, tear so brutally to pieces the same ones who practise them? Customs and traditions practised with such skewed precision, choosing when and when not to slam its steel gavel with its deafening verdict of 'GUILTY'. You are permitted to work with, befriend, be treated at the hospital by, eat meals prepared by, and wear clothes ironed by an outcast. But if your relative joins an outcast in matrimony, you are prohibited from every form of association with such a person.

'He cannot go against the Igwe… that's what he said.' Ifeatu's eyes were two pools. Her voice sounded hoarse and far away.

From Ifeatu's house, Jide and Fiyin stopped at the store to buy gourmet popcorn and juice. Afterwards, they went to Ikoyi. Once they arrived at Jide's family home, Fiyin asked Nsikan to prepare oven-roasted cinnamon chicken drumsticks and have two plates sent upstairs to the lounge. She ate a hearty portion, but Jide managed only a few bites. Fiyin's mobile phone rang. It was Omo. Jide walked away to the balcony. Fifteen minutes after, he came back in, but Fiyin was no longer in the lounge. He found her on the floor of his bedroom, her back to the foot of his bed. Jide settled beside her, turning her wet face towards himself.

'Ben is in Nigeria. He proposed to Omo. She said yes, and I'm over-the-moon happy for her,' Fiyin said, her voice a whisper, her chest heaving, ready to burst open.

Jide took her in his arms, and they cried together. When her shoulders stopped shaking, he said, 'Let us pray, sweet pea...

'Dear God, we come to you, flawed and fearful, yet resting in the certainty of your unfathomable love for us... and for this we are eternally thankful. In every way we have erred, in pursuit of our happiness, we beg for your mercy. We ask you to show us the... Lord, Fiyin came into my life, and I thought you sent her to me... I still believe you sent her to me... but... but if... but if this is not...'

Fiyin prised open one eye. Tears were trickling from the sides of Jide's closed eyes, down his face. She squeezed his hands, and he resumed his prayers.

'If you are not in this... help us align our will with yours... and please... please, God... please take away the hurt it will bring. This we pray in the name of Jesus.'

But rather than the customary 'Amen', Fiyin's response was, *'And oh Lord, please remind us that you are THE-RED-SEA-PARTING GOD. In the mighty name of Jesus.'* This time, the echo of a fervid 'Amen!' floated through the room. A tangle of arms and legs, Jide and Fiyin cried some more before exhaustion charmed them into troubled sleep. And in the morning, they went window-shopping for the equipment for Fiyin's catering outfit. Since fate had expended all its resources on warring with his most desired intentions, Jide committed to investing his remaining emotions in sculpting Fiyin's big dream.

'Married or not, I intend to look into your eyes, with confidence, on the opening of your outfit, and many years after, and ask if you are happy, my sweet pea.'

～

'Sir, very sorry for disturbing, sir. Is my wife, sir. She say them rush my daughter go to hospital.' I.G looked at his driver like one would stare at fresh cow dung.

'Carry my box from the dining table. We are going to the airport... sorry about your child,' he said, slurping the rest of his orange juice. Alfonso scurried to the dining table, lifted the travel case with both hands and placed it on his right shoulder.

As usual, Abuja Airport Road bustled with vehicles. Alfonso always wondered where everyone was going. Through the rear-view mirror, he slid glances at his boss. I.G's flight was not until 4:00pm, but he liked the tranquillity and the pleasant expensive air in business lounges and would often sit for countless hours before his flight time, sipping, eating, or reading whatever piqued his interest. Alfonso snatched another glance at I.G and realised he had never seen him smile. His boss's constant adornment was a scowl.

The car temperature read fourteen degrees, but beads of sweat hung on Alfonso's forehead. He swiped them with his right palm, swallowed. He glanced at I.G again and started to tell him about his child who had been diagnosed with an inflamed appendix. How he needed to make a down payment of NGN50,000 to the hospital for her surgery, but I.G cut him off.

'You must think I am an idiot. Doling out money at every scenario you manufacture. One day, it is your father's burial. The next, your mother sprained her hip. The day after, it is—'

'No, sir! No, sir! Is not for dash. Please, I will pay back, sir. Am begging for advance of my salar—'

'Look at this buffoon! How many times will I tell you never to interrupt me? I'm talking and you are talking! Anyway, like I have told you before, I don't have any spare cash! Every spend is pre-planned. There is no floating cash anywhere.'

It was inevitable. Like that first gulp of water by a drowning man. No matter how long he held himself from breathing, that first gulp was inescapable; Alfonso slammed the brakes.

'Alfo... why... wha... what are you... what is wrong with this buffoon!' For several moments, Alfonso sat unmoving, inhaling and exhaling, absolute in his disinterest in the countless horns blaring their disapproval of his abrupt halt in the middle lane of the expressway. Like contestants in a turbo car racing game, drivers swerved and screeched and swore. Alfonso peered into the rear-view mirror, and an indolent smile pulled at his lips. For the first time in a long while, satisfaction spread from his chest, down to his toes. Why couldn't facial expressions be laminated? The look of sheer panic on the face of his boss of six years. Priceless.

'What nonsense is this, Alfonso? Why did you stop?'

Alfonso leaned over the gear stick, to reach the foot of the passenger's seat, picked his mobile phone and nylon bag of bits and bobs. He served I.G an icy glare and said, 'I am going to find money. Make my daughter no come go die for hospital... and... and let me tell you, eh, I am not a buffoon!' Alfonso got out of the car. He did not bother to shut the door. I.G's mouth hung open as he watched his driver navigate his way to the other side of the road and flag down a keke. After a full minute, he was at last able to marshal the chaos in his head into structured thinking. Shrugging the thought of climbing over to the front, I.G, with his left sleeve, wiped sweat off his forehead as his eyes drew lines from his car door to zapping vehicles and back to his car door. A white saloon missed him by the breadth of a thread as he ambled out of the car. Once in the driver's seat, he let out a long sigh.

When I return, this buffoon will regret ever crossing me. I will make Abuja unbearable for—

Everything happened within nanoseconds. A man in a black SUV stole a quick glimpse, to hit the 'answer' icon on his phone. He slammed his foot hard on his brakes, missing a pedestrian by a whisker. 'Why don't these people ever use the bloody pedestrian crossing for heaven's sake!' A female voice filtered through the man's phone speakers, 'Chairman, I'm so sorry I won't be making it to Abuja again... the money... someone else gave me the money... for free. Thanks for everything.' The lorry behind saw the black SUV at the last possible minute and swerved to the right, into I.G's car. Metal grating on metal, horns blaring in a frenzy and distant cries of anguish were I.G's last memories before nothingness engulfed him.

EPILOGUE

A service lady rolled a trolley with tiny saucers of spicy meat to their table. 'What's this?' Afulenu asked.

'Asun, ma,' said the lady and began placing saucers before the occupants of the table.

'Oh, none for me. I don't eat goat meat,' said Bree, passing her saucer to Auntie Nkechi.

Jide mouthed, *I love you, Fiyin.* Fiyin's lips parted, poised for response, but she sucked a sharp breath, and they slammed of their own accord. They parted again for her to say, 'You know I love you too.'

'No, Fiyin! You hesitated!' Jide pulled down his lips in mock dismay.

'I did not! All right, all right, I did… but only to soak in the beautiful moment, my love!' Now Fiyin was giggling.

'You have the most amazing friends, Fifi. Imagine every one of them bright with untainted happiness for you.'

'Yeah, all but one.'

'Yes, Anita. But she is gone for good causes, did you not say?'

'True. Her mother's surgery. But Jide, now you'll agree that sometimes, though unknown to the parties involved at the time, hanging around a barber's shop may be for the ultimate good of someone else… to remind them to go in for a haircut. Hmm?'

'Perhaps. Are you happy, my sweet pea?'

'With every cell in me. Jide.'

'Mmm?'

'If you were there, would you have done everything to save him?'

The Hippocratic oath came barrelling through Jide's lips, but Fiyin's steady gaze stopped his recital. In truth, Jide did not know and offered silent gratitude to providence for his absence on the ill-fated day. The day I.G's near-lifeless body arrived at Soma-Williams Hospital, Abuja.

He linked his hands with hers, lowered his head and planted a soft kiss on her temple. With eyes shut, they swayed to Sadao Watanabe's 'When We Make a Home', utter in their oblivion to the hundreds of eyes watching in admiration as they performed their first dance as husband and wife.

<hr />

"It is devilish and most uncharitable to brand any human being with a label of inferiority due to the accidents of history." – Dr. Nnamdi Benjamin Azikiwe; 20th March 1956.